Treasonous Behavior

In The Beginning

by

Robert A. Johnson

Treasonous Behavior
In The Beginning

TBBooks may be ordered through booksellers or by contacting the author via e-mail:arizonadesertdogg2@yahoo.com

ISBN: 978-1499681864

This book is dedicated to freedoms fought
and died for by our brave soldiers…

…and to those Americans who have forgotten
the privilege of living in a nation blessed by God.

A grateful nation

FOREWORD

Frank F. Buchanan
Biblical Historian/Researcher

Although what you are about to read is a fictional account of probable scenarios soon to be facing the American Nation and its people, it still sends chills up your spine and causes you to re-think your day to day activities and re-evaluate what is truly important in your life. It will cause you to question what is real and what is simply a fantasy you've been fed by the "powers that be". Much of the story is based on actual proposed procedures, laws and government orders unilaterally and covertly set in place, as well as recent actual events largely ignored by the "mainstream" media.

The treasonous behavior of the "players" involved in the plan for complete destruction and re-structuring of America is unfolding before our eyes! From the slimy scum (Globalists/Banksters) controlling our President and the "tools on the hill" (Congress), to the greedy Corporate cockroaches here and abroad, all expecting to be rewarded handsomely for their seditious actions. Needless to say, the names have been changed to protect the guilty.

The human condition is a complex conundrum. There are those who sit silent and watch. Those who only talk a big game. And others who say, "Somebody should do something about this!" And the few who possess leadership qualities, take action, and make things happen. Then there are those who seemingly come out of nowhere. They are the ones who step up and rise to the level heretofore thought unachievable.

Treasonous Behavior documents many of these conditions through a variety of characters and circumstances throughout the story. It is easy to imagine yourself in the situations both main characters, Raz and Cody, find themselves in. What would you do if faced with the takeover of the country you loved? What would you do if you witnessed the utter destruction, literally overnight, of life as it was? How would you cope? Who would you trust? And when the time came, who would you kill?

The author asks these questions and more as he takes you on one hell of a rollercoaster ride through all the twists and turns Raz and Cody experience in their quest to restore the Republic and regain their freedom, only moments ago taken for granted.

Wake up America! Before it's too late.

Definition of <u>Treason</u>:

The Constitution of the United States

Article III, Section 3

Treason against the United States, shall consist only in levying War against them, or in adhering to their Enemies, giving them Aid and Comfort.

Webster's New World Dictionary:

treason, noun

1. betrayal of trust or faith
2. betrayal of one's country to an enemy

Oxford English Dictionary:

treason, noun

The action of betraying: betrayal of the trust undertaken by or reposed in any one; breach of faith, treacherous action, treachery

Definition of <u>Treasonous</u>:

Collins English Dictionary

treasonous, adjective

Relating to or involving treason; traitorous to your country

In The Beginning...

"Gentlemen," the bellowing voice cut through the quarrelsome clamor in the grand meeting hall. Silence blanketed the room with due respect for the eloquent speaker. The man slowly gazed into the eyes of his fellow countrymen.

"We are living in a time of difficult and dangerous decisions." The room full of statesmen and lawyers and merchants and land owners gave their full attention to the distinguished leader. It was time for words to give way to action.

"What man amongst us dares to stand strong against the evil that suppresses us? Who is willing to sacrifice all that he has for his sons and daughters, his fellow citizens, his future generations? Is there a soul here today who is prepared to risk all his worldly goods, his reputation, even his God given life, in order to right the wrongs he has so long suffered? Who is willing to come forth to speak his mind against overwhelming adversity, to denounce tyranny, to let it be known to the world that he shall fight to the very end to preserve the divine human desire to be unshackled as a truly free man? What man before me pledges his word and bond toward the independence of a new found sovereign nation dedicated to the needs and wants of its own populace? Is not human liberty a natural right, deserving of every man's effort to preserve?"

Cheers rose among the distinguished men in the meeting. For weeks they had argued and debated, deliberated and contested, discussed and questioned a formal statement of principles as an expression of the American mind.

"Together, as free men from each of the separate colonies, as voices of our citizenry, our families, our neighbors, we have set forth a list of grievances against the laws of a government which no longer represents our rights as human beings. We shall from here forward live under the laws of nature and the self-evident truths endowed by our Creator. We shall endure tyranny no longer and live by certain unalienable rights. Among these are life, liberty, and the pursuit of happiness."

The likes of John Adams, John Hancock, and Benjamin Franklin, along with the other fifty two colonial statesmen, had put their differences aside and showed their support for the document they were about to sign, one of the "greatest statements of human liberty ever written."

"In the name of the good people of the colonies, as unified peoples under divine Providence, we shall declare our independence and our right to be absolved of all allegiance to the British Crown.

"I ask you, gentlemen and statesmen," Thomas Jefferson concluded. "Shall we at this moment in history side with one another, pledge our lives, our fortunes, and our honor, in declaring our faithfulness to a new land governed by the people and for the people?"

Early Summer, 1776

The Declaration of Independence

In Congress, July 4, 1776
The unanimous Declaration of the thirteen united States of America,

When in the Course of human events, it becomes necessary for one people to dissolve the political bands which have connected them with another, and to assume among the powers of the earth, the separate and equal station to which the Laws of Nature and of Nature's God entitle them, a decent respect to the opinions of mankind requires that they should declare the causes which impel them to the separation.

We hold these truths to be self-evident, that all men are created equal, that they are endowed by their Creator with certain unalienable Rights, that among these are Life, Liberty and the pursuit of Happiness.-- That to secure these rights, Governments are instituted among Men, deriving their just powers from the consent of the governed,--That whenever any Form of Government becomes destructive of these ends, it is the Right of the People to alter or abolish it, and to institute new Government, laying its foundation on such principles and organizing its powers in such form, as to them shall seem most likely to effect their Safety and Happiness. Prudence, indeed, will dictate that Governments long established should not be changed for light and transient causes, and accordingly all experience hath shown, that mankind are more disposed to suffer, while evils are sufferable, than to right themselves by abolishing the forms to which they are accustomed. But when a long train of abuses and usurpations, pursuing invariably the same Object evinces a design to reduce them under absolute Despotism, it is their right, it is their duty, to throw off such Government, and to provide new Guards for their future security.--Such has been the patient sufferance of the Colonies, and such is now the necessity which constrains them to alter their former Systems of Government. The history of the present King of Great Britain is a history of repeated injuries and usurpations, all having in direct object the establishment of an absolute Tyranny over these States. To prove this, let Facts be submitted to a candid world.

He has refused his Assent to Laws, the most wholesome and necessary for the public good.

He has forbidden his Governors to pass Laws of immediate and pressing importance, unless suspended in their operation till his Assent should be obtained; and when so suspended, he has utterly neglected to attend to them.

He has refused to pass other Laws for the accommodation of large districts of people, unless those people should relinquish the right of Representation in the Legislature, a right inestimable to them and formidable to tyrants only.

He has called together legislative bodies at places unusual, uncomfortable, and distant from the depository of their public Records, for the sole purpose of fatiguing them into compliance with his measures.

He has dissolved Representative Houses repeatedly, for opposing with manly firmness his invasions on the rights of the people.

He has refused for a long time, after such dissolutions, to cause others to be elected; whereby the Legislative powers, incapable of Annihilation, have returned to the People at large for their exercise; the State remaining in the mean time exposed to all the dangers of invasion from without, and convulsions within.

He has endeavoured to prevent the population of these States; for that purpose obstructing the Laws for Naturalization of Foreigners; refusing to pass others to encourage their migrations hither, and raising the conditions of new Appropriations of Lands.

He has obstructed the Administration of Justice, by refusing his Assent to Laws for establishing Judiciary powers.

He has made Judges dependent on his Will alone, for the tenure of their offices, and the amount and payment of their salaries.

He has erected a multitude of New Offices, and sent hither swarms of Officers to harass our people, and eat out our substance.

He has kept among us, in times of peace, Standing Armies without the Consent of our legislatures.

He has affected to render the Military independent of and superior to the Civil power.

He has combined with others to subject us to a jurisdiction foreign to our constitution, and unacknowledged by our laws; giving his Assent to their Acts of pretended Legislation:

For Quartering large bodies of armed troops among us:

For protecting them, by a mock Trial, from punishment for any murders which they should commit on the Inhabitants of these States:

For cutting off our Trade with all parts of the world:

For imposing Taxes on us without our Consent:

For transporting us beyond Seas to be tried for pretended offences:

For abolishing the free System of English Laws in a neighbouring Province, establishing therein an Arbitrary government, and enlarging its Boundaries so as to render it at once an example and fit instrument for introducing the same absolute rule into these Colonies:

For taking away our Charters, abolishing our most valuable Laws, and altering fundamentally the Forms of our Governments:

For suspending our own Legislatures, and declaring themselves invested with power to legislate for us in all cases whatsoever.

He has abdicated Government here, by declaring us out of his Protection and waging War against us.

He has plundered our seas, ravaged our Coasts, burnt our towns, and destroyed the lives of our people.

He is at this time transporting large Armies of foreign Mercenaries to compleat [sic] the works of death, desolation and tyranny, already begun with circumstances of Cruelty & perfidy scarcely paralleled in the most barbarous ages, and totally unworthy the Head of a civilized nation.

He has constrained our fellow Citizens taken Captive on the high Seas to bear Arms against their Country, to become the executioners of their friends and Brethren, or to fall themselves by their Hands.

He has excited domestic insurrections amongst us, and has endeavoured to bring on the inhabitants of our frontiers, the merciless Indian Savages, whose known rule of warfare, is an undistinguished destruction of all ages, sexes and conditions.

In every stage of these Oppressions We have Petitioned for Redress in the most humble terms: Our repeated Petitions have been answered only by repeated injury. A Prince whose character is thus marked by every act which may define a Tyrant, is unfit to be the ruler of a free people.

Nor have We been wanting in attentions to our Brittish [sic] brethren. We have warned them from time to time of attempts by their legislature to extend an unwarrantable jurisdiction over us. We have reminded them of the circumstances of our emigration and settlement here. We have appealed to their native justice and magnanimity, and we have conjured them by the ties of our common kindred to disavow these usurpations, which, would inevitably interrupt our connections and correspondence. They too have been deaf to the voice of justice and of consanguinity. We must, therefore, acquiesce in the necessity, which denounces our Separation, and hold them, as we hold the rest of mankind, Enemies in War, in Peace Friends.

We, therefore, the Representatives of the united States of America, in General Congress, Assembled, appealing to the Supreme Judge of the world for the rectitude of our intentions, do, in the Name, and by the Authority of the good People of these Colonies, solemnly publish and declare, That these United Colonies are, and of Right ought to be Free and Independent States; that they are Absolved from all Allegiance to the British Crown, and that all political connection between them and the State of Great Britain, is and ought to be totally dissolved; and that as Free and Independent States, they have full Power to levy War, conduct Peace, contract Alliances, establish Commerce, and to do all other Acts and Things which independent States may of right do. And for the support of this Declaration, with a firm reliance on the protection of divine Providence, we mutually pledge to each other our Lives, our Fortunes and our scared Honor.

signed by Thomas Jefferson
and 55 other colonial statesmen

Prologue

I t's a naturally, and frequently, occurring phenomenon which, under ideal conditions, can kill nearly every human being on the planet. It's called an Electromagnetic Pulse, commonly referred to as an EMP.

An Electromagnetic Pulse occurs by natural forces emitted from our solar source, some ninety-three million miles from earth. These solar flares are produced by an abrupt release of magnetic fields stored within the gaseous core of the sun. The huge amounts of energy released can reach the equivalent of 160,000,000 megatons of TNT. The recurrent fiery explosions eject invisible clouds of charged electrons and ions upward to heights of nearly 500,000 kilometers. Flare-up temperatures can reach highs of 100,000,000 degrees Kelvin.

Corona mass eruptions from the outermost atmospheres of the sun trigger geometric storms sending pulsating waves of destruction throughout our solar system. X1 class events, the most severe storms emitted from the sun peaking in eleven year solar cycles, quickly distort the ionosphere. The imperceptible effect of the EMP reaches the earth with the speed of light producing radiation across the entire electromagnetic spectrum.

It is one of the most devastatingly destructive attacks on a planet and its inhabitants ever imaginable. At over 186,000 miles per second an EMP hits its targets without warning. On earth's surface it strangely causes no perceptible colossal explosion. It creates no menacing fireballs, no torrential wind storms, no massive flooding, no destructive earthquakes. It destroys no houses, no buildings, no infrastructure. It swiftly and silently sweeps through cities and villages, fields and farms, leaving no discernible damage. It leaves no lasting effect on earth's plant life, its forests, or sea life. It directly injures no animals, nor openly kills a single human being. It is neither seen, heard, nor felt by its unfortunate victims. Yet it is still the most deadly force ever envisioned.

Electronic waves a million times more powerful than any radio signal on the planet destroys all electronic devices in its path. All power grids turn off as if a simple switch were suddenly flipped. Like a silent weapon the EMP carries with it damaging voltage surges burning out semi-conductor chips in any electrical equipment within its line of sight. Every one of the more than 300,000,000 personal computers and laptops in America will shut down within a fraction of a second.

All forms of telecommunication ends. Three hundred thirty million cell phones power down in the blink of an eye. Hard wired land phones fail, radios go silent, and televisions go dark. Untold numbers, perhaps billions of memory micro-chips, logic circuitry, SIM cards, and integrated circuits cease to function as the unseen pulse of death burns up the magical powers of silicon innovation. Every technologically advanced digitized piece of equipment and energized system developed over the last decades instantly become useless hunks of metal and plastic.

All means of land transportation screech to a sudden halt without warning. Millions of automobiles, trucks, and SUVs slow to a stop. Commercial haulers charge forward with their weighted momentum, crashing into stationary structures. Police cruisers, city buses, fire engines, and motorcycles stop dead in the streets.

Tens of thousands of accidents occur at the same moment. City intersections become massive pile ups as thousands of traffic lights go down and engines fail to respond. Law enforcement and military vehicles as well, become disabled, failing to respond to cries of help and increasing chaos. Millions of motorists become confused, angered, disoriented, stranded at their work places or from their homes.

Freight trains pulling miles of loaded containers coast to a long but quiet stop. Passenger trains traveling cross country end up forsaken in the open scrub western deserts or the flat central plains of America. Packed commuter trains speeding along the metro corridor between Washington, DC and New York City roll to an end of their journey, still far from their destinations. Subway trains deep beneath the asphalt of Chicago and Boston and New York leave their hundreds of thousands of travelers isolated in the pitch black maze of tunnels.

Ships hit by the pulse drift aimlessly without power. Monstrous oil tankers run aground in the Gulf. Cargo ships entering ports on both the east and west coasts float helplessly in the ocean currents. Cruise ships out of Miami flounder without purposeful direction. Naval aircraft carriers, cruisers, and battleships lie dormant in the San Diego and Newport News shipyards, unable to protect our shores. Pleasure boats and decked out yachts float adrift in open waters.

Within seconds every aircraft in flight goes quiet and falls to earth. More than five thousand planes, including commercial airliners, private craft, air cargo carriers, helicopters, and military jets, are in the air at any given time over the skies of the United States. All are instantly doomed as the powerful pulse ruptures their vulnerable systems. Redundant backup systems fail just as easily.

At an altitude of 35,000 feet, a cross country jetliner instantly loses power to its engines. Seasoned pilots frantically attempt to restart the turbines, but with no working controls their efforts prove useless. Hundreds of passengers strapped in their seats scream in horror when the lights go out and their plane begins to drop like a stone. Travelers and flight crew have a mere forty-six seconds to pray before they crash into the earth. Hundreds of thousands of other air passengers meet the same fate as planes hopelessly drop from the sky simultaneously.

Elevators in large apartment houses, office buildings, and government centers stop mid-floor. Some free fall straight to crushing death. With no lights, no working phones, and no manner of escape, the poor souls remain in their stainless steel coffins. Heart pacemakers shut down, killing seniors blindly. Hospital ventilators stop ventilating patients. Critical monitors quit monitoring. Life saving devices cease saving.

Every financial institution in the land is affected. Banks turn dark and completely unprotected. Alarm systems become worthless deterrents. All credit cards and debit cards and wire transfers are ended in mid-transaction. The New York Stock Exchange streams into mayhem as the giant money boards dim. Every company stock and every corporate or government bond simply vanishes into thin air. All bank account amounts disappear into cyberspace, as if they never existed. Savings and checking and pension plans are instantaneously wiped out, as if they never registered. Every dollar of government funding ceases to exist. No financial record in the path of the EMP survives.

All retail stores in the country lock down without operating computers. Throughout the nation grocery stores hurry customers out of their businesses as the registers bind up, the frozen foods begin to melt, and the perishable products begin to sour and decay. Food soon becomes a major concern.

In all homes and businesses, apartments and civic buildings, the electricity shuts off as the power grids burn out. Even daylight turns dark in residences and workplaces. Water pipes run dry, natural gas for heating quits delivery, refrigerators turn warm as houses turn cold in the lasting winter cold.

Every single factor of modern living comes to an end in an instant. A total shutdown of the computerized age takes hold. Digital progress disintegrates. Within seconds of a solar electromagnetic pulse an entire advanced civilization is thrown back some two hundred years to when kerosene lit houses and steam drove machines. A thriving, rich country, once the envy of the world, becomes paralyzed and unprotected, people dying from the effects of an unseen force, and the rest running scared to death in anticipation of what might be coming next.

Most people are ill-prepared for such a catastrophic disaster. Only days after the EMP strikes people run out of drinking water and turn to their toilets. Meager pantry food supplies are exhausted in two weeks time. Food, once plentiful, becomes a precious commodity. Medications are used up as patients gasp for air or fall to chest pains. Families are separated, most likely never to be reunited. News of the event remains nonexistent for the lack of power. Cries for help go unanswered and mayhem sets in and is common.

People panic and live in fear. Alarm and chaos rule the day. People die from dehydration, and more from starvation. Soon others fail from untreated ailments. First the elderly and the sick, then young children. The devastation and lack of electricity continues for at least six months, perhaps much longer. Should the systems which inhabitants and businesses and governments once so casually relied on stay shut down for a full year, almost ninety percent of the American population will perish from starvation, disease, or societal chaos, and its ensuing collapse.

But the normal phenomenon of solar flares is not the worst catastrophe inflicted upon an unprepared nation.

Solar disturbances are but one cause of an EMP, a regular occurrence completely beyond control of mankind. Scientists, astronomers, and astrophysicists monitor and study the sun's surface, constantly fearful of a massive flare up, a giant sunspot which can shoot out six times the diameter of the earth. World leaders aware of the catastrophic potential, pray a solar induced electromagnetic pulse will never come to pass on their watch. Common citizens following their mundane and trivial days ignore the possibility entirely.

Equally devastating, though by far vastly more abhorrent than any other devious act of man conceived in history, is when an EMP is intentionally triggered. A first possible scenario is an EMP being created by sophisticated and well funded enemies of a state intent on paralyzing its foe.

In the midst of the Dark Ages the widespread outbreak of the insidious black plague killed a mere fraction of those who could be wiped out by a strategically initiated EMP. Over a thousand centuries of man butchering his own kind pale in the shadow of an EMP aftermath. Millions were slaughtered during the Great Crusades. Millions more were massacred by the dictators of oppressed countries. Millions again were selectively eradicated by mad men in power, or starved to death by obsessed rulers intent on self-idolization, or enslaved and annihilated by fanatical godless men. Such historic carnage in total would barely reach the potential death toll of a single electromagnetic pulse perfectly executed.

An EMP event over the central plains of the United States would cause a staggering death toll of the American population. Upwards of 300,000,000 people on the continent would die from the long term aftermath effects of an intentional EMP explosion. There would be no bloodshed, no shots fired, no traditional killing, no death by standard warfare.

Instead, the millions of citizens—men, women, and children—would perish from ultimate starvation, pervasive diseases, and eventual societal disintegration. In the hands of a radical group determined to annihilate the United States, an electromagnetic pulse would be the perfect weapon.

Russia's military has largely been dismantled since the breaking up of the Soviet Union. However, it still has the capability to slip a stealth nuclear submarine within a few miles of the American coasts and deploy a missile over the American continent. Russia would have no qualms in attempting to wipe out the western superpower in its striving to once again gain super status.

A top secret Russian strategic submarine known as the SSBM, slips beneath the calm waters of the Gulf of Mexico fifty miles off the shores of New Orleans. It carries a one megaton nuclear warhead on the tip of a medium range ballistic missile. This specially designed weapon is an enhanced super EMP, or E-bomb.

The missile is aimed near the center of the continental United States, over the Nebraska-Kansas border, approximately one thousand miles in distance from the Gulf. Once deployed, it takes the missile only six and a half minutes to meet its target, too quick for U.S. domestic defenses to react. The nuclear devise explodes two-hundred miles above its ideal coordinates. The High Altitude EMP will have an effective range of over fifteen hundred miles rippling across the nation. It spreads into the southern portions of Canada and the northern sections of Mexico. The vast American shorelines of the Pacific and Atlantic Oceans and hundreds of miles of sea will be affected as well. Most of the Gulf of Mexico will also be covered by the pulse. Results of the intentional attack will be similar to those caused by a solar flare EMP, only more sinister.

Except, it would open America to even more devastation. It would clear the path for Russia's other mortal enemy, China, to stand tall in the number one spot of worldwide domination.

Of course, China, the Red Dragon, with its huge, unmatched military force, could initiate its own assault against America. Its advanced EMP bombs are aimed at the eastern seaboard of the United States—the political, financial, and defense centers of the country. Long range intercontinental missiles or nuclear liftoffs from nearby secluded submarines could inevitably give Communist China the edge they have long desired. Such an injured nation could easily succumb to an invading naval force and savage takeover.

In the end, China would lose its prominent economic trader, its favored trading status, its monetized security on trillions owed it by the U.S. But China would gain much, much more.

Another rogue, dogmatic nation, North Korea, has secured the technology from Russia capable of launching ICBMs carrying 300 kiloton nuclear bombs. They are able to fire a preemptive long range nuclear missile orbiting over the South Pole, and detonating it over specific regions of the North American continent.

Iran is another nation with an intense hatred toward the West, and in particular against Americans. It and any number of mobile terrorist groups are ever preparing to pull the trigger to annihilate the White Devil once and for all in an attempt to fulfill their prophetic destiny.

The world is full of American enemies ready to eradicate the Great Satan. Most of them foreign, many of them domestic. But, there are even more malicious forces determined to stamp out the American way, if that is even feasible. As enemies within, they will eventually reveal their heinous and treasonous behavior to the astonishment of the American people and those who thought it could never happen.

Which leads to the second possibility of an EMP being deliberately activated.

It is something beyond comprehension to the average citizen. It shows the true evil nature of man in the pursuit of power and riches. With the backing of a small group of insiders, a leader of a nation resolute to use weapons of unspeakable destruction against his own people for his own designing agenda, could accomplish it. Such vile actions can only be halted if the citizens of a nation remain vigilant against the inherent wickedness of man and decide to take control of their own fate.

There is only one question to ponder.

Will the people stand up to such terror?

Chapter 1

T he arctic freeze swept farther south over the high southwestern deserts and into the northern Mexican states. The uncommonly frigid air had taken a deadly grip on the entire North American continent. Climate changes and peculiar weather cycles continued to wreak havoc on the population days before the joyous Thanksgiving holiday.

Cody Gordon drove his pickup truck into his driveway, hit the garage door remote button, and pulled into the garage next to his wife's car. Although it wasn't four o'clock yet, the heavy overcast and below freezing temperature made it feel much later. He was looking forward to the long weekend at home, a wonderful turkey meal with his family, and four whole days away from work. Tonight would be a great time to put some logs in the fireplace, build a roaring fire, and relax.

But Cody couldn't rid his mind of what had happened earlier that day.

As he entered his house through the garage door, a strong smell of sautéed onions and garlic hit him. His wife Robin was cooking up the makings of a sausage stuffing for tomorrow's bird. He removed his overcoat and hung it on a hook behind the door. He could hear the furnace running up his gas bill, but the heat from the kitchen felt good.

"Smells wonderful, hon," he mumbled automatically to Robin as she stirred the contents of the pan with a long-handled wooden spoon. He took in a long whiff of the pleasant aroma, though he was preoccupied with things other than food.

Robin gently pushed him away. "This isn't for you now." She had a pot of tomato soup simmering on the stove and a grill pan heating up.

"Since I'll be cooking all day tomorrow we're going to have soup and grilled cheese sandwiches tonight. And don't you dare touch the pies. They're for tomorrow."

He forced a half-hearted smile. "Okay," Cody solemnly answered. "It's dreadful out there," he added, nodding toward the kitchen window. The wind was picking up and blowing the last of the autumn leaves off the tree branches. He gave his wife a quick kiss on her cheek and picked up the few pieces of mail from the breakfast counter. Nothing but bills and junk mail.

He thought about what had taken place at work. How could such a horrible thing have happened? He wondered.

"What's wrong?" Robin asked Cody. After ten years of being married to this man she could easily tell when something was bothering him.

He quickly blew off her question. "Not now, okay?" He glanced around the kitchen and small dining room, a lost look in his eyes. "Where're the kids?"

"They had half a day at school. They're in their bedrooms getting their pajamas on. I told them they could watch TV after we eat dinner," Robin said. She looked at her husband again. *What's wrong?*

"I'm going to get some firewood," he told her. "It's cold in here."

Cody looked out the back slider door near the dinner table. The small thermometer attached to the door frame indicated the outside temperature had dropped to nineteen degrees. It was unusually cold for southern Arizona in November. *Should be in the fifties this time of year*, he thought. He didn't own warm winter gloves, so instead he went back into the garage to find his old leather work gloves.

After a minute of searching he couldn't find the damn gloves so he went back through the house, out the back door, and up to the pile of firewood against the side fence. *Why the hell would he do that?* He kept wondering. Cody loaded up his arms with dried mesquite logs and carried them to the back patio. He dropped the wood near the doorway and went back to get another load. The freezing wind numbed his ears and cheeks. It cut through his button down shirt. He should have worn his jacket.

He carried the second armload into the house, moved through the living room, scattering tiny pieces of mesquite bark on the floor, and placed the logs into the brass wood bin on the hearth. He methodically placed scraps of kindling sticks on the metal fire grate, stuffed a few pages of rolled up newspaper beneath them, and struck a match. The fire caught and he slowly stacked several smaller logs on the flames.

The heat of the fire felt good. The blaze began to warm his body. He ran his hands close to the flames to take the chill off. He smelled the smoke swirling up the chimney. It reminded him of the last time he had started a fire. It was Christmas last year when the children were opening their gifts. They were excited that Santa had come to their house and given them most, if not all, of what they had wished for. He watched the fire for another minute and listened to the crackling of the wood as it burned and threw off glowing sparks.

He wondered how things could change so much in one year.

"Dinner's ready," Robin called out.

From her bedroom Jennifer heard her mother. She came into the dining room and sat at her usual chair. "Mom, Jeffrey's not coming. He's still playing in his room."

The six year old girl was always trying to get her older brother in trouble because he picked on her every chance he got. "Want me go get him?" she asked, just to make a point.

Before Robin said another word Jeffrey ran into the dining room, flannel Spiderman pajamas on and cotton socks on his feet. He slid into the room like Tom Cruise in his movie *Risky Business.* "Tada!" he said, stretching his scrawny arms to the sides as if he had just magically appeared.

"Okay, Tada, take a seat. It's soup and sandwiches tonight," Robin said. She and Cody had taken to calling their son 'Tada' because of his 'magical' entry every night at dinner time. Jeffrey thought it was pretty cool being called Tada. His sister thought it was a dumb name and made fun of it at least once every hour when they were home together.

Satisfied with his fire, Cody went to the dinner table. "How're my favorite kids?" he asked the two. He was trying to keep the conversation light, even though things weren't right with him. He walked over to his seat and kissed both of them on their heads.

"Daddy!" Jennifer said in an attempt to correct her father. "We're your only children, so we have to be your favorite kids. That's how it works."

"Sorry, you're right," Cody corrected himself. He looked at his wife who was setting the bowls of tomato soup and plates of buttered grilled cheese sandwiches in front of everyone. He tried to give her a genuine smile, but it came across like a ton of bricks. "So, no school today?"

Jennifer shook her head as if she were a mother disappointed in her own youngster. "Daddy, we went to school this morning. You ate breakfast with us. We got out early. Didn't you know that?"

"Oh yes. I forgot," Cody said. He wasn't thinking straight ever since he received the word about his good friend. Her husband's actions immediately confirmed to Robin that something bad had happened at the college where he taught.

Jeffrey jumped into the conversation. "Pop, we got out early today, you know, because of Thanksgiving." Two years older than his unbearable sister, Jeffrey was the complete opposite of her. Unlike Jennifer, who was very fussy about keeping her room clean and careful about doing things the right way, Jeffrey was more footloose and fancy free, so to speak, where very little bothered him.

"Okay Jeffrey, now I get it," his father commented.

"Call me Tada," the little boy said as he took a big bite out of his warm sandwich.

Robin had to grin, but she looked at her troubled husband. After dinner they had to talk.

After they had eaten, Robin cleaned up the kitchen and gathered a few cans and boxes of food from the pantry for tomorrow's turkey dinner. Jeffrey and Jennifer went into the living room to watch *The Wizard of Oz,* the classic holiday special. They lay down on the carpeted floor with their blankets and got comfortable as the movie began. Cody retreated to his tiny office, which was really just a small

closet-sized, windowless room at the far end of the hallway. He had to
jot down a few things he wanted to finish by next Monday's class.

Cody had been teaching U.S. History classes at the local
community college for the past eleven years. That was where he had
met Robin Whitney, a young and beautiful second year English
teacher. He had enjoyed teaching back then. It was his passion, his
purpose in life. His students were great. They wanted to learn. They
were eager to discover. It was a truly rewarding profession.

But gradually the whole educational system began changing. There
seemed to be more emphasis on filing reports and filling out lengthy
surveys and submitting lesson plans for college approval than there
was for actual teaching. Standards were being altered to
"accommodate" students' changing needs rather than to enhance the
learning process and preparing young people to succeed in the world
beyond college.

Political discord and the demands of ever decreasing budgets
became more important than the dispensing of relevant knowledge
with tangible results. Instructors were told to limit challenging issues
in the classroom, to initiate sliding grade scales, to de-emphasize the
outcome of tests over the mere experiences of the students working
their way through college.

Pulp over substance. That's what Cody had seen happening.

Even the teaching books had been altered over the years. U.S.
history was being changed by the textbook writers and publishers.
Based on their agendas, politicians and educational leaders were able
to input their own views into the books and subject matters which
were being taught. Truth was being redlined, propaganda was being
inserted into the fabric of American history.

Cody was uncomfortable with these alarming changes, as were
other instructors. They were reminded, however, of "what was best
for the students" and how "any dissention within the ranks of
educators could result in specific downsizings." Most teachers,
including Cody Gordon, toed the line, even if reluctantly. A few
instructors, not only at the community college level, but also in high
school classes and four year universities, refused to adhere to
Common Core liberal standards. They were there to teach, not to
dumb down.

There were no official lists of the numerous, so-called radical teachers who were "let go due to their failure to follow internal policies." But people working in the college knew. There were some educators who plainly could not tolerate the deceptions any longer. Some moved on by choice, while others simply vanished.

Cody's friend and fellow teacher, Jonathan Campbell, was one of those who had ended his teaching career, not by choice or through attrition, but by reportedly committing suicide.

Chapter 2

It was almost six in the evening, well into the darkness of an early November winter. The cutting wind was gusting up to forty miles an hour and the temperature was plummeting toward zero. Possible snow was in the forecast, but the weatherman said the current storm conditions might be too cold to produce snow. That's what Cody heard on the weather report from a small radio on the desk in his office space. The old house furnace kept blowing warm air through the vents, fighting desperately to combat the freezing air seeping through cracked seals around the aged windows and doors.

After checking on the children watching their show in the living room Robin went down the hall to see her husband. "Hi," she said, standing in the doorway, pulling her wool sweater tighter around her. "What's up?"

"Just writing down a few things for school," Cody answered, trying to avoid what she really meant. His books and papers and lesson plans were piled neatly on the desk. He liked things organized, where everything had its place and was easy to find. That's why years earlier he had chosen history as his profession. History had a sense of order, a precise lineage of time, place, and events.

A handful of sharpened pencils and ballpoint pens stood up in a soup can wrapped in a strip of pink paper and labeled "PencilS".

Jennifer had made it in her first grade school project for her dad on Father's Day. Hanging on the wall above his desk was Jeffrey's hand made sign which read, "Dad's Office." The capital 'O' in office was a smiley face. Another sign beneath that one warned, "Don't Touch My Stuff!" Cody had made that one. To either side hung framed reproductions of the United States Constitution and The Declaration of Independence. He loved the things in his office.

Robin remained silent, waiting.

"You know Jonathan Campbell," Cody said, realizing that Robin knew him and his family well. For years Cody and Robin had spent many an evening at the Campbell's home. Informal dinners, weekend card games, a few casual drinks, sometimes just coffee and pie. They were close friends until Jonathan had changed and their marriage had broken up.

"Of course," Robin answered. "He teaches history with you at the college. We haven't seen him for…what…at least six months, ever since his…"

"Divorce." Cody ended her sentence.

"Did something happen to him?"

Cody had a difficult time saying it, but he did. "He was found dead in his office on campus."

Robin looked shocked. "Oh, dear! How? What happened?"

"The police said he killed himself. They interviewed me and a number of other potential witnesses on campus." Cody shook his head in disbelief. "I don't understand. It just doesn't make any sense."

"You witnessed it?" Robin asked, horrified at the news.

"No, but I heard the shot, a loud noise came from his office two doors from mine."

"Maybe he couldn't handle being alone. Maybe he was too depressed," Robin speculated. "Maybe…"

"No! I don't think so, but they said he shot himself!" Cody shouted.

"Poor man."

"He wouldn't have done that. I knew Jonathan. There's no way he would have taken his life," Cody tried to defend his friend.

"When his wife left and took their son he was devastated. He had to take a leave of absence from the college. You filled in for him.

Don't you remember that Cody?" Robin said, keeping her voice down so their children couldn't hear.

"Of course I remember," Cody said sharply. "But something is terribly wrong, Robin," her husband continued. "Yes, Jonathan had problems, not the least was his family leaving him. He was working through that. He was beginning to accept the fact it was his fault. For god's sake, I saw him every day after he returned to his classes. We talked about our work. We shared plans and projects. We had coffee together several times a week. He was the head of the history department. He was my boss. He was my friend, for crying out loud."

"I know," Robin added. "I didn't mean…"

"He didn't like the way things were being run at the college. He saw what they were doing. He saw what was happening to his students, to the entire system. It was tearing him apart."

"Then why didn't he just quit? He could have retired. He's been there for nearly thirty years. Even if he didn't agree with the school's policies he could still teach. You told me he had made tenure a long time ago. His job was safe. They couldn't fire him," Robin reasoned.

"This time he must have pissed off the wrong people. He kept telling me over and over again to watch out," Cody said. "He told me they were out to get him, to quiet him, and if they got too close he was going to go up the ladder so the higher ups knew what was going on."

Robin pulled back. "What did that mean?"

"I know he sounded paranoid, but maybe there was a good reason. He was fighting the dean, the college president, even the state department of education. The whole thing, top to bottom. In our department meetings he'd speak his mind no matter who was there. He didn't care. He just wanted to do what was right." Cody stopped. He admired his friend, but he believed sometimes Jonathan did go over the edge to make his point. Sometimes he was too in-your-face for his own good.

"You knew Jonathan. He wouldn't back down. To him, what was right was right, and he'd never give in," Cody insisted.

Robin took a second before answering. "Maybe that was part of his problem. Maybe he should have backed off and let things go."

Cody hesitated, and then he decided to tell his wife what had been bothering him for the past couple of days. "On Monday he told me something that scared the hell out of me."

Now Robin felt frightened. "What did he say, Cody?"

"He told me he couldn't go up the ladder. There was nobody he could tell about how the education system was destroying our country. He could prove how students were being dumbed down. He had evidence that the citizens of this country were being lied to every time they heard or read the news. He could corroborate how every new law was written to empower the government and gradually take rights away from the people. He had hard proof that every government educational report was manipulated or completely falsified to give the citizens a false sense of things getting better and safer."

"But Cody...."

He put his hand up to stop his wife. "Jonathan also told me the changes came from the top down, not from the bottom up. It gets even worse," Cody said, still having a difficult time believing what Jonathan had told him last. "A new constitution has been signed. Do you know what that means? The highest powers in the country are behind this massive fraud. The country has been taken over, Robin. It's all about money and power. Real education isn't important any longer. People don't matter to them anymore."

"You're scaring me now," Robin said. A worried look formed on her face. She knew enough about American history and its dirty politics. But at that moment she didn't care. "Cody, please let this thing go. You have a family. Let someone else get in trouble, if that's what they want."

Cody shook his head and bit his lip. "Robin, I love you, you know that. I don't want to get into an argument, but on this you're wrong. Jonathan tried to fix the system and he got killed for it. Someone has to do something about this."

"Someone else, not you."

Her husband sat quietly at his desk. He looked at his wall. Some of the most important words ever written stared down at him.

"Cody, I'm sorry about Jonathan. But you said he shot himself. It was suicide. Maybe there was something else bothering him."

"No, that's what the police said. It wasn't suicide, Robin. Someone killed him to shut him up."

"How can you even say that? The police said…"

Cody stopped her. "They lied. Someone is trying to cover this up. I know it."

"But how do you know for certain?" she asked. By this time she was on the verge of tears.

Cody looked up at his wife with a clear sense in his eyes. "Because, Robin. Jonathan never owned a gun. He'd never even touched a gun. He hated guns."

Chapter 3

Cody rose from his chair and took his wife's hand. He kissed Robin on her lips. "Everything will be fine, honey. I won't do anything stupid." He promised himself he would call the police on Friday to see if they had any more information about his friend. He wanted to put the situation with Jonathan behind him, at least for the Thanksgiving weekend. "Let's go watch the *Wizard of Oz* with the kids," he said.

He shut the hallway light off as they went toward the TV room. The wall light flickered and then popped like a small firecracker. "Hell," Cody said. "Where are the extra bulbs, Robin?"

"In the kitchen, top drawer on the right," she hollered back as she settled on the living room floor with Jeffrey and Jennifer.

Cody pulled the drawer open, moved aside a couple flashlights, a few small tools, and found a box of 60-watt bulbs. He went back to the hall light, changed the bulb, and threw the burnt out one in his office trash bin.

He then went back to the kitchen, opened the pantry door, and picked up a metal canister filled with mini-chocolate chip cookies. "Who wants cookies?" he shouted as he entered the living room.

"I do. I do," both kids screamed with joy.

"How can it get any better? Munchkins and mini-chocolate chips." Cody gave the container to his wife. The kids laughed at their father's silly joke. He was referring to the part of the movie already playing where three short Munchkins from the Land of Oz strolled up to Dorothy and sang their lollipop theme.

That was Jeffrey's cue. He threw his blanket aside and got up off the floor. Then he re-enacted the funny dance scene and bowed when he was done. "Tada!" he said, and got comfortable once again under his blanket.

Cody went to the fireplace and put a few more logs on the fire. He looked at his children and his wife nibbling on cookies. "How about some hot chocolate too?"

A chorus of 'yeses' filled the room. He went to the sink, filled the tea kettle with water, placed it on a stove burner, and turned the front knob to 'on.'

This was how it was supposed to be.

Suddenly the television turned off. The house lights shut off simultaneously as well. Jennifer began screaming. She was always afraid of the dark, even though the burning fireplace cast reassuring light throughout the living room.

"It's okay," Robin tried to calm her daughter. "The lights will come back on in a few minutes."

Jeffrey liked it. He stared at the fire and smiled. "Cool."

Cody reacted quickly. "It's just the storm. I'll go check the electrical panel. Probably tripped a breaker."

Robin rose to her feet. "I'll get the candles out of the cabinet. You children remain where you are, and stay covered."

Cody found his way back into the kitchen and retrieved a flashlight from the light bulb drawer. He checked to make sure it worked. The wind was still blowing hard, so this time he pulled his jacket from the door peg and put it on. "I'll be right back, save me some cookies," he joked with the kids.

He went out the back door and walked to the side of the house where the electrical box was. With the help of his flashlight he opened the panel and looked for any tripped circuit breakers. It had happened a few times over the years, an electrical surge, too many appliances running at the same time, too many Christmas lights on one circuit.

Just flip the switch and that was all it took. But this time all the breakers seemed to be on. He flipped the main breaker just to be sure. Peeking around the corner he could see that no lights had come on.

Had to be the storm, he figured. During the few minutes he was outside, his fingers were beginning to freeze. When he went back into the house Robin had set up several lit candles. The kids were still in place and the fire was going strong. "It's not the breakers," he said to his wife. "The storm must have knocked out a transformer nearby, or snapped some electrical lines."

Cody shook the cold from his jacket and rubbed his hands together to warm them. A hot cup of coffee would go well right now, but their stove was electric. No hot chocolate either. "Guess we'll have to make the best of it," he said to no one in particular.

"I don't like the dark," Jennifer said, keeping a tight grip on her blanket.

"It's fine sweetie," her mother said. "Let's sing a song."

"Okay," Jeffrey said, and he began. "We are the lollipop kids, the lollipop kids..."

"Let's choose another song," Robin smiled.

"I'm calling the electric company. They should know what happened and might be able to tell us when the lights will come back on," Cody said. He moved toward the kitchen again, pulled out his cell phone, looking for his long list of saved numbers. His phone didn't light up. It didn't even turn on. Frustrated, he called out to his wife. "My phone's dead. It must need a charge. I'll have to use your phone."

Robin went to her purse and handed her identical phone to Cody. He flipped it open, and it too was dark. "What the ...? Neither phone works."

"That's odd."

Cody looked at her in the dim candle light flickering from the drafts coming through the windows. "I'm going out front to see if anyone has lights." With his jacket still on he went through the front door, walked down to the sidewalk, and looked around at his neighbors' houses. It was pitch black. The entire street was quiet and blanketed in solid darkness. Instead of going back into his house he decided to walk across the narrow street to see if his friend Jack was home.

It felt strange walking into the night completely socked in by fast moving thick clouds. No lights, no traffic, no sounds except for the wind. The light from his flashlight led him to Jack's front door. He automatically went for the doorbell, and then he remembered there was no point. Cody rapped on the door. In a few seconds it opened and Jack appeared.

"Oh. It's you Cody," the old man said, looking through his bifocals. "Come in, come in. Terrible weather we're having. And now this." He slowly pointed to the burning candles in his front room. Cody noticed Jack had leaned a baseball bat back against the inside door frame. For being an eighty-seven year old man, he was still fairly strong, but a bat in his hands wouldn't really discourage a serious intruder.

"Thought I'd stop by to see if you lost your power, but it seems it's out everywhere," Cody offered.

"Thanks for coming by Cody. We're doing just fine," Jack said. "Edith is in bed. She's still sleeping." Edith, his wife of fifty-three years, was in frail health and seldom ventured outdoors now. Jack had been caring for her for a long time. They'd lived in this house for fifty years, ever since it was built. The elderly man meticulously maintained his yard, was a friendly old guy, and all around good neighbor.

Cody nodded his head. He liked the old fellow who was a World War II veteran who insisted on walking in every Veteran's Day, Fourth of July, and Christmas parade. "I'm glad to see you are okay," Cody mentioned. "Just hope they get the electricity on soon."

"Except, now we have no heat," Jack added. "The gas heater won't work without electricity to turn it on and run the blower."

Cody had completely forgotten about the furnaces not working. In this bitter cold he hoped everything would get back to normal soon. He had to ask Jack, "Can I use your phone? Our cell phones are down for some reason."

"I'd let you, but our home phone doesn't work. It went out with the lights too," the nice neighbor said. "Never owned none of those damn fancy cellular type phones myself. Too much of a bother if you ask me."

"Okay Jack. You take care and stay bundled up. Say hello to Edith for me. I'll find out what's going on and let you know tomorrow," Cody said as he headed to the door.

"Good to see you Cody. Go stay with your family," Jack said. "We'll be fine. Been through much worse over the years."

He opened his door and automatically went for his bat. "Good night my friend," Jack said. "Oh, Cody, don't let them get to you," he said as the door closed.

Cody wondered what the old man meant by that, but it didn't really matter. It was too cold outside in the howling night wind to stand there thinking, so he rushed back to his house.

Inside he smelled the burning wood. It was comforting in a strange sort of way, but he also sensed the house temperature had dropped a bit. The candles were still burning and threw off enough light to get around. Robin and the children were having a good time singing Old McDonald songs in front of the fireplace.

Cody broke up their fun and explained to his wife what he had found out about the blackout, which was absolutely nothing, except that the entire street was without power. And it definitely didn't help the situation. "We'll have to make the best of it until tomorrow, but…"

"But what?" Robin asked.

"We won't have any heat. The furnace can't start up without power."

"Well, we have the fireplace. But Cody, there's something else," his wife mentioned.

"What more can go wrong?" Cody asked, shaking his head.

"There's no water. I turned the faucet on when you were out, but there's no water."

Cody stopped to think for a minute. *How in the hell could that be?* Then it came to him. Water systems were delivered by pumps, electric pumps. Another thought popped into his brain. The radio in his office also worked on batteries. He could listen to the news to find out how bad the storm was. Carrying his flashlight he rushed to his work space, unplugged the radio, and switched it to battery power. He dialed the station selector along the full AM spectrum. Nothing, not even static. He then turned the knob to FM and increased the volume, getting the same results. He opened his laptop, but even on battery power it refused to boot up.

"Damn!"

Cody sat back for a second, thinking. He picked up his truck keys and hurried through the kitchen into the garage. The radio in his truck would give him information he needed. He opened the pickup's door and jumped in. He couldn't believe how cold it was in the garage. He inserted his key to start the engine. It refused to turn over. He tried it again, then again. He turned the radio knob, but it too was dead.

Confused, Cody dashed into the house, and without saying a word, grabbed Robin's car keys out of her purse. He had installed a new battery in her Nissan not two months ago. He desperately went through the same motions over and over. Her car was dead too. *But that was impossible,* he thought. *Wasn't it?*

He sped back inside and saw his wife looking anxiously at his erratic actions. "Robin, I don't understand what's happening. There's no electricity, no phone service, no computer hook up, no heat, no water. Now the cars won't start and the radios don't work. I've never heard of a winter storm knocking out everything. Something weird is going on, Robin. I don't know what it is, but I'm going to find out."

Chapter 4

That evening Cody had made several more trips to the woodpile. He dumped a big heap of frozen, but dried wood on the patio and stacked the fireplace bin full for the cold night ahead. He thought it best for the whole family to sleep together in the living room since the fire was their only source of heat and the bedrooms in the back of the house would get colder.

Robin had laid most every blanket they had down on the carpet near the hearth as a cushion for her and the children to sleep. Cody tried to sleep on the long sofa, but at best he slept off and on through the night. Each time he woke he topped off the fire with more logs and made sure his kids hadn't kicked off their covers. The house was getting colder by the minute and he started to get concerned for his family's well being.

Early in the morning he stoked the fire for the umpteenth time. He looked at his watch and was surprised to see it was keeping time. It was six fifteen on Thanksgiving Day. He tried the light switches; however, the power was still off. The faucets ran dry too. He checked his cell phone once more, but it didn't light up.

Walking about the house, the temperature felt like it was fifty degrees. Outside, fifty degrees was not too bad. Inside, it was a raw, bone chilling level. Cody opened the living room curtains enough to look out. There was a thin layer of white frost on the graveled front yards and the street looked slick with a film of ice. The winds had died down and all the trees had lost their leaves to last night's blowing gusts.

From the window he glanced both up and down the road hoping to see repair crews in their big rigs and yellow gear working to restore power. No one was out there. It appeared that no traffic had even traveled the slick icy roads. The storm clouds, still dark and threatening, hung low enough to block the early sun. The southern mountains, usually in full view, were lost in the weather. Touching the window pane, Cody could tell the outside temperature was probably close to ten degrees. By all accounts it appeared the cold was with them for at least another day.

Robin woke up, rose from the bedding on the floor a bit achy from the ordeal, and cuddled up against her husband looking out the window. Her thick woolen robe was warm from the blankets and she felt good next to his side.

"It seems that nothing has changed since last night," Cody commented.

"Brrrrr. It's cold," Robin said.

"Yeah, everyone needs to bundle up today," Cody said. "I can make some hot water on the barbeque grill. It will help a lot. The kids can have hot drinks and hot cereal for breakfast."

"Good idea, Mr. Gordon," she teased. "That will work. But where are you going to get the water?"

"Mrs. Gordon," he threw it back to her. "I had a full kettle of water on the stove last night, if you remember. Is the cold making you forget?"

"Ah…ah," she mumbled. "Hey, I'm sorry about Jonathan."

"Yeah. Me too."

"Doesn't look as if we'll be eating a traditional Thanksgiving meal today," Robin remarked. "I'm not even sure if we have a hand can opener to open the peas."

She patted Cody's backside, went into the kitchen and opened the refrigerator door. Inside was dark, but remained cool. The defrosted turkey was still good and could be cooked outside, although she would have to cut it into pieces to cook on the grill. The freezer compartment on the bottom was cold and there was a full tub of ice, as if they needed more ice. That would last for a day or two. But by then the electricity should be on. In the meantime, any perishable foods, like the milk and fresh vegetables, could be stored outside in the colder patio.

"I could use a coffee," Cody told his wife. "How about you?"

"Right now, anything warm will do," Robin answered.

Cody took the tea kettle filled with water out to the gas grill at the far edge of the back patio. He reached under the grill and turned the propane tank valve on. Another full tank sat next to it. Then he turned the gas knob controlling the side pan burner to the 'on' position. He pushed the starter button to ignite the gas without success. "Not this too!" he shouted. He had a foolish thought that the propane gas might have frozen over night. He pushed the button again a bit too hard. This time the orange flames kicked up.

Cody went back into the house to wait for the water to boil. The kids were up and running around in their pajamas and stocking feet. Robin was folding and putting away the night's blankets. After several minutes Cody retrieved the kettle and poured an instant coffee for himself, a green tea for Robin, and two hot chocolates. Enough hot water was left for two bowls of instant oatmeal for the children.

He checked the fire and peered out the front window. Still no repair trucks. "What the hell is going on?" he said aloud. He felt he had to do something. This situation was getting ridiculous. Where were the police? Wouldn't a person think that under these dire circumstances the local police or sheriff department would patrol the neighborhoods making sure the citizens were safe? Especially when there was no way to communicate. What about the National Guard, the Red Cross? People pay their taxes; they should be able to rely on emergency services.

He was getting upset, maybe a little crazy. Annoyed. Definitely impatient. It had only been twelve hours since the power outage, though it seemed much longer. He started doubting that the electric would ever come back on. What if this abnormally severe storm and its effects lasted for more than a few days. Or maybe longer. The dismal possibility concerned him.

Robin returned from the linen closet. "It might be a good idea to think about our situation," her husband said without warning. "What if the electric stays off for any length of time? We need water. Each person needs at least a gallon of water per day. We don't have that. The house will stay cold, even with the fireplace burning. Our cars don't run. We have no means of contacting anyone. The only good thing is we can cook on the grill. Hell, where is everyone?"

"It will be okay," Robin said. She didn't like when Cody got this way. He was normally calm, reserved almost. Not too many things actually bothered him. He generally went with the flow and almost never got aggravated.

He softly grabbed his wife by the shoulders. "There's something I need to do. I'm going out. I have to go to the police station. They must know what's happening. If this weather continues, people are going to need help soon."

"The police station?" Robin said. "That's four or five miles away! You can't drive there. You definitely can't walk. It's freezing outside. You'd freeze to death trying to walk that far."

Cody stood solid. "I can't simply wait here. Wait for what? What if there is no help coming? What will happen when we run out of water and food? Do you know what will happen to us and the kids when we run out of firewood? There's enough wood for a few more days. Then what?"

"Things will get better by then. I'm sure of it."

"Well, I'm not so certain." Cody went down the hall to his bedroom closet. He pulled a sweater over his shirt and grabbed a heavy winter jacket from the back rail. He found an old winter hat that he never wore and tugged it over his head. Then he picked up his wallet and cell phone.

"Robin," he began when he entered the kitchen again. "I'll be gone for awhile. Maybe I can get some more water at the store. We need water."

"But Cody!" Robin tried to protest, although she knew once her husband had his mind set, there was no use trying to change it. Maybe he was right.

Cody looked her square in the eyes. He was serious. Serious as all hell. "There's a half case of bottled water in the pantry. Heat it up and have the children drink plenty of hot chocolate or tea. It will keep them warm. I'll be back in a few hours. Trust me Robin. I have to go."

"Okay. Are you warm enough?" she asked and buttoned his top two jacket buttons. He looked funny in the hat, but Robin still felt nervous

"I'll be fine. Don't worry. I'll have my phone with me, just in case we get service again."

All of a sudden Jeffrey ran into the kitchen yelling. "Mommy, Daddy, I can't go to the bathroom. There's no water. I can't go poop."

Cody smiled at his son. "Daddy will fix it Jeffrey. I'm going to get it all fixed."

Before he went out the front door he told his wife, "Lock the doors and don't open them for anyone. You hear me?"

"Yes. Here," she said, handing him his leather work gloves which were in kitchen drawer. "You'll need these. Be careful."

"I'll be back as soon as I can." He stepped out into the cold and shut the door. He had no idea what he would discover, but he knew he had no other choice.

Chapter 5

Thus far, exactly twelve hours into the scheduled blackout, everything was going precisely as planned. It was still too early to see the results of this grand operation, but they would most certainly occur within the allotted time. Another thirty-six hours was all that was needed. That's when everything in normal everyday America would begin to collapse.

And collapse they would.

The entire coordinated scheme will begin as confusion sets in almost immediately. Irritation and discomfort will arise during the minor annoyances inside the initial twelve hours. Within eighteen hours in the extended cold and deepening darkness, uncertainty and a growing sense of urgency will most certainly develop. One full day into the event, people will begin crying for help and cheering at the sight of uniformed relief. In two days most of the populace will be accounted for, one way or another.

All essential forces will be firmly in place. Every facility will be up and ready. Each conceivable contingency will be anticipated and covered. Those in charge of this enormous undertaking will be keeping a watchful eye on the complex mission as they anxiously follow the prescribed phases so meticulously laid out and as they patiently wait for the end.

Every electrical device and computerized component and automated element in a three thousand mile perimeter will be damaged beyond repair. Replacement components and alternate systems will be unavailable. Citizens of the land will quickly realize their misguided reliance and unfettered addiction to modern world inventions and conveniences. Their woeful dependency on such vulnerable, advanced technology will soon be known. Their so called easy life will disappear in a second. People all across the nation will curse their imprudent ways and regret their reckless conduct. Being ill-prepared will carry no excuse, but will only offer frustration, confusion, and despair.

For most, it will be too late.

All manners of communication will revert back two hundred years, well before the invention of the telephone and light bulb and electricity. Messages across any distance will take weeks by carrier, if not months to share. News will become irrelevant and useless, obsolete when sent, outdated when received. Information of all sorts will be dispensed only as needed by those who deem it so, and controlled by the few.

Travel will be limited to foot and beasts. As in ancient times, backs will tote people's tattered bags and wagons will haul their meager belongings. Only those few things of necessity will be carried. People will leave their homes, forsake their properties. All other possessions, once thought so valuable, will be left behind, non-essential for life to continue. Journeys will be checked at frequent points, on all highways and exits, waterways and seas, either to be denied or tolled. A great exodus of citizens will follow the crowds in front and end up lost in places even more desolate than from where they had departed.

Commerce will be restricted to local bartering for those with few things of value. Trade will be for those allowed it. Commodities will be restricted and dispensed in small units by those who have. Food will become scarcer by the hour. It will be hoarded by the few and hunted by the many. Water, the vital source of life, will be more precious than oil and more prized than sacks of gold. Supplies will dwindle through fear and greed and bedlam.

Only the strong shall sustain. From the masses a mere handful of determined souls shall be fortunate enough, or determined enough, to survive.

All stores will be stripped of supplies, depleted of essentials, ransacked of every conceivable item. From food goods to daily supplies, from medicines to the last bag of grain, from TVs to the newest DVDs. Businesses will be shuttered and closed, but soon destroyed by marauders intent on destruction for its own sake, and by those in search of hope.

Banks will be emptied of cash and coin. Vaults and drawers and trays cleared down to the last piece of copper. Paper dollars, once the most sought after of dear possessions, will be trumped by silver tenfold. And silver trumped by gold ten times again. Those with real coin will trade to survive. Those without will go without.

Churches and temples will be chained closed to those of faith and those praying for hope. Houses will be boarded or burned, raided and looted. Schools will become temporary prison quarters packed with once common citizens, parents of the children and teachers of the students. Camps and centers of the grandest scale in the most obscure and secret places will be overtly contained, guarded to hold those distrusted.

Hospitals and clinics, once havens of care and promise, will be shut to injured and sick. The injured and sick will slowly disappear as their ills are not met. Those seeking help will find none. Those offering help will be barred.

Lands will lay barren as if never touched. Farms will dry up into dust bowls never seen before. Crops will decay on their vines and stems. Lakes and rivers and streams, once jewels of the land, will be poisoned and made toxic.

Diseases long contained and cured will spread again and cover the land, leaving no one unscathed. Infections and unknown maladies will multiply and spread from the dead to most living beings. Those living will fester and spread to the rest, until few remain whole as before.

Ruthless gangs of criminals, intent on terror and revenge, will run unleashed. Mobs of youths and those of color once denied their chance, will scatter and right their social injustices. Desperate men, once kind and civil, will terrorize in search of sustenance as the streets become feared danger zones. Soldiers in mass squads of unknown origin will by force and violence enter the homes to clear those who remain and dispose of those who resist. And for their vigilance they will be promised great riches.

From shore to shore and wide boundaries to the north and south, an entire population, which through all recorded time had once reveled in comfort and wealth unrivaled throughout the world, will be decimated to a tiny fraction of its former self as catastrophe is thrust upon them. Those left will be secured and monitored, enslaved and worked, confined and tortured, until it is no longer practical.

The few sorry survivors still free to roam and hide, chased by legions of paid warriors loyal to their fortunes, will silently join in battle against the evil makers of death. But they too will be crushed if divine righteousness abandons their souls.

And as the grand event continues, the bitter weather altered by science and maneuvered by man will hasten all by design and with a touch of sheer chance. Every person within the grand circle will soon believe in the concept of hell on earth. The fortunate ones who endure the event may wish they weren't so lucky.

Chapter 6

The cold air blasted Cody like a solid brick wall. He looked at the empty street and moved toward the sidewalk. He was already freezing and flapped his arms against his sides. He smelled burning wood from nearby chimneys. Wisps of white smoke escaped his house chimney flue. To his right on the street corner he saw someone bundled against the freeze walking his way. The man waved at Cody and came closer.

"Thought that was you," the man said.

"Didn't recognize you with that coat and hat," Cody said. It was Nick, his neighbor from three doors down the street. They weren't exactly close friends, but they had run into each other several times ever since Nick and his family had moved into the neighborhood last summer. Mostly they simply waved at one another from inside their vehicles on their way to work or on their way home.

"Brutal weather, huh?" Nick said, his teeth chattering in the cold.

"Tell me about it," Cody remarked. "Your phone working?"

"Nope, must have gone down during the blackout. My car won't start either," the man added. Nick was a contractor working for the Army on Fort Huachuca, the huge military intelligence base adjacent to the city. As far as Cody could figure, Nick was some kind of computer whiz who worked on high tech, secret government projects well beyond Cody's comprehension. He too had the long four day Thanksgiving week-end off from work.

"You and your family doing okay?" Cody asked him.

"They're doing fine so far, as long as we have heat."

Cody looked up and saw smoke rising from Nick's fireplace chimney. Nick had twin daughters, Caitlin and Tanya, who were about six years old. Cody had seen them all dressed up in their cute costumes when they came by his house on Halloween. Their kids played together frequently.

"I stepped out to see if there was anybody moving out here. Haven't seen nor heard a car drive by since yesterday afternoon," Nick remarked. Some ice still covered the road and there were no recent tire tracks. It was odd not to see or hear any traffic driving through the neighborhood.

Cody nodded. "Something's wrong. I can't understand how everything could shut down at the same time. I mean, the phones and the cars should still work. We've had snow storms and cold spells here before. We're at an elevation of nearly five thousand feet, so being in the high desert we can expect some bad weather on occasion, but I've never experienced anything like this."

"I agree," Nick said. "What baffles me is there's no running water too. And no radio signals. That doesn't just happen because of an arctic sweep." Clouds of warm vapor escaped their mouths as they spoke. "There is one incident that could have caused this," he added.

Cody stared at him in the sub-freezing conditions. "What do you think it is?"

"Well," Nick began, "I can see the electricity going out. That's not uncommon in weather like this. But since everything that seems to be affected is electrical, there has to be some sort of interference with electromagnetic components. You know, electric and phone service, car engines, even radio transmissions."

"That sounds logical," Cody said. "But how?"

The two men both wished they were in a warmer place, instead of standing on the roadside freezing their asses off. Nick started to explain what might have happened. "In today's digital age nearly everything we rely on is controlled by computers. Try to think of one modern convenience that isn't dependent on micro-chips and semiconductors. We've turned every aspect of our lives over to electrical devices and tiny silicon chips capable of handling billions of functions. Hell, even the old style hand-cranked pencil sharpener and can opener have gone electric."

"So you think the computer systems that run everything have somehow failed because of this unusual weather?" Cody questioned.

Nick tried not to think of the worst possible scenario, but he knew the unlimited potential of complex computer systems. That was his job. He worked on super computers everyday developing networks and software that only a few years ago seemed farfetched and futuristic. Some of the advanced programs he'd seen would make recent science fiction movies look like children's games. But he also knew of their weak spots.

"No," Nick stopped for a moment. "I don't think the weather has caused this problem. Not all of it, anyway. I think maybe it was an intentional event."

Cody looked shocked. "You mean someone or some group may have caused this blackout on purpose? This whole thing is turning into a crisis. People's lives could be at stake. Why in the world would someone do such a thing?" It was beyond his grasp that someone would, or could purposely instigate such a disaster.

Nick nodded his head. He knew what he was suggesting was a feasible, but unlikely possibility. Carrying such a test to this extent was almost unbelievable to him too. He threw his arms into the air. "I'm just saying it could be that. Maybe so, maybe not. No matter what, I can't come up with any other explanation."

He didn't mention what he really thought, because it would be too terrible. Terrorism was still a major threat in the world, especially to the United States. Ever since the 9/11 attack the whole world had changed and America wore a big target on its back.

It was too cold to think straight. "It had better be fixed, whatever it is and by whoever caused it," Cody said, his mouth almost useless at this temperature. He was unconvinced by Nick's theory. That would never happen. Besides, he thought, to what end would it lead?

Cody dropped the conversation about unlikely plans to inflict pain on citizens of his small city. He turned his thoughts to the reason he was out in the cold in the first place. He was heading to the city's police station. "Since there's no way to communicate and it seems no help is on its way," he told Nick, "I'm going to the police to get some answers."

"Mind if I come along? I want to know what's really going on too."

"Of course," Cody said. "I'd welcome the company. But first I want to check in on Jack. See how he and his wife are doing. I told him last night I would stop by sometime today."

Nick turned to look back at his house. "Okay, I want to let Lisa know where I'm going. I'll meet you at Jack's in a couple minutes." Nick turned and walked toward his home.

Cody went straight to Jack's front door. He almost reached for the doorbell again. Old habits. The smell of burning wood got stronger. But it smelled different as he was about to knock on the door. It had a more pungent odor than the prevalent smell of mesquite or juniper in the air. It reeked of the acrid scent of burning oil. He knocked on the solid door, waiting for the old man to answer. There was no sound. So he knocked again, this time a little bit harder. Still no response. The next time Cody removed the leather glove from his right hand and banged on the door with force.

He could smell the caustic smoke lingering near the doorway. Something was wrong. One more time he rapped on the door, then he tried the handle, but of course it was locked tight.

He called his neighbor's name.

"Jack! Jack!"

Maybe the man was in the back bedroom and couldn't hear him. Maybe he was sleeping. Whatever the reason, Cody was getting concerned. He looked through the front windows, but the drapes covered every inch, making it impossible to see inside.

Then he decided to do the crazy thing. He rammed the door with his shoulder, padded by his thick winter jacket. It barely budged. He hit it again and the frame cracked a bit. The smell of smoke seeped through the small fracture. One more time, with all his strength, he stepped back and slammed forward into the door, crashing it open.

A sudden wave of caustic smoke was quickly sucked out the open doorway nearly knocking Cody over. With a gloved hand he covered his mouth and nose the best he could and entered the dimly lit room. His eyes sprinted around looking for the fire. But there was none. Not in the front living room, anyway.

He called out again.

"Jack! Jack!"

There was only silence.

The smoke was thinning as it escaped. The smell was like that of a chemical fire. The house was as dark as night, accept for the faint light from the doorway. Each window was covered with heavy drapes to seal out the daylight and cold. The inside was nearly as cold as the outside. Two barely lit candles rested in pools of melting wax.

"Jack! Edith! Where are you?" Cody continued to shout.

The house had two bedrooms, Cody remembered. One on either side of the main entrance. Cody opened the door to the left. It was even darker inside and contained a chilling freeze.

He called out again.

"Jack! Jack!"

Quickly moving inside the room he found the bed and felt around, but it was empty. Then he turned and ran across the house to the second bedroom.

That door was locked. A visible stream of smoke was oozing under the door's threshold gap. In one fell charge Cody kicked the hollow core door back. The room was filled with smoke making it difficult to see the furniture. The scathing smoke made him gag and he almost threw up from natural reflex. Moving farther inside with his arms extended he touched something soft. Bed covers. Then he felt something solid, like a person's leg or foot covered with blankets. Immediately he went to the window and yanked the drapes back to let some light in.

Some of the layered smoke swept out the open bedroom door. Cody's eyes were stinging and tearing from the poison. His throat was gasping for clean air. He could not believe what he was seeing. Lying on the bed were Jack and Edith.

"Cody! Cody!" He heard a voice from the other side of the house. It almost startled him to death. Then he realized it was Nick.

"In here, Nick. In the bedroom."

Nick entered the second bedroom and saw the two old people in their bed. "Oh, no!" he mumbled. "Oh, no!"

Cody wiped his burning eyes with the back of his hand and coughed. "Jack," he whispered. "Edith." He removed his other glove, reached over and touched Jack's neck in hopes of feeling a pulse, but it was too late. The old man's lips were a dark blue, his eyes were closed. Then Cody did the same to poor Edith. The skin on her neck was cold and rigid. Her lips were a deep purple. Her eyes were also closed, as if she were sleeping comfortably.

"I'm no expert, but I'd guess that she's been dead for some time now," Cody said to Nick. "Longer than Jack."

Jack's body was lying cuddled up close to his dear wife, their faces nearly touching. A small pillow rested awkwardly against Edith's forehead. Cody immediately thought, *Jack, what have you done?*

Several blankets and a heavy quilt had been tucked around her in loving comfort. Jack's left arm was wrapped around his wife in a lasting hug as they drifted off together toward a better life.

"Christ."

Cody looked around the room. Sitting on the floor on the other side of the bed was a kerosene lantern; the kind often used outdoors, its wick still burning, its stained glass flue still spewing deadly smoke. Nick went to the lantern and turned the brass knob to extinguish the flame.

Cody noticed something crunched in Jack's outstretched hand. A white tag, a small piece of paper.

"He's holding something," Cody said to Nick.

"Leave it," Nick said, nervous just being in a room with two dead people.

"No," Cody whispered.

He took Jack's frigid hand and gently unclenched it. Cupped in his neighbor's thin, wrinkled palm was a key with a scrap of white paper taped to it. Cody removed the key and moved Jack's hand back to Edith's side. Cody's name was written on it. He looked confused and glanced up at Nick.

"What do you think this goes to?"

Nick shook his head and shrugged his shoulders.

"Must be important," Cody remarked. "Maybe it goes to a cabinet or closet."

"Did he have a safe?" Nick asked.

Cody had no idea. "Let's look around."

The two men slowly moved through the cold house. For added light they pulled open the rest of the window drapes. They looked in the kitchen and every closet, but none had locks. They rambled through the living room, then the front bedroom and found nothing.

"This feels creepy," Nick said.

"Keep looking," Cody said. It did feel disturbing, almost invasive. But Jack wanted Cody to find whatever it was he had left.

"I found something," Nick called out. "There's a safe in here."

In Jack's bedroom closet there was a small portable safe stuck in the back corner under some bath towels and folded blankets. The safe was about a foot tall and a foot wide, with a dial tumbler and a key slot. It was heavy, but Cody was able to rock it away from the wall allowing some shadowed light from the bedroom window to filter in on it.

The men looked at each other. Cody got on his knees and inserted the key, then pulled the handle. The safe door opened without having to use the combination dial. Though dark inside, Cody could see a piece of paper on top of some odd shaped items. He removed the paper and brought it up to full light. It had Cody's name scribbled on the outside fold.

Cody unfolded the paper. It was a brief letter to him from Jack. He read the letter aloud:

Cody---

These are bad times we live in. We have forgotten there are always terrible people out there. We have ignored past events and are destined to relive them. Being a teacher of history, you should know that. We have forgotten how to fight for what is right. I know. I've been there. All the things in this safe are for you, Cody. Over the years you have been a dear friend to Edith and me. Take them and protect your family. If anything, remember what a great man once said, "Bad things happen when good men do nothing."

Jack

"Wow," Nick uttered.

"Yeah. Wow," Cody softly responded.

"What was that last part, about bad things happening?" Nick asked Cody.

"That," Cody said in a broken voice, "was what Thomas Jefferson said while he was writing the Declaration of Independence."

"Holy mackerel!"

"Exactly," Cody answered.

After a long moment Cody stuck his hand in the safe and found a pistol, an older model it seemed, though Cody was completely unfamiliar with firearms. There was a small box of ammunition, apparently for the pistol too. Behind it was a woolen sock filled with what felt like coins. Cody picked it up. It was very heavy. He untied the top of the sock and poured out a few coins. There were old silver dollars from the late 1800s and the early 1900s, mixed with older quarters. These were pure silver, unlike the plated coins of today, and their value had steadily risen over the past decades. Three additional heavy socks, equally filled, rested on the bottom of the safe.

"Jack must have been saving these coins for a long time," Cody said.

"Apparently," Nick said.

"I'm going to leave this stuff here for now. We need to go to the police," Cody said in an urgent tone. He put the socks and pistol back in the safe, locked it with the key, and tossed the blankets on top. He slid the key in his pocket, and then also put the letter in his pocket.

Both men looked at each other. "This shouldn't have happened," Nick said with a twist of rage in his voice.

"Damn straight," Cody said. "Somebody needs to do something about this."

Chapter 7

S omebody *was* doing something about it.
     Two hundred eighty heavily armed troopers stood motionless
awaiting their orders at the command center. The new regional high
school five miles on the outskirts of the city was an ideal headquarters
for this small district. It had been commandeered at the start of the
event, not a full day earlier. All the facility's ingress-egress ports were
easily guarded. It was far enough from the main population area to be
tightly secured. The building and parking lots were large enough to
accommodate the massive number of transports and detainees that
were expected. It was the perfect facility with only one way in and
one way out.

     The soldiers were geared up for action with their semi-automatic
AK-47 assault rifles and SIG P226 Elite side arms. They wore all
black, cold-weather uniforms and were protected by full-body Kevlar
vests and Blackhawk ballistic Kevlar helmets different from any
military garb ever seen on the street. The uniforms showed no forms
of identification. There were no badges or shields or emblems or
patches of recognition. There were no signs of rank attached to their
sleeves or lapels or helmets. And of course there were no name tags.

     They weren't the usual security type personnel hired by banks or
research buildings whose purpose was mainly as a visual deterrent to
potential illicit behavior. They weren't regular soldiers ready to fight
for and defend their nation. They weren't National Guard weekend
warriors working outside their zones. They weren't part of local

police forces who had taken oaths to serve and protect their citizenry.

These professional units were hired for one thing, and one thing only.

The forces comprised of well-trained, rogue American soldiers and a much larger, but less qualified, foreign militia. The Americans were well compensated for their services. Most of them were active duty military soldiers, the ones who had, for selfish reasons, broken away from their main corps whose purpose was to protect the nation.

Others were hard cases, disgruntled retired veterans who had, in their opinion, been done a great disservice by their government, either through neglect or outright disregard. The rest of the Americans were reassigned law enforcement officers who had figured the odds and moved to the dark side. These men had no allegiance to their country. They were loyal only to the people who paid them. They had forsaken their oaths to defend their native land in turn for the chance to alter the nation's path with the possibility of getting rich.

The foreign troops, imported under the guise of international cooperative training programs underwritten through subversive treaties, came from various countries around the world. They numbered nearly half a million, surreptitiously hidden from the general population in various preparation stations throughout the country.

The largest contingency of imported militia was from China. Most of which were low level communist soldiers anxious to fight the White Devil and eager to make more than two dollars a day. Their homeland government had worked out a deal to supply second rate troops to the new American forces in return for future agreed upon favors and rights in the fertile western states.

Brigades of Russian troops similarly transported to secluded Army bases had gladly taken up arms against their American counterparts. They too were determined to wipe out their decadent foe with the assurance of getting rich doing it. Other employed militia enticed with the promise of amnesty and untold entitlements included tens of thousands of undocumented soldiers from south of the border. They willingly joined the private ranks to battle the soft and rich residents they were assigned to gather.

There were several advantages of using foreign troops. They took orders well from their American superiors, expecting their just rewards in the end. They worked extremely cheaply when compared to American soldiers or experienced 'for hire' mercenaries. They could be vicious in the field, and having no loss of love for their target population, they had no second thoughts about brutalizing their marks.

Plus, and most beneficial to those in charge, these blended misfits were ultimately easily expendable when the proper time came.

The soldiers' mission was to clear the entire district of all citizens known to have harbored unpopular opinions against the newly established leadership. There were many to be dealt with. Tens of thousands resided in this tiny southwestern district alone. Having been secretly monitored and scrutinized by various 'national security' agencies, some for many years, most of the people here were on the dreaded list, though, without their knowledge.

The infamous list is quite extensive. It had been devised by various governmental agencies whose main focus is to identify extremists and potential terrorists, both foreign and domestic. The inclusive and exhaustive list, backed by newly signed laws under the wide auspices of national security, covers all partisan sectors of the population. Conservatives, right-wingers, constitutionalists, gun owners, educators, business owners, and Christians are among the most watched over.

Fort Huachuca, the sister city of Sierra Vista, and surrounding towns are located in the southern portion of what is officially referred to as FEMA Region 9. Arizona, Nevada, and California make up this geographic region of the continental United States. The Federal Emergency Management Agency had been established back in 1978 under guidelines which differed today. Its main mission was to respond to natural disasters in the U.S. and attempt to aid those citizens affected by the disasters. All told, ten regions in the country were established for similar purposes.

But, like many official government agencies, FEMA's function had been drastically changed. In 2003, FEMA was absorbed by the newly established Department of Homeland Security, altering its fundamental mission. National security had become its mainstay.

The projected numbers of dissidents is unusually high in this corner of Region 9 due to the strong affiliation with Fort Huachuca, home to a major military intelligence contingency and the Electronic Proving Ground. The base is the economic anchor of the large county, and as such, controls the financial viability of the area. The huge Army base is situated at the foot of the Huachuca Mountains near the southern tip of the Rockies, a picturesque area not far from Mexico. Established in the 1880s, the post had over the years become a key military facility focused on national defense and an attractive spot to thousands of retired veterans and their families. Because of the close proximity to the military facilities and its services available to those who had served, many ex-service men and women reside in Sierra Vista, the mid-size city located just outside the fort's main gate.

It is generally recognized that most military personnel, retired and active, tend to be loyal to the older form of national allegiance. They had devoted their lives to their beloved country. They had served and were wounded and many died for the principles they believed in. They were patriots of their nation, aligned in the truths which they had been taught and learned and respected. They believed in the sovereignty of their country and the greatness of their homeland. Not lightly, they had taken oaths to protect this country of theirs from all enemies, both foreign and domestic.

And so, they were considered suspicious and dangerous.

These sons and daughters of America had an obsessive disposition toward national pride, historical integrity, and self-reliance. Despite any personal differences, as a group they would stand tall to protect their country. That was the main reason they were targeted out as potential opponents to the good of the new leadership's agenda, what some would call the New World Order. They were essentially all on the list held by those in charge.

The combat ready troops at the high school knew what their orders were and exactly what was expected of them. Their training for this event had been intense and clear. Their task wasn't so much to defend and protect as it was to intimidate and secure. Their job was to aid in changing the face of America, no matter at what costs. All forms of aggression were considered acceptable to the end.

They were called to order, about to enter the first phase of the new nationwide offense. Operation Rescue was prepared to kick off. The people of this small community, just like thousands of others throughout the United States of America, would soon learn of the sweeping changes to come.

Chapter 8

Cody and Nick looked at the bodies of their neighbors, Jack and Edith, frozen as one into eternity. The men slowly backed out of the house. Nick snuffed out the candles in the front room with his fingers. Cody pulled the front door shut and drew it tight enough to stay closed. Later he would return to gather the items which Jack had left him.

It was mid-morning, the sun remained hidden behind the storm clouds, and the cold seemed to worsen.

"You ready?" Cody asked Nick.

"Yeah."

"Well, let's go."

Cody looked over at his house. Robin was looking out the living room window through the drawn curtain. She smiled and waved at her husband and he waved back. In a few hours this whole fiasco should be over and done with, he said to himself. Soon he'd be enjoying a nice turkey dinner with his family.

The two walked up the road toward the top of the hill. They had a long hike to the police station. It could take an hour or longer to get there. The sidewalk was slippery in places and the persistent cold wind didn't make it any easier to navigate their way.

"That was horrible back there," Nick said.

Cody didn't say a word. It was more than horrible. It was disconcerting. A lot of questions began working their way into his mind. Why did Jack and his wife have to die? The answer was, they didn't. Why did he have a gun and all those silver coins? Maybe he was paranoid or just cautious. Why did he leave them all to him? Cody didn't believe Jack and Edith had any children. And what did Jack mean in his cryptic message? What was all that about this being bad times and terrible people and protecting his family? Why were these bad times? And who were the terrible people?

The old man was losing it, Cody thought.

The men reached the top of the hill. They would head north at the Coronado intersection up to the main road. Several cars were parked haphazardly in the middle of the street and along the curbs. The drivers must have lost power when the blackout hit. The cars were simply abandoned where they had died, blocking the streets from all directions.

Up ahead, Cody could see Coronado Drive. It was usually thick with traffic, but this morning he didn't see or hear any. *Well, it was Thanksgiving morning,* he thought.

"This feels strange," Nick said.

"Very peculiar," Cody replied.

At the corner of the intersection he looked both ways. There were dozens of deserted vehicles scattered everywhere. Some had their car hoods open. A city police car with its driver's side door still open, rested at an awkward angle against the sidewalk.

"Very peculiar," Cody repeated himself.

He saw a couple of people bound in overcoats and wrapped in blankets walking north toward town. Cody nodded at one of them as he passed. He and Nick weren't the only ones searching for answers. The two men walked without speaking, their hands jammed deep in their jacket pockets, their faces looking downward for ice slicks. Their ears and noses were red from the cold. Their eyes squinted nearly shut as if to stay warm. Puffs of hot vapor escaped their mouths as they continued.

Cody's mind returned to Jack's letter. The old man had written that Cody should know about past events being ignored because he was a history teacher. It was as if Jack was chastising him for allowing something to happen. What exactly did the old man mean by that? Cody had an idea, but he didn't really want to accept the truth.

The most pressing thing that bothered Cody about the letter, however, was the quote Jack had written. *"Bad things happen when good men do nothing."* Cody had taught that actual Jefferson passage in his history classes. He had skimmed over it along with many other pertinent sayings attributed to great American leaders. Washington, Franklin, Adams, Hancock, Jefferson, and more. He had glided over significant historical events in American history in a perfunctory manner. Names, places, events, dates. Mere lists of information required to pass the course.

That was the kind of history he had been teaching his students. But Cody knew there was something much more than plain facts taken from a text book. He was bothered by what Jack had written and what he had been reminded of.

By this time they had walked over a mile.

"The traffic lights are out up ahead," Nick mumbled. "The blackout is wider than we expected."

"Let's keep going," Cody said. "We'll go to Safeway farther up. Maybe they have electricity." The cold wasn't affecting him as much now. Maybe because his ears were numb and he was still thinking about that damn letter in his pocket.

Once they reached the intersection of Coronado and Golf Links a loud noise caught their attention. It sounded like an engine on a sick lawnmower. In the morning overcast they saw two lights coming down the street going too fast for the slick road conditions. It was a car, or a truck, or some odd shaped vehicle. Headlights were weaving around abandoned cars stranded on the street like it was moving through an old pinball machine. The vehicle drew closer and hit the corner barely slowing down.

Cody and Nick jumped from the sidewalk to get out of the way from the reckless driver. It was a van and it swerved sharply and slid onto the walkway, stopping inches from the astonished men. The vehicle was one of those old Volkswagen bus vans. It had once been painted a two-tone green and white. But that was at least fifty years ago, back in its heyday as a hippie mobile. The side panels were beat to hell and several windows were held in place with layers of duct tape.

The driver manually rolled down his side window. "Whoa, dude! That was intense! Hope I didn't freak you out. Friggin' brakes need a tune-up." Earsplitting noise from an ancient eight-track tape player filled the van and drowned out what he was saying. "You guys okay?" the driver asked.

Cody and Nick couldn't hear a word this crazy dude was mouthing. The driver finally figured it out.

"Oh, yeah. Sorry about that." He stretched over and lowered the music to a less piercing level. "Hey! You dudes want a ride?" he asked.

The two understood and nodded.

"Well, hop right in," the driver said. "Use the back door, the side ones don't work. And don't mind the crap inside. I've been meaning to clean it up."

Cody and Nick jumped into the back and crawled forward over piles of boxes and clothes cluttering the inside of the stripped out van. Cody climbed over the bench seat and sat down. Nick found a solid box in the back and sat on it close to the front. The men introduced themselves to the odd driver. The heater was cranking in its attempt to keep the van warm, but it was losing the battle.

"Thanks," Cody said. "Damn cold outside."

"Friggin' glacial dude. Been tooling around town all morning, checking out the scene. It's wild, man. My name's Zeke, but my close friends call me LuNar."

Zeke must have been in his mid-sixties. He had a long gray ponytail, a scraggly white-gray beard, and a crazy look in his eyes. He wore a baseball cap emblazon with 'PEACE' on the front and a vintage Army fatigue jacket from the Vietnam War era.

The first thing Cody thought of was this weirdo was a remnant from the free-spirited, make-love-not-war days of the 1960s. LuNar was an appropriate name for this senior whacko on the loose. Cody and Nick introduced themselves as they tried to rub some life back into their ears. As they began warming up they could smell a distinct, though faint, smell of marijuana inside the van.

"Nice to meet you," Zeke said. He steered his way back onto the road and drove north along Coronado Drive. "Where you dudes headed to?"

Nick told Zeke their plans to reach the police station to figure out what was going on and find out if help was on its way.

"Haven't seen a single car on the road. Not one that's running, anyway," Zeke commented. "Friggin' weird, man. No lights, no traffic, no nothing."

Cody had to stop him. "Ah...Zeke. How is it that no other cars are working in this entire area, but your van is?"

"Oh, that," the old hippie said, as if it was obvious. "Betsy's an oldie. She's..."

"Betsy?" Nick interrupted.

"Yeah man," he said patting the top of the dashboard with tender loving care. "This is my girl. Might not look pretty right now, but she's special."

"Why's that?" Cody asked the lunar man. He looked back at Nick and rolled his eyes. *Maybe they should get out and walk the rest of the way,* he thought. Nick caught his drift and shook his head.

"The solar flashes have been acting friggin' peculiar lately. I mean really weird," Zeke said out of the blue. His body shivered, as if he had felt something strange enter it. "You can feel them, man, like the waves are blowing right through your soul. Can you sense it, man?"

In unison, both Nick and Cody looked at the guy and said, "No." It was definitely time to get out of the whacko's van. But it was so warm.

"So the solar flashes are erupting, like they're really pissed off at something. And they're sending out these strong rays. When the rays hit our planet they kind of fuck things up," Zeke was telling them. Another unearthly shiver rattled his body.

Nick tapped Cody's arm and put up his index finger as if to say they should maybe listen to what the guy was talking about.

"Whoa! Just got a rush, man," Zeke blurted out. "Anyway, these invisible rays infiltrate electrical things and shut them down. The rays definitely cause havoc on computers, like with a vengeance. Colossal melt down for silicon city, dude."

Zeke was still driving and dodging the disabled vehicles all over the street as he was going through his story and crazy antics.

"Okay," Nick began. "But why is your van...ah...Betsy still running?"

Zeke smiled. "Because my Betsy is a classic lady. She's never even seen a computer." He patted his baby again. "Now, haven't you, Betsy?"

"Oh," Nick said. "So these rays you're talking about don't affect simple old engines like this one?"

"That's what I've been trying to tell you dudes," Zeke said.

"Can't be too many of these classics around," Cody added.

"Oh sure there are, especially here in Arizona. Not like Betsy, of course, but the weather is kind to the old beasts. No salt on the roads, usually gentle winters. Lots of people down here collect the older models, you know, those built in the '50s and '60s. Simple mechanics. Nothing can stop these babies." He leaned forward and stroked the dashboard again, muttering something.

Nick and Cody nodded their agreement. Maybe they should stay with Zeke the LuNar man. Whacked out or not, he may have figured out a few things that were happening in the area. Plus, he had a working vehicle to get them around. And it was actually getting warmer.

"Hey, dudes!" Zeke yelled. "Want to hear some *Who*?" Without waiting for an answer he grabbed an eight-track cartridge and inserted it into the player. Then he cranked up the volume to *Pinball Wizard*.

Chapter 9

Z eke had a difficult time threading his van through the stalled traffic as he got closer to town. At some points he drove onto the sidewalks to get around the backed up cars. A few times he tore across front graveled yards to detour around the chaotic lines of useless vehicles. He was still the only one driving on the roadways.

Cody yelled to Zeke over the loud music. "Let's stop by Safeway to see if it's open."

Somehow Zeke understood him and nodded his head as he grooved to the blaring tunes. Safeway was one of the larger grocery stores in town. It was set in the middle of a spread-out shopping plaza anchored by a Walgreens on the corner of Coronado and the town's main street, Fry Boulevard, running east-west.

Zeke lowered the music down to the sonic boom level. "Maybe if it's open, we can get some beer and Twinkies."

Whatever, Cody thought. This guy had no idea how disastrous this storm and its strange occurrences were. People were dying and all this pothead could think of was getting some beer and junk food.

Half a mile from the plaza the three men heard a rumbling crash from behind them. Zeke looked in his side mirror in amazement. Cody and Nick turned and looked through the rear door windows.

Despite the dirt and grime and strips of duct tape they were astonished at what they saw.

Two sets of headlights riding high on the cab of what appeared to be large dump trucks emerged over the ridge through the gloomy morning air. They were moving at a steady, but strong pace north on Coronado toward the main boulevard. Mounted on the front of each massive truck were oversized plows, similar to the ones that are used to clear northern roads of snow. The trucks were riding low and heavy as they continued straight up the road.

The men in the van couldn't believe what they were watching. The trucks roared through the abandoned cars as if they were children's Tonka toys. The cars piled up like tin play things. Some hit the sides of houses along the road. Others knocked down street light posts and electric poles. The monstrous trucks rammed straight through the stalled vehicles shoving them aside like discarded junk metal. The noise from the crashes and pilings was tremendous. Plowing onward they cleared the street of all vehicles, making the road open for other traffic.

But what other traffic?

Zeke kept glancing in the side mirror watching the demolition coming closer to old Betsy. He couldn't move fast enough around the thick congestion of stalled cars to keep a safe distance from the raging destruction gaining in his path. The blaring lights were getting brighter in his rear view mirror. The clamor of gratuitous damage drew ever closer to the aging van.

Within minutes the relentless trucks were on Zeke's bumper. Side by side the plows continued tearing up a straight and even path along the four lane road, unyielding to anything in their way. The men in the van were blinded by the harsh lights behind them. They could smell the diesel fumes overtaking their ride. If Zeke couldn't maneuver around the cars ahead of him blocking his escape, Betsy would soon be a heap of worthless scrap with three dead passengers.

"Step on it, Zeke! Step on it!" Cody yelled.

"I can't get through," Zeke screamed back. "Friggin' traffic, dude."

"Go through it! "Nick shrieked. "Plow through the god-damn cars!"

Zeke's body shivered. He didn't want to hurt his girl, but at this point he had no other choice. "Okay, man. Hang on, here we go." He nudged the dead car in front of him, but Betsy didn't have enough power to plow through a four-wheeled road block.

"Ouch, ouch. Sorry girl," he whispered as he floored the gas pedal and slowly inched past the first car.

The two trucks were almost on them. A plow blade struck the back of the van and thrust it forward. Zeke steered around another vehicle and found an opening in the road. But the second plow had pushed a car into his side. The scraping and crunching of the van's body brought Zeke to the verge of crying.

Cody yelled again. "Hard left Zeke, hard left! There's some room. Move it! Move it LuNar man!"

Zeke did what he was told, shifted into high gear, and roared away from the oncoming slaughter. The two trucks stopped after crashing into the traffic jam. They had to back up to get a better run through the congestion. This gave Zeke and the guys enough time to whiz down the opposite side of the road unscathed, except for poor Betsy, which looked as if she had gone through a shredder.

A hundred yards ahead Zeke pulled into the Safeway plaza. He stopped to catch his breath and assess damages to his pride and joy. As he walked around his van, the only word that came out of his mouth was, "Bummer."

They then drove closer to the grocery store. There were no lights, no evidence of the store or any other business being open. Several dozen cars were still parked in the lot. But there was lots of activity at the food storefront. Probably fifty or sixty people were pulling at the locked doors and pounding on the large plate glass windows. If there was anyone inside they refused to acknowledge their presence, whether by orders of the manager or for fear of their being harmed. Besides, without electricity no business could be conducted anyway.

"People are getting distressed," Cody mentioned. "This whole thing is getting way out of hand."

"No kidding," Nick added. "Every time we turn around there's more problems."

"Guess I can't get any snacks now," Zeke mumbled, very disappointed.

They heard a loud grinding of metal and the breaking of glass. The plow trucks had pushed their way pass the shopping plaza and turned west on Fry Boulevard toward the Army base two miles away. In their wake lay hundreds of demolished vehicles cast off the major byways of the small town.

"Now what?" Zeke turned and asked his passengers.

"The police station," Nick said.

Cody interrupted. "I've got three concerns. I'm wondering why those trucks were so maliciously tearing up the streets with no regard for personal property or safety. Doesn't that seem a bit drastic? The cars could have easily been pushed to the side or towed away without causing any damage."

"That was pretty lame, man. See what they did to my Betsy?" Zeke said.

"Someone is in a damn hurry to get the roads cleared," Nick said. "And it's no secret that property damage or even the possibility of killing people isn't a concern of theirs."

"Also," Cody continued, "why is it apparently so urgent to clear the major streets if no vehicles are working? I don't believe in conspiracy theories, but this has all the signs of being one."

"It has to be the government, man," Zeke said as if he were zoned out while driving.

Nick jumped in. "But there are at least two trucks running. How in the hell is that happening? Maybe there are other vehicles capable of operating. Maybe for some reason or other they weren't damaged or affected by this strange turn of events."

"It's a conspiracy, man," Zeke said with conviction.

"That was my third question," Cody commented. "How in the hell are they still running? From what I could see, they weren't no fifty years old. They were modern big rig diesels. Aren't they computerized just like every other newer vehicle?"

"I would assume so," Nick agreed.

Zeke looked at the two men. "Freaky, huh?"

"More than freaky, my friend," Cody added. "It's inexplicable."

"To the police station," Nick said again.

"Buckle up dudes, we're going to the fuzz shop," Zeke said as he turned out of the shopping plaza past the crowd still banging on Safeway's windows. He straightened out the van and headed toward the city hall complex on North Coronado. "I could sure use a beer," he uttered, entering the newly cleared metal carnage leading to the police station.

The road was littered with shattered safety glass from numerous windshields and side windows. It glistened in the dull daylight and looked as if ice crystals blanketed the asphalt pavement. Chunks of ragged plastic bumpers and bits of odd shaped rubber were strewn along the sides. SUVs and sedans, pickup trucks and mini-vans, motorcycles and several small city buses lined the street shoulders. Some were barely scratched while others were twisted into unrecognizable hunks of metal. At once busy corners cars were piled two or three high like giant snow mounds in the winter.

Clearly, it was imperative to clear the roads, Cody reasoned. But to what end?

Everywhere they looked there were no lights. The communication towers along the mountain range no longer blinked red. There were no sounds of military aircraft running training sorties from the far off runways. Every storefront was shut down. Every traffic light and speed camera was disabled. But there were still some people walking in the bitter cold to places unknown.

Minutes later they were approaching the city hall-police complex in the north central part of the city. The battered VW van slowly rolled off the pavement onto the soft shoulder some hundred yards or so before the police department entranceway.

"Ah…guys," Zeke said weakly.

"What's wrong?" Nick asked. "Engine trouble?"

Zeke looked at him through the rearview mirror. "Um…this is as far as I can go. You can walk from here. The fuzz shop is right over there," he pointed.

"Just pull up to the front doors, Zeke," Cody instructed.

"Ah…no. It's best if I don't go there. I might be seen."

"And there's something wrong with that?" Cody asked suspiciously.

Zeke looked at him sheepishly. "Me and the cops don't get along so good. I mean, they're cool and all that, but…"

Nick asked, "But what?"

"They're kind of looking for me on account of a few little things."

"A few little things? Like what?" Cody had to ask.

"Like a few tickets."

"Hell, Zeke. They don't care about some traffic tickets during a crisis like this. Don't worry about it. So let's go."

"Well." Zeke was hesitant. "They kind of caught me selling some weed and I haven't exactly gone back to see them."

"How much weed are we talking about?" Cody asked. He knew some of his college students smoked grass and the punishment for possessing small amounts was generally lenient.

"Not much," Zeke said.

"How much?"

"About a pound."

"A pound of grass? Zeke, are you dealing?" Cody asked again.

"Well, maybe it was closer to two pounds. Hey, I have friends, you know."

"Okay," Cody said with a roll of his eyes. The scent of weed was all of a sudden much stronger. "You stay here. Nick and I will go inside and talk with the police."

"I'll stay right here," Zeke said.

"We won't be long, okay. Just keep the engine running and wait for us."

"I'll keep the engine running and wait for you," Zeke repeated. Another spastic shiver ran through his body.

Nick and Cody exited the van out the back doors. Cody raised one finger toward Zeke as if to say 'we'll only be a minute.'

"Hurry," Zeke said through the window. Then he cranked up the music in Betsy's eight-track and tried to chill out.

Chapter 10

The guys walked up to the police station. "He's one crazy bastard. Isn't he?" Nick said to Cody.

"No kidding. L-u-N-a-r all the way," Cody answered. "But he got us here."

"That he did."

Approaching the station they saw lights inside the modern two-story southwestern style building. "Hey, they have electricity," Nick shouted with excitement.

There were about a dozen police cruisers in the parking area. They saw no police officers outside, but it was too cold to be outside anyway. A couple other pedestrians were entering the double doors in front of Cody and Nick. Once inside the massive foyer the men were surprised at the number of people standing at the counter listening to a young officer. At least a few dozen people were talking at the same time asking for answers from the cop.

Cody noticed the lights in the building weren't real lights. They were battery operated portable lanterns set on far sides of the long reception counter. They threw off a harsh fluorescent illumination turning everything in the room into black and white shadows. So much for having electricity, Nick realized.

"Please quiet down folks," the cop said. "I know you are wondering what has happened. I know you are wondering when the lights will be turned back on. You're also wondering when help will arrive for those who need it."

"No shit Barney Fife," someone yelled out from the back.

A few laughs echoed in the cold building.

"My family is cold," another voice said.

"What about the cars on the streets?" a different person yelled out.

"None of my cars will start."

"Yeah, and the stores are closed."

"We have no water."

Some idiot in the mob grunted, "I can't watch television."

"You dumb shit, who the hell cares about television when nothing else works," another voice echoed.

There were some muffled chuckles from the gathering.

Cody shook his head. It took all kinds.

The crowd was getting restless. They were impatient, tired, and cold from their trek to the station. They were mostly frustrated not knowing what was happening. They were concerned about their families and their homes. At this early phase they weren't thinking about any possible long term effects, though they should have been. It wouldn't have made a difference for most of them, however.

The cop held up his hands as if that would stop the barrage of questions. But it didn't, and the barks of shouts and screams continued to fill the room. Another police officer came through a staff's door to rescue the younger recruit. This cop appeared to be a senior member of the force. He had an air of confidence and emitted a practiced sense of authority.

Cody recognized him as the officer who had interviewed him regarding the probable suicide of Cody's friend and work associate, Jonathan Campbell. It seemed like a month ago, although it was only yesterday. Maybe this guy had answers, even though he was one hundred percent wrong about Jonathan, as far as Cody was concerned.

He stood in front of the group in an attempt to calm them down. "Okay. Let me explain what I know," he started. The crowd simmered down, hoping for everything to be fixed in the next few minutes. "Our entire police force is on alert. They understand the gravity of the situation which has hit our city. Every one of our officers and staff members are doing the best they can under the circumstances. As we speak patrols are canvassing the neighborhoods to assist. But there are priorities which must first be met. Our elderly and sick are our first focus. Then families with young children. The general population will have to stay calm and remain in their homes until this storm passes through and the electricity can once again be restored."

He waited a brief moment, then continued. "I've personally been in touch with the people at the electric company. You can understand they are inundated with inquiries and overwhelmed with determining the cause of the outage. They have assured me that all of their repair crews are on the job attempting to fix the problems."

"When did they say the electric would be back on?"

"What about the phone service?"

"When will the water be on again?"

"My house is freezing."

"I haven't seen any cops on the streets."

"Yeah, and I haven't seen any repair crews out there either."

"This is Thanksgiving. How can we cook?"

Cody and Nick listened to what the cop had been telling the crowd. It didn't sound right to them. Something was wrong.

The officer watched the pack of irate citizens. They didn't want promises, they wanted action. They didn't want feeble assurances, they wanted something to be done, now. "Just bear with us folks. We have lots to do with very limited resources."

Someone in the pack asked, "So you're in touch with your men. I mean your phones or radios are working."

The cop's eyes dropped to the floor looking for an answer that would satisfy the furious mob. "Ah...yes...our radios have a back-up system and we are in communication with our forces throughout the city."

"Bullshit!" a loud man's voice soared over the crowd. "Then how come I haven't seen a single cruiser since this thing started? Every other day I see them all over town giving traffic tickets, but so far I haven't seen one damn squad car since yesterday. And how in the hell did you contact the electric company?"

Cody didn't believe a word the officer was saying. He and Nick had seen that disabled police cruiser on South Coronado. Most likely every one of the other cop cars had met the same fate of all the other vehicles left on the streets.

Cody stood tall and yelled above the noise. "Then tell us, why are the abandoned vehicles being bulldozed off the streets?"

All heads turned to Cody. This was news to everyone, since Cody had just witnessed it not ten minutes earlier.

The cop looked dazed. "We have no knowledge of such activity at this time. I'm certain you're mistaken about that sir. All I can tell you at this point in time is that the entire police force is diligently working to protect its citizens."

Cody was getting pissed off at the run around they were hearing. It was obvious nothing was being done. There were no cops on the street, because they had no working cruisers and no means to communicate. They were all in the dark just like everyone else. And there were no electric crews out in the field repairing damaged lines or transformers or whatever. That's because there were no working phones, no working radios, no working vehicles. This cop was following the emergency procedure manual line for line. His sole purpose, at this point in time, was to stem the fear of the people and make them believe there really was help on the way.

"What about the dead people?" Cody shouted loud and clear. Because of the things he had seen, he was unusually vocal. Every person quieted in an instant and opened a gap in the packed room to see Cody. "What about the people who are dying, while absolutely nothing is being done?"

The group of angry men joined in. "Is that true?" many of them asked.

The officer was startled by Cody's questions. There was no easy, clear cut answer written in his manual. "I can assure you that no one is going to die from this inconvenient electrical blackout."

"And I can assure you, sir," Cody spoke up again in an uncharacteristic assertive manner, "that there are dead people. There are two of them in fact, my friends and neighbors froze to death in their bedroom across the street from my house."

"We will check into it as soon as our resources allow it," the cop answered, hoping it would quell the mob. "I recommend you all return to your homes and care for your families until this is over."

Cody wasn't his typically calm and quiet self. He generally let others ask the questions or deal with head on confrontations. He liked to go along and get along. But this just wasn't right. He moved toward the front, getting almost face to face with the officer in charge. He had never felt so…so out of control, so damned pissed off. He stuck his finger into the cop's face. "And what you call an 'inconvenient electrical blackout,' sir, has turned into a god-damn catastrophe."

"That's enough, mister. As I said we are doing the best we…"

Cody didn't let him finish. He wasn't done with this guy. "No, it's not enough. You don't have a fucking clue what's going on out there," he said pointing toward the street. "I'm not staying here listening to your lies and false promises. People's lives are at stake and I'm going to find out who is responsible."

The mob grew wild and noisy again. This guy taking on the police officer was right. More questions and accusations were thrown at the officer.

At that, hotter than he's ever been in his life, Cody pushed through the crowd and slammed the two front doors open. "Come on," He motioned toward Nick. "I've heard enough of this shit. It's for damn certain we're not getting any answers here."

Nick and Cody exited the station leaving the rest of the crowd arguing with their law enforcement professionals. Cody was convinced they would get no straight, nor truthful answers in this place.

On the steps of the station Nick turned to Cody. "I would have never expected that from you. It was good, but completely unexpected."

Cody, feeling the outside cold calm him down a little, said, "Thanks. Sorry. I usually don't swear like that. I just felt so helpless and frustrated. You know he's lying."

"Whatever it was, you put him in his place. And yes, I know he was lying. Now let's go find Zeke and get out of here."

They walked back to where Zeke had parked his van out of sight from the police station. The van was gone. "Where the hell is that dope head?" Nick asked.

"He most likely freaked out and drove away."

"Well, looks like we're walking again." He checked his watch. It was almost noon. "It's a long way to the house," Nick remarked.

After walking two blocks the men heard a high pitched beep. The VW's horn sounded like a sick roadrunner in that popular kid's cartoon. Zeke quickly pulled out of a side street and stopped for the guys. "Get in, dudes!" he yelled. "Hurry!"

"Where'd you go?" Cody asked, once he and Nick had crawled in through the back.

"I'd rather be safe and out of sight," he answered.

"Hey, how'd it go in there? What's up? The fuzz offer any help?"

"You been smoking that shit?" Cody asked him. A thick layer of marijuana smoke filled the van.

"Dude, just to take the edge off."

"It was a wasted trip," is all Cody said.

"Bummer."

"Yeah, bummer," Nick repeated.

"So," Zeke began, "where to now, dudes?"

"How about you take us back home, Zeke." Cody said. "I want to see my family and we have some things to work out."

Nick nodded his agreement. They had to take care of their families, because it was apparent no immediate help was on its way.

Zeke felt a shiver run down his body. He turned up the music and sped south on the cleared road.

Chapter 11

The First Phase of Operation Rescue was a go. The soldiers in the high school gymnasium were double checking their gear and weapons. The commander of the local operation was preparing to brief his men. Lieutenant Colonel Carl J. Fielding, Retired Army, had gladly accepted the charge over his newly assigned mission.

He had put in twenty-six years in the service of his country. During that time he had been in both Gulf Wars as a junior officer, survived three tours of duty in Afghanistan, and four tours in Iraq, mostly during the hot and heavy days of Saddam Hussein. There, he was wounded twice, commanded major battles against the rag heads, and had received the Congressional Medal of Honor from then President Bush. His record was impeccable and he was undeniably one of the top notch combat officers in the military.

In the heat of battle in some Afghanistan mountain outpost, his company of seasoned soldiers had attacked and killed an entire enemy force identified by American intelligence as members of al-Qaeda, the radical terrorist group recognized as the most serious threat to American national security. After the firestorm had ended, the body count was thirty-two enemies dead, no friendlies hurt.

Or so he was told.

Once he and his men had returned to base he was immediately arrested for war crimes against the people of Afghanistan. The colonel was charged with murdering civilians and allies of the United States. Somehow military intelligence had mistaken the village as a haven of extremist combatants and orders were sent to destroy and purge the region. It wouldn't have been the first blunder by MI.

Because the incident had created an international uproar caused by a media frenzy against American troops killing innocent civilians, the top brass needed someone to blame, a scapegoat to take the fall. Lt. Col. Fielding was quickly accused, court-martialed, and sentenced for the offense. He was immediately retired from the Army under duress and dishonorably discharged for his egregious errors of command.

He was allowed to retain his long earned pension at his current rank under the stipulation that he never discuss the case with the media. In turn, his sentence of life imprisonment in a military prison was suspended. With that done, the United States Army swept the whole incident under the rug. Betrayed by his country, the proud officer found it relatively easy to take sides against good old Uncle Sam. In the ranks of battlefield officers, what had happened to him wasn't an uncommon scenario.

"Men, we are about to embark into new territories," the Colonel began. He knew the background of each of his American soldiers. "Changes are in the making and a new future awaits us."

His men stood straight, eager to begin their task. The foreign troops barely understood a word. All they had to do was follow simple orders given them by their American squad leaders. Hand signals and a few key words were all they needed to know.

"You are to follow your orders in a swift and thorough manner," the Colonel continued. "We have a long couple of days ahead of us, but remember, timing and proper execution of your mission is critical. Also, it is imperative to conduct yourselves in a, let us say, 'a gentle approach,' as you rescue the residents in need. Such conduct will ensure a quicker and much easier roundup."

He strode past his men, looking at each one of his American troops, inspiring them to swiftly and systematically complete their duties. Satisfied with their readiness he asked, "Are there any questions?"

One tall, rugged American soldier stepped forward. "Sir, what if we should encounter strong resistance?"

The Colonel answered. "If you follow through as ordered, there should be very little opposition. However," he paused so the men would understand his intent, "you are to deal with it swiftly and without hesitation. If your lives are threatened, then you know what to do."

Lt. Col. Fielding gazed at his force. They were not the best he had ever commanded, but they would do against a bunch of unarmed civilians. He looked at his watch. Twelve noon. "Men," he barked. "Let Operation Rescue begin."

The troops fell into their assigned squads. Each squad was made up of four members. There were two American soldiers, each in charge of their two-man team. The other two were a random mix of foreign troops, Chinese, Russians, and Latinos. They lined up and exited the building toward their awaiting buses.

Each squad entered their numbered school bus. One of the American soldiers drove the bus out of the school grounds. They knew exactly which neighborhood they were to first enter. A complete list of streets congested in manageable sections hung from the bus dashboard. The roads were cleared, although there was some minor debris scattered in spots. A few hardy souls were walking on the road sides. They were surprised to see the school buses speeding by on otherwise quiet streets. Frantic efforts by the hopeful citizens to wave them down went unnoticed.

The buses veered off into different neighborhoods. It looked similar to a school day when long caravans of yellow buses cruised through the areas picking up school children for a day of learning. These were the same school buses, but today they weren't driving the streets looking for school-aged tots. They weren't as welcoming as the innocent daily rounds stopping at designated corners where mothers waited, lunch bags in hand, with their offspring.

Somehow protected from what Zeke had called 'solar rays,' the forty buses were in perfect running condition. Just like Zeke's VW. One bus turned onto Cody's street. It stopped at the first house on the corner. The bus came to a halt in the middle of the street and the men jumped out. Two of them, an American with his foreign troop backup, walked up to the house, while the other two went to the residence across the street. This was practiced routine.

One man knocked on the door of the first house. The American had a clipboard of addresses, names, and other information. The door opened and a young woman appeared. "Yes, can I help you?"

The American spoke up. "We're with law enforcement, miss, ah…" He stopped to check his roster.

"Robinson," the woman automatically gave her name. "Charles and Annette Robinson."

The soldier noted something on his ledger. "Is everyone okay here?"

The woman was intimidated by the soldiers dressed in what appeared to be some sort of S.W.A.T. uniforms with threatening rifles. One of the officers looked strange, non-American. "Yes, we're doing fine, considering the circumstances. Do you know when the power will come back on?" She was holding the door partly closed as protection.

"I'm afraid it will be several more days, ma'am. And the weather isn't going to break for awhile as well," the soldier answered in a calm, almost sweet voice. This is what they were taught to say. Get the people to believe you. Get them to trust you and they will go peaceably. Most of them will be happy to accept help. Most of them will be glad to be rescued during these terrible times. Particularly if the electricity was going to be out for days longer and the cold weather persisted.

"Oh dear," the lady said. "My children are cold, we have no heat."

The soldier moved on to the next question. "I can appreciate your situation, ma'am. Many of your neighbors are going through the same difficulties. Mrs. Robinson, is your husband at home?"

"No, he was traveling this week and was supposed to be home last night. But I haven't heard from him. I can't get through to him either. I've been worried sick, officer."

"I understand. We're doing our best to help everyone and find those who have been stranded because of the storm," the soldier explained. He smiled as if he were a friendly neighbor.

"I need help finding my husband," she said, almost in tears. "Where could he be?"

The soldier eased into his routine. "That's why we're here, ma'am. We'll locate your husband. We're asking everyone to come with us to a safe place."

"But I can't leave. What if Charles comes home and the house is empty?"

"We'll stake an officer here just in case Mr. Robinson shows up. But in the mean time we'd like for you and your children to board the bus," the trooper said as kindly as he could. "The buses are taking

everyone to the high school. They have lights and heat there. There're cots, hot food, and doctors if you or your children are in need of medical attention."

What the officer was offering sounded good. It sounded safe. It was good for her children. She saw her neighbor across the street, old Mrs. Gunther, being gently escorted to the bus out front. "Well," she hesitated. "Okay."

The soldier told her she could bring a small overnight bag and leave a note for her husband. "One last thing, ma'am. Are there any weapons in the house? We need to log them in for safety purposes."

"No, we don't have any weapons. My husband and I don't really like guns."

The man made another notation on his clipboard. It took Mrs. Robinson a few minutes to gather her two children and what they needed in an overnight bag. She left a short handwritten note for Charles, telling him where they would be. Then she stepped outside, locked the door behind her, and rushed the little ones to the warm bus.

The school bus moved down the street going through the same procedure with every homeowner. There was very little trouble given the security officers. After all, they were there to help. The promise of warmth and food and water drew the desperate residents into the bus. Lead by the kind men in uniforms the people carried their small bags for the overnight stay. Most of them had been in the high school before. Some to talk with their older children's teachers, or to see a basketball game, or maybe watch a student play in the massive theater. It was a safe and comfortable place.

At houses where no one answered, the uniforms broke down the doors to make sure people weren't being stubborn. It was understood that some inhabitants would refuse to vacate their residences and decide to stay in their homes. The rescue plan simply would not tolerate that kind of behavior. A few muffled popping sounds echoed in the cold from nearby houses, like caps being burst off from kid's toys. Uncooperative home owners would not be tolerated. The street was almost cleared as the loaded bus pulled in front of Cody's house.

One squad went to Jack's house. There was no answer, but the front door was unlocked. The soldiers found the frozen bodies in their bed, and with indifference toward the deceased, did a quick walk through the house and found nothing of value. They were on a tight schedule and needed to keep moving.

At Cody's house an American soldier banged on the front door. Robin had seen the bus and law enforcement officers out her living room window. The same questions were asked of her. Mostly the same responses were given back. "But my husband should be back home soon," Robin protested to the trooper. "I'm not leaving until he returns," she insisted.

The soldier explained the serious situation to Robin and told her to leave a note for her husband. She was getting into the bus whether she liked it or not. Robin scribbled a brief note for Cody and left it near the door.

After a second mild attempt to get Mrs. Gordon and her children out of the house the Chinese soldier grabbed her arm firmly. Having dealt with these submissive Americans the foreign soldiers rapidly became bolder in their actions. The American soldier's voice turned hostile. He was already growing weary of this babysitting gig and was in no mood to patty-cake these pampered housewives and rotten kids.

"Mrs. Gordon, we've tried the easy way. Now we'll do it my way." He nodded at the foreign soldier who forcibly removed Robin and her two screaming kids from the house. He let Robin lock the door and then rushed the pain in the asses to the bus. Six year old Jennifer began crying. She knew something was wrong when these mean men started hurting her mommy.

Robin kept yelling at the soldiers while holding her children close to her side. "It will be okay, kids," she tried to reassure them. "Daddy will come see us as soon as he gets home."

"My daddy's going to get you when he gets back," little Jeffrey shouted at the American soldier. The soldier laughed at the boy's spunk. The kid was never going to see his daddy again.

The bus was overloaded as Nick's family also stepped on board and sat near Robin and her children. Some people were crying and sniffling. Others were glad to be saved from the horrible weather. A few of the men were defensive, not completely sure if this was the right thing to do. They had watched the rough treatment bestowed on several of the families.

There was standing room only in the bus with fifty-seven residents on board and logged in. It had taken just shy of an hour to fill up the bus. Seven street residents were unaccounted for, lost somewhere without a vehicle. Five were dead, including two old people from the freeze and three from resisting lawful orders. A satchel of guns had been collected, three pistols, a shotgun, and two hunting rifles. The bus driver turned the rig around and drove toward the high school with the first load of evacuees.

The other buses in town had by this time completed their runs as well. Results from those squads were similar to the first. Most people were accounted for, some were lost in the wind, a few wouldn't need transportation. It was going to be a long day and night for everyone involved.

Chapter 12

Leaving the police station, Zeke drove his passengers back into the Safeway Plaza. On their way home the men wanted to see if the store had opened. That would be a promising sign, though the guys knew it was unlikely. Zeke pulled into a vacant parking spot close to the store's entrance. The pack of hopeful shoppers outside had grown larger than before. Several people turned to see the van drive up, but they were more intent on forcing the grocery store to open its doors.

The three men sat in silence with the engine running to keep the heater going. They noticed that the Walgreens pharmacy several storefronts away had a gathering of people also. They were burning piles of advertisement papers from a rack outside the door. It was unknown whether their actions were in protest or simply to stay warm. Some of the grownups were throwing plastic water bottles taken from outside displays against the solid glass windows. It was obvious the crowds were growing impatient and more violent as time passed.

"What do you think?" Nick asked in general.

"I think there's going to be trouble," Cody said. "Those people are getting rowdy."

"Yeah, and there's no cops around," Nick added.

"You know what happens when there's no police in sight."

"Anarchy, dude," Zeke added. "When the man is gone, the natives run wild. Mayhem, man. Pure mayhem."

Cody looked over at Nick. He hated to admit it, but Zeke was right. He realized history had shown over and over again that when any semblance of authority breaks down, the natives do indeed cause havoc. When there is no army, no police, no law enforcement to maintain rule and order, other factions will always fill the gap and attempt to take control. It was a sad commentary on the human condition, but it was a documented fact.

The crowds were getting louder, encouraged by a couple loud mouth instigators. "Open the doors. Open the doors. Open the doors," the crowd chanted in unison, as if they were at a rally of some sort.

"Let's boogey, dudes," Zeke said. "What if the fuzz do show up."

"Wait!" Nick yelled. "Look over there." He pointed to a rabble of teenagers entering the parking lot through a side alley. There were at least ten, maybe fifteen of them, and like a swarm of trouble, they quickly moved to the crowd banging on the grocer's windows.

"Speaking of trouble," Cody remarked. "Sit tight."

The men watched as the encounter between the older group and the teens developed. The younger boys first stuck their faces against the windows and began cursing at anyone inside, though by all accounts, not a soul was there.

"Open the god-damn doors. We cold and hungry."

"We bust down these damn doors, you don't open up."

"I kick the fuckin' windows in."

"I'll fuckin' shoot the windows out," one kid shouted loud enough for the rest of his gang to hear him. He acted like the leader of the hooligans and wanted to show off.

The loud mouths of the original group that had been waiting outside for some time spoke up. "Hey, you punks, back the fuck off," one man shouted.

"Go harass some little kids your own size," another yelled.

The gang leader, a kid no older than sixteen, dressed in a hoodie with his pants hanging halfway down his ass, stepped up. "Say what? mutha fucka!"

"I said back off asshole," the boisterous guy built like a linebacker said straight to the punk's face. Some of his buddies backed him up by moving closer to the hoodlums.

The rest of the young punks moved into the circle of action also. "You don't know who you messing with, old man," the kid threatened.

"I know exactly what kind of low life shit I'm dealing with," the linebacker snarled. "The likes of you and your friends are all talk and no action. These people here have families and all they want is to get some food. So punk," he drew face to face with the teen, "why don't you take your little friends and go home to your mommies."

The tall, lanky kid was edgy. He had his boys with him and couldn't back down. A leader takes control and that's precisely what he was going to do in order to maintain his position and earn respect from his young followers. "All talk, huh? All talk, huh, mista? I'll show you who the man around here. You find out who you fuckin' with."

At that moment he pulled out a pistol from his saggy trousers and aimed it at the guy's fat head. Their eyes met. The linebacker's glance dared the punk to try it. "Go ahead asshole. You haven't got the balls."

The rest of the crowd slowly backed off.

The kid, growing more agitated by the minute and put on the spot in front of his friends, turned his hooded head toward a few members of his gang. Watch this, he wanted to say to his homies.

The big man smiled and said, "Just as I thought."

The blast startled everyone in the parking lot. At point blank the man's head exploded. His body was thrown back into the standing crowd like a sack of potatoes dropped from the back of a speeding truck. The gang of teens stopped in their tracks. Even the kid with the gun was shocked. Then he grinned. "Told you not to fuck with me," he said to the dead man lying on the pavement. "All talk, huh? Now who the punk?"

Then he whirled around, a brazen look on his face, emboldened by his action. He fired at the plate glass windows of the grocery store. Nearly emptying his clip, he sprayed the glass until entire sections shattered and collapsed. The older crowd of shoppers scattered. The mob down at Walgreens ran in different directions too. Crazies were on the loose.

The men in the van watched through the closed windows in horror. "What the hell is going on?" Cody said to no one in particular. "He just shot that guy for no reason."

"Told you," Zeke said, affirming his theory on social chaos.

"We should get out of here," Nick whispered.

Zeke nodded. "Right on, man."

He threw the van into reverse and slowly backed out of his parking space. He tried to be inconspicuous so the gang of teens wouldn't see them. But the lawnmower engine in the back of an old VW bus rattles like a warped tumbler filled with ball bearings.

"Oh, oh!" Nick said. The gang had noticed the moving van and they stirred closer. "Hit it, man!" Nick motioned to Zeke.

The van was probably the only running vehicle the boys had seen since yesterday. They wanted it and were going to take it. There were no cops in the city and a van would be perfect to get around. There was a free-for-all on the streets. Anything they wanted was theirs for the taking.

Zeke raked the van's gears and went for the closest exit.

"Hurry, hurry!" Nick screamed. "They're on our ass."

Cody was the first one to hear the gun fire. He instinctively ducked down in his seat. They felt the rear passenger tire pop with a loud burst. The van slowed a bit, but Zeke kept the gas pedal to the floor. "Oh, Betsy," he mumbled.

A second shot came through a side window, narrowly missing Cody. Zeke's body shuttered. "Bummer," he softly wheezed. Then the van, finally out of sight from the plaza, gently rolled to the side of the road. The bullet had struck Zeke in his neck and he slumped over the steering wheel.

"Oh shit!" Cody screamed.

"My god!" Nick said.

Unaware if the teenage gang was after them, Cody and Nick swiftly moved Zeke's body to the back of the van. "We have to keep moving." Cody said.

Nick jumped into the driver's seat and took the wheel. "We'll go the back way. I think we can still make it home with the flat."

"What about Zeke?" Cody asked.

They both took a second to look at the crazy old hippie. It was obvious he was dead. "There's nothing we can do for him now. We have to get out of here first." Panic had overtaken Nick.

They drove through some of the back streets of unfamiliar neighborhoods, going home in a roundabout way. The damaged tire was tearing away as they pushed forward. Turning back toward Coronado Drive, they were surprised to see moving vehicles coming their way. Two school buses raced north past the van. They appeared to be loaded with people.

"There's some sort of help going on," Cody commented. "The cops must be taking people to shelters. Maybe one of the schools or churches."

"That's a relief," Nick said.

It was growing more difficult to steer the beat up van. The shredded tire had all but disintegrated and it was running on the metal rim. Finally, the VW turned on their street. Something was different. The abandoned cars had been pushed to the side, just like on the main streets. Several bags of clothing littered the sidewalks and roadway. Then Cody saw something that scared the hell out of him. Every front door along the street had a big red X spray painted across them.

"Dear God! Hurry Nick!"

"What is it?"

"I don't like this!"

Nick stopped the van in front of Cody's house, just beyond the mailbox. "What should we do with Zeke?" he asked.

"We'll leave him here for now. Sorry Zeke. Nick, you go check on your family," Cody said, an anxious tone in his voice. He stepped out of the van. Old Betsy had seen her last journey. He looked up at his house. Robin wasn't peeking out the window. He hoped against hope to see her there.

Quickly, he looked across the street. Jack's front door was wide open. He scrambled up the walkway to his front door. Red paint defiled it.

"Robin! Robin!" he shouted.

Chapter 13

The buses began approaching the high school grounds. "Red Leader, this is Rescue One." The American soldier from the first bus was calling into headquarters. The walkie-talkie radios which were issued to each unit had, like the school buses, also been protected from whatever electrical waves were in the air. However, they only had a short effective range.

Lt. Col. Fielding was handed a mobile radio by a subordinate. "Red Leader here. What is your status?"

"Sir, we are returning to HQ. Section A10 has been rescued."

"Rescue One, did you encounter any resistance?"

"Nothing we couldn't handle, sir."

"Good job Rescue One. Bring your transport in and do your turn around as quickly as possible." Fielding was pleased with the first response. He expected nothing less. Within the next ten minutes each of the other thirty-nine units would contact HQ with essentially the same results.

As the buses rolled in they formed a long line at the high school main front entrance. The passengers were rushed to disembark with their few things they carried. Some were upset in the way they were treated so abruptly. A few were crying. Some of the children had fallen asleep during the short trip. Several of the men were growing uncertain about this rescue attempt. But they went along without causing any disturbance.

Robin Gordon's arm still hurt from when the security personnel forced her out of her house and onto the bus. She remained quiet and watched every move of the soldiers. She knew this wasn't an ordinary rescue mission to relocate and protect innocent victims from a natural disaster. There was more going on, but so far she couldn't figure it out yet.

Her son Jeffrey ran from the bus as the passengers were being routed through the doors of the school. He kicked a guard in the shin and dashed inside. Another guard instantly grabbed the rascal by his jacket collar and held Jeffrey up like a trophy deer, ready to head slap the miserable brat.

"Please, please. Let him down," Robin cried out. "He'll behave and do as I tell him."

The guard dropped the scrawny kid on the floor and laughed. Robin tapped her son on his head. "You stay near me young man, and do exactly as I say. Do you understand me?"

He readjusted his jacket. "Yes," he said, somewhat reluctantly.

"I told you so," his sister Jennifer said. Then she stuck her tongue out at her brother.

All passengers were directed into the large gymnasium. Men, women, and children. It was policy to keep the men with their families. If they had been separated, possible outbreaks could occur. By staying with their families, it was surmised, the men would be more concerned with the safety of their wives and children and would more likely remain passive and less troublesome.

Before all the passengers had even entered the gym, the buses were on the road again, destined to their next sections of town. Several armed guards blocked the entrances to the sports arena located in the center of the school. The lights were on, but there was no heat. There were no cots, no blankets, no food or water. The evacuees were lied to.

One middle aged man spoke out. "What is this? These people need water. You told us there would be food too."

A foreign guard went up to the man. He grunted, then slammed the butt of his rifle against the man's forehead. People screamed at the assault. The man's wife went over and helped her husband back to his feet. A warning had been sent. Don't ask questions, just follow orders.

The entire group of more than two thousand city residents felt more like prisoners in their own high school, rather than casualties of a terrible winter storm. Waiting for something to happen, they huddled in friendly groups. They took up spots in corners away from the guards. They rested on the cold wooden floor. The few who had carried small blankets wrapped up their crying children. Most of them were hungry and thirsty. Many had to go to the bathroom. But nobody was allowed to leave. And clearly, no questions were tolerated.

Another man went to a guard near the door. He tried the calm and sensible approach. "Excuse me sir, but some of us were wondering if we could use the restrooms." The man received a similar solid head bash as the previous do-gooder.

A hushed murmur filled the room. No one wanted to talk too loudly. They knew the penalty. Questions ran swift in their minds. Who were these people holding them? Why were they being held here? What did the guards intend on doing with them? How long would they be locked up here? Was a doctor available? Were the guards terrorists? And if they were, where were the real police? Another raging question among many of them was: Why did they allow themselves to get into this dangerous situation?

Time dragged on in the contained gymnasium. No questions were answered. No assistance offered. Some people cried themselves to sleep. Others tried to block out the nightmare they found themselves in. A few, including Robin, kept their eyes open, searching for possible means of escape.

Almost an hour later they heard doors across the hall open to the thousand seat theater. More buses had arrived, the same buses on their second return trip. Another two-thousand plus local inhabitants were being stuffed into the school. They heard the doors being locked. Shouts in the other room were quickly silenced.

Robin's group realized they were in a perilous position. What now? They silently wondered. Robin constantly worried about her husband. Was he safe? Where could he be? Has he been to their house and seen her note? She wished she had brought some food with her. She should have thought this thing out before leaving the house. But she was rushed. She was scared. She wanted to care for her kids. She checked her cell phone for the hundredth time. But of course there was no service.

The side gym doors suddenly opened with a loud bang. The guards stood at attention as an American soldier in the same uniform as the detainees had seen earlier, entered the room.

"Ladies and gentlemen. I am Colonel Fielding. I am sure you are wondering what is happening. Please hold your questions. First I'd like to thank you for your patience and understanding while we are all going through this very unusual period."

Two men and a woman stood up to ask something, but the guards rushed to them and pushed them back to the floor.

The Colonel continued. "I apologize for any inconvenience and for the rather uncomfortable setting. However, for your own safety and well-being it was necessary to relocate you and your families. People have already died from this brutal weather and we intend to keep the loss of life to a minimum. Since this disaster came upon us so suddenly, we have not as yet received our full supplies of food and water as you were promised. I assure you we have every intention to make your brief stay here as painless as possible. But under the tragic circumstances you can appreciate our position."

Half the people in the room looked around. People have died from the cold? Maybe being taken to the high school was, although very unusual, the best thing that could happen to them. Others cast a suspicious eye toward their rescuers. The whole process just didn't look right. They didn't believe a word from this man in charge and were justifiably apprehensive.

"Since we have more residents being brought to these facilities than were initially expected," the Colonel added, "we are forced to transport you to another designated location nearby."

There was shouting and screaming from most everyone in the gymnasium. Most of them stood up as they heard the news. Questions bombarded the commander from all corners.

"What do you mean, you're moving us again?"

"Where are you taking us?"

"But my children are hungry."

"Will there be food and water there?"

"How will my husband find us?"

"You can't treat us this way."

The crowd was turning unruly. Several of the men appeared ready to charge the Colonel. There was outrage in the air which could quickly lead to mob action. This kind of behavior was not going to be tolerated.

Lt. Col. Fielding glanced at a guard nearest the main gymnasium door. In two seconds extra guards entered the room, their AK-47s ready at their sides. Fielding raised his hands to the group as if he were stopping traffic. "Okay people. Sit down now and shut the hell up or someone will get hurt."

Four men from the group remained standing. They took orders from nobody, at least not since they had retired from the Army a long time ago. They weren't going to be treated like common criminals.

"Who the hell are you to talk to us that way?"

"Do you think we're your prisoners or something?"

"I demand you release us."

"Well, I'm leaving right now, whether you like it or not."

The Colonel had a smart grin on his chiseled face. He enjoyed this part of the game. He stood in front of the agitated crowd and stared at the troublemakers. He slowly lifted his right hand and gently scratched his right temple. All hell suddenly broke loose. Within a split second the guards raised their rifles, took aim, and shot the four standing men in their foreheads.

The blasts echoed in the closed off gym like several rounds of thunder. Every one of the two thousand evacuees in the room hugged the floor. Cries and screams and whimpers mixed with the reverberating gun shots. The dead bodies fell on people near them. Blood and brain matter splattered into the bunch. Some people went into silent shock, unable to accept what had just happened. All eyes grew wide with fright as they witnessed the brutal reprisal.

The Colonel smirked at the commotion. Just as expected. People could be put in their place so easily. A little pressure, a little assertiveness, a few dead bodies. Then when they realized the consequences, they would fall in line like cattle being prodded through the slaughter pens. So predictable.

"Now that we understand each other," the Colonel said. "Please form a line and follow the guards to your new transportation. Oh...and thanks for participating in Operation Rescue." He laughed to himself, then directed two guards to get rid of the mess on the floor. More folks were expected any minute now.

A long line of large Army green buses parked on the back side of the high school were being filled with detainees. They weren't destined to another nearby facility. Instead, they were preparing for the two hour trip to a massive detention center southwest of Tucson, in the middle of the desert.

Region Nine, Camp 49, would be the new home for this first round of detainees, courtesy of FEMA and the Department of Homeland Security. The Colonel grinned as the people were being moved out.

Chapter 14

The red paint on the wood door was still wet and running. Cody tried the doorknob, but it was locked. Good, he thought. Then he called out again. "Robin, Robin. It's me, open the door."

No answer. He was getting frantic and dug in his pocket, but remembered he didn't have his house keys. He banged on the door again, this time loud enough for the neighbors to hear. That is if there were any neighbors around. His family had to be home.

The back door, he thought. He dashed to the side gate and entered the yard. He ran past the firewood pile and went to the back patio. They never locked the slider except at night. He tried the latch, but it was locked.

"Robin, Robin," he called out again. Cody looked through the glass door into the dining area. There was no movement. He grabbed the cheap handle and jimmied it up and down a few times. He had done this before and the door lifted off the track and easily slid open.

"Robin, Jeffrey, Jennifer, it's Dad," he said as soon as he entered his home. He ran through the house, slamming doors, tripping over throw rugs, knocking over a flower vase. He looked in every bedroom, the two bathrooms, the laundry area, then the garage. He rushed back toward the living room. Blankets and pillows were on the floor again. The coffee table was covered with coloring books and crayons. Some reading books were left open on the sofa next to half empty cocoa mugs.

There were hot embers glowing in the fireplace, but the fire had gone out. In the kitchen Cody found their Thanksgiving turkey on a cutting board, partially chopped up. They had planned on cooking it on the outside gas grill. Something or someone had interrupted Robin.

He was beside himself with worry. Where would they have gone? And why would they leave? He went through the entire house once again, hope against hope he would find his family. But they weren't home. They were out in the cold someplace.

Then Cody noticed a piece of paper on the small table near the front door. In the tray where he kept his keys was a note. He picked it up and read it. It was from Robin.

Cody, The police came through the neighborhood and insisted we be evacuated. They're taking us to the high school. Please come get us as soon as you return home.

Love—Robin

A sense of relief swept over him. At least they were safe. But he had this odd feeling in the pit of his stomach. It seemed strange to him that the authorities would evacuate people after less than a day since the blackout occurred. There were too many questions left unanswered, but for the moment Cody let them pass. It was probably nothing, though he still felt an unsettling sensation deep inside.

He decided to go see Nick. First he locked the back slider, and then he picked up his house keys from the tray and locked the front door as he exited.

Nick opened his door at the first knock. It had been sprayed red as well. "They're gone," Nick said. He was holding a scrap piece of paper from his wife with similar information about their being relocated.

"The high school," Cody said with an intense look in his eyes. "Let's try the van."

"We can't get there in that," Nick insisted. "The high school is at least seven or eight miles away."

"Let's try anyway," Cody insisted. "You want to walk that far?"

They went to the van. This time Cody got in the driver's seat. He instinctively looked in the back and gazed at Zeke's cold body. Nick slid over to the passenger seat as Cody started the VW. He slowly drove away from the curb and circled through the cul-de-sac in front of Nick's place. The steering was difficult with the missing rear tire. The metal wheel grating on the pavement caused a shrieking sound. Then as Cody straightened out the van there was a loud pop.

The van fell at an angle in the middle of the road. The guys got out and inspected the damage. The ruined wheel had snapped off from the axle due to the added strain.

"Shit!" Cody screamed out.

"Now what?" Nick asked, not really expecting an answer.

Cody looked around. "Guess we're walking. But first, let's check out Jack's house again."

A white X was spray painted on the door. They entered the opened door into the frigid living room. In the back bedroom Jack and Edith rested undisturbed. "I should get the gun," Cody said. He remembered the gang of punks on the loose and the fact that there were no police on the streets.

"Might be a good idea."

They went into the closet and threw back the blankets covering the safe. Cody took the key to the safe from his pocket and opened it. He pulled the gun out and held it tight. He didn't know how to handle a weapon, but now might be a good time to learn. He picked up the bullets, slid open the box, and dumped several into his hand. They felt like steel ice cubes.

"Open that part," Nick explained, "then slide the bullets in one by one."

Cody did that and spun the cylinder of the old pistol back in place. The gun was now loaded, although Cody hoped he wouldn't have to use it. He stuffed the weapon in his jacket pocket. The dead weight of the loaded gun surprised him. He then put the boxes of ammunition in his other pocket.

"What about the coins?" Nick asked.

"What about them?" Cody wondered aloud. "I don't need them. Not now. Besides they're too heavy to carry."

"Put them in your house. They'll be safer there."

"Well…I suppose." Cody lifted the socks as the coins clinked. He handed two socks to Nick and carried the other two. It was amazing how much they weighed. The men left the house and Nick pulled the door tight again.

"Let's drop these off, then we can go," Cody remarked.

As soon as the men turned from Jack's they saw a truck in Cody's driveway. "Who the hell is that?" Nick asked.

It was a 1965 Chevy pickup, most of its paint faded and bleached away from years of sitting in the desert sun. The hood and roof were iron red from decades of rust. Stuck on the rear bumper were remnants of ancient bumper stickers endorsing the NRA, denouncing the FED, and promoting Liberty. A gun rack in the back window held a hunting rifle.

"That's Raz!" Cody said, somewhat excited to see his old friend, but also confused as to why he showed up now.

"Who's Raz?" Nick wanted to know.

"You'll see." The two men went up to the truck, their arms loaded with socks full of silver coins.

The old man must have pulled up to Cody's while they were in Jack's house. He was sitting in the driver's seat, thinking. Cody rapped on the driver's window. Raz looked at him as if to say, "What the hell ya want?" He rolled down his window.

"This piece of shit still running?" Cody said, kidding.

Raz pulled at his gray whiskers. "This piece of shit, as ya call it, can save ya life, sonny."

Cody laughed. Whatever Raz said, he was usually right. "Well, come into the house," Cody invited his good friend. "It's not much warmer, but it will do for now."

Raz opened his door. The rusted hinges squeaked and the door rattled as he closed it. The three went into Cody's house. He and Nick placed the heavy socks on the table near the door. Cody went to the fireplace and stoked the fire back to life. As he was stirring up the radiant embers he said, "Raz, this is my friend Nick. He lives a few doors down."

Nick reached over to shake the old man's hand. "Nice to meet you."

"Yeah, well, not so nice, considering," Raz grunted. He shook Nick's hand almost grudgingly.

"Yes, this damn weather is terrible," Nick added, a bit put off by the unfriendly geezer.

"There," Cody said as he stood up from the growing fire, "Should be better in a few minutes."

"Ain't 'bout the weather, boy. And it ain't gonna git much better, sonny. Fact 'tis, gonna git worse. Much worse," Raz grumbled through his beard.

Raz Hunter was a unique individual. At sixty-three years old he had been retired for five years. He had put in his twenty as an Army military intelligence officer and was stationed at the local Army base prior to his discharge. His specialty was interrogation, mostly with captured soldiers during the various wars which America had been involved in. He also used his honed skills to grill wayward U.S. troops who had been court-martialed. On occasion he had also sat across from legitimate spies, mostly foreign, but several home grown, facing espionage charges against the country. Later, in his second career, he worked as a contractor hired by the government to gather intel as needed.

Raz had grown up in the Appalachian mountain country, on the Kentucky-Tennessee border. His good ole boy manner of speech and laid back approach to handling people were treasured assets in his line of work. Although his back woods demeanor appeared to make him less intimidating and somewhat uneducated, he was extremely intelligent and hard-nosed persistent. He had a brilliant mind and could remember things that most people would take lightly. In a nutshell, Raz was an extraordinary 'military consultant.'

During his entire career, and life, for that matter, Raz remembered every person he had ever met. He remembered every detail about that person, every conversation ever shared. He remembered every book, every story, every newspaper article, every report, every contract, every memo, every file, every piece of testimony, and every written assignment he had ever read. He remembered names and dates and times and events and locations and numbers. Like a simple flip of a switch he could access his computer-like mind and retrieve any or all information he had stored in that resourceful hillbilly brain of his.

Hunter's ability to squeeze the truth out of his adversaries was uncanny, almost legendary. Barely a single one of his cases had failed to discover the hidden facts and agenda of each enemy combatant or subversive agent. Many American lives had been saved as a result of the hard-core determination, perseverance, and patriotic fortitude of Raz Hunter.

Eighteen more years as a highly sought after civilian 'consultant,' Hunter worked diligently in his pursuit and apprehension of active and suspected terrorists determined to annihilate the American population and wipe out the western culture. Since the attacks of 9/11, terrorist groups had rapidly grown in strength and numbers, supported and funded by American 'allies' in the Middle East and other radical Muslim cells scattered throughout the world.

Hunter had grown progressively suspicious of the 'coordinated workings' of his own government with known terrorist factions as well. He had revealed through his investigations that many of the sworn enemies of his nation were actually on Uncle Sam's payroll.

Al-Qaeda rebels were trained by the CIA to protect the massive poppy fields in Afghanistan and to keep the Russians in check from expanding oil pipelines through the harsh terrain. Afghanistan insurgents fighting American troops were supplied weapons by mysterious sources controlled by the highest level of United States elected officials. Syrian 'freedom fighters' were funded by the American military-industrial complex to overthrow the standing leader in favor of one more open to American policies and commercial interests.

The list went on and on.

Billions and billions of dollars passed hands from the American government to brutal and corrupt dictators within strategically significant third world countries. Plane loads of money were funneled through hundreds of charitable groups with unassuming names like, Save the Afghan Children, Peace for Africa, Better Living for Southeast Asia, and People of the World, and more.

There was always more.

The entire geopolitical process of starting wars, promoting internal civil unrest, establishing debilitating trade sanctions, assassinating troublesome and uncooperative leaders, allowing widespread poverty and starvation, even civilian massacres, and pitting allies against allies could all be attributed to the one source. The people Raz worked for.

Hunter was disgusted by what he had learned. There was no mistaking the fact that, funded by the Congress, the U.S. government and its top leaders were in the thick of things for the obvious benefit of the few running the country and their politically wealthy and powerful supporters. Hunter felt the work he had been involved in for nearly forty years had all been a farce, a front to defraud the American people, a hoax to steal trillions in order to line the pockets of the social elites and to maintain their power over global forces.

When he could finally verify all that he suspected, he had resigned his position and retired for good from government service. From then on, he had been preparing for this eventual catastrophe.

"I'll go over that later," Raz said about things getting much worse.

Cody eyed his old friend. "So why do you all of a sudden show up here?"

"Figured ya might need some assistance. Got some things ta take care of too. And ya boys are gonna help," Raz grunted.

"We have to get our families, Raz. They were evacuated to the high school while we were gone," Cody informed him.

"We need a ride," Nick said almost apologetically to the gruff old guy.

"Suspect ya do. That's if ya don't mind ridin' in a piece of shit."

"Sorry about that," Cody answered.

Raz eyeballed the two men. He couldn't do this alone. "Well, git ya asses in the truck. We have places ta go."

Chapter 15

"Now what in the hell ya doin?" Raz asked Cody before they got out the door.

"I'm putting these away," he answered, picking up the coins.

"What ya got there Cody?" the old man asked.

Cody told him the story about Jack, the gun, and the coins.

"Might be a good idea ta take 'em with ya. Could come in handy later."

"You think?" Cody said.

"I said it, didn't I?"

Cody handed two socks to Nick, held on to the others, and with his free hand locked up his house.

As they loaded themselves into the ancient pickup Cody looked at the broken down VW bus across the street. He had seen five people die this week, including his friend Jonathan, and it was only Thursday. He and Nick dropped the sacks of coins on the pickup's floor boards. From now on his full focus was on getting his family back.

Raz shifted his truck in gear and slowly backed out of the driveway. "Ta the high school, huh?"

Cody nodded. "Yes, that's where they took them."

Raz drove up the road. "They? Who the hell are they?"

"I don't know," Cody responded. "They. The cops, the sheriff's department, the Army. They!"

"And ya let 'em take 'em?" "I wasn't home!" Cody yelled in defense. "I, ah…we went to find out what was going on."

"Best hope it was one of 'em," Raz growled.

"What do you mean?"

"Just sayin'."

"What the hell happened here?" Raz asked about the dozens of vehicles smashed to the sides of the road.

Nick explained what they had seen earlier when the dump trucks cleared the streets of abandoned cars.

"Ahh," Raz cleared his throat. "That gun ya picked up. Ya got it with ya?"

Cody felt the heavy revolver in his jacket pocket. "Yes."

"Good, might just need it too."

They turned north on Coronado Drive.

"So, Raz," Cody broke the silence. "You have a pretty good handle on things. How could this bad weather affect so many systems? It seems the whole city is without power."

"Ain't just the city."

"You think the whole county is down?" Fort Huachuca and the city of Sierra Vista were secluded in the high desert of the south-eastern portion of Cochise County. It was a huge geographical land area, larger than the two states of Rhode Island and Connecticut combined, although the population was barely over a hundred thousand, most of it concentrated near the fort.

"Hell, boy. Don't ya know what kind of mess we're in?" Raz grumbled. "It's bigger than that. The whole damn country is unplugged."

Cody and Nick stared at the old man. That was impossible. How could a storm shut down the entire nation? They wondered. "Is that possible?" Nick asked. "How could a storm shut down the entire nation?"

Cody nodded. It was a farfetched explanation. One he had a hard time believing too.

"It ain't 'cause of the storm, boys. That's just an added bonus,"Raz said.

"So what actually caused the lights to go out, and the phones to stop working, and the cars to quit running?" Cody asked. "Oh yeah, and tell me how is this old jalopy still running."

"One thing at a time, sonny, " Raz said. "First, nothin's workin' 'cause of the pulse."

"You mean like the sun rays hitting the earth?" Nick asked, remembering what poor Zeke had explained about the solar flares and rays.

Raz laughed and scratched his bearded chin. He shook his head, a mop of unkempt white-gray hair flopping side to side. "Ya boys. Don't ya know nothin'? Ain't ya been readin' the stuff I've been sendin' ya?" He looked over at Cody.

He was referring to the tons of information about recent government activities, some overt, some very much kept under wraps, that were affecting every American citizen. Most people paid no attention to the back door antics happening in Washington, D.C. People just went to their jobs, got paid, spent their money, watched television, surfed the Internet, and got lost in Facebook.

Every day for the longest time Raz had forwarded articles to Cody's computer via email attachments. Some were about chem-trails and poisons in the water and genetically modified food supplies. Others described how the U.S. government was incrementally erasing citizens' rights guaranteed by the Constitution, one by one going after the Bill of Rights. Many stories emphasized the attack on people's rights to freedom of speech and assembly and religion. Even more discussed the erosion of people's right to bear arms. They told of FEMA internment camps and death squads and SMART grids and subversive operations against the American people, the threats of martial law, and the final takeover.

Yes, Cody had received Raz's emails. Sometimes there were five, ten, maybe fifteen per day. At first, Cody would read them. Interesting articles, but to him they seemed to be nothing more than conspiracy theories. Science fiction blabbing put out there by anti-authority radicals, tax rebels, even whackos and crazies.

As time went on and Cody continued to receive even more trash talk on his computer, he just spammed the mail into oblivion and chalked it up to the misguided thoughts of a once brilliant man who had basically lost it when he retreated from the world.

"Yes Raz. I read some of the things you sent," Cody said timidly.

"Well, it's apparent ya ain't learned a damn thing," Raz scolded the young man like a fed-up teacher tired of his student not doing his homework.

Cody sank into the truck's bench seat feeling reprimanded.

"The sun had nothin' ta do with what's happenin'," Raz began.

"Not this time anyway. It's one of 'em god-damn EMPs that got us. That's why everythin' is wiped out. The whole continental United States of America has been hit.'"

Nick spoke up. "But if the EMP wasn't caused by the sun, then what caused it?"

"For bein' so damn educated ya boys are dumber than two sticks," Raz jumped on them. "This electromagnetic pulse was intentional. Somebody done this on purpose. They're tryin' ta take us out, and so far they're doin' a damn good job of it."

"You really think so?" one of the men asked.

"Ain't ya been listenin', boy?" Raz loudly grumbled. "We're under god-damn attack."

No one in the truck said another word for a minute or two.

Raz tried to explain. "Someone, or some group, or some country exploded a nuclear bomb hundreds of miles above our nation somewhere. Most likely over the central states. Better coverage that way. The radiation won't kill ya. Not quick, anyway. The pulse spreads at the speed of light. Ya don't see it and ya don't feel it. But it's there alright. Ya can see part of what it does right in front of ya eyes."

Nick looked at Cody and rolled his eyes. Another Zeke.

"Lots of countries have the capability ta launch such a weapon. Hell, ya know for damn sure we do. Then there's the commies, China and Russia. They'd love ta take us out. That lunatic in North Korea would do it too if he had the chance. Then there's the sand people in the Middle East. Ya can't trust 'em son-of-a-bitches. Ya don't think they want ta git rid of us? Hell, that's their damn mission in life."

If what Raz had proposed were true, Cody thought, what would happen next? All hell would break loose. What if all that crap that Raz was sending him was really happening? Martial law. Gathering up citizens. Confiscating guns. Selling America. Gradually making it easy for a take over. Was Raz really crazy or was he smart enough to know the difference?

Cody's mind began churning a million miles a minute. Too many questions were rattling inside his brain. Visions of old war movies and brutal documentaries dominated his thoughts. Past history lessons sprung up in their gruesome scenes. Pictures of his family passed by too. Robin. Jeffrey. Jennifer. He was completely lost in thought and was close to the point of not knowing what to believe.

The pickup ran over a large piece of metal on the road and the sound jarred Cody back to the moment. He looked around to see where he was and remembered. Raz was glaring at the roadway. Nick was quietly sitting in the middle, most likely thinking the same thoughts as Cody.

"Step on it," Cody said to Raz. "We need to get to the high school fast."

"Goin' as fast as we can, son. I'll getcha' there alright."

As they got closer to the main street, known as Fry Boulevard, Raz glanced into the Safeway Plaza. "Somethin's brewin' over there, boys."

He slowed down to watch. Crowds of people were smashing the huge windows in several of the stores. They were crawling over each other attempting to get inside. Safeway and Walgreens were being inundated. Some of the mob was pushing grocery carts filled with food items out the door and toward the street. It was obvious the darkened stores had been closed, if not for the blackout, at least for the holiday. No police cars were in sight. It was just a mad horde looting and rioting in the grim daylight.

Cody said, "We saw someone get killed there earlier today."

"It's startin' pretty quick," Raz advised.

"What?" Nick asked.

"The bedlam," Raz answered. "In just one day ya see what can happen," the old man commented. Suddenly the men in the truck saw two school buses racing east on the main road in the direction of the high school.

"See, see," Cody yelled. "They're taking them to the school just like Robin said."

"I see 'em, boy. I might be old, but I ain't blind yet."

Cody thought for a second and asked, "Raz, if this EMP thing destroys every modern electrical and computerized component, then why are those buses running?"

"Old vehicles like this one ain't affected on account of it ain't got no computer devices. Just like that beat up Volkswagen van ya was tryin' ta drive. But those buses have been protected," Raz said.

He began to explain how it works.

"There's a thing called a Faraday cage. It's a pretty simple contraption, easy ta make and use. It's really just a shield, generally made with metal screenin' or even common chain link fencin'. The cage blocks external electrical fields by channelin' electrical pulses through the conductive mesh or screen, makin' it a protective cage. It protects electronic equipment from the dangers of an EMP. Microwave ovens and MRI machines do the same thing, only in reverse. They keep the energy inside the cage instead of keepin' it out."

Cody nodded, understanding what Raz was saying.

"Every damn thing is run by computers these days. I sent ya information 'bout 'em, but I don't suppose ya got around to readin' it. I have some cages set up at my place. I suspect whoever is runnin' this show did the same with 'em buses. Wouldn't be too surprised if they had more vehicles of sorts on the road as well."

Nick had a question. "But why wouldn't the cops have this type of equipment? Cody and I went to the police station. None of their cruisers were running. Wouldn't you think they'd have this cage protector on their cruisers and radios? It almost seemed as if they were lost for answers too."

"Hell, Nick," Raz growled. "The local cops ain't part of this thing. At least not in this small city. They're like everyone else. They don't have a clue 'bout what's happenin'. If they did, don't ya think ya'd see flashin' lights all over the place? Every cop on the force would be patrolin' the streets. Sure as hell that shit goin' on in 'em stores wouldn't be happenin'."

Nick just shook his head and eyed Cody.

"Tell ya one thing, though," Raz continued. "Someone's got themselves workin' communications. Can't run an operation this big without communications. CB radios like the truckers have. They work okay. Got one back at my place. Git lots of good information from fellas around. Walkie-talkie radios too. They ain't affected by the pulse either, but they only work short range."

"Follow those buses, Raz," Cody said anxiously.

Raz grunted again. "That's 'xactly what we're doin', boy."

Chapter 16

R az was right. There were more vehicles out there in excellent
running condition. In fact, there was an entire fleet of them. It
wasn't only the buses used to evacuate the residents that were
working. There were armored troop carriers as well. Forty of them
had been assigned to this local operation. They were essential in
accomplishing Phase Two of the grand design. It was called
Operation Clean Sweep, because that's exactly what it was intended
to do.

The army green fortified military Humvees idled in the high school
parking lot, clouds of smoke and vapor escaping their exhaust pipes.
Each vehicle had a two-man team, an American leader and a foreign
troop. They were assigned similar streets and neighborhood routes
through the city just as the rescue buses had. Each team was to sweep
the rescued areas as soon as the buses returned to HQ.

As scheduled, the first Humvees entered their designated positions.
The soldiers weren't looking for stragglers or late comers. Some
missing residents may have found their way home after the buses had
left. A few may even have hidden in their premises, feeling safer in
their own homes rather than being saved by the police. Neither really
mattered to the two-man units. They weren't combing the

neighborhoods for survivors. In fact, according to the plan, there would be no survivors once they had completed their clean sweep.

Front doors with a red X signified they had been cleared of all personnel by the bus squads. A white X indicated no one was found in the property, no live persons, anyway. Those were the houses where the Humvee soldiers would have to be more cautious. Empty houses could be dangerous should owners unexpectedly return, or come out from hiding places, and find themselves face to face with armed intruders.

An Army vehicle stopped at the corner of Cody's street and the men exited. The American soldier let the Chinese trooper force his way through the Robinson's red scarred front door. He hated working with these illiterate, ignorant, foreign mercenaries, but they were good for the grunt work. Their first move was to ensure no people were in the houses. Their task was comparable to that of a tactical search and destroy mission. Many people remained unaccounted for during the evacuation attempt, and if found they were to be dealt with. Husbands stuck in stalled highway traffic. Families traveling for the holiday. College students returning home for the long weekend. Loose ends.

If anything, the soldiers' duties were very specific. They were to search and seize anything of value from the vacant homes. Money, coins, jewelry, gems, silverware. And of course, guns. Wars were expensive and an influx of viable funds was needed to feed the hungry monster. Each team carried a black canvas duffel bag to collect the loot. The American in this unit instructed the Chinaman to carry it, but he would keep a close eye on the bag and its contents. The foreign soldiers couldn't be trusted. And when finished, the team leader would be accountable for the booty upon reporting back to Lt. Col. Fielding.

Cash money was the easiest pickings for the troops. Americans kept their money in obvious places at home. Purses, wallets, desk drawers, cookie jars, kid's piggy banks. There were a few problems with cash, however. These days most Americans carried very little cash with them or in their houses. Debit cards, credit cards, and bank checks were the preferred means of buying things. On line too. Cash had almost become an inconvenience. Even coffee drinkers used plastic to buy their four dollar cappuccinos. So, the overall cash taken from this operation could be relatively meager when compared to other valuables found.

The ultimate concern with the American dollar was its vulnerability in the world market. For generations it had been the favored medium of exchange. Backed by the almighty United States government, the dollar, and the strength of the nation's economy, American greenbacks were used and unconditionally accepted for all commerce in every market, every bank, every transaction within the confines of the nation and in most other countries.

That would change over night.

Within one day after the event had begun, two days tops, every country in the world would recognize the devastating effects set upon the United States. Its central government would cease to exist, at least for the time being. Its monetary system would instantly collapse. Its worldwide trade would come to a complete and sudden halt. In effect, there would no longer be a United States government. Which meant the dollar would be essentially worthless.

But, there was a positive side to collecting cash, at least for the ones in charge of these massive operations. The Humvee soldiers were told they could keep all the cash they found. Sort of a bonus for their good work. All other valuables were to be turned into the HQ commander, ultimately to be used to further fund the effort, if not the commander's personal needs. The soldiers thought this was terrific. They would be very motivated to scour the properties for everything of value in return for their special incentives. But they had absolutely no sense of financial intricacies and would soon learn of their valueless booty.

All confiscated silver and gold, including coins and jewelry, were to be collected. Large and bulky items, such as valuable paintings and sculptures, if there actually were any to be found in this modest income city, were to be left behind or discarded. It was at the troopers' discretion to destroy them or not during their raids. All types of sidearms and rifles were to be removed from the premises so no one else could have access to them.

The soldiers began ransacking the Robinson's house. They tore through the rooms searching for their fortunes like a hurricane torrent hitting a trailer park. First, the master bedroom. That's where most household valuables were likely kept. Drawers were ripped out of the dressers and nightstands. Socks and underwear and scarves were dumped on the carpeted floor. Nothing was worth stooping down for. Jewelry boxes were emptied into the duffel bag to be sorted later. Shoe boxes were swept from the closet shelves onto the floor and quickly looked through. There was a woman's purse, but it had less then twenty dollars in it. The American stuffed the money in his uniform pocket anyway, grumbling. No safe was found.

They continued their search in the kitchen. They smashed a chicken shaped cookie jar on the counter with the end of a rifle. Canisters of sugar and flour and coffee were shattered in search of any cash. The leader checked the refrigerator freezer section. He knew some people often stashed cash there. But there was none. In the room used as an office the Chinese soldier opened the desk drawers while the American went down the hall. The foreigner was getting excited in his search. He was going to get rich stealing from these degenerate Americans.

In the bottom drawer of the desk he found a thick envelop with some English writing scribbled on it. He couldn't read it, but he opened it. Inside he found five crisp one-hundred dollar bills. His eyes grew wide with excitement and a crooked smile creased his face. In his hand was a year's worth of wages back home. He unintentionally let out a soft squeak at his good fortune. The American walked through the hall and peeked into the office. He saw the soldier slipping an envelope into his shirt, stuffing it behind his Kevlar vest.

"What the fuck you doing?" the American asked him.

The Chinese soldier shook his head and got up. He instantly lost his smile.

"What you got in there?" the leader asked, seeing part of the envelope sticking out of his uniform.

The subordinate tried to be sneaky and pushed his fortune farther into his shirt. He said something unintelligible in Chinese.

The leader shouted back, "I don't speak Chink."

The American grabbed the little man by his jacket collar, then pulled the envelope out from his shirt. He opened it and took out the cash. Five bills. Nice score. He tossed the empty envelope in the Chinaman's face and slipped the bills into his pocket. The Chinese soldier looked up at the much taller trooper. He tried to smile, but he knew he was caught.

"Son-of-a-bitch!" the American yelled. "You sneaky little thieving bastard, you!"

The Chinese soldier put his hands up to his face, as if to protect himself from a solid blow to the jaw. He had no idea what would happen next.

The American drew the pistol from his holster and without a moment's hesitation aimed and shot the Chinese man in the temple. "Fucking commie bastard!" He removed the dead soldier's weapons and tossed them into the bag. More for me, he thought as he continued his search of the house alone.

He returned to the back of the residence, hoping to find more cash. The likelihood of locating anything of value in the kids' rooms wasn't good, but he wanted to be thorough. Then he heard a sound in the front. It was a man's voice.

"Honey? Honey?"

The soldier assumed it was the husband, lost in the fray of things and returning home. He moved quietly toward the front door, rifle raised at a shooting angle.

"Honey, I'm home. Where is everyone?" the husband asked, stepping into his own house a bit cautiously.

The American soldier inched down the hall. He could hear the man moving in the living room still calling out to his wife. The soldier swiftly turned into the front room, ready to shoot.

The homeowner came face to face with the soldier. "What... what? Who are you? Where is my fam...?"

The soldier shot Mr. Robinson once in the heart before he finished his question. An easy shot from such a short distance. The man fell backwards onto his sofa and quickly began to bleed out. Then, the soldier ripped the wallet from the dead man's pocket and pulled out fifty-seven dollars, which he greedily stuffed into his own pocket.

"They're waiting for you in hell," the American said. "And stop calling me Honey," he laughed out loud. He had more work to do.

Chapter 17

I n the next five minutes Raz steered his Chevy onto the half-mile
long high school drive. Over the last several moments he had
been thinking privately.

He pulled to the side of the road.

"There're lights on in the school," Nick mentioned. From a quarter
mile away he could see they weren't battery operated lanterns either.
The entire outside of the complex covered in a thick gray sky was lit
up like a ballpark at night. There were two uniformed guards with
weapons at the main entrance turn off. They had stepped aside and
waved at the drivers as the school buses which Raz was following
entered the lot.

"Let's go in there and get our families, Nick," Cody blurted out in
frustration, his voice somewhat dry and anxious.

"I'm with you, buddy," Nick added.

"Now hold ya horses, boys," Raz said. "Ya think ya just goin' go
up to 'em guards and ask if ya can git ya families back? And they're
goin' say, 'Well sure boys, go right on in and find 'em.' Then they
goin' escort ya in there and wave as ya go on ya merry way with the
wives and the kiddies."

"Hadn't thought of that," Cody admitted.

"They ain't goin' let ya waltz right in there, ya damn fools. Those
people inside ain't comin' out that easily. Believe me."

Nick became irritated with Raz's theories. He was a crazy old
man, maybe even demented. "Raz, the people inside were evacuated

from the cold. You know what that means? They were saved by whoever is in charge here. I'm getting my family, god-damn it."

Nick tried to push his way out of the cab past Cody who reached to open his door.

Raz growled like he does and turned sideways next to Nick. He held a pistol in his hand aimed at Nick's chest. "Just simmer down, boys. Ya ain't goin' nowhere. Least not yet. Ya go in there and ya ain't comin' out. How in the hell is that gonna help ya families?"

Both Nick and Cody were shocked to see the gun. Cody cocked his head. "Raz? What's this?"

"Just savin' ya lives," the bearded driver groaned. He pulled the pistol away and returned it someplace inside his jacket. "We need a plan ta git in there, and then ta git out."

Cody thought about it. Raz was right. Again. The old man was so damn irritating with his common sense arguments. "So, what's the plan?"

"Ain't got one yet. Give me a minute," Raz said, deep in thought.

Both Cody and Nick threw up their hands.

Another school bus passed them and entered the grounds. Two more left empty, heading back toward town.

"We have ta figure those people in the school are bein' held against their will at this time. They're more like prisoners than evacuees," Raz began processing his plan.

"Why do you say that?" Nick wanted to know.

" 'Cause, the cops ain't on the road. This ain't their show. Ain't seen no troops from the army base, neither. I'd feel more relaxed if they was involved. So my question is, who are those guys drivin' the buses and collectin' the families?"

"No clue," Nick remarked.

"The only logical answer is that they ain't the good guys. That's what I suspect."

"If that's true, Raz, and I'm not saying it is. What can we possibly do about it?" Cody asked.

"Shush! I'm thinkin'. It's a step by step process, just like effective interrogation. Move from one theory 'til ya discover the facts. Another theory leads ta more facts. Do it over and over. In the end ya have the answer. Well, most of the time."

"What are the facts?" Nick asked.

"Well." Raz was organizing his intricate estimations. "It's a fact that the people are bein' detained as if they was prisoners. So, what do ya do if ya have, what, thousands of prisoners in a small, inadequate space?"

Cody and Nick shrugged their shoulders. They had absolutely no idea.

"The first thing ya do is ta relocate 'em ta a larger facility. Someplace unfamiliar ta the detainees. Someplace possibly far away where they can be better watched over. Ya git too many people in there," he pointed toward the high school, "there's bound ta be trouble."

"Sounds reasonable," Cody said. "That means we have to get them out now."

"Not so fast, sonny." Raz's thoughts started to come together. Guards at the main entry road, probably have guards at the other doors around the building. Lights are on. Still daylight. Most likely there are troops inside with the detainees. Maybe not that many. Buses coming in. Buses leaving. They'd be filling up the building pretty damn quick. Time to move some of the people.

"What are you thinking?" Nick asked.

Raz held up his hand. "Wait a damn minute, will ya." Trees and bushes along the far side of the building. Blind spot. Then he remembered something.

"Ah huh!" Raz said with a wicked grin. "Years ago when we still lived in town there was some days I took my son, Jacob, ta school. He could never wake up on time. Teenagers, ya know. So I'd drive him here before goin' ta work. He didn't want ta go in through the front door. They had someone stationed there who would write up the late ones. So he would sneak in through some back way. There's a single door on the far side near the student parkin' lot. Apparently only the janitors use it. Jacob would tell me how he could jimmy the lock and git in without anyone catchin' him. Damn kid."

Raz nodded his head. "That's how ya get in."

"Okay," Cody said, happy to have half a plan. "But how do we get out?"

"Ya'll have ta figure that one on ya own," Raz said. "Improvise ya way out. Ya have ya gun, don't ya?"

"Ah…yeah."

"When ya git ta the door, use a knife ta slide back the latch. There's no metal brace protectin' it, if I recall correctly. Should be easy. Just pry the lock open and ya're in," Raz explained.

"I'm not sure if I can do it," Cody admitted. He'd never broken into any place before.

"Hell, my boy got inside in less than two seconds. Ya smarter than a tenth grader, son?"

"Okay," Cody said again. "But I need a knife."

"Ya don't even have a damn knife?" Raz grumbled. "Jesus H. Christ," he huffed. Raz reached into one of his pants pockets and pulled out a four inch pocket knife. He handed it to the school teacher. "Here. Ya know how ta work it?"

"Yes."

"Well, that's good. Don't cut yaself. It's sharp."

Cody gave the old man a weird face, like he wasn't completely incompetent.

"I'll back the truck down that there dirt road. I think the grounds crew uses it. See that small storage buildin' over there. No one will see us 'cause of the trees. Ya guys can scoot around ta the door and git in without any guards noticin' ya," Raz explained to them.

Cody and Nick nodded in agreement.

Then Raz slowly backed the pickup down the dirt path and stopped on the blind side of the storage shed. "Okay boys. This is it. Remember, stay low and be quiet. I'll stay here in the truck waitin' for ya. Be quick, but don't get caught."

Cody looked at the mastermind behind this rescue attempt. "Duh!"

Both Cody and Nick exited the truck, closed its door quietly, and moved through the trees toward the back corner of the school. They were scared to death. They stopped at the last clump of bushes, looked around for guards and saw the coast was clear. They then ran to the door Raz told them about. Single door, no brace protecting the locking mechanism. This was it.

Cody opened the jack knife while Nick kept an eye open for any nearby movement. Cody slipped the blade between the door jamb and the locking bolt. The knife slipped and hit his index finger. "Shit!" he yelled, after realizing he had just cut himself. It was a minor gouge, but it was bleeding.

"Shhh! Quiet," Nick said, worried that a guard would hear them.

"Sorry. I cut myself."

"Yeah, I see that. Want me to open it, Indiana Jones?" Nick mocked.

"I can get it."

On the second attempt the door lock released and the two entered the janitor's dark room. They were in.

Inside the crowded gymnasium the first group of detainees was being formed into a haphazard line. Guards pushed the evacuees toward the double doors. People were crying and shouting. Some complained, but were convinced by the back end of several rifles to shut up. They were being moved to some other part of the school.

Cody and Nick slowly opened the janitor's interior door into the bright gymnasium. They cracked the door a few inches to peek inside. They heard jumbled noises. Cody pushed the door open two more inches, hoping not to be detected. Then they saw thousands of people wrapped up in their coats and hoods and tight blankets. The room was as cold as outside. A line of sorts was being organized. Guards were pushing people in place, their backs to the door.

Cody leaned on the door and opened it enough so he could stick his head inside and look for his family. There were too many of them. The column of people was being slowly led out of the room.

"I see Robin," he whispered to Nick. Robin was carrying little Jennifer. Jeffrey was holding onto his mother's coat. They were being shuffled along. "Your family is right behind her," Cody added. There was hope in his eyes. But how was he going to get to them?

A guard walked near the opened door. Cody saw his back. He was a big man. He was close enough to touch. Cody quickly but quietly closed the door several inches. He felt the pistol in his jacket, but let it rest there. Seconds later he dared again to look inside. This was his only chance. Robin turned to Nick's wife, Lisa. She appeared to be lost. Anger had reddened her cheeks, Cody thought. Or was it just the cold? Still moving in line, Robin was about to say something to Lisa. Then she saw the janitor's door slightly cracked open a bit farther, her husband barely visible.

Instinctively she yelled out, "Cody!" Then she caught herself, but it was too late. Young Jennifer parroted her mother with a question. "Daddy?"

Cody put a finger to his mouth, as if to say 'Quiet.'

But the guard nearest the door saw Robin's reaction. He swiftly turned and saw the door partly ajar. He barked something in a different language. Russian, maybe. He grabbed the door knob and pulled, but Cody held onto it with both hands. Thinking quickly, Cody then slammed the solid door outward into the guard which pushed him off center. Cody glanced up at his family. They had disappeared into the outside hall.

With Nick's help, Cody yanked the metal door shut. They felt it being pulled from the other side. Two sets of hands were yanking at it. The two pulled it tighter and heard the lock finally click in place.

"Run, man, run!" Nick shouted.

They dashed through the room toward the exit. Bam, bam, bam. Bullets pounded the metal door panel. Most of the lead lodged in the steel, but several bounced off. More bullets rained against the door like fireworks popping incessantly.

One bullet squeezed through the weakened metal and struck flesh. There was a spastic shriek. Nick went down just steps from the outside exit. It was dark and Cody almost tripped over his friend. "I'm hit," Nick whispered. The bullet had penetrated the back of his left leg, just below the knee.

Cody reached down and hoisted his friend to his feet. "We have to go!" Cody said as calmly as possible. The door was being riddled with more hot lead. Several shots entered the small room, but missed the men. They heard loud and hysterical screaming echoing from the other side of the door.

Cody and Nick crashed through the outside door. They didn't bother looking for any security forces. They just ran, Nick leaning on Cody. They raced to the bushes, then through the clump of trees. Any minute they expected to see armed guards shooting at them. They could easily and swiftly be picked off before they reached the landscaper's storage shed. But they heard no shots. There were no alarms. But it didn't mean that the soldiers wouldn't be outside any second.

Cody helped get Nick to the shed. Nick's leg was bleeding badly from the running. Cody ripped off his belt and wrapped it around Nick's thigh. "That should help slow the bleeding," Cody said. Right now they needed to get to the truck.

Raz saw the men make it to the shed. He knew something had gone drastically wrong. He took a fleeting glance at the corner of the school building. Two huge uniformed soldiers had burst out the door and were crouching low, searching the grounds for the fleeing invaders. Raz flung the passenger door open.

"Hurry boys," he said, as if he were late for church. "We got company comin'."

Cody dragged Nick to the truck, his injured leg giving out. He threw his friend into the cab and jumped in just as Raz put the pickup in gear. The old man heard gun fire and felt several slugs hit the back panel of his truck. He pushed the Chevy to its limits as he bounced down the dirt path onto the pavement.

Moments later he swung left and raced away from the high school grounds. In his rearview mirror he saw something very strange. Behind the guarded entrance Raz saw a row of four large Army buses waiting in convoy to leave the premises.

What he had feared most, and somewhat predicted, was happening.

Chapter 18

Nick groaned from the piercing pain in his leg. He lifted his pant leg to look at the wound. It was the first time he had ever been shot and it hurt like a son-of-a-bitch, but it wasn't as bad as he had first thought. The bullet had torn through the fleshy part of his calf. It was a nasty looking injury, but he would survive.

Cody tore off a strip of his shirt and wrapped it around the bloody mess. He then secured the improvised bandage with the two end strips of cloth. "There," he said. "That should hold for awhile."

"What the hell happened back there?" Raz asked after watching Cody tend to his buddy. "I heard some gunfire from inside and thought ya guys was goners."

Nick bit his lip against the pain. "Then why did you hang around, old timer?"

Raz grunted. "Knew ya'd make it."

"We saw them, Raz. We were so close. But they were being moved out. Then the shooting started," Cody explained.

"Yup, thought it might be a long shot."

"It's impossible to get our families out this way. They're heavily guarded inside. Thought I heard a foreign language. Could have been Russian," Cody said.

Raz nodded. "Makes sense. Russian guard, I mean. They've been known ta use foreign troops for the dirty work. Word is, there's lots of 'em throughout the country. 'Em and others. Gettin' harder ta find true blue Americans ta fight against their own kind."

"We need to find another way, Raz," Cody said, hoping the old man had a Plan B.

"Workin' on it now, sonny." He turned to Cody. "Damn good job ya done with Nick's leg, kid. Damn good."

Cody cracked a small smile. All he wanted to do was to get his family back.

"Appears things are movin' faster than I thought," Raz began. "I saw a row of buses back there preparin' ta leave. Not school buses, neither. Army buses for long distances. I reckon they're fixin' ta relocate the whole lot. Take some doin', but like I said before, they can't keep 'em all locked up here."

Cody thought for a moment. "Maybe Robin and the kids, along with your family, Nick," he turned to his friend, "were being loaded into those buses. Makes sense."

Nick grabbed his leg, loosened the belt tourniquet for a second and re-tightened it. "The big question is, where are they being taken?"

"We should pull to the side of the road and wait for the buses. Then we can follow them," Cody suggested.

"Good idea," Nick seconded.

Raz shook his hairy head and snarled. "Bad idea, boys. Those guards are pissed off at ya for what ya done. They might send out a search crew lookin' for ya. Don't want ta take the chance. They know what we're drivin'. We'd be easy pickins' if we stay too close."

"But we don't want to lose them," Nick said.

"And we have no idea where they're going," Cody added. "Let's chase them."

"Yup. And we catch up ta 'em. What we gonna do? Ask 'em ta pull over? Think boys, think. They'll have guards in the buses. Maybe in jeeps or somethin' escortin' the caravan. And what do we have? Two pea shooters, an old rifle, one guy with a bad leg, 'nother who don't have a clue. Ya want ta stick 'em up with ya little pistol?"

Cody shut his mouth. He felt frustrated and insulted.

Raz kept driving farther away from the school. He was staying off the main streets as best he could by using the back roads. The guards could have radioed ahead to other crews around the city to keep a look out for his Chevy truck. There were no other civilian vehicles on the road, as far as he knew, so it would be easy to spot.

He glanced over and saw Cody's bloody hand. "Looks like ya're bleedin'."

Cody stuffed his hand with the cut finger into this jacket. "It's from Nick's leg," he lied.

Raz knew better. "Seems ya got cut."

"It's nothing," Cody answered, ready to drop the issue.

"Yeah, right," Raz scoffed. "Can I have my knife back?"

Cody dug into his pocket for the knife and without a word returned it to Raz.

"Told ya it was sharp," Raz said, just to get in the last word.

"I have a pretty good idea where they're headed," Raz mentioned. His bearded face showed wrinkles of deep thought running through his calculating brain. He scratched his wiry whiskers and looked straight ahead. A few seconds later he spoke again. "Here's how I see it, boys. The Army buses are goin' ta one of 'em FEMA camps. The people need ta be moved. What else would they do ta 'em? I mean. It's unthinkable and it could happen. But...I believe it's too early in the game ta...ah...eliminate 'em."

"Are you suggesting that whoever is conducting this...this fiasco," Cody said, outraged at the extreme possibility, "that these guards would stoop to killing innocent people? Women and children?"

"Just thinkin' out loud, sonny. Seen it before. Not here in this country, mind ya. But lots of other places."

Cody looked at the old man with utter disbelief in his eyes. "How could all this be happening, Raz? I mean, this is America. This kind of thing doesn't go on here."

Raz had a serious frown. "Not 'til now."

"But...," Cody said, before being cut off by Raz.

"Wake up boys. This ain't no movie. This is real and sometimes real ain't good. Ya think ya live in a Johnny-be-good world? Ya and ya nine-to-five jobs with weekends off and four weeks vacation. Goin' out ta eat five times a week, orderin' in the rest of the time. Watchin' the idiot tube six hours a day, ya faces buried in Facebook, ya ears smothered with ya cell phone. Ya spend more time on the damn computers than ya do with ya own families. Everything is hunky-dory. La-de-da! 'Til one day somethin' goes wrong. The cable goes out, ya lose phone service, price of gas goes up. Ya paycheck is one day late, ya credit cards git maxed out, ya car needs fixin'. All hell breaks loose. Life ain't worth living. Oh, whoa is me!" Raz stopped to wet his lips.

"But all that shit ain't nothin' compared ta the real thing. I'm tellin' ya boys, there're bad people out there tryin' ta do ya everyday. Every large business, every country, every government. They want what they want and they'll do whatever they have ta in order ta git it. Our government is the same. Fact is, it's probably worse, 'cause people, the fools that they are, tend ta believe what they're told. They forgot what self-reliance is, so they let the government slowly take away what is rightfully theirs in order ta feel safe and secure.

"Well, safety and security are out the window, boys. Ya got what ya got, 'cause we let it happen right under our noses. Mark my words. Things are gonna git much worse before they git better. If they git better. There's treachery and deception and subversion and betrayal everywhere ya turn. And if ya ain't part of the solution ta end this…this treasonous behavior, then ya part of the problem."

Raz shook his head. That was the most he had ever said about this whole event. He wondered to himself if it was too late to stop the madness. Then he blew the thought away. Hell no, it wasn't.

"Give me one of 'em damn beers from behind the seat there, kid," he motioned to Nick.

Cody gazed out the windshield, his breathing short and rapid. His heart beat racing. Despite the cold, his hands were clammy, his mouth dry. Still staring out the window he said, "Somebody needs to do something about this."

Raz let loose a rasping chuckle.

"What?" Cody said.

"*Somebody* always needs ta do somethin' about it," Raz said with conviction. "The damn question is always, who?"

They drove through small neighborhood roads until they came to Buffalo Soldier Trail, the major bypass which ran from Fort Huachuca's main entrance down to the southern edge of the city. Raz intentionally detoured around Nick's and Cody's houses. No need to drive through trouble. Raz suspected there might be clean up teams working their way through the rescued areas.

Cody recognized the fact that old Raz had purposely avoided his street. He thought to himself. He might never see his house again. He might never get to drive his truck or the car again. All the things he owned meant nothing to him at this point. He simply wanted to be with Robin and the children.

Their three TVs, the expensive stainless steel refrigerator and the matching stove, dishwasher, and microwave. The California king size bed, his desk computer and laptop. The small motorboat parked in the driveway, the ATV in the garage, the four-burner BBQ grill out back. None of those things meant anything now. He'd give up everything he owned just to save the people he most cared for. At that moment he vowed he would, no matter what it took.

Raz's truck screamed down Buffalo Soldier to the tail end of the Huachuca Mountains. At upwards of seventy miles an hour he weaved and swerved around damaged vehicles heading toward his destination. There was no other moving traffic on the road.

Cody snapped out of his trance. "Where're we going, Raz? What about the buses?"

"There're a few things we need ta pick up first. Have ta be prepared ta go after those bastards. Can't go half-cocked."

Nick was bobbing back and forth in the middle of the seat. His leg was throbbing. He stayed quiet in an attempt to stem the pain, but it wasn't really working.

A few miles farther Nick shook out of it. "I'm dying of thirst. Need something to drink."

Cody realized Nick was right. It was nearly four in the afternoon. The skies were getting darker as the storm clouds hung low. "I haven't eaten all day," Cody said. Then he thought about his family. Most likely they haven't eaten today either.

"Should take us less than half an hour ta get ta where we're goin'." Raz grumbled. "Let's make a quick stop for a few things."

Both Cody and Nick were relieved. They could get some real bandages for Nick's leg too.

"Ah…Raz?" Nick said.

"Yeah."

"Back there at the school. You weren't really going to shoot me. Were you?"

Raz took his sweet time answering. "Hadn't thought that far ahead at the time."

Nick's eyes widened. "You didn't have bullets in your gun. Did you?"

"Only a damn fool would point an unloaded gun at someone," Raz commented, like anyone should know that.

Nick slumped into the seat. He reminded himself not to piss off the old guy again.

Shortly after turning off BST onto the Highway 92 leading south, Raz noticed a Circle K convenience store to the left. He drove into the empty parking lot a little too fast and hit the concrete stops a bit too hard. The sudden stop jolted Nick, causing him to scream. The store was closed, which was no surprise. The shocking thing was there wasn't a crowd trying to break in. Not a single person was around nor any car drove past the store.

Cody suddenly burst out. "I have no money with me." Then he remembered he had a ton of silver coins.

"Don't worry 'bout it," Raz mentioned. "Save ya money." He flashed a menacing look. "We have these." He held up his pistol and grinned ear to ear.

Cody looked at the crazed man. "Are you serious?"

"Why the hell not? Ain't nobody here and this store ain't never gonna' open again. Besides, it's time for ya ta practice with ya piece."

At first Cody didn't get it. Then he realized Raz wanted him to use his gun. Sort of a mock robbery where there were no consequences. And they did need a few things. Before he knew it Cody saw Raz standing in front of the locked store door firing his pistol at the glass panels.

"Try it. It's fun," Raz said to Cody.

From inside the truck Nick thought to himself. Oh shit! The crazy old bastard's gun was loaded.

Cody stepped out of the truck and moved closer to Raz. He pointed the pistol at the store and pulled the trigger. Nothing happened.

"Release the safety first," Raz commented, barely shaking his head.

"Oh...okay." Cody flipped the lever and the gun went off, shattering a window above the door. "Touchy trigger," he said.

Raz bent over and laughed like a fool. "Oh, ya'll do just fine."

Cody tried it again and shot twice fairly close to where he was aiming. Still in the truck holding his leg, Nick was enjoying the bizarre show.

"Okay, 'nough fun. Let's git what we came here for."

Raz and Cody slipped through the glassless door. It was dark inside. Cody went one way while Raz went another. Cody gathered packs of gauze and bandages, some antiseptic creams and alcohol. He then picked up several plastic bottles of water from the refrigerated section. They were still cold.

Raz ambled to the back of the store and grabbed several pre-made sandwiches wrapped in plastic. He picked up a few Sara-Lee snacks and two bags of potato chips. He found plastic bags behind the cashier counter and dumped his shopping into one of them. On the way out of the store he lifted a six-pack of Bud Light beer. "For my troubles," he said to nobody in particular.

He threw the bag on Nick's lap. Where the hell was Cody? He asked himself. Back in the store he saw Cody loading up the counter as if he was going to pay for his purchases.

"Put a fire under ya ass, boy," Raz growled. "Time ta git."

Cody snapped out of it and figured out this was a free shopping spree. He stuffed his take into bags, gathered them up and went to the truck. He tossed the bags on the floor leaving little room for his and Nick's feet. Then he ran back into the store.

"Jesus H. Christ," Raz yelled. "Now what?"

Cody returned to the truck. He had three Baby Ruth candy bars in his hand, tossed one each to Nick and Raz, keeping one for him. "I love these things," he commented.

They drove away to the south. "We'll git ya leg fixed up as soon as we git there," Raz said to Nick. The boys had no idea where they were going. But for the moment they didn't care. They were content with their water and candy bars.

Chapter 19

Hordes of people from the gymnasium were being forced to board the large Army buses waiting in the back of the high school. The guards were in an irritable mood after the break in by two would-be intruders. Three of them had exited the building firing on the escaping truck as it bounced out of range. Lt. Col. Fielding was told about the incident and with his walkie-talkie radio alerted all patrols within range to keep a lookout for the Chevy pickup. Their escape didn't really matter much to him.

Just a fly in the soup.

Everything else was going as planned.

The guards rushed the detainees into the overloaded buses. Orders were barked at them in Chinese and Russian and Spanish. The soldiers kicked the slow movers and butted several heads as an example of their authority. The moaning and groaning, mixed with constant crying, filled the buses. The transports were originally fitted to carry sixty people. Close to one hundred were jammed into each one. Three to most bench seats. Mothers carried their children in their arms. Some dropped on the floor near the back door. Many had to stand.

Robin quickly scanned the passengers. They had been diverted to the last of the buses. Nick's wife Lisa and their two young daughters were about ten seats back. The women silently acknowledged one another. Their eyes and curt smiles indicated they were all unhurt. But just minutes earlier, Robin knew she had seen Cody at that open door. He was trying to rescue them. She worried for his safety, hoping he had escaped the shooting. How did he get this far out of town? She wondered. And where would he go now? For that matter, where were these buses taking them?

The transports, fully loaded, each one with a driver and an armed guard sitting in front, slowly pulled away from the school grounds. As they made the first turn Robin could see there were four buses, with an escort vehicle that appeared to be an Army Humvee leading the way. There were no other vehicles behind them. She paid attention to every stop, every turn. She wanted to know which way they were headed.

On the straight away along the northern by-pass, she glanced around the inside of the bus. She was searching for possible ways out, weak points, maybe. Not that she and her kids could escape a fast moving bus. But nevertheless, she wanted to be aware of any potential exits. She saw two men, strangers, looking her way. They made eye contact and there was a sense of unity among them. Each nodded slightly like they were ready too, if a chance arose to jump off the bus.

The release handle to the rear door emergency exit had been removed. Robin had no idea whether the door was locked from the outside, though most likely it was. The windows on both sides were tinted to stop the harsh summer desert sun. Today there was no sun. Cross bars covered the windows also, like those seen on county prison buses. There was also very little heat in the bus. The front was warm from the blowing heater in the dash, but not much of the warmth seeped toward the rear.

Robin sat next to a window. She looked at the release latches. They were screwed in place to prevent the windows from being opened. She looked up, but there were no roof vents which could be possible escape routes. This was crazy thinking, she thought. No way could they leave the bus unless they were allowed to. She prayed that her husband and Nick would somehow find them and save them.

That was if their husbands were still alive.

The convoy of buses roared past Fort Huachuca's east gate and turned north on Highway 90. It was twenty-eight miles straight to Interstate 10 which stretched from coast to coast, east to west. At that point Robin would have a better idea which way they were going. Before then, though, they would stop at the U.S. Border Patrol check-point ten miles north. And they may stop at the intersection of Hwy. 90 and I-10. Both places were possible opportunities for escape.

From the outside landmarks she knew they were getting close to the check-point. It was one of many similar stations in southern Arizona established close to the international border. They had been an issue of much controversy when the Border Patrol converted temporary check-points for vehicles going north into well-manned, permanent highway pull offs. This particular BP check-point was a full thirty miles north of the Mexican-American border.

Why in the world, it was argued, did the BP need another inspection station so far in country? Did they expect to apprehend illegal immigrants or drug runners from the south? Everyone knew of the check-points. Those who didn't want to get caught found other unmonitored routes.

Most people driving from the Sierra Vista-Fort Huachuca area toward Tucson and beyond saw it as a method to harass American citizens, a means to intimidate the average law-abiding resident. Some claimed it was a long term scheme to display the presence of law enforcement and get the citizens accustomed to routine interference in their daily lives. At any rate, all traffic traveling through the check point was casually inspected.

At the permanent stations every vehicle was stopped. Every passenger was asked about their citizenship status, although most Americans carried no proof of their birthplace. Some were asked about their final destination, as if it were essential for federal officers to know a person's itinerary. All travelers were looked upon suspiciously, like they were criminals or illegals attempting to pass through to the promised land. Citizen profiling, though vehemently denied by the BP and DHS, was considered a legitimate means of checking on travelers. Trained German Shepherd drug dogs sniffed every car, truck, and bus in search of illegal drugs and contraband.

The check points were a clear infringement on every American's rights, but nothing was done to stop them.

Robin glanced at the men toward the front. Two others and a woman, none known to her, did the same. There was a silent alliance established amongst strangers. When the bus stops we all do something, was the unspoken agreement. Jump the guard, take his weapons, storm the driver.

Do something!

Robin put up one finger as a signal for the upcoming stop. Some of the men stood up in the crowded aisle, waiting to pounce. The rest grabbed the chair bars in front of their seats, prepared to charge. But instead of slowing down, the convoy raced through the check station without question. Several BP agents, dressed in their olive green uniforms, simply threw sloppy salutes to the bus drivers as they breezed on through.

The tension inside eased. Robin held her sleeping daughter on her lap. Jeffrey clutched onto his mother's side and squeezed into the tight seating space. Inside the bus was quiet. There was some whimpering and sniffling, but most everyone had settled down, waiting for the unknown. Every once in awhile the guard in front stood up and peered down the rows of seats. Satisfied there was no problem, he sat back down again.

Less than fifteen minutes later the buses began slowing down. The silent alert had roused those willing to fight. The buses were gearing down as they reached the wide turn to the interstate. Robin looked up, hoping against hope the buses would veer off and stop. Maybe they would change guards, discuss their final plans, make sure all was going well, stretch their legs.

Something!

"Stop the bus. Stop the bus," she whispered as if praying. By now the dozen or so who had committed their alliance in doing something to escape, confirmed their positions through fleeting eye contact. We can't just wait to be saved, Robin thought. We must rely on ourselves, on our instincts. We have to take control now to save ourselves and our children.

The cluster of bold people stood up. The bus was still slowing a bit, but not stopping yet. The guard turned and yelled something in Russian to the brave men and women standing. He wanted them to sit down and remain silent. One last glance among the committed and they were ready to roll. Then the bus took a sharp left turn and raced up the long entrance ramp to the highway. They were on Interstate 10 going west toward Tucson and the lower deserts.

The bus people would have to wait until they had another chance.

Chapter 20

The old pickup truck rattled as if it was falling apart when it turned west onto Coronado National Monument Road, named after the famous sixteenth century Spanish explorer who had traveled the region in search of Cibola, the City of Gold. The road wound around the southern most tip of the Huachuca Mountains through the sloping mesquite and oak covered foothills. The valley drained into the San Pedro River lined for miles with ancient cottonwoods, some five miles farther south.

"I've never been down here," Nick commented. "Where are we going?"

"My place," Raz said. "It's down the road a piece on t'other side." Actually, his home was quite a ways down the road, past where the pavement ended and the gravel road began. Then it turned into a single lane dirt trail that climbed over the mountain in switchback fashion. It wound down the back side of the Huachucas into the lower forest and rocky landscape. Near the bottom of the mountain's sunny side, the trail hugged along the international border which comprised of a simple four-wire barbed fence separating the two countries. The land was pristine and remote, just as Raz liked it.

Cody spoke up. "I thought you went through the Army fort on the west side to get to your house."

"Usually do," Raz answered. "But ya can be sure the fort's locked up tighter than a drum. Soon as this event happened they would have shut 'er down. Anyway, my place is harder ta find comin' this way, and that suits me just fine."

He meandered through the trail for a few more miles, dodging large boulders, scraping the sides of his truck against clumps of creosote brush and low hanging trees. The shadows were getting thicker in the late afternoon. Slick sections of ice that never saw the light of day caused Raz's truck to slip off the path more than a few times. He made a sharp turn into the bush. "This here's Forest Road, number 284. Not much of a clearin', which is good. Makes my place almost impossible ta locate."

"You sure we're not lost?" Cody had to say. Nick was thinking the same thing, but he didn't dare say anything, remembering the old guy carried a loaded weapon and was touchy about a few things.

Raz didn't respond to the stupid question. In a minute he steered onto a rutted road that used to be a lumber trail from the turn of the previous century. He rolled up a short ridge and stopped. "This is it," he said. The path opened to a large clearing with an old doublewide house trailer, probably built in the 1960s, set in the middle. Tall junipers and black oak trees growing in the higher elevation surrounded the flimsy structure, making it impossible to see from three sides.

Raz parked his truck and got out. There was a rusted padlock on the door and with his key ring he struggled to open it. Cody jumped out and grabbed the bags of medical supplies. Nick slowly slid out of the truck holding his leg.

"Let's git ya inside ta look at that leg of yours," Raz said to Nick. Cody walked over to the wobbly wooden stoop leading to the front door. "Don't look like much from the outside," Raz said. "That's how I like it. If someone happened ta stumble on this place they wouldn't bother with such a dump."

"No doubt," Cody said under his breath.

Raz removed the lock, entered, and switched the lights on. Nick limped through the door. "Wow!"

Cody stepped inside and looked around. "Raz, this is nice."

The interior was well maintained, clean, and generously filled witholder, but comfortable looking furniture. A wood burning stove was in the back corner close to the kitchen. "Let me git a fire goin'," Raz said.

"You have electricity, Raz. How's that?" Cody asked.

Raz got the logs burning. "Told ya before. I have cages protectin' my stuff. Everythin' here works. The well pump, my lights, my computer."

"Oh yes. Those Faraway devices," Cody remembered.

"Faraday," Raz corrected him. Damn young people don't pay attention. "They're basic devices that protect electrical equipment, but they work," Raz said, about the uncomplicated protective cages. He moved toward the back of the house turning on more lights.

"Cody, think ya can take care of Nick?"

Nick slumped in a stuffed chair. Cody found some scissors, cut his pant leg up past the wound, and in a few minutes redressed the injury. The bleeding had stopped, so there was no need for the belt tourniquet any longer.

Raz tossed Nick a bottle of aspirin. "It's all I got, but should take the sting off a bit."

Nick swallowed a few pills and in several minutes felt better even though the throbbing sensation was still there. Then the three men sat near the hot stove and began eating their sandwiches. Raz reached for a Bud Light.

Nick and Cody grabbed one too. "Don't you think we should go now? It'll be nightfall soon," Cody said.

"Nah, I know where 'em buses are headin," Raz said. "Best if we leave when it's dark. We got a long trip ahead of us."

Cody wondered. "Hey Raz. What's with the beer. You seem more like a straight whiskey guy."

Raz nodded. "Usually am. But I have this thing about Bud Light."

The boys watched Raz and knew he was about to say something else.

"Back in the war we was chasin' this band of Viet Cong in the jungles north of Saigon, near the Cambodian border. Vietnam's a big country when ya're slashin' through it. A band of gooks had captured eight of our boys in a fire storm. Most of our men died there, but the VC kept t'others as prisoners. Figured they wanted ta drag 'em ta

Hanoi and maybe trade 'em for somethin'. They moved farther inta the bush every day headin' north. My company kept trackin' 'em. There was fifteen of us GIs hackin' through the jungle, fightin' the insects, sufferin' from the heat and damn humidity. We was all young, don't ya know. I was just a kid too. Wars are fought by the young 'cause they believe in things."

Raz took another pull from his beer bottle. Cody and Nick sat back watching Raz ramble on about his war days back before either one of them were even born. They let the grizzled old man take his trip back to his earlier days.

"So, after weeks of chasin' 'em bastards we knew we was gettin' closer. We could smell their fires from miles away. Stank like road kill, the shit they was cookin'. Eight miserable days later we caught up with 'em. Flanked the assholes while they was eatin'. Caught 'em by surprise, we did. A few of our guys they had was tied up ta some trees like they was livestock. They was in real bad shape."

He stopped his story telling for a brief pause and snorted. "My whole company fired on those no good pricks until they was sprawled all over their camp site. Killed 'bout thirty of 'em gooks. Some of the men emptied their clips inta the bastards ta make sure they was dead. My guys was hot and tired and pissed off. I went ta cut our boys free. By that time there was only four of 'em left. The looks on their filthy, desperate faces still haunt me." Raz stared into the stove's fire for a few seconds, remembering forty year old nightmares.

"Anyway, when we went up ta the dead bodies we seen what the gooks was eatin'. They was eatin' our boys, one at a time as they headed north. They chopped 'em up and was eatin' 'em. Can ya believe that shit? What kind of human bein's could do that? Makes me sick ta this day. That's what the horrible smell was we was gittin' over the past week or so." Raz dropped his head down.

Cody saw his red eyes. How could somebody live with that? He wondered.

"Well, one of the guys in our company, Buddy Light, was a crazy bastard. Ya know, all gung-ho and the like. Not sure if that was his given name or not. Didn't really matter, but that's what he was called. He carried a flame thrower on his back the whole while. It was heavy, but he insisted on keepin' it with him for when he found the VCs with our guys. When he seen what we seen he went berserk. He torched that camp site ta hell along with all them dead Viet Cong. He didn't let up 'til the whole friggin' jungle was burnin'. It was holy hell. He'd burn up the whole damn country if he coulda. The rest of us just stood back and watched, covering our noses from the god-awful smell."

Raz stood up and walked to the kitchen. " 'Bout a week later Buddy got killed in a mortar attack," Raz finished. "So that's why the beer, boys."

Cody and Nick remained silent. There was nothing they could say.

Raz went to the kitchen, made a pot of coffee, and set it on the table with three clean cups. The coffee was so strong it could be stirred with a fork, but it was hot and went well with the last of the sandwiches and the Sara-Lees.

"We can't waste much more time," Raz said. "Help me with the supplies before it's too dark."

The guys followed Raz outdoors. "We'll need gasoline. Don't expect Texaco will be open anywhere. Some water, too. It will be a long trip."

Cody and Nick filled several five gallon cans of gas from a huge storage tank out back behind the trailer house. Then they filled two five gallon potable containers with fresh water from the well. Because of his leg Nick couldn't lift them, so Cody carried the cans to the truck and loaded them into the bed. Raz went to his utility shed, unlocked the door, and gathered more things.

He grabbed a coil of thick rope, a bolt cutter, three rolled up sleeping bags, a loaded tool box, two shovels, some gloves, a small gas propane burner stove, extra blankets, and a large canvas tarp.

"Give me a hand with this stuff," Raz yelled at the boys. In minutes the pile was secured in the truck bed and covered by the tarp.

"There's more inside," Raz directed. In the trailer he opened a closet door off the living room. It wasn't very large, just deep enough to hold a few jackets. Raz stepped in and slid a panel in the back wall to the side. Another room. He pulled the light string and disappeared for a minute. "Git in here boys."

Cody and Nick looked in the hidden space. Raz had at least six rifles hanging on the wall. All automatics. Opened drawers built into the wall revealed a dozen or so pistols and enough ammo to fight a war. Six big shiny, sharp hunter's knives were in another drawer. A plastic first aid kit was on a narrow countertop.

"Welcome ta the jungle," Raz snickered. "Load 'em up boys. We're gonna' need 'em." The weapons and ammo were jammed into two long army-type duffel bags and zipped up.

Cody and Nick stared at each other. What in the hell does he expect us to do with all this? That was the common question.

"Ya okay Nick?" Raz asked him. He liked the young men, but if it came to battle they wouldn't have been his first choice.

"Yes sir," Nick answered.

"Git another bag out of that bottom cupboard," Raz ordered Cody as he pointed toward the kitchen cabinets.

They filled the bag with foods stuff from the generous pantry. Peanut butter, crackers, cans of beans and tuna, a box of energy bars, and several bags of venison jerky which Raz had made himself. They packed a few pots and pans too, just in case they were needed.

"Come over here, boys," Raz insisted. He turned a key to open a double door in one of the cupboards. "Couple dozen should do," he said. Cody and Nick dug out two dozen MRE containers. Meals Ready to Eat. They were complete meals prepared for the military while on extended duty in the field. Just add hot water and they were edible. They tasted like shit, but they were full of essential nourishment.

"Think we have everything," Cody said, overwhelmed with the load.

"Not quite." Raz went to his secret hiding place in the kitchen and retrieved an unopened bottle of Johnny Walker. "For the long ride," he added with a wide grin. "Didn't have no Johnny Walker in my unit, but he's still a good buddy of mine."

They packed everything in the truck's bed and tightened up the tarp. "Okay. Looks good, boys," Raz said, looking about to make sure he hadn't forgotten anything important. "Almost forgot," he added. Raz went back inside and came out with two flashlights, a handful of maps, and other papers.

Then he remembered. "One more thing before we hit the road. Follow me."

The trio moved toward the shed that Raz had gathered supplies from. Inside he kicked at the dirt and straw on the floor. The boys wondered what he was up to now. Raz stopped and stomped his foot one more time.

"That's it," he said. He bent down and found a metal ring, pulled it loose from the dirt and yanked on it. He raised a false floor door, creating a cloud of dust. Raz let the door slam back against a work bench. Then he stepped into the dark hole.

Chapter 21

The boys leaned over and stared down the opening. Suddenly a bright light came on. A set of steep wooden stairs lead into a cave-like space. "Don't be afraid, boys. Come on down," Raz said from farther back in the cavern.

The men climbed down the stairs into a dirt walled dungeon. "Must have been a root cellar some time ago, I figure." Raz explained. "Used ta be a log cabin on the property behind where the trailer is. Got me ta thinkin' some years back."

Raz motioned for the boys to follow him. He moved a row of rotting planks held together as a makeshift door. Behind it was a solid steel door which he unlocked with a key. He stepped into another room and turned on the lights.

Cody and Nick followed closely behind and were amazed at what they were standing in. It was a long tube-like bunker with fluorescent lights running along the ceiling from end to end. "Welcome ta the home of the future, boys."

The space was at least fifty feet long, twelve wide, and seven feet tall. In a strange sort of way it resembled the inside of a commercial passenger airplane, without the seats. There were no windows, of course, but the bizarre bunker was divided into functional spaces.

Raz moved farther in as the boys tagged along. The front roomwhere they stepped into was the living area. It was crammed, but looked relatively comfortable with bench seats covered with cushions attached to the outer walls. Two fold-down tables locked in their upright positions stored away to offer more room. A worn CB radio set and hand-held mike hung on the wall with antenna wires running up the metal siding through the ceiling.

Next was a kitchen of sorts. A tiny electric hot plate was set up to cook the few foods that needed cooking. A small counter space extended three feet to a tiny stainless steel sink. Top and bottom cabinets, like those in a compact recreational vehicle, held various pots, pans, dishes, cups, and utensils for everyday use.

"I got me a generator hid in the woods where no one could ever find it. It supplies me 'nough power for what I need. There's 'nother smaller back-up one in the rear closet. There are two air filtration systems which supply recycled fresh air. Good for six months. Got water too. Thousand gallons buried underground in a sealed container with pipes runnin' here." He pointed at a shut off valve and small faucet sticking through the kitchen wall.

He continued the tour past the kitchen.

"Here we have the sleepin' quarters. Comfortable 'nough for a long stay." Four double bunk beds lined the sides of the main aisle. Two on either wall. The beds were made up with starched, folded-over sheets and army blankets square cornered like those in a military boot camp barracks. Old habits never die. Raz opened small doors and cubby holes above and beneath the bunks to reveal extra storage spaces filled with food supplies similar to those in his trailer. A taller closet, barely a foot wide contained more rifles and side arms.

"Raz," Cody said, astonished at what he was seeing. "This is absolutely amazing. You have everything you need here. But why?"

"Why what?" the old man growled. It was apparent the young man didn't have any concept as to what could possibly happen. What was happening. "Survival, boy. There needs ta be some of us left ta fight, ta get back what's ours. 'Nough people survive the takeover, maybe we can beat 'em back." Fire raged in his eyes and spittle dripped from his beard.

Cody noticed a small framed picture on the interior wall. It was a faded family photo with Raz, his wife Mildred, their son Jason as a young boy, and an old black dog. Raz was wearing an Army Special Forces uniform with a chest full of medals. *Things can change so quickly*, he thought.

Raz turned toward the end of the tubular structure and pointed behind a plastic curtain. "There's the john. Small and self-contained, but good 'nough to take care of business. Got it leechin' out ta an underground field. The bunker is ten feet underground, made of reinforced steel, encased in cinder blocks and concrete with rebar. It can hold eight people for six months, a bit longer if need be."

"This is unbelievable," Nick remarked. "Must have cost a fortune."

"Yup," Raz began. "Took a chunk of my savin's, mostly from when we sold the place in town. But I figure it's worth it. Beats the alternative."

"And nobody knows about this place?" Cody asked.

"Not a livin' soul," Raz said. "Ya the first ones seen it finished."

"Wow."

They exited the bunker, shutting off the lights, and climbed out back through the shed floor. Raz made certain all locks were secured and the false wooden wall reset. With his boots he scraped dirt and straw back over the drop down door.

Raz looked at the gray sky. "One last thing and then we'll be goin'." He took the maps he had thrown in the truck and spread them out on the hood. It was getting darker so he grabbed a flashlight. "This is where we are," he pointed to a spot on the atlas near the border. The boys looked on. "This is where 'em buses are goin'. I guarantee it." He drew a line on the map with his finger up to Interstate 10, west toward Tucson, then south again to some barren location in the middle of the desert. "Ya can see there's nothin' on the map."

"How can you be certain that's it?" Nick asked, stepping back from the man.

Raz shot him a glance. " 'Cause I been there before. I know what it's used for."

"What?"

"It's a secret detention center hid off the grid. A few buildings, lots of fences. Not much else. Kinda sets back in the mountain out of sight in a dip between two ridges. Can only see it from the air. Been there once for work. Somebody, I don't know if it was the CIA or DHS, or even the NSA, had twenty three prisoners hold up there. Corraled 'em from three different airports on the east coast lookin' suspicious and carryin' plastic explosives. I was flown in by chopper ta ah…question the men. They was all Muslim, Jihad terrorists from various Middle Eastern countries, we was told. Not too friendly ta the United States, don't ya know. So me and my team did what we do, interrogated the group 'til we got what we wanted." Raz grumbled. "Took some time, but they talked."

A slight grin formed on his hairy face. "In the end they always talked."

He shifted his body. "Well, I was sent back home after we finished. No questions asked. That's how we worked. That was the only time I been there, but I seen 'nough ta know what was goin' on. All I know is ya don't have prison buildin's in the middle of a god-forsaken desert capable of holdin' lots of people just ta question a handful of suspected terrorists."

"When was that, Raz?" Cody asked.

"Five years ago. Seems longer, though. When I came back home I went ta work the next day and quit on the spot. It was all over for me. Found out I was part of the system I thought I was fightin'. Couldn't do it no more. That's when we sold the house in town and I got this place."

A slight smile escaped his lips. "It was fun at first. Me and the wife livin' off the land, enjoyin' our time together, walkin' through the woods, a big burden off our shoulders. Blackie my dog was still with us. Life was real good. Then," he stopped and nodded toward Cody, "ya know what happened next with Mildred. After that it just made sense ta stay here and live the best I could."

Cody knew what Raz meant about his wife. Mildred was best friends with Robin's mom. They saw each other everyday, not living too far from one another. They were inseparable. Cody and Robin would frequently spend time with Raz and Mildred. But when Mildred passed, they gradually went their own ways as the Gordon's kids were getting older and Robin's mom passed away.

After that, Raz would drop by Cody's house maybe twice a year to say hello. He was aging badly and mostly kept himself busy working on his 'research'. The last time Cody had actually seen Raz was about a year ago. Cody liked the guy, even admired him, despite his quirks and crazy theories and bothersome emails. *Maybe Raz wasn't all that wrong after all,* Cody thought.

Raz returned to his plan to rescue Cody's and Nick's families. "We can't drive on the highways. There could be road blocks or checkpoints. Be easy ta catch a lone pickup out in the open. Have ta take the back routes. Be a lot longer, but our chances of gettin' there are better."

On the map he traced a back way from town through the desert to the detention camp. "Still have ta run on some smaller highways, but this is the best route."

He folded the maps up and went to lock the front trailer door. Everyone got in the truck. It was pitch dark by now and the cold seemed to worsen. "Ready ta kick some ass?" Raz asked.

"Let's do this," Cody said. Nick agreed.

Raz slowly weaved his truck through the black woods. "There's one more thing I want ya ta know. Both of ya."

The boys looked at him, just a silhouette in the pickup.

"If anythin' happens ta me, move ya families here. They'll be safe. It's yours. Ya understand?"

They both nodded.

"Ya understand me?" he said again more forcefully.

"Yeah."

They knew exactly what Raz meant.

Chapter 22

The residents of Sierra Vista, Fort Huachuca, and the surrounding areas weren't the only ones dealing with the extreme weather, the devastating blackout, or the forced evacuations. Neither were the problems only restricted to Cochise County in the southeastern corner of Arizona. The massive power outage had affected all of Arizona, all of the Southwest. In fact, the event, just one day old, had affected every point in the entire continental United States.

Thousands of Operation Rescues were in place running similar scenarios throughout the nation. Thousands of Operation Clean Sweeps were simultaneously in action in every village, town, city, suburb, and large metropolitan district. Virtually no place in America was spared the sudden and unexpected aggressive measures.

Hundreds of thousands of citizens had already died from exposure, freezing to death from the vicious cold front while attempting to reach their homes or waiting for civil assistance. Millions more would meet the same fate as the bitter air flow blanketed the nation and the electromagnetic pulse destroyed the country. The people controlling the event actually projected these substantial body counts. They rationalized that the more deaths caused by the effects of the storm alone, the better. It meant fewer resources were necessary for the ongoing local operations.

'Rescuing' and 'sweeping' the smaller, less populated districts were reasonably easy when compared to the mammoth undertakings in the densely inhabited metro areas. Large cities like Los Angeles, Chicago, New York, and Boston were strategic nightmares. The smaller cities of San Francisco, San Diego, Dallas-Fort Worth, Philadelphia, Atlanta, and Washington, D.C. were no easy task, however. Tens of millions of people still had to be dealt with in one way or another. Large military facilities with their 'patriotic following' were of special concern and designated top priority targets because of their 'high stakes resistance rating.'

The Fort Huachuca area clearly fell into that category.

The general consensus by those in control was that the cold weather, combined with the lack of home heat and essential supplies, would eliminate ten to fifteen percent of the cities' populations within three or four days. Most people, especially in urban settings, were completely unprepared for such unexpected circumstances. These were encouraging numbers to the event coordinators, but more needed to be done. Much more. After a full week, the numbers should geometrically increase to upwards of thirty percent, a more optimistic figure, leaving the actual number of active survivors more manageable for the operation commanders.

The people running the show, however, did not have to brave the weather or chaos above ground. They were safe in their luxurious bunkers well protected below the earth's surface. Two of these protected zones were largely undisclosed to the general public, kept secret from the American populace under the guise of national security. Sheltered in their twenty billion tax dollar subterranean hideaways, their families and close friends and essential business associates and allied political proponents remained secure and comfortable in their assigned quarters. Between the two zones, the privileged inhabitants numbered less than three thousand, plus servants. A minuscule fraction of the entire population.

In the western portion of the country the chosen ones were transported to an underground safe zone forty-eight hours before the event began. Forewarnings were covert, transportation secretive.

Deception was the key to ensured security. The bunker, identified as Station Two, was much like a self-contained city some two hundred feet beneath a well known mountain in the Denver, Colorado area. It had been built decades earlier to protect essential personnel involved with critical national defense operations against any potential nuclear blast. That was during the Cold War period between America and Russia. Over the past several years Station Two had been extended and renovated to accommodate the influx of prospective new residents and updated with modern technological equipment.

The second, and even more secured bunker, was located in Washington, D.C., which should be of no surprise. Identified as Station One, it was located not far from the Capitol Building, several hundred feet beneath the surface of land owned by a private, unidentified corporation. It was only accessible through a concealed tunnel under the capitol, and controlled by the strictest of safekeeping.

Station One was reserved for the more important commanders and leaders of the operation. These people were considered to be experts in their fields and supporters of the new policies being implemented now and after America, or what was left of her, rose from her death bed in a new and stronger form, more condensed and centrally controlled. The expansive network of command centers, work stations, conference rooms, living quarters, and storage sections, far surpassed the smaller one in Colorado.

Both Stations were completely equipped with functioning electrical generators capable of running indefinitely, telecommunications which could connect all essential forces, and satellite links feeding information to the command posts. Everything necessary for the efficient operation of this immense attack on the country had been set in place nearly twenty years previously as the plan was being developed. All essential electrical and computerized equipment, both above and below ground, had been properly protected from any nuclear or EMP event. The private satellites orbiting the earth had remained in perfect working condition and were critical for all domestic and international communications.

Communications was the vital key in this mission, as it is in all tactical maneuvers. Being the central headquarters of the nationwide exercise, all information on every aspect of the mission was funneled into Station One. Station Two was linked directly to One. All other outlying regions' communication systems were patched into Station One via satellite through a tiered system similar to that of a military chain of command.

The country had been mapped into ten regions, starting from the eastern seaboard. The regions were then divided into a different number of sectors, depending on the population count. Those sectors were lastly split into districts, which were typically identified as secluded cities—much like the Sierra Vista-Fort Huachuca grid—large suburbs, or geographically restricted portions of large metropolitan areas.

During the entire event all districts would report a glut of information and data regarding their progress in the field. Such data would include: number of detainees 'rescued,' number of inhabitants eliminated in direct confrontation, number of missing and presumed dead, and any unresolved 'situations' occurring in their particular sectors. All sectors, then would report the same to their regions. Every region would finally report their accumulated information and numbers directly to Central Command at Station One.

On the American east coast it had been exactly one day since the blackout and destructive event was initiated. Operations Rescue and Clean Sweep would not be finalized until the next few days, but reports were coming into Station One as scheduled from all ten regions as the local operations continued their tasks. The numbers looked very good.

The first analysis meeting of the general council deep beneath the Washington, D.C. cold was in progress. Eleven men were seated around a large conference table in the private Command Center. They were a mix of military commanders, political leaders, high ranking information specialists, and of course, the top man. All dedicated friends of the cause.

"Good evening gentlemen," the executive said in a demanding voice from the head of the table. He looked confident in his expensive suit and power tie, but tired around his eyes and a bit apprehensive before hearing from his trusted associates. He forced a brief smiled and scanned a quick look at each person before him.

To his immediate left sat four-star General Joseph E. Wells, U.S. Army, Secretary of National Defense, and second in charge only to the lead man. Next, in clockwise direction, was Lt. General Howard

P. Clayton, U.S. Marine Corps, Military Operations Commander. Then in succession, there sat the Deputy of Transportation, Deputy of Energy, Deputy of Communications, and Deputy of Foreign Affairs.

On the opposite side of the table sat the Secretary of the Department of Homeland Security (DHS), the Undersecretary of the Federal Emergency Management Administration (FEMA), the Deputy of the National Security Agency (NSA), and the lead scientist in charge of the top secret weather control program known as HAARP.

Detailed files with up to date reports were on the table in front of each men.

"Let's begin," the executive said.

"Yes, Mr. President," came the unanimous response.

Chapter 23

Raz worked his truck through the black forest and over the bumpy mountain terrain. He eventually turned off the Forest Service road and headed west. Instead of retracing the route taken to his house earlier he decided to take the longer, but less likely to be watched, road along the southern side of the mountains. It was a gravel road which ended on the far side of the army fort through Canelo and Elgin, small villages tucked in the western hills. From there he traveled through vineyard country surrounding Sonoita, a sleepy little ranching town. Then he continued west on State Route 83, a two-lane highway winding toward the border city of Nogales.

When on the straight runs of pavement Raz kept a keen eye looking for vehicle headlights miles ahead. Fortunately, none were seen and he drove quickly through the cold night. A few cars were left abandoned on the road side, but there was no human activity. It was a strange scene, though after so many miles it had become commonplace. Nick groaned, holding his calf. The injured leg caused him a slight, though steady throbbing pain, like a mild toothache that wouldn't go away. He just grimaced and willed the hurt to vanish.

Cody sat quietly, thinking of his family. A lot had happened in one day. Today was Thanksgiving. It was supposed to be a relaxing, enjoyable time at home. By now he should be eating too much turkey with homemade stuffing and all the trimmings that go with the traditional dinner. He should be having a mug of hot chocolate and a big slice of pumpkin pie topped with whipped cream with Robin and his children. He should be sitting by the fireplace, warm on a cold early winter night, watching *The Wizard of Oz* again with the people he most loved in this world.

Instead he was searching for them with no idea where they might be. Were they warm? Were they safe? Had they eaten? How were Jeffrey and Jennifer handling this traumatic experience? He knew his daughter would be scared. Even the darkness in her bedroom scared her enough that she needed a night light left on and her bedroom door cracked open a bit. Jeffrey, on the other hand, might consider their trip an adventure. It seemed nothing frightened the 'Tada' man.

How was Robin holding up? He wondered. She was a strong, sensible woman, and could care for herself. But with the kids she would be cautious. She must be wondering what happened to him, Cody thought. She must be wondering if he was coming for her. After briefly seeing each other through the slightly opened door in the high school gymnasium, Cody was certain that his wife knew he was in pursuit. She had to know that somehow he would come for them. And somehow he would.

From the center of Sonoita at the only intersection in town Raz turned north and drove several miles to Continental Road. It was a side road which meandered through dense forest land, past numerous worked-out silver mines, territory now mainly used by local cattle ranchers. This route avoided Interstate Highway 10, which Raz was positive would be closed down, or at least monitored or patrolled. It was a dark and narrow road leading toward the far south side of Tucson, some forty miles away.

The long ride gave Cody time to think, time to generate a bunch of questions which popped into his head and hadn't yet been answered. He wondered out loud. "Raz, you think those Army buses are taking everyone to a camp of sorts in the desert?"

"Pretty sure."

"I was thinking," Cody continued. "Why wouldn't our families and all the others be taken to some place closer? It'll be a lot easier."

"Ya'd think," Raz snorted. "But there ain't no other closer place ta handle that many. 'Cept maybe Fort Huachuca."

"Yeah, the fort," Cody jumped, disturbing the resting Nick. "Already filled up, is my guess."

"Filled up?" Cody asked, totally confused.

Raz at first just nodded, then he answered. "Where'd ya think all 'em soldiers went ta?"

"Hadn't thought of it," Cody said. "With all that's happening I never really gave it a thought."

"I'm sure somebody has," Raz assured him. "Bet my bottom dollar that every one of 'em soldiers and their kin, 'cept for the few who mighta turned ta the other side, are held up inside."

"Why in the world would you say that? They're soldiers, they have guns, they're patriotic and all that. If what you're saying is right and there is a foreign group or radical faction responsible for this...this attack. They'd be on the streets, in the neighborhoods, helping people, fighting back." Cody caught himself. He finally realized what had been happening was actually some sort of unbelievable attack on his country.

Raz knew he had to explain, and now was as good a time as any, considering the long dreary drive ahead of them.

"First, soldiers don't carry weapons around all day. Firearms are secured and used for drillin' and trainin'. No guns, or very few, would be readily available ta the troops on post without authorization. Second. Ya're right, sonny. Most of 'em are devoted and loyal ta their country. Most of 'em would fight ta the death in the face of danger. Lots have. Patriotism is in their blood. They breathe it. They bleed it. I know. I've worked with 'em for a long, long time. I knew a lot of boys who gave up their lives for what they thought was right. They're the true believers and every one of 'em took a solemn oath ta defend this country and its citizens."

He stopped for a second. "Damn right they'd fight back. If they could."

Cody waited. "Well...?"

"There're places on the fort ready for such a situation. Lots of buildings capable of holdin' captives. NCO clubs, the officer's club, a few gyms, schools, several warehouses. They can be easily converted inta detention centers. But there is one place off the beaten path, set back toward Garden Canyon up in the back hills, away from the rest of the base. Been there a few times too, years back. It's a large facility, very secure, and fully equipped.

"My suspicion is the soldiers on base was ordered ta assemble at that facility before all hell broke loose. Of course, they'd follow orders. That's what they do. Just over five thousand troops are stationed at the fort. Maybe a third of 'em are deployed overseas at any one time. So that leaves 'bout thirty-five hundred or so on site. Be pretty easy ta keep 'em contained. It don't take too many guns ta keep unarmed people, even soldiers restricted."

"You really think so, huh?" Cody asked.

"Said so, didn't I?" Raz barked. "So that's why ya families ain't there. All the soldiers who are there are prisoners by now. They won't be helpin' nobody. We're on our own right now."

"Jesus, we're screwed," Cody commented.

"Ya got that right," Raz said. "This country is bein' taken over. Everyday a little piece of it gits stolen from us. Bits and pieces. Most people never notice what's goin' on. They're like those giant birds…what the hell ya call 'em? Oh yeah…ostriches, who stick their heads in the ground and never look up. Outa sight, outa mind attitude. They think if they can't see nothin' then nothin' can bother 'em. People don't want ta be bothered 'cause they're stuck in their own miserable little worlds. So, without much resistance, the powers that be keep takin' and takin'."

Cody nodded, partly in agreement. He was thinking as Raz rattled on.

"Do ya have any idea what's happenin' ta our nation, boy? Our country is bein' torn apart, piece by piece. We're losin' our civil rights protected under the Constitution. Freedom of speech, freedom of religion, freedom of the press, freedom of peaceable assembly. 'Ems all been taken away. Try voicin' your opinion against the government. Call your senator a liar, call the president an asshole. Try printin' up somethin' against the thievin' politicians who are pickin' us clean. Ya just try that nowadays, boy, and ya'll have the FBI or NSA up ya ass. Worse yet, the fuckin' IRS will camp at ya doorsteps 'til ya give in or git stripped ta the bone. Things will happen ta ya, boy."

Raz turned angrier. "Hell, just t'other day the feds set up restricted first amendment zones for anyone who wanted ta complain. Bet ya haven't heard of that one. Like ya can only speak ya piece in certain approved areas. What the hell's with that? Show me in the Constitution where's that's allowed."

"Well..." Cody began.

"Well, shit! You're a history teacher, ain't ya? Don't ya know what in the hell is happenin'? The United States Constitution, the supreme law of our land, is bein' ignored. Hell, if anythin', it's bein' completely disregarded, circumvented for evil purposes. We're all bein' turned back inta subjects of the king and the royals. Serfs ta the elite. Slaves ta the rich. And ya know why? 'Cause nobody done shit ta stop it."

Cody knew the Constitution inside and out. It was his business to know. But over the years, as textbooks changed and written history was altered and pressure came down from higher up about procedures and policies and lesson plans and agendas, funding for the 'right types' of classes and curriculum became supreme. State and private education boards bowed to the feds in order to get their share of funding. Go against the system and they got nothing. That was understood. Arm twisting techniques and compromises allowed the nation's education system to slip into the ranks of third world countries. The two almighty evils of power and money had trumped learning. Americans were getting dumber and dumber. The kids were being turned into fuckin' retards and social misfits.

Raz had lots more to say.

"Then there's the big push ta confiscate our guns. They want us defenseless. Don't ya see all the big cities and spineless states doin' whatever they can ta git the guns out of the hands of law abidin' American citizens? Cash for guns. Food for guns. Turn in your armed neighbors. It's the patriotic thing ta do, they try ta convince ya. Every time there's a shootin' the libs want ta make ownin' guns illegal. For our own protection, don't ya know. But of course they can keep theirs for their own protection. And the criminals won't ever stop havin' guns.

"Hell, the problem isn't too many guns in our citizens' hands. It's not enough guns," Raz went on. "Did ya know it has even been suggested that every gun owner should wear a bracelet of some sort ta control the use of his gun? I can just see the government gittin' their filthy hands on that information. All I can say for sure is if they want ta take my guns away from me, they're gonna' have ta pry them from my dead hands. I will never give up my guns because I love my country, and I need ta stand ready ta protect it. Ya know the Constitution states that it's the citizen's right and duty to fight a spoiled government? Well hell, of course ya know that."

Raz continued driving along the deserted road periodically glancing in the rearview mirror for lights. Cody remained quiet. He was taking in Raz's rantings.

"Yup. Then there're the hundreds of executive orders. Did ya know that if the President don't agree with the Congress or the Congress won't side with the President, the Prez can simply bypass the lawmakers and sign in his own laws? He just said t'other day that he has a pen and will do whatever the hell he wants ta do. Of course ya know all that too. You're a god-damn history professor."

"Yes, I know that," Cody said, getting madder by the minute at Raz's accusations that he didn't know his history, that he wasn't aware of recent political irregularities. But, in truth, he also knew that much of what Raz was saying made sense.

Raz squinted into the darkness. "Secret treaties, back-door alliances, hidden agendas, illegal wiretaps, unlawful NSA snooping, criminal IRS shenanigans, sanctioned killin's, illicit gun runnin', clandestine death squads, martial law, the list goes on and on."

Maybe what Raz was saying really was true, Cody thought. The old man knew things. He seemed to know what was happening and what might be coming. He looked over at his long time friend, not certain what to believe. In some ways Raz reminded Cody of his dead friend Jonathan who used to talk about some of the same things.

"I know ya think I'm one of 'em conspiracy type nuts. A little crazy talkin' 'bout all this shit that can't be real. Think what ya like, sonny. It's all fact and I got proof. They want ta git rid of us 'useless eaters.' That's how they see the majority of the earth's population. Worthless consumers at worse, indentured slaves at best. Submission and ultimate annihilation is their long term plan. Problem is, it ain't long term no more. It's right now. Everywhere ya turn there's interference and intimidation, threats and conditionin', mistrust and lies. High rankin' people go missin', outspoken people have 'accidents,' free thinkers get incarcerated."

Nick was rocking back and forth in the seat between the two men, apparently asleep. "How much farther?" Cody asked.

Raz pulled at his beard. "Reckon about two more hours, once we hit Route 19. The road will be a lot slower and rougher the nearer we git. Might be a bit uncomfortable for ya friend."

"He'll be okay," Cody added.

"He's kinda a wimpy fella, ain't he?" Raz said, referring to Nick.

"Yeah, well, he's a computer nerd," Cody answered.

"He's awake," Nick said, overhearing the conversation. "Just been resting and listening to you guys. Nice talk about your sleeping friend."

Within ten minutes the Chevy truck merged onto Highway 19 heading south. Mexico was a half hour away, but Raz knew where to turn off before the border. The six-lane freeway was smooth and fast. Cars had been shoved to the shoulders. There were no lights on the road, no moving traffic. They were about fifteen miles from the abandoned dirt road leading to the camp Raz was sure the Army buses were headed.

Inside the cab nothing was said for the longest time. Raz was staring over the steering wheel, avoiding broken glass and pieces of car parts. He watched the highway marker signs written in kilometers flash by. It pissed him off seeing U.S. roads leading to Mexico measured in metrics. "God damn it," he said to no one in particular.

Nick was resting his eyes again trying to sleep, but with the constant swerving of the truck and Raz's continuous bitching, it was impossible. Cody was calculating all this new information inside his rational mind in an attempt to figure out what was real and what wasn't. He gazed out the side window into the one-dimensional darkness.

Just as they peaked over a hill in the road Raz looked in his rearview mirror. His eyes went suddenly wide. "Oh shit, boys!"

Chapter 24

"What? What is it?" Nick said, sitting up in the seat.

"We got company, boys," Raz barked, his eyes scanning the road ahead, flicking back and forth to the image in the rearview mirror. A bright set of headlights kept popping over the hilly roadway bouncing off the mirror from about a mile behind them.

Both Nick and Cody turned around to see what Raz saw. A fast moving vehicle with glaring lights was racing toward them. The lights were set far apart, like those on a wide vehicle. Then a pair of fog lights mounted high above the vehicle flashed on, flooding the road in front of it in dazzling daylight.

"What do you think?" Cody asked.

"Think we got us some trouble," Raz said. "That ain't no civilian vehicle comin' that big and that fast. Sure as hell can't out run it in this." The lights were getting brighter and brighter, sporadically reflecting off the mirror, causing Raz to squint and move his eyes away. The next exit off the highway was six kilometers south, almost four miles away. No way in hell could they reach the turn-off before the vehicle chasing them caught up.

"Who do you think it is?" Cody wondered aloud. "Maybe they can help us."

"Don't know, sonny." Raz looked over at the young men. "Could be cops, highway patrol. Soldiers, maybe. Security of some sort. Whoever they are, my guess is they ain't here ta help us."

Now the fierce lights were about a half mile from the Chevy and moving ever faster. Cody and Nick had no idea what to do. They just looked at Raz, hoping he had a plan, an escape route.

And he did.

"Gonna have ta pull on over, boys. Figure out what these guys want." Raz shifted into a lower gear, slowed his truck down, and coasted onto the graveled shoulder of the road.

"But Raz," Cody protested.

"But nothin'. We need ta handle this head on. Deal with the situation as it progresses." Raz stopped his truck, leaving the engine running and the lights on.

The chase vehicle flashed its burning high beams several times and pulled up twenty paces behind the pickup. The glaring sets of lights blinded the three men in the Chevy. All they could see through the back window were blistering lights blanketing them and the inside of their truck. Everyone sat and waited.

Whoever was in the heavy vehicle took their sweet time exiting. Raz heard two solid doors slam shut, then, through his side mirror he saw a figure dressed in serious gear crunch his way on the gravel. Still blinded by the lights, Raz assumed the other guy was holding back near the rear of the pickup. "Keep calm, boys. I'll do the talkin', but stay alert."

Nick and Cody nodded their heads in rapid succession. They were scared to death and had no alternative but to follow Raz's lead.

"Cody," Raz said with a severe glare.

Cody stared back at him like a toddler about to be punished.

"Keep ya hands in ya pockets. Ya hear me?"

"Yes, sir."

A huge shadow approached Raz's driver's side window, then there was a loud rap on the glass, strong enough to almost crack it. Raz saw the figure through the fogged pane. It appeared to be a soldier dressed in a black uniform and black helmet. There were no noticeable insignias on the uniform. The man held what looked like an AK-47 rifle aimed at the glass. He made a hand motion for Raz to open the window.

Raz held up his hands to assure the man he was no threat. The boys copied him. Raz then slowly rolled down his window and a blast of frigid air filled the cab. The cold made them more alert, like a sharp slap in the face. "What can I do for ya?" Raz asked. He watched every move made by the soldier.

"Where you going, gramps?" the man asked in a casual, almost friendly manner, with a hint of an accent.

Raz didn't trust the guy one bit. He didn't trust anyone pointing an assault rifle at him. "That a ways," he said, pointing straight down the road. He wanted to size the soldier up, see what he was after, get a feel for his reaction. Then, after he learned a few things, maybe Raz could do something.

"To Mexico?" the soldier asked, realizing that some Americans would try to escape across the border. But nobody was going to get pass him.

Raz noticed the man had dark skin and wore a thick, black mustache. Probably Mexican, he reasoned. Raz had to determine if the soldier was a good Mexican or a bad Mexican. It gave him an idea. "Nah, don't much like Mexico. Filthy country run by a bunch of inbred drug dealers. Ain't too safe down there nowadays."

Apparently he pushed the right button. The soldier shouted, "Get the fuck out of the truck. Now!" His angry voice produced a more pronounced accent.

It was exactly what Raz expected. He couldn't do anything while stuck in the truck cab. He opened the driver's door as the soldier backed off, his weapon aimed at Raz's head.

"Damn cold out here, Jose," Raz said, adding to the fire.

The soldier shoved the old man against his truck and stuck the icy cold rifle muzzle deep into Raz's neck. Nick and Cody sat still in the cab, frozen in place wondering what to do. *Why in the hell was Raz trying to piss off this guy?* They both thought.

"One last time before I shoot you," the soldier yelled. He hated redneck gringos, especially ones with an attitude. "Where were you going?"

Raz knew it was time to regain control. "We was takin' our friend here ta the hospital. He's got a hurt leg."

"The hospital's closed," the soldier said with a devious grin. "They're all closed."

The second soldier at the back of the pickup banged the side of the truck and yelled inside. "You two, get the fuck out of there." Nick and Cody jumped in their seats, then they slipped out of the cab through the passenger door.

"Over here," the soldier ordered, directing them to stand next to the tailgate. The boys obediently moved.

Raz was bent over the bed of his truck when the first soldier asked him, "What's under the tarp?"

Raz looked at the boys opposite him. In the bright lights their eyes showed they were scared stiff, as if they were about to be shot on the spot. Raz knew that could happen at any moment if he didn't do something.

"It's my stuff," he said in a defiant tone. String the bastard along as far as he could go. Bit by bit. Look for an opening. Be ready. Be two steps ahead of your adversary. Thoughts were rapidly racing through Raz's mind. He knew how to handle situations like this.

"What's your name?" the soldier asked. He was coming to the end of his rope, getting impatient, irritated with this backwoods hillbilly.

Raz cracked a smile and answered sarcastically, "Heyward." He sneaked a peek at Cody letting him know to be ready.

"Heywood?" the soldier said. "Heywood what?"

"Heywood Jablowme. And stop askin' so many fuckin' questions," Raz chuckled, ready to make his move.

Cody and Nick immediately cringed.

Rage exploded over the soldier's face at Raz's remarks. "I've taken enough shit from you, you fucking old geezer." The soldier backed off half a step, finger on the trigger, about to blow Raz's head off.

"No! No!" Nick screamed. He then did something very stupid. He jumped from the rear of the truck, leaping toward the soldier in an attempt to protect the old man.

But it was too late.

Bam! A gun blast tore through the deadly night silence.

Bam! Another shot went off.

Bam! Then a third.

Before Nick could grab the soldier, Cody had pulled the pistol out of his jacket pocket and promptly shot the soldier in the head from across the truck. Instant death hit the man as the soldier went down firing a wild shot missing Cody by inches.

The second soldier was slower to react and he was taken down by Raz with his old pistol drawn like a seasoned gunslinger. A big hole blew through the soldier's unprotected chest as he fell backwards, bouncing off the hood of his Humvee and onto the raw ground.

The rapid explosions had taken less than a second. The blasts left clouds of smoke in the air, the smell of burnt powder in the cold, and echoes of recoiling thunder receding into the night. Raz and Cody looked at one another, as if to congratulate each other for their quick reaction. The two soldiers lay dead on the frozen shoulder.

But Nick wasn't standing. He was on the ground behind the pickup truck. The soldier's errant shot had pierced Nick's right side, tearing a gaping hole through and through.

"Nick!" Cody yelled. He ran to his friend and knelt next to him. Blood was gushing from the wound, soaking his shirt and jacket and forming a thick muddy red puddle beneath Nick's body.

Cody held his buddy's head trying to comfort him, helplessly attempting to keep his friend alive. "Nick," he whispered, working to stay calm. But it was impossible to remain composed. "I got you, Nick. I got you."

The old man moved toward Cody. Nick looked real bad.

"Raz!" Cody yelled, looking for help.

Nick tried to say something. "Co…Cody…."

"Yeah, buddy. I'm here."

"I…I only wanted…to see my wife…and kids," Nick struggled.

His eyes looked up at Cody, but they were blank. A steady stream of dark red blood seeped from his side. A trickle of blood spilled from Nick's mouth. Gasping short breaths he could barely breathe, his heart ripped apart by the bullet. "Sa…save my fam…." They were Nick's last words.

Cody held his friend, crying as if he had just lost a child. "I will, Nick," he answered. "I promise." He rocked back and forth with Nick in his arms, as if that would bring his friend back. But all the crying and all the rocking in the world would do Nick no good.

Looking on, Raz grunted. "He's gone, Cody."

"No!"

"Let him be, son."

"But why? Why did this have to happen?" Cody howled.

Raz went to Cody and patted him on the back. There were no good answers. Bad things happen to good people. " 'Cause there's always bad people around us," Raz answered.

Cody shook his head. It wasn't a good enough reason.

"He just saved us," Raz said. "If it weren't for Nick, we'd both be dead."

"What should we do?" Cody asked.

"We'll have ta leave him here, son."

Cody shook his head. "But it's not right."

"I know it ain't right," Raz said. "He didn't deserve this." Raz turned away so Cody wouldn't see the emotion in his face. He had seen too many good men die like this.

"Damn, damn, damn!"

"We can say a few words," Raz added.

"Yeah."

"Dear Lord," Raz began to pray. "Please take this young man, Nick…ah." He stopped and had to ask Cody, "What was Nick's last name?"

Cody thought for a second. "I…I don't know," he answered shamefully.

Raz began again. "Please take this young man, Nick, ta ya glorious heaven. He was a good man tryin' ta do good things. May his soul rest in peace. Amen."

"Amen."

Cody gently placed Nick's head on the ground. He had lost a good friend, a brother. He rose to his feet and rubbed the tears from his eyes. The pistol still in his hand he walked over to the dead soldier he had killed, the one who was going to kill Raz, the one who had murdered Nick.

Bam! Bam! Bam! Bam! Bam!

Without thinking Cody's primal rage had taken over his rational body. Primitive vengeful wrath had emptied the remaining bullets from his pistol into the son-of-a-bitch who had killed his friend and changed his life forever. With each successful blast of the gun Cody had lost his innocence, his naïveté, his trustworthiness, hiscontentment, his indifference to what has been going on in the world.

Cody had become a changed man. He was now a part of the high stakes game of life and death.

Raz watched the young man transform before his eyes in the time it took to fire five shots. Raz knew the rage and guilt and agony Cody was going through. At some point in his life each real man would experience it.

"Ya done killin' bad guys?"

"What?" Cody said, his warm breath escaping in short, fast vapor clouds.

"I said, are ya done killin' bad guys?"

Cody looked at the bloody mess beneath him and at the soldier Raz had shot. Then he turned toward Nick's body. His friend was gone, like so many others today. "I've just begun," he said in a determined voice.

Chapter 25

"We should be goin' now. It's dangerous out here and it's gettin' late," Raz recommended.

Cody looked around at the death they had caused. The scene was surreal, like a late night action movie where the good guys had just won a small battle against evil. But the losses had far outweighed the victory, and the war was only beginning. "Let's take the Hummer," he suggested.

"That's a damn good idea, Cody. These guys won't be needin' it no more," Raz growled. "We might be able ta outrun other patrols if we run inta 'em and the truck will be useful travelin' through the desert."

"Sounds good," Cody agreed. "Let's transfer our load into the back."

The men took five minutes unloading the Chevy. They lugged the cans of gas and the jugs of water to the back of the carrier's cargo bed and secured them. The sleeping bags, boxes of food, duffel bags, and the rest of the supplies were thrown into the military vehicle's back seat. Raz shut his pickup down, turned off its lights, and removed the keys which he pocketed. He then grabbed his papers and maps.

Raz stopped for a second, then retrieved a gas can from the Humvee. He opened it and poured a few gallons of fuel on his beloved Chevy pickup, dousing the inside seats, the engine hood, and the empty bed.

"No need leavin' the truck for someone else." He took out his pistol ready to shoot the old piece of shit truck and ignite the fire. Then he thought it better to drive a safer distance before blowing it up. He bent over the dead soldiers and retrieved their rifles and side arms, and threw them in the Hummer. "Can always use the extra power," he smirked.

The two looked at Nick, and with their eyes saluted their goodbyes. "I'll save your family," Cody whispered his promise.

"All secure, Cody. Let's go."

Cody went to the driver's side of the Humvee. Raz gave him a strange gaze. "What ya think ya doin' boy?"

"I'm driving this beast," Cody answered with commitment.

Raz shook his head. "No ya ain't. Not yet. I know where we're goin'. Ya'll git ya chance later."

Cody gave in to the old man without complaining and moved to the passenger side. Perhaps Raz was right. He hadn't been wrong yet, Cody thought.

The engine was still running. Raz climbed into the bulky vehicle and settled into the driver's bucket seat. The interior was warm from the humming heater. He found the light switches and flicked off the overhead beams. Maintaining a low profile was still his best bet. He was familiar with the vehicle, but never had one of his own.

"I think I'm in love," Raz chimed as he got comfortable.

"One of the best high mobility multi-purpose vehicles ever built," he said, slamming the steering wheel. "Camouflaged and low profile ta hinder detection, sixteen inch ground clearance for rugged territory, wide wheel base for low center of gravity stability runnin' on thirty-seven inch run-flat tires, turbo-charged V-8 diesel engine with 190 horsepower, armor-fitted on laterals and below, capable of a three ton payload, high-maneuverability and the ability ta climb sixty degree slopes. Can be mounted with a variety of interchangeable armaments, includin' the M134 Mini-gun capable of firin' up ta 6000 rounds per minute, a grenade launcher, light and heavy machine guns with a remotely operated weapons station controlled from inside the vehicle."

Raz finally caught his breath and let loose with a grand smile.

"Sounds as if you really like this thing," Cody remarked. He couldn't help but smile too.

"Oh yeah. I know everythin' 'bout 'em. Never owned one, not 'til now," Raz said.

"Guess what, Raz," Cody said. "You don't own this one either."

"That's what ya think. Like ta see someone try ta take it from me."

"I see your point," Cody agreed.

"Only one thing this beauty don't have," Raz conceded.

"And what's that?"

"There ain't no AM radio."

Cody just shrugged his shoulders.

"And no cup holder," Raz ended.

He began turning onto the roadway ready to light up the Chevy, when Cody suddenly yelled. "Wait!"

"Now what?"

Cody opened the door and dashed toward the pickup. He yanked the passenger door open and leaned inside. In less than thirty seconds he returned to the Hummer, his hands filled. "I almost forgot," he grinned and dropped the socks full of coins on the floorboard near his feet. He slipped them safely under the seat.

Raz smirked. "Good thinkin', boy. Can we go now?"

"Yes."

He pulled onto the road, passed his old Chevy and the human carnage. From twenty yards away he stopped, raised his pistol, and shot at the pickup. The bullet hit solid metal creating a spark. In seconds the truck was ablaze. The rusted hood blew off from the sudden blast, lighting up the roadway. Watching the raging blaze for several seconds, Raz then continued south. "I'm gonna miss that wrinkled old girl."

Cody stayed silent for a minute. "I'm gonna miss Nick." He scratched the stubble of his day-old beard and rubbed his cold ears. Raz knew something was bothering him.

"Ya done good back there, Cody," Raz said in a fatherly tone.

"Yeah, I know."

"Ya saved us from 'em soldiers. If ya hadn't took the shot we'd both be lyin' there with Nick."

"Then how come I feel sick inside?" Cody asked.

"Ya just lost a good friend, that's how come."

"It's not only that," Cody admitted.

Raz looked at the young man. He knew exactly what was bugging Cody. "It ain't fun killin' a man, is it?"

"No, it ain't…ah…isn't."

"It sticks in ya gut, huh?" Raz said.

"You ever kill a man, Raz? I mean before tonight."

Raz looked into the darkness. "Only when they had ta be killed."

"Yeah." Cody thought about that for a moment. "Do you ever get used to it?" Cody had to ask.

"Nah. Ya never git used ta it no matter how many times ya do it."

They drove down the highway in the Humvee. It was a strong, solid ride with its wide tires hugging the pavement as Raz swerved and weaved around abandoned cars. On the road side he noticed dead bodies frozen to the ground. People who couldn't get to where they were going, succumbing to the brutal elements, helpless in the face of extraordinary circumstances. He kept driving.

"Cody, look on this map," Raz said, handing the man a folded atlas of Arizona. "See if ya can find the turn off up ahead. Should be a few miles farther up, off one of the next exits."

Cody flipped on a flashlight and searched the faded map for their location. "Here," he pointed. "Is this it?" he asked. "Off exit fifty-eight, there's a small dotted line that runs northwest into the desert."

"That's it, boy. A few more minutes and we'll be safe."

Less than thirty seconds passed on the quiet stretch ahead of them when Raz saw something else he hadn't anticipated. "Son-of-a-bitch!"

A line of cars were blocking the road not two kilometers away. There were at least three sedans angled across the highway, though there was no traffic to stop. Except for the stolen Humvee. Their red and blue emergency lights swirled in the pitch blackness, casting eerie kaleidoscopic laser-like shadows over the drab desert landscape.

Raz slowed down his armored rig. The flashing lights reflected off the vehicle barricade. Raz squinted hard and made out the green striped cars. "Looks like Border Patrol."

"Why would the Border Patrol be here? Wouldn't you think they'd be at the port of entry in Nogales? Especially with all that's going on," Cody said.

Raz grunted. "Don't be stupid. There ain't nobody at the border. It's wide open by now. The border agents have either been pulled away by DHS for other purposes or simply melted into the woodwork. Some people are tryin' ta go south thinkin' it might be safe down there. But it ain't. My guess is more people are tryin' ta come north where the pickin's are ripe."

"What do you mean by that?" Cody asked.

"Haven't ya learned by now, sonny, that at the point when civilization is no longer controlled by legitimate law enforcement, anarchy raises its ugly, sinister head. Even law abidin' folk turn to their sinister ways. But the criminal elements, those people who live a life of crime and feed off the weak and unprotected, they're the first ones ta hit the streets. Ya saw the group at that grocery store. That's exactly what we're about ta run inta up yonder," Raz explained.

"Cockroaches! That's what I call 'em. No good stinkin' cockroaches. They come out in the dark searchin' for scattered crumbs. They target anyone who has what they want, anythin' that looks like easy pickin's. But these kind of cockroaches work together, in gangs, numbers that can put the fear of God inta anyone who has the unfortunate bad luck of bein' in their path." Raz stared straight.

Cody just looked at the colored streams of lights ahead bouncing off the low hanging night clouds.

"But these roaches are the worst," Raz warned.

"How so?"

"These low-life cockroaches are armed to the teeth with nobody ta stop 'em," Raz ended.

As they inched closer to the road block Raz and Cody could make out a dozen or so men with rifles watching them, their weapons at the ready. "Have ta git ta that side road," Raz mentioned. "I ain't turnin' back for nothin'. We don't have the time."

Cody watched his old friend thinking. Another plan was in the making. He could almost hear the wheels in Raz's brain moving, the genius mechanism working its magic. "What should we do?"

Raz chuckled. "Let's see what they want. They'll think we're on their side in this green tank. Might let their guard down long enough."

"Long enough for what?"

"Long enough ta take 'em out," Raz explained.

Cody pulled the gun from his jacket, got a box of bullets from his other pocket and began reloading his weapon. After dropping two cartridges on the floor he finally settled down and put the loaded gun back in his pocket. It was likely, he figured, that he'd be using it again, real soon.

"Here," Raz said. "Load mine too." He handed Cody his pistol and some ammo which Cody loaded faster this time and returned the gun to Raz. Then Cody reached into the back seat, grabbed one of the dead soldiers' automatic assault rifles, and placed it on his lap.

Just in case.

Raz slowed down to about twenty-five miles per hour. He wanted to scope out the ambush situation ahead and be prepared once he came up to them. "There's lots more of 'em than there are of us this time," he advised Cody. "Ain't gonna' be no turkey shoot like before."

That was a turkey shoot? Cody thought. "Are the sides of this Humvee well armored?" he asked.

"Against small arms," Raz nodded. "The glass ain't bullet proof though, so be careful."

Cody had a crazy thought. He was starting to think like the old man. "What if you pull up to them in the middle, like we're friendlies? We'd have a good shot at most of them from both sides, maybe catch them by surprise."

Raz turned to Cody, a shocked grin on his face. "Ya got some balls, boy. Just go up ta 'em like we want ta shoot the shit and have a beer, then mow 'em down. The whole bunch of 'em?"

"Well, I was just thinking. At first they won't know what to think. Then, bam! Blast our way through."

"Ya got the fever, don't ya boy?"

"No," Cody answered, trying to control his rage and fear. "I just want my family."

"In that case," Raz went on. "Let's go say hello."

Chapter 26

Bill Bennett sat on the edge of his bus seat, third row back from the passenger door. His wife of forty-two years sat next to him holding their four year old grandson who had the misfortune of staying over at grandma's house for the Thanksgiving holiday. The boy was wrapped in his grandmother's arms, having cried himself to sleep during the ordeal. The heat from the front of the bus had kept them relatively warm, but food and water were priorities on their mind. They hadn't had anything to eat or drink since they were abducted from their home more than eight hours earlier.

The entire bus reeked of stale urine. Women and children who were awake whimpered and moaned. Everyone was trying to fight off the cold, thirst, and hunger. Sniffling and bouts of coughing came from most every section of the shadowy Army bus. No one spoke above a whisper as the loaded transport raced westward along I-10 between Benson and Tucson.

Bill looked forward to the driver and guard next to him. If they, the passengers, were lucky, they might have one final chance to break toward the soldiers. What was waiting for them was a complete unknown, but for Bill and the others it would not get better. Maybe they were being taken to a detention site of sorts. Maybe a prison camp. Whoever was in charge wouldn't go through all this trouble to gather and then transport them if they didn't have an ulterior motive. And it couldn't possibly be good.

There was no way in hell Bill was going to be imprisoned. Not again. Images of his prisoner of war days crept into his mind from long locked up memories. Fifteen months as a POW in Vietnam, right after the devastating '68 Tet Offensive, flashed before him. It was sheer hell for him and ten other American soldiers and airmen being shuffled through the jungle, forced to labor in the fields, living on sustenance barely enough to keep them alive. By the time they were rescued there were only two of them left. His buddies had died from either disease, starvation, exhaustion, or a bullet in the back of their brain. The lasting part about the nightmare was that Bill had lost his right arm during the firefight which had actually saved them. Still, even back then, he would have rather been a crippled man than suffer what he had been forced to live through.

He would do anything in his power to stop these bastards and to save his wife and grandson. *Who the fuck were these assholes?* He wondered. They would have to stop the bus sometime, maybe take their eyes off their human cargo long enough to rush them. Bill searched the bus for his fellow allies. Again, with the eyes Bill spoke to three men across the aisle, another sitting on the floor of the bus, and Robin mid-way back.

Robin saw Bill's fixed gaze and silently acknowledged his plan with a slight nod. She held onto little Jennifer and made sure Jeffrey had his coat buttoned up. She leaned over and whispered something in her son's ear. Jeffrey looked at his mother with a confused stare. "Just do as I say, okay. I'll let you know when," she said.

Jeffrey smiled like the superhero he was. He could do this.

The five or six people who were ready to fight stayed alert, waiting for the right moment. The longer they rode in the bus the less time they had. As luck would have it, within twenty minutes the brake lights of the forward buses lit up. The caravan was either coming to a stop or to a slow turn. Robin's bus stopped. This was the 'do or die' moment. Suddenly the brake lights on the visible buses out front went out and the green transports moved forward.

The driver of Robin's bus grinded the gears and released the clutch too fast. The bus chugged and stalled in the middle of the road, as the rest of the convoy continued into the darkness. The driver cursed in an undecipherable language. The armed guard standing next to him laughed and slapped the driver on his head. It sounded like he said, "Idiot," only in a rough, foreign accent.

Being closest to the front, Bill Bennett did a quick head jerk. The others nodded back. It was time. Robin said to her son, "Now!"

Jeffrey began screaming like a wild banshee. It sounded as if a jungle animal had been wounded, injured by a hunter's true aim. He kept up the ungodly noise, drawing everyone's surprised attention. Including the soldiers'. Simultaneously, Bill and his squad of men rose from their seats and raced toward the standing guard, stunned by the screeching sounds and the shadowy force moving upon him.

With Bill in front, the hulk of humanity squeezed through the narrow aisle shouting and growling. Screams of death were in their voices. Hatred and revenge drove the unarmed men forward into the path of fury. They were all in. Some might die, but not all of them. Robin left her children and followed the men. Such a sweeping, determined force could surely overtake just two soldiers.

The guard yelled something in Russian at the top of his lungs, his eyes grew large with a mix of fear and anger. Before the guard could bring his rifle in line, Bill and the man beside him grabbed the man and kneed him in the stomach. The soldier fell forward, but managed to steady his balance. His Kevlar vest had absorbed the deadly kick. He used his helmeted head to butt the men back, but they were too strong, too many, and too close to push back.

The driver screamed holy hell as the attack made headway. He attempted to draw his sidearm to stop the madness, but was unexpectedly stopped. Just inches away, the woman sitting directly behind him swiftly removed her woolen scarf from her neck, threw it over the driver's unprotected head, and twisted it into a knot as tightly as she could.

A man behind her reached over the bench seat and took the scarf ends from the lady. He yanked it full force, putting every pound of his huge frame into the effort. He could hear the driver gurgling, sucking for air, almost pleading for his life with his bulging eyes. But this was no time for mercy. The man coiled the scarf so firmly he could feel the driver's throat collapse. With one final powerful twist the driver's neck was snapped and he slumped dead in his seat.

The standing guard dropped his assault weapon and inched his free hand toward his holster. He was a strong, muscular trooper, a dedicated and seasoned soldier. These petty American prisoners were not going to take him down. Robin and other passengers standing in the seats, pushed at the attacking crowd, trying to overwhelm the soldier through sheer weight and body mass.

The soldier finally caught the handle of his pistol, his fingers searching for the trigger. Several men were on top of him by now, kicking and punching anywhere they could. The burden of bodies was suffocating the soldier.

Everyone in the bus was yelling and screaming.

"Kill the bastard!"

"Break his fucking neck!"

"Kill the god-damn Russian!"

"You can do it!"

But with all the energy and spirit of the saving forces up against just one man, they couldn't do it. The soldier triggered his weapon and started shooting. Muffled shots filled the bus as they ripped through bellies, chests, and heads. Hushed groans and agonizing cries shrieked out from the pile of men. More shots blasted away as the soldier slowly climbed out from under the heap of dead and injured civilians, like a super hulk emerging from the depths of hell.

Some of the passengers moved back to safety. Others stayed tall and fought the mangled soldier. But feet and fists were no match for hot lead, and the number of attackers quickly dwindled. Scarred and hurt, the soldier yelled at his attackers, threatening them with words they didn't understand. And with his gun. He shot wildly into the retreating crowd. Every one of them could die for all he cared. Blood splattered bodies toppled from the pile and into the crowded aisle. Others went limp on top of their fellow saviors. Mayhem ruled the moment.

Robin fell backwards over a heaving body and crawled back to her children. Jennifer just sat there in a trance, a young child's way of handling such unbelievable horror and carnage. Jeffrey had stopped yelling and was crying for his mother, but through all the noise he could not be heard. Nick's wife had stayed put with her daughters during the battle, too afraid to move. They remained unharmed physically, but undoubtedly psychologically scarred for life.

The soldier got to his knees, then finally stood up. He had welts on his bare head, gashes on his face, bruises on his legs and arms. He holstered his pistol, picked up his AK-47 with little resistance this time, and screamed a death cry. He then let loose a wide surge of automatic fire through the entire bus, like a flame thrower drenching his targets with molten fire. The sounds of dying passengers, old and young, filled the transport. Injured fell in their seats and onto their neighbors. Death came mercifully quick for some, unbearably slow for others.

After the soldier had emptied his thirty-round clip, he dropped his rifle. He then pulled an extra magazine from his belt clip and slammed it into his pistol. He stood there in front of the horrified group of housewives and retirees, faces frightened beyond imagination. His eyes warned each and every soul remaining to not fuck with the demon. Those still alive hid behind their seats, foolishly thinking thin seat fabric would save them from high-powered 9mm slugs.

Hysterical screaming and crying filled the bus. Parents were praying and children were weeping. The injured howled with unbearable pain, crying for help which would never come. Windows were shot out on both sides of the bus letting in the deep freeze. Bullets had peppered holes in the roof in an arched formation. The front third seats were torn to shreds from the firestorm.

People were dead or dying in the forward half of the bus. Bill Bennett was one of the first to meet his maker. His wife and grandson, unable to move, were shot and killed as well. Most of the other men who forced themselves on the soldier lay quiet in their pools of blood spilling on the floor and nearby seats. Some who had turned to run toward the rear of the bus had been shot in the back. The brave scarf woman was ripped in half by the assault fire power, as was the man who helped her strangle the bus driver.

The death toll was at least eleven people. The number of wounded was higher. Finally in control, the armed soldier waved his weapon toward the cowering crowd, but ceased firing. They wouldn't dare come at him once again. A wicked grin forced an evil laugh from his beat up body. "You die," he said in fractured English. "You all die."

The first three buses were by now approximately a quarter mile ahead of this battleground. Their back brake lights lit up, indicating they were stopping again. Within seconds the front escort vehicle had swung around and was racing toward the shot-up fourth bus. It stopped against the bumper of the green transport and two soldiers jumped out with their rifles raised to kill. They kicked in the side door of the bus and one of them yelled in English, "We saw you stop. What the fuck is going on here?"

Climbing aboard the steps they looked at the gruesome sight inside. "What the fuck?"

The Russian guard, his face still red with rage and dripping with blood from the pounding he had endured, turned his hand gun toward the American soldier, prepared to shoot rather than try to explain.

"Put that fucking gun down now, asshole!" the American ordered.

It took several seconds before the Russian lowered his weapon. He then stepped off the bus pushing the American soldier to the side. The American peered into the dark bus. "Holy shit! Looks like a fucking war zone."

The guard pulled the Humvee driver away from the bus and explained in his language what had happened. "They jump me. Fuckin' people try to kill me,' he said in between his agitated Russian.

The American stepped off and screamed orders to the two standing Russians. "Get rid of these bodies. Now! And get back in the convoy. You got one minute."

It took more than one minute to drag the corpses and wounded off the bus and throw them on the roadside. Some of the bodies were still moving and groaning. A few asked for help. But they were all left to die in the freeze. Twenty three bodies were dumped off the bus as the surviving passengers looked on in shock. *Murdering animals,* most of the civilians thought to themselves, but not one dared to say it out loud.

The American soldier pointed at the Russian Humvee driver. "You! You drive the damn bus. And you, you sorry piece of shit," he glared at the soldier who had inflicted the damage. "You watch the passengers. If there's any more shooting I'll come back and personally put a bullet in your fat, stupid head. You understand?"

The guard tried to compose himself. He nodded his understanding. This was another American he'd like to take out if he ever got the chance.

The American returned to his Humvee, shaking his head at the Russian's fuck up. The guy did take out more than twenty troublemakers, which was pretty damn good, he thought. He then got in the vehicle and drove back to the waiting buses.

The Russians looked at one another, as if to say, "Don't fuck up again." The driver threw the bus in gear while the battle scarred soldier sat in the empty, blood soaked front bench seat, glaring back at his living cargo. They wouldn't dare try it again.

Robin's hope of escaping the bus, or hijacking it, were over. Her, her children, and everyone else on this bus to hell were destined to wherever they were being taken. Her only hope of being found was her husband Cody.

But now, that seemed a farfetched possibility, as well.

Chapter 27

T he President sat in his luxuriously padded chair at the head of the highly polished wood conference table hundreds of feet below the frozen and deserted streets of Washington, D.C. He looked at his newly appointed cabinet of commanders, deputies, and department secretaries waiting for their commander-in-chief to commence the briefing.

Inside he was smiling at the immediate success of the operation. Under the all encompassing blanket of national crisis, this time a legitimate call, swift and widespread martial law had been established by his authority an hour prior to the electromagnetic event being set off. With the swift brush of a pen he had signed over to himself absolute control of the entire nation.

All systems were a 'go' before the deadly pulse had swept the nation. It was unimaginable how such a small explosive device could devastate such a huge geographic area in a matter of milli-seconds. This aggressive move was going to be much easier than he had figured. The President would soon personally thank the Chinese Chairman for his fine work, though the President's degree of appreciation would ultimately not meet the Yellow Bandit's expectations. To hell with the Chinese and the Russians, he thought.

They were mere pawns in the grand scheme of things, suitable partners helping to create and assist with the event. But none of them would be around long enough to enjoy the spoils of victory. They would be ignorant victims of the event, much like the millions of other people above ground.

To hell with the hundreds of true-blue, patriotic generals who refused to follow orders for the promise of new visions. Instead, in the face of danger, they faithfully stood by their futile oaths to their country in its declining days. And for their misplaced loyalty their positions had been newly filled and they had been dispensed with.

To hell with all the top-notch scientists who stood by their research and findings on the dangers of potential man-made electromagnetic pulses, genetically modified food products, and toxic chem-trail saturation in the skies. To hell with their warnings of the inherent perilous hazards, the impending perils. They too were disposed of, traitors to the new and rising regime.

To hell with the senators and representatives, the Democrats and Republicans, the Independents and the fucking Tea Party, who failed to back him and the inevitable machine. They would go down as enemies of the state in the newly written archives of history, the President silently pondered. Only those few who sided with him would survive and see the new vision rise from the ashes.

And especially, the President thought to himself, to hell with the American people who would vote for anybody promising them a bunch of free shit and believe what they read in the newspapers and saw on the television. To hell with their folly and self-centeredness and sheepish mentality. They were their own worst enemy, allowing the few to take from the many, forsaking their past and selling their future, discarding their religious beliefs, their personal morals, their once cherished integrity.

And because of their shallow ways, every one of them being expendable, they would either perish or serve. Each one of the fools truthfully deserved what they got.

The President smiled outwardly this time. He was pleased with the plan, thrilled with the potential, ecstatic with the godly control which would soon be his. He sat tall in his throne-like chair and began listening to his comrades.

"Mr. President," General Wells, the Secretary of National Defense acknowledged his superior.

"Gentlemen," the highest ranking soldier recognized the rest of those in the room. "As you know, the EMP event began yesterday precisely at nine PM Eastern Standard Time, as scheduled. It has affected every inch of the continental United States, including portions of Canada and Mexico and, as planned, has destroyed all means of electrical grid power, communications, and transportation. All except for those units and components which were previously protected from the pulse, which of course, are under our control."

Those at the table nodded with joy. The President looked on with restrained glee. This was really happening.

"All regions in the country have reported tremendous success. The element of surprise and lack of preparedness by the general population has made the execution of the first phases, Operation Rescue and Operation Clean Sweep, nothing less than exceptional accomplishments," the General continued. "Within the next forty-eight hours the entire country will be fully constrained and ninety percent of the population will be accounted for."

The high-powered men applauded the welcomed news. Each one of them had their own reports filled with encouraging intelligence to share, and their own riches to reap as well.

General Wells went on. "I have complete confidence in my generals and commanders in the field. Thus far, every one of them has done an outstanding job in carrying out their assigned tasks despite the difficult situations they find themselves in. I have no doubt," he addressed the President, "that our mission shall be completed as planned and on time. With that, I would like to turn it over to the Military Operations Commander, Lt. General Howard Clayton."

"Thank you Mr. President, General Wells," General Clayton commenced without fanfare.

"We currently have over two million uniformed and armed troops on the ground, including regular soldiers, bands of National Guards, and foreign militia. Troops have earlier been proportionally attached to command centers in every population core throughout the nation. That includes over fifteen hundred cities with census counts over 25,000. Larger metro regions, have of course, been much more challenging than the smaller towns and rural areas. However, with the coordinated efforts of all active agencies, and you gentlemen," he pointed around the table, "we can expect excellent results within the time frame allotted."

The President had one question. "General, have you encountered any form of resistance so far?"

The General was hoping he would not be asked that question, though he had no choice but to tell the truth. "Nothing we can't handle, sir. We've had isolated pockets of resistance, mostly in the outlying areas. They're nothing but a few groups fluffing their feathers. A small number of our soldiers have been killed in the round-ups, mostly foreigners, so it's not a big loss."

"What about out west?" the President asked. He knew Texas and the sparsely populated sections of the western portions of the country could be thorns in his side, as they had been throughout his presidential elections and administrative terms.

"Well...well," the General stuttered. "There are clusters of resistance throughout Texas. As you know they still allow people to own guns out there. Some of them won't go down without a fight, but we have enough military forces nearby to contain and snuff out the rebels."

"And down south?" the commander-in-chief wanted to know.

"Hillbillies and rednecks. They have no leadership, no structure, no serious forces. They're always a royal pain in the ass...ah, excuse me sir. But I believe we have them under control also, sir."

Fire burned in the President's eyes. Nobody was going to slow down, never mind stop this essential mission, least of all a bunch of inbred, toothless wonders living in trailer houses down near the creek. "Damn rednecks. No good Texans. They always want to start a fight. What the hell is this, National-fucking-Pride Week?"

No one dared to respond.

"Listen to me everyone, and listen good," the President blasted, as he stood up. There were no smiles at the table now. "I want this operation to be completed as planned. I don't care what has to be done. I don't care who gets trampled on or who dies. Most of them are going to die anyway. I don't give a shit what it costs. If you have to wipe out a whole town or an entire city, then do it. There will be no surviving subversives. These mobs of rebels, these backward revolutionaries, these ill-advised patriots must be swiftly and aggressively dealt with. I want them completely exterminated.

"Gentlemen, these people are nothing more than domestic terrorists, homegrown insurgents. I want them hunted down 'til they have no place to hide. I want them squashed to a pulp, burnt to a cinder. There will be no mercy, you hear me? Each of you gentlemen have been selected because of your special skills, your years of experience, and your pledge to the new order. Now do your god-damn jobs."

General Clayton shrunk into his seat and timidly bowed to his commander, letting the next man pick up the briefing.

The Deputy of Transportation straightened out his pile of top secret documents, giving the President time to simmer down.

"Mr. President. All traffic came to a stand still when the pulse hit. Millions of running vehicles stopped in their tracks without warning. All aircraft were permanently grounded." He nearly snickered at the double meaning. "Ocean vessels have been rendered useless. All major roads critical to the mission have been cleared. Reports have come in that some older vehicles have been seen traveling about, but the numbers are considered insignificant.

"Our fleets of necessary military vehicles and transport buses are operational, thanks to the protective shields installed. More buses could have been used due to the large number of detainees. However, the transports are running around the clock as we speak. Air Force One and your helicopters, sir, are in perfect condition as well, and are ready for your use once it is safe above." The Deputy finished his reporting, relieved the President didn't rip him a new one too.

But the President did have a question. "Mr. Deputy, what happened to the planes in the air once the pulse spread?" He knew the answer, but he simply wanted to hear the gruesome details from an expert.

The Deputy cleared his throat. "At the moment of the EMP impact all power would have been lost to any aircraft in flight. There would be no survivors."

"What about the flights outside the perimeter of impact, the planes en route to the United States?" the President clarified his inquiry.

"Oh," the Deputy mumbled. "Aircraft flying safely beyond the force of the pulse would not be affected. However," he took a long pause, "they would still have to land. Most aircraft inbound from overseas would not have sufficient fuel levels to turn about. A few may have been able to change course to places like southern Mexico, farther north into Canada, or perhaps one of the islands in the Caribbean, but for most of them that would be impossible. And as you are aware sir, per the devised mission, it was standard procedure to block all major runways with abandoned vehicles, heavy equipment, and debris to prevent any landings at the larger airports."

The President released a wide smile. "Yes, I know."

An aide, an Army Major, tapped lightly on the double doors, opened them and entered the conference room. He moved toward the President, his head lowered. He excused himself and gave the commander a small piece of paper which the President quickly read. From his chair the President looked at his cabinet with an extended silence.

"Gentlemen, I regret to inform you that the Vice-President has been killed."

Chapter 28

The VP was dead. A stunned hush filled the room at the sudden news.

There wasn't much love lost over the demise of the Vice-President. It was generally agreed that he was more of a liability than an asset to the administration and for the new order. His absence from this committee meeting was painfully obvious and pleasantly noticed. If the truth were told, the Vice-President was kept on a short leash simply to pull in some of the senior constituents and the white vote. Except for those limited benefits, he was actually looked upon as a moron whose numerous misspeaks and foolish antics had caused unwarranted issues for the political party in general and the administration in specific.

The President mulled over the memo. He was glad the dimwit was gone. In fact, it had been he, the President, who had sent the VP on the scheduled emissary trip to the United Nations just minutes before the pulse was set off. Great timing. The fool had no idea what was about to happen.

After a moment of silence the President nodded toward the next man at the table to continue. Rest in peace you moron, we have work to complete.

The Deputy of Energy spoke up.

"Mr. President, I am pleased to report that all command posts have adequate power to complete their tasks. Generators, shielded from the anticipated blast, are in proper working order. The main electrical grids and power plants, are, of course, out of commission. However, additional backup generators placed in storage prior to the event are ready for quick installation and reactivation of any or all power transmissions throughout crucial portions of the country when the time is right.

"All nuclear power plants were safely shut down yesterday and are capable of maintaining their integrity once we open up for business again. You will certainly be able to restrict their upstart as you deem necessary, sir. And finally, the White House can be up and running with the flip of a switch. In conclusion, all systems are proceeding as smoothly as can be expected."

The President nodded his approval. He liked hearing good news.

It was the Communications Deputy's turn to share his information.

"Mr. President, the telecommunications we had installed in Stations One and Two are working perfectly. Our satellites were well beyond the range of impact and were not affected by the EMP. They continue to function as designed and the satellite phones are operating as planned. The feed allows us to send and receive encrypted data through our secured network. All sectors, districts, and regions relay their status through the proper levels to our communications Command Center here at Station One. Local communiqué exchanges between the men in the field and their section headquarters have been restricted due to the limited range of their equipment. But, I believe, sir, that the majority of the information we are receiving is current and accurate."

The Deputy quickly turned to the man next to him, hoping the President didn't have any questions or concerns. But, as every man in the room knew, the commander-in-chief understood the basic workings of every system in play.

"Thank you Mr. Deputy," the President added. "Tell me. Are there any active civilian communication systems?"

Damn! The Deputy thought to himself. The President was better briefed than he had believed. "Yes sir. Some citizens band radio transmissions have been monitored. Apparently, patchy groups were able to cage their equipment allowing them to work over long distances. However, these rebels are ill prepared and fragmented in such a manner that they should be of no danger to the completion of your plan."

"If they're so 'ill prepared' as you say," the President interjected, "then how is it they knew enough to shield their transmission systems?"

The Deputy had no answer and sat in his seat like a dummy.

The President held his cool this time. "I told you men to put a stop to any insurgents, any dissidents who may cause problems. That, gentlemen, includes knocking out their CB capabilities."

"Yes sir," the deflated Deputy responded, knowing it was impossible to stop every CBer in the country from freely broadcasting.

After a short pause, the next member, the Deputy of Foreign Affairs, moved quickly into his lengthy report.

"Mr. President, the entire world has been watching America over the past twenty-four hours. Many of our European allies have declared states of emergencies themselves, fearing a similar EMP event may hit them as well. Canada and Mexico are most concerned since significant portions of their nations have already been affected. Both countries are on full military alert. Several other allies, including Great Britain, Japan, South Korea, and Israel have initiated first steps toward martial law as precautionary measures, while maintaining their military forces in critical defense maneuvers. Our allies are scared to death, Mr. President. And rightfully so.

"America's financial networks no longer exist. It is in complete shambles. The Federal Reserve is shut down and has lost control of the government's monetary system. All banking has ceased, leaving citizens without pay checks and cash. The New York Stock Exchange is dark, and I dare to say, all financial instruments—stocks, bonds, hedge funds, commodities, pensions, both private and public—have been suspended, if not entirely wiped out. Expectations are that none of the mentioned systems will ever recover. All of that leads to the U.S. dollar having lost more than fifty percent of its value in the international market over night. It is projected that the American dollar will be worthless in no time.

"Conversely, the quote on precious metals has skyrocketed in the past day. Speculation is causing demand to out-pace the supply. Gold is trading thirty-five percent higher than yesterday. It is projected by the major London banks that gold will reach three thousand dollars per ounce should America fail to turn around in the next week. Silver is following the same upward swing and may hit three hundred dollars an ounce."

The Deputy took a deep breath. "We all know it will take upwards to a year for the country to regain any substantial ground. But most of the nation will never recover, at least not under the old methods."

"What about our enemies?" the President asked.

"They're coming out of the woodwork. Nearly every country in the Middle East is celebrating our dilemma. The Emirates, Saudi Arabia, even Kuwait and surrounding kingdoms who we've worked with have remained silent, though the word from that region is the White Satan and the infidels have finally succumbed to Muslim radical terrorism. North Korea is rattling its sabers, forcing South Korea and our troops stationed there to stand at the highest level of readiness. Iran, too, is causing trouble, which should be no surprise. That nation is preparing to launch its first round of short-range missiles toward Israel which would spark full out regional war.

"The nine hundred pound gorillas in the room are, of course, China and Russia. Both nations have their nuclear subs within striking range off all our shores, with heavier presence along the eastern seaboard, most notably at the mouths of the Hudson River and Chesapeake Bay. Although we have certain agreements with the countries' leaders, neither one can be trusted to hold up their end."

The President grinned. He knew every aspect of the Chinese and Russian working relationship with the U.S. He had been the one to initiate the temporary treaties. And yes, he expected them to renege on their deals once the giant appeared to be down for good. They could never be trusted to hold true their agreements, and so too was he, the President thought.

The Deputy of Foreign Affairs concluded his formidable account. "In effect, our allies are too involved with their own self preservation to offer any form of assistance to America. Our adversaries are prepared to swoop in once the country shows no proof of life and its inability to defend itself. We have perhaps four or five days at most before World War III begins."

"Thank you Mr. Deputy," the President said. "A very informative report."

The Secretary of the Department of Homeland Security was next.

He could not match the previous speaker's intensive briefing. "Sir, DHS, working in conjunction with the new Army, has focused its efforts on the preliminary operations, which I might add once again, are functioning beyond our expectations. Our first task was to initiate the Internet kill switch to ensure no one except for authorized insiders would be capable of spreading news of the event or coordinating grass roots militia forces against our operations.

"We have also, in coordination with the Department of Transportation, set up checkpoints along every major roadway corridor and highway in the country to control the potential civilian and unsanctioned militia movements. The southern borders have been left unmanned since it is anticipated that very little northbound traffic will be encountered. Quite the opposite, if anything, it has been reported that undocumented immigrants and some U.S. citizens are trying to flee into Mexico, probably due to the blackout and arctic sweep. Very few of those traveling southbound will survive the trip.

"The American roundup, as determined by the NSA's Threat Matrix Score, or 'Red List,' has assisted in the streamlining of final disposition for potential dissidents. The mission has proceeded relatively smoothly with the assistance of Russian and Chinese troops, with whose nations we have bilateral agreements," the Secretary added.

"There is a lot going on simultaneously, much of it hand-in-hand with the Federal Emergency Management Agency, a contingent of DHS. So, with that, I'll turn to the Undersecretary of FEMA to expound on the situation."

The man in charge of FEMA was ready.

"Our major Readiness Exercise 84 is in full procedure. As General Wells had mentioned, Operations Rescue and Clean Sweep are moving along fine as sub-programs of Operation Garden Plot in their movement and control of the population. The more advanced process of Operation Cable Splicer, Mr. President, involved in the orderly takeover of state and local governments by the new order, had been established prior to the pulse event. Cable Splicer has appointed low level military commanders to replace the local elected officials in order to guarantee the continuity of government and the ability to monitor the regions' populace."

The Undersecretary reached for a glass of water and took a small sip. "As for the nearly twelve hundred incarceration facilities scattered around the regions, they are filling up quickly as the buses, trains, and trucks are shuttling in their cargos from local temporary detention centers. Once the camps reach maximum containment we'll have to contend with the excess prisoner populations as earlier discussed. I suggest, Mr. President, we look closely at the United Nation's Agenda 21 plan to deal with the massive influx of captive civilians and loose dissidents. Otherwise, the centers and camps will be well beyond capacity within the week."

The President nodded toward the FEMA chief. "Thank you. I'll look into that." Massive executions at the detention centers were an option previously arranged. He glanced at General Wells, as if to say, take care of this potential mess.

The Deputy of the National Security Agency was next and he didn't waste a second.

"Our decades-long monitoring of potential undesirables within the country has paid off. All of those on 'The List' have been tracked through various Internet, social media, telecommunication, and personal means. Through our dozens of intercept centers we have collected over twenty trillion transmissions. Our surveillance of domestic, as well as foreign contacts, has gathered incalculable data-mined intelligence.

"We know everything we need to know about everyone we need to know. We know who they are, their familial situation, their financial status, their political position, and their affiliations. We know where they live, where they work, what they read, what they watch, and what they think. We even know how much they cheat on their taxes."

There was a muffled laughter in the room.

"Some have slipped through our nets, however, the majority are accounted for and are being rounded up as we speak. The few loose cannons will be pursued to the fullest extent." The Deputy took a deep breath. "We know what our allies are doing. We know what our enemies are doing. We also know what foreign terrorists and those in between are doing. In other words, gentlemen, the NSA knows everything about everything, and we're damn good at our job."

He addressed the President directly. "Sir, I think it would be prudent to review my more sensitive information with you in private at your earliest convenience."

The committee members looked on, feeling left out of the loop. What in the hell did this head spy have to discuss confidentially with the commander-in-chief?

The President nodded toward the NSA Deputy. "As soon as this meeting is adjourned."

Finally, the last man at the table was about to speak. As the lead scientific engineer of the government's Weather Modification Program he knew everything concerning geo-engineering of the world's climate.

"The bitter cold encompassing most of the United States," he began, "has perfectly enhanced the main mission we are involved in. Our manipulation of the weather locked in over the country through the modification of Cirrus clouds has given us full control over atmospheric pressure systems, the planet's jet streams, and changes in the environmental climate.

"Through exhaustive scientific research and extensive experimentation focusing on ionospheric, electromagnetic, and global electrostatic fields, we are capable through military endeavors of creating localized weather systems and worldwide climate alterations. For those of you who are unaware of how this occurs," the scientist paused, assuming the other men had no concept of what he was talking about, "let me briefly explain.

"Our HAARP project, or High Frequency Active Auroral Research Program, has allowed us to use radio frequency energy to create atmospheric heat directed toward targeted portions of the ionosphere. In turn, this affects the earth's weather patterns, precipitation, and temperature. I'm certain you have seen the so called 'chem-trails' in the skies over every populated area of the globe. Those aerial sprayings of various chemical and biological agents work in conjunction with HAARP to modify the climate as we deem necessary."

There was a heavy silence in the room. Of course each committee member had seen the 'trails', commonly mistaken as commercial airline's vapor contrails, delivered by high altitude military jets and stealth drones. But few of them knew exactly how the airborne mists interacted with HF waves to change the weather. Now they knew. Sort of.

"We can, Mr. President," the scientist said with pure confidence, "maintain the frigid air over the nation as long as you need to complete the mission. Alternately, if desired, deadly freeze, desert heat, heavy precipitation, or the lack of can be controlled. Also, high winds, tornadoes, hurricanes, even earthquakes can be established at the flip of a few levers. In conclusion, sir, our weather manipulation program is operating precisely as expected."

Everyone in the room sat quietly for a moment. The reports they had just heard were intense, to say the least. To some, they were almost
unbelievable. Each one of the men felt privileged…no, honored, to be a part of the most rigorous world changing military coup in human history.

The President stood up. He was damned pleased at the progress. "Thank you gentlemen for your fine work. I must be going now. Please keep me updated every two hours. Good night."

The meeting was over. But there was more work that had to be done. The Chinese Chairman and Russian President were standing by for the American President's update of the critical event.

Chapter 29

The Humvee moved toward the string of headlights blocking the roadway. Sure enough, Raz and Cody could visually verify the cars in front of them were commandeered Border Patrol vehicles. They weren't there to check passports, either.

"Fuckin' cockroaches," Raz growled once again.

"Think we should be ready," Cody mentioned. He reached into the back seat and found two semi-automatic rifles which Raz had tossed in. "You know," Cody eyeballed his friend, "just in case."

Raz grinned at the kid. He was all right as far as the old guy was concerned. "Good idea. Keep ya pistol handy too."

"You think they're trouble?" Cody asked, referring to the dozen or so armed cockroaches waiting for them.

"Ya can bet on it, sonny."

"So what should we do?" Cody asked nervously.

"I kinda like ya idea. Go in as friendlies, then blast our way through," Raz laughed. "Just let me do the talkin'. Don't say nothin'."

Cody looked at him, trying to figure out if the crazy old man was serious. He couldn't tell. He slid the rifles between his seat and door frame to keep them hidden from any nosy cockroach sticking his head into the vehicle, if any of them got that close. "Okay."

Raz rolled the Humvee to within a car length of the lit-up sedans crowded with gun-totin' thugs. Cody lowered himself in his seat, remembering the side panels of the vehicle were bulletproof, but the windows were not. He watched Raz come to a stop.

Two young men stepped out of their 'government' car, one carrying a shotgun, the other a pistol. The one with the handgun motioned for Raz to open his window. Raz had one of those deja vous moments, but this time he planned on remaining in the vehicle.

"Que paso?" the man yelled through the closed window.

Yup. Just as Raz figured. Mexican cockroaches. The criminal type who come out at night when nobody's looking.

Raz lowered his window. It was still too damn cold outside. "Que paso back ta ya," he said in his worst Spanglish. "Como estas?"

Cody rolled his window down too, following Raz's lead. He was ready.

"Where you go?" the man switched to broken English after seeing the hairy, white gringo in the driver's seat.

In his usual manner, Raz played along. "Goin' that a ways," he explained while pointing straight through the windshield beyond the roadblock.

The man didn't understand a word Raz said. Must have been Raz's relaxed form of speech. He asked again. "No comprende gringo. Where you go?"

"Just told ya, ya dumb son-of-a-bitch. Down ta Old Mexico ta get me some tequila and one of them hot senoritas. Been a rough night."

A few of the other bandits shouted something in Spanish to the man grilling Raz. He waved them off. He could handle a crazy old drunken fool. "Nice car, mister. I like you car," he said.

"Yup, it's a beaut. Great for desert travel or for runnin' road blocks," Raz grunted, attempting to rattle the trouble maker. If the bastard could understand him.

The man looked inside the vehicle and motioned toward Cody. "Who you?"

Cody waved at him, determined to stay silent.

Raz answered before Cody could say anything. "He's my boy. Gonna git him drunk and laid in Nogales. It's his birthday."

"No, no," the man shook his hand. "Nogales not open. Not open. You go back. Now."

"What in the hell ya mean Nogales ain't open? How in the hell is a city closed?" Raz kept pushing.

"Not open. You go back. You walk back," the man said. "I keep you car."

Raz gave the man his go-to-hell stare. "Listen amigo, I need a drink real bad and my boy needs ta pop a cherry. So that's where we're goin'. Besides, it's too damn cold and no way in hell are we leavin' the car and walkin' back home. Comprende?"

The gunman caught enough of what Raz was saying and couldn't believe the whiskered gringo. He shoved his pistol into the cab of the vehicle and connected with Raz's neck. He looked frightened, but this punk was fool enough to pull the trigger.

"Don't cotton much ta guns bein' pressed against my body," Raz remarked. "Last person ta do that didn't git too far."

"Who the fuck you?" the cockroach asked in a think accent, his gun hand shaking.

"Me?"

"Si, you."

"Well," Raz began, shifting a glancing signal to Cody. "I'm generally nobody special. Just an old man goin' 'bout his way, lookin' for no trouble and not wantin' ta cause no trouble. Just tryin' ta git a drink in this god awful weather. But ya know what always seems ta happen? Every time I'm just tryin' ta go 'bout my own business someone with a gun and a big mouth tries ta ruin my day. And wouldn't ya know it, on occasion I happen ta run inta some assholes who wanta stop me from gittin' ta where I'm goin'. I really don't like that." His eyes squinted at the lights in front and the men beside his door. Another few seconds is all he needed.

"You one loco hombre," the man said and laughed as the other members of his cockroach gang laughed too.

"I might be a lot of things, amigo. Been called a lot worse in my day. But there's one thing I ain't. Damn sure I ain't loco," Raz answered. "Ya want ta know what I really am?"

"Si, loco gringo. You tell me."

Raz formed a wide grin on his grizzled face and locked a death stare on the asshole. "I'm the monster in ya nightmare, the boogeyman under ya bed, the reaper at ya doorway."

The gun man looked surprised. He either didn't understand the words or if he did, he couldn't believe what the old man was saying.

"Now Cody!" Raz yelled.

Raz pulled his gun from the seat and shot the punk point blank, throwing him back into his partner. Instantly Raz aimed and shot the second man. In one smooth motion he flipped the toggle switch for the high powered roof lights and the barricade cars were bathed in searing light, momentarily blinding the rest of the cockroaches in their warm vehicles.

Cody wasted no time.

He emptied the pistol into the Border Patrol cars. Then he grabbed a rifle, stuck it out his window and blasted away with automatic fire. Bullets ripped through the cars, glass shattered under the torrent of lead, tires exploded, metal caved in pitted plugs from the onslaught. Cody's aim had improved in the dark.

The thugs weren't ready for such an assault, their weapons useless against the lightning fast attack. Cody's shots hit four cockroaches jumping from their stolen cars. Two had died on the spot, never having the chance to take aim. The other two fell to the ground and limped behind the metal blockade, waiting for their compadres to take out the damn gringos.

Raz kept shooting out his window as he put the Humvee in low gear and rammed the cars blocking his way. The crunch of fenders and popping of windshields didn't silence the screams and shrieks coming from the dying cockroaches. The three ton Humvee pushed through the parked cars like a bulldozer rolling over a pile of aluminum cans. Raz continued firing as the cars were shoved aside. The roof lights blinded the remaining cockroaches as Cody wildly swung his rifle, peppering the young crew, keeping them low or mortally wounding them.

Incoming bullets hit the Humvee from several directions. Shots striking the front and sides of the armored troop carrier bounced off the reinforced panels and ricocheted into space. For Cody, the battering was terrifying. He had never been shot at before today. It had only been less than an hour since he actually shot a pistol at a living being for the first time in his life. A blended mix of fear and necessity forced Cody to keep shooting. There was no way he was going to be stopped after coming this far. He wasn't a low-key college professor tonight. Instead, now he was a maniacal warrior fighting to stay alive and doing a damn good job at it.

Raz shouted. "Ya okay, kid?"

"Yes," Cody answered. "You?"

"Just dandy," Raz added. "Keep shootin' the assholes. We'll git outa this."

"A turkey shoot, huh?"

"Well, more turkeys than I expected."

"So I noticed," Cody commented.

"For a quiet Thanksgiving night, I mean." Raz chuckled.

Several bullets smashed through the windshield, showering bits of shattered glass into Cody's face. "I'm shot! Raz, I'm shot!" Cody yelled above the steady gun fire echoing in the air and throughout the Humvee. Cody dropped his rifle out the window and it bounced to the ground. Raz kept ramming his way through the cars.

Cody slapped a hand against his forehead, felt the hole. He pulled his hand away smeared with blood. More blood trickled into his left eye making it hard to see. He began to panic. "Raz!"

Raz ceased shooting and looked at his friend. He grabbed Cody's head and roughly squeezed his forehead where the blood was leaking.

"Ouch! Hey! What the hell?" Cody screamed.

"Ha!" Raz snorted. "Ya ain't shot, boy."

"Then what's this?" Cody said, holding up his blood drenched hand.

"Ya got cut from the glass, that's all."

Cody felt his forehead again. It hurt like a son-of-a-bitch. He wiped his eye and held his jacket sleeve up to the wound to help it stop bleeding.

Raz remarked, "Ya'll know when ya git shot, boy. It's the worst pain ya can ever imagine. It don't feel like no sliver of glass stuck in ya forehead. Believe me, ya don't want ta git shot."

"It still hurts like a bitch," Cody admitted.

Raz laughed. "Yeah, I know. Been there. Keep shootin'."

Cody went for the next rifle and aimlessly fired into the mangled cars and the highway outlaws. With only one good eye his shots went high, but they allowed Raz to plow through into the safety of darkness.

"We did it," Cody shouted. "You got us through."

"Stay down," Raz suggested. "The rest of 'em are still firin'."

Sure enough, a number of rounds pinged off the rear of the vehicle until it moved out of range.

"Whew!" Raz exhaled. "Quite a rush."

"You can say that again," Cody added, the adrenalin in his body still running strong.

Raz looked ahead. "Two more minutes and we'll be off this damn road."

"Drive faster," Cody said. "Drive faster."

Chapter 30

"How's ya forehead?" Raz asked Cody.
"Throbbing."
"Ya'll be fine."
"Yeah?"
"What's ya count?" Raz asked.
"Count?"
"Ya body count?"
"What?"
"KIAs."
"What's KIA?" Cody had to ask.
"Killed in action."
"Oh. I don't know."
"I figure it's four, maybe five. Good shooting Cody. Blasted right through 'em bastards."
"We almost got killed," Cody yelled, as if it were Raz's fault.
"But we didn't."
"That's good."
Raz looked over at his young friend. He was proud of how Cody had handled himself. How he had stayed cool under fire. How he did what had to be done under difficult and deadly circumstances. He was a man who could get things done when everything around him

seemed overpowering and hopeless. He was still inexperienced, but he had what it took. Raz felt like a father watching over his anxious son. A man helping his boy to learn, to grow strong, to be self-assured when life's moments were overwhelming. *This world would be a much better place if there were more men like Cody Gordon,* he thought.

"It was five for sure," Raz ended, referring to Cody's KIAs.

Two kilometers farther Raz turned off I-19. "Check the map Cody," he said.

Cody turned the flashlight on the map and found the dirt road identified by dashes and spaces. It led westward into the desert along a mountain range. "Here it is, about a quarter mile up the frontage road."

Once Raz found the road he stopped the car. "Let's take care of that nasty gash," he said to Cody. From the first-aid kit in his bag Raz tended to the glass cut. He cleaned it, rubbed some ointment on it, and applied a large bandage over the minor wound. Cody felt his forehead. It didn't hurt as bad.

"Ya look better with that," Raz said. "Like a bad ass. A real soldier with a medal of bravery under fire."

"I don't feel brave," Cody remarked. "I feel scared."

"Sometimes it's the same thing," Raz said, off handedly. "Hand me one of 'em waters, will ya. We still got a ways ta go."

They drove along the narrow, unused road. There were no directional signs, it was pitch black, and there were no points of reference to help them determine their direction. "Keep an eye on the map, Cody. I ain't never been on this road and want ta make sure we're goin' right."

After ten minutes of traveling Cody spoke. "What do you think they're going to do with the people on the buses? You're certain the buses are headed to that camp, but, I mean, why would they move so many people so far away?" Just thinking about it and his captive family made him nervous. He looked at Raz waiting for an answer he could live with.

Raz peered into the deep darkness beyond the range of his headlights. He knew what the desert camp and all the other detention centers in the country were set up for. He had been there and in many others during his interrogation sessions when he worked for what he believed was national security, the good of his nation, and his patriotic duty. But these FEMA camps had nothing to do with national security in the real sense. They weren't established for the good of his nation, the America he truly loved. His American duty and the pride he held so dearly in serving his country had been twisted into something horribly gone wrong.

The detention complexes were essential prisons to every unfortunate soul dumped into them. They were holding facilities for quick retention during the crucial first week of the population roundup. They were compounds filled with political undesirables, government subversives, domestic terrorists, liberty lovers, and sympathizers of grass roots anti-administration factions, and for anyone else vaguely connected.

Raz knew the camps were hopeless places where families would be torn apart, where people would starve from the limited or lack of food supplies, where they would freeze from the unnatural cold, protected only by what they had carried with them. He knew most of them would die an appalling death.

Every human right once guaranteed and protected by America's two hundred twenty-five year old Constitution no longer existed within the dismal fences and walls of the camps. Or anywhere else in the country. Every ounce of dignity once cherished by free and unencumbered peoples of the greatest nation ever conceived in the history of mankind would suffer in the muck of anguish and distress. Every possible inkling of hope clung to by the frantic captives would be ripped from their clutches just as their homes and possessions and lives had been.

To every man, woman, and child, the centers were death camps, plan and simple. They were not unlike the gulags of inhumane wars in the previous century. They were similar to the concentration camps of history's madmen determined to rule the world. They were comparable to the re-education centers of oppressive tyrants willing to kill millions in the name of ideologies and profits. They were reminiscent of the killing fields created by maniacal despots devising their own ill-fated destinies.

Raz did not want his friend Cody to know the truth. The young man's family was locked in one of those hell holes and their final outcome was almost a certainty.

But Raz would have to tell him.

"Every one bein' detained in 'em camps is in one way or 'nother considered a threat ta the new government," Raz began his lengthy explanation.

Cody stopped him. "What new government?"

"Ya don't think the people doin' all this are good old American patriots concerned for the citizens of this country? Do ya? Ya think they follow the laws that helped ta create this land? The government we know, boy, is gone. Dissolved. Expired. A republic of the people, by the people, and for the people. Hell, that's all over my, friend. Our Constitution is dead. Everythin' the foundin' fathers risked their lives and wealth and reputations ta establish is no longer in effect."

"But...." Cody tried to talk.

"But nothin'," Raz grumbled. He was getting pissed off just speaking his piece. "Ya of all people should know about the Constitution. Don't ya teach it in that damn college of ya's? You're a history professor, for cryin' out loud. A government for the people, the Bill of Rights, We The People, citizen representatives in the Congress, Life, Liberty, the Pursuit of Happiness, citizens' rights. None of it matters no more."

"But who is doing this?"

"Who?" Raz grunted. "Ya asking' me who is doin' this ta us?"

Cody looked on as Raz drove the Humvee slowly through the desert brush following what appeared to be a dusty, winding path. He really didn't know who exactly was responsible for the crisis at hand. Not yet, anyway. But he had his suspicions of who was in the snake pit.

"Who do ya think ordered martial law as a means ta round up and control the American population? Wasn't the Army. Wasn't the Congress. Who do ya think wants ta take every single gun away from the citizens so they won't have the ability ta protect 'emselves from the very people who are supposed ta protect 'em? Ain't the good, law-abidin' citizens. Ain't the hard workin' folk who just want ta be left alone ta live and ta provide for and ta protect their families. Who do ya think wants ta take God out of the equation? We're a nation born under God. We live through divine intervention. Ya think the founders just came up with our Constitution by 'emselves? Well, I don't.

"Who do ya think has unmanned drones spyin' on everyday people lookin' for domestic terrorists? Ain't people concerned with national security as we know it. Who do ya think has been disarmin' our military and turnin' the country inta a defenseless target for our enemies? Sure as hell ain't patriots tryin' ta defend our sovereign country and its people. Who do ya think is sprayin' poisonous chemicals inta the air every damn day? Ain't nobody who gives a shit 'bout the people breathin' in the lethal toxins causin' unprecedented numbers of asthma and cancer cases and killin' people. "

Raz stopped to catch his breath.

"Who do ya think is destroyin' our once thrivin' economy by killin' jobs, forcin' industries out of business, and turnin' over our technological secrets and economic advantages ta countries resolved ta destroy us both militarily and economically? Sure in hell ain't our business people, our entrepreneurs, our fathers and mothers, grandfathers and grandmothers who want their children ta have a better life than they had. Who do ya think saved Wall Street and the large banks with our own tax dollars, only ta have 'em turn on us? We had no say in the deceptive practices. Who do ya think caused the real estate collapse that wiped out the most valuable assets of millions of Americans, killin' their dreams and future hopes and wishes?

"Who do ya think initiated that Common Core crap in the nation's schools ta dumb down our youngsters so they'd be easier ta control and dominate, sedated ta the fact that the government and all its trappin's would promote 'learned helplessness'? Who do ya think lets our borders stay wide open ta encourage illegal immigrants and subversives, and drug dealers, and arms runners ta come on over. Oh yeah, and when ya git here we'll show ya how ta collect welfare checks without workin' and git free housin' and food and medical help and schoolin' and damn cell phones. Who do ya think's payin' for all that free shit? Ain't nothin' free."

Cody listened, taking in all these issues. He was getting upset. Not at Raz, but instead, at the truths he was forced to acknowledge.

Raz continued his tirade. He was hot and ready to do something about it.

"And who do ya think bought more than two billion, that's billion with a 'b', rounds of high tech ammunition ta control the American people? Sure the fuck wasn't the NRA or the local cops, or the

National Guard soldier down the street. Who do ya think handed over power ta the United Nations and the World Bank so they could coordinate their ultimate agenda over our country and the rest of the world?

"Who do ya think ran up the national debt ta over seventeen trillion dollars makin' us virtual slaves ta foreign governments like mobsters holdin' the note on our assets and collectin' their vig every week? Who, by the way, just happen ta be our military and economic enemies. Who do ya think recruited hundreds of thousands of foreign troops ta handle the round-ups and executions of loyal American citizens 'cause they knew most dedicated American-grown soldiers would refuse ta fire on their own if ordered ta?"

"But Raz," Cody said, trying to stop him.

"I ain't near done yet," Raz blurted, shutting Cody down. "Who do ya think allowed foreign entities ta out right purchase our shippin' ports and oil fields and power plants and manufacturin' facilities and technology centers? The very things that are vital ta us as a nation. Who do ya think backs the major GMO food producers 'cause the profits are astronomical and the kickbacks are beyond belief? Who do ya think is takin' control over the national health industry, clearly one sixth of our entire economy, to divert even more money and control through the central purveyor? Who do ya think is plannin' on eliminatin' the U.S. Constitution all tagether, callin' it a useless, out-dated document, soon to be replaced with a unilaterally written twenty-four hundred page decree aimed not at the freedoms of the people, but at the dictatorial control of those who are left?"

Cody didn't know what to say. Much of this was new to him.

Raz wasn't quite done. He left the worst for last.

"There's more, my friend. And it does git worse. Who do ya think developed the National Defense Authorization Act or the Patriot Act allowin' the military the right ta kidnap, interrogate, indefinitely detain, and even murder American citizens? Wasn't nobody I ever voted for. Who do ya think established the Readiness Exercise of 1984, known as REX 84, givin' 'em the illegitimate right ta imprison good Americans, like your wife and daughters and Nick's family? All of this goes way back, my friend."

Cody was in shock. How could all of this have happened without him ever hearing about it? How could he have been so uninformed, so unaware, so naïve?

"And finally," Raz added to the heap of destructive news. "Who do ya think ever came up with the ultimate plan of domination, Agenda 21, which is bein' implemented right before our eyes this very moment? It's truly the demise of our great nation and all that we hold dear."

Cody squirmed in his seat. Thousands of images rattled through his mind. His friend and associate Jonathan being killed on campus for what he believed. Old man Jack and his wife dying in their frigid bedroom at the mercy of evil forces. Thousands of his neighbors being kidnapped, traumatized, and perhaps even killed. And there were street riots, thugs on the loose, foreign troops patrolling the highways, armed gangs at road blocks, nationwide blackouts, buses full of people being relocated, shoot outs at the high school, secret detention camps, Raz's underground bunker, Zeke being killed, Nick dying in his arms, him shooting and killing other killers.

But most importantly there were Robin and Jeffrey and Jennifer in the hands of some evil bastards. He would find and save them, and he would kill anyone who tried to stop him.

Cody returned to the moment. He asked Raz the same question again. "So, what do you think they're going to do with the people on the buses?"

Raz turned to his friend and shook his head. "I think they're fucked," he blurted out.

"Yeah?" Cody mumbled.

"Unless we do somethin' about it," Raz added.

"Yeah," Cody said.

Chapter 31

R az was drained from his venting. He rattled off all the things which were bothering him about his country and its government and the way things were being handled far beyond the lawful parameters of the U.S. Constitution. It seemed the more he knew about the lies and deceptions and schemes scattered by the new order of leaders, the more aggravated and frustrated he became. Simply knowing what was happening in plain sight wasn't enough. In fact, just being conscious of it was enough to drive him crazy.

He was certain there were many people like himself who were aware of the taking over of America by treasonous forces. But there were far more clueless citizens, like Cody and his generation, as to what was occurring. Two things would have to happen, Raz believed, if there were any chance in hell to change the course of American history.

The first was the non-believers, those who were frequently referred to as 'low information voters,' would have to learn of the grave situation they were in. It would be a monumental task to convince them of the dangerous state of affairs, particularly, at this moment, without any conventional forms of communication in operation. And, most of those in this group would sheepishly follow the recommendations of the governing forces in return for promised food, shelter, and safety. They could not be relied upon as part of the solution.

The second option was more promising, though far more difficult to launch. All over the nation there were people in every region, every state, every city, town, and village, Raz was convinced, who would fight for their country and families. When push came to shove these truly independent, well-informed, self-reliant Americans would dedicate their efforts toward battling for their historically imbedded principles and personal freedoms.

Raz knew these kinds of people. He had worked with them his entire life. He had seen them fight for values instilled within them since birth. He had witnessed them die for what they really believed in. They were out there. Somewhere. Everywhere. The only obstacle was how to gather them into a counterforce to take back their country. It was a formidable undertaking. One Raz had absolutely no idea how to bring about.

Cody was on the verge of being distraught, worried for his family after what Raz had said about their capture. He took in several deep breaths to calm down and gain control over his rational thought process. Yeah. Some of what Raz had mentioned Cody had heard before. He knew of several of the disdainful policies set in place by the government. He was aware of some of the restrictions being placed on the citizens, in particularly in regards to the first and second amendments of the Constitution. But, at the time they seemed innocuous, hidden behind the obscure umbrella of national security or safety precautions for certain factions, like children, or police officers, or various ethnic groups.

He should have known better.

American history was a part of his makeup. He lived and breathed it everyday, teaching the battle scars of a developing nation, the triumphs and defeats of a people hungry for self-reliance, the heartaches and blessings of a diverse group of immigrants working individually and jointly to create a democracy where all people were supposed to be equal and all life was sacred. He had taught the proven pillars of American democracy: free will, self-determination, and rugged individualism—characteristics vital to a free people.

But Cody, like many educators, had forgotten the important lessons of our history. He had merely gone through the motions of teaching the hardships and sacrifices of early Americans striving for what the Declaration of Independence had been so valiantly based on: the truths of life, liberty, and the pursuit of happiness. He had lost his passion for the very principles he had devoted his life's skills to. He had failed to inspire his charges with the sense of greatness, and the privileged fortune to be an American, and the fragile balance between democratic rule and government control.

Cody thought about his past actions leading to his future measures. He chastised himself for having failed in his promises to his vocation, his students, his country, his family, and especially to himself. It was time to turn around, to join the legendary men he had read about. It was time to stand and be like the early American heroes he had once revered and shared in their amazing stories.

It was time for Cody to become part of the solution rather than a piece of the problem.

He had often heard, and frequently said, that in a troubled situation somebody should do something about it. Somebody should try to fix it. Thomas Jefferson was correct in his assessment. 'Bad things happen when good men do nothing.' His neighbor Jack knew of it too. Cody stared at old man Raz. It was time for Cody to become that good man he wanted to be and do something about it.

Raz was struggling to keep the Humvee on the crooked path which occasionally dropped off into the adjacent dry wash. It was getting late into the night and he was growing tired. But he was more pissed off than fatigued.

Cody asked him, "Want me to drive for awhile?"

"Nah."

"Come on, Raz. Time for you to relax a bit. Let me take over."

Raz crooked his tense neck and gave in. "Okay, but when we git closer ta the camp I take the wheel again."

"That's a deal," Cody agreed. They both got out and reversed seats.

"I've been thinking," Cody said as he threw the Humvee into gear.

"That's a good thing," Raz mentioned. "Most people don't take the time ta think."

Cody nodded.

" 'Bout what?"

"About what you were saying," Cody answered. "All those things you brought up."

Raz said, "Scares the shit outta ya, don't it?"

"Of course it does."

"That's a good thing, too. Makes ya take your head outta your ass and look around. If more people had paid attention ta what was happenin' ta 'em, we wouldn't be in this god-damn mess."

"I should have seen it, some of it anyway," Cody said, ashamed at his lack of awareness. "I'm a history professor, for god's sake. People who forget their history are doomed to repeat it. That was pounded into my head for years. I know what happens when we take our eyes off the ball, when we don't speak up against what's wrong, when we refuse to hold our leaders' feet to the fire. History books are filled with the dire results."

Raz rested in his seat watching the road. He listened to the young man coming to terms with himself.

"Everyday we lose a small piece of our lives, of our freedoms. We let them take from us, a little extra tax here, more regulations there, new laws when we're not looking. We're told it's for our safety, so we say okay, because safety is good. Right?"

Raz smiled.

"We're told it's to protect our children, because every parent wants the best for their kids. So we sign on. We're told it's for a more secure nation, because there are terrorists under every rock. So we let them set up their road blocks and searches and nets. We're told the government will care for us and the food is safe and the air is clean and the schools are good and the vaccines are necessary and coal is bad and climate change is caused by humans and small snails are more important than people and the polar bears are threatened and guns are evil and our enemies are our friends. And we say little."

The smile on Raz's face grew wider.

"And we line up like obedient citizens as our constitutional rights melt away one by one. If you say something against them you're marked. You're scorned by people around you because you cause waves. You get fired because you just don't fit in the mix any longer. You're persona non grata in your field because you are too difficult to work with. You get killed because you get too close to the truth."

Cody glanced at Raz who was absorbing every word.

"And they never stop," Cody ended. "They never stop." An air of frustration caused his voice to waiver.

Raz smirked. He was getting to like this kid even more. The boy sounded a lot like him. He had a fire in his stomach, a burning passion. He had a strong sense of right and wrong, of moral principles. He was beginning to learn the truths hidden among all the lies and wanted to do something about it. Now, Raz realized, Cody had a purpose in life. People needed a purpose. They needed something bigger than themselves. He would save his family and his country at all costs. Raz had no doubt that Cody would succeed or die trying, and Raz wanted to be with him when he did.

"Hey kid. You're okay in my book," Raz said to Cody.

"Thanks," Cody responded with surprise. "You too."

"I'm truly proud ta know ya Cody."

"Ha." Cody stopped, struck by Raz's words. "Nobody ever said that to me."

Raz said, "Well, I'm sure ya'll hear it again."

Cody focused his tired eyes on the dirt path, but he was thinking about what Raz had said to him.

"Wish more men felt the way ya do," Raz added. "Ya're correct. Our rights are bein' suppressed, ignored, and violated everyday by unendin' government regulations, laws, treaties, and hush-hush deals. It's what they do and they don't never intend on lettin' up unless we the people put a stop ta it." Raz was working himself into a frenzy again.

"Ya travel by plane and ya're defiled fifteen ways ta Sunday. They say it's ta prevent terrorists attacks. Takin' my damn shoes off prevents terrorists intent on killin' Americans? Give me a fuckin' break. Then they have ya take off ya belt and ya watch and dump the change from ya pockets. Hey! They say. That stopped the bad guys, so let's squeeze the toothpaste tube and forbid nail clippers. Makin' us all safe, don't ya know. Why stop there? Next they zap us with X-rays and oogle at our naked bodies on the screens. No weapons there, but we need ta go a little bit farther.

"Ya refuse ta be radiated or ya have a piece of metal in ya skull from the war, so they take ya ta the side and frisk ya. Oh, they love that part. Ya stand there like a common criminal for everyone ta see while the TSA perverts grope your junk and fondle your ass hopin' ta find somethin' suspicious, like a ball point pen or a key stuck up your ass. All in the name of security. So they slip on the latex gloves and go ta town checkin' places that ain't never been checked before 'cept by ya doctor. If his god-damn fingers gone any deeper ya woulda had ta marry the guy."

Cody couldn't help but smile. Raz wasn't shy about his opinions.

"Hey! They say, we ain't never been blown up so far. This shit must be workin'. How 'bout we check grandma's skivvies and that guy's wheelchair and the baby's shitty diaper. Can't be too cautious. And they tell us over and over that all that probin' and violatin' catches terrorists and saves the country, hallelujah. Bull shit! They just want ta mess with us and show us who's the boss."

Raz looked at the map once more. The road had all but disappeared as they followed what seemed to be nothing but a beaten animal trail. He reached back and retrieved bottles of water for himself and Cody.

"There's one thing I'd like to know," Cody asked the old guy.

"What might that be?"

Cody shook his head. "How in the hell do you know all this stuff?"

Raz cleared his throat. "I read and listen and watch. But mostly 'cause I got their damn book."

"Book? What book?" Cody asked, shocked as hell.

"The *Internment and Resettlement Operations Manual*," Raz divulged. "It's their god-damn secret playbook. Tells everythin' 'bout the takeover, right down ta a gnat's ass."

"Really?"

"Yup. And I got me a copy of it," Raz smiled.

Chapter 32

T he small convoy of four military buses from the Fort Huachuca area moved along the roughly graded road toward the halo of lights hovering over a protected valley. Dust clouds kicked up as the transports moved closer to the desert camp. Within minutes they rolled down the steep mountain inclines and slowed as they approached the guarded gates.

Most detainees on Robin's bus stirred, looking out the windows as the massive compound came in sight. The wind blew gusts of cold air through the shattered windows. Some rested in their troubled sleep, hoping the nightmare of a dream would soon end. But for all of them it was just the beginning. This place would be their new home for the foreseeable future. Whimpers and subdued cries filled the bus as the captives viewed the prison. Food and water were on everyone's minds, but the most urgent concern was, where were they now?

"Mama. Where are we?" young Jennifer asked her mother as they bumped to their stop. Robin had no idea, but she didn't want to worry her children more than necessary. "A building where we can sleep more comfortably," she said to ease her daughter's growing fear.

"I'm hungry," Jeffrey said. His stomach was making constant growling sounds.

"We're all hungry," Robin agreed. "When we exit the bus you two hold onto to me. You understand? Do not leave my side." Both kids nodded.

The guard at the front of the bus rose from his seat. He yelled something in mixed English-Russian to the passengers. They understood enough to stand up and gather their few possessions. The guard barked another order and the folding bus door opened to the freezing air. He stepped down to the ground and motioned everyone to move out. People were exiting the other buses up ahead.

Robin grabbed her children and slowly followed the rest of the scared passengers off the bus. Nick's wife and children were a dozen people behind. Her girls were complaining and crying. Grownups tried to shush the little ones unsuccessfully, hoping not to enrage the guards. Mere hours earlier, the captives had witnessed the merciless killings of many of their neighbors. They did not want it to happen again.

The ragged mob of evacuees lined up in jumbled lines outside their buses. One guard from each transport watched over them as the second soldier entered the buses looking for stragglers. The Russians could be heard screaming and shouting at several people still in their seats. Moving too slowly for their own good, the guards shot the detainees where they sat. There was no time for patience, no time for humane treatment, no time for mercy. Those outside began crying louder as the guards exited the buses. Several of the men were forced at gun point to pull the dead bodies off the buses and drop them at the feet of those waiting for something else to happen to them.

The captives were freezing from the strong mountain winds and bitter cold. Several of them fell to the hard ground, exhausted and hungry. The guards brutally kicked them to the side. Three of the tired souls were shot without a second's warning. The foreign troops were vicious in their actions and seemed to enjoy their power over the great Americans.

A sixty year old man who Robin knew, approached a guard. "Please, sir. We are thirsty and hungry. No one has had anything to drink or eat all day." The guard stared at the older man without a spark of pity in his eyes. The stock of his rifle violently smashed the man's face, breaking his nose and rendering him unconscious. More screams and whimpers followed. He too was shot like a rabid dog.

The prisoners were left to stand in the late night freeze. Robin looked around, taking in the layout of the camp. She had to keep her wits about her as she scanned the landscape for future reference. Harsh bright lights on poles twenty feet tall cast eerie shadows amongst the imprisoned. The lights were staggered about every forty feet along the chain fences surrounding large wooden buildings. There were no lights on the inner side of the fences topped with razor wire. There were no other people looking on, just those from the newly arriving buses.

Robin pulled her children closer to her side. People kept their heads down so as not to draw attention to themselves or cause trouble with the blood thirsty guards. The building they stood before was huge, with few windows and a single front door closed tight. It was the end building of a long row of similar roughshod structures. Robin glanced behind her, counting at least ten rings of lights surrounding other buildings. For all she knew there could have been many more around a bend in the hidden contours of the foothills.

The massiveness of the complex was overwhelming. It was at least a half mile long, with buildings on either side of the bus road. Smaller shacks, guard outposts, and twenty foot tall guard towers were scattered along the outer edges of the compound on the patrol road. The entire camp appeared to be double-fenced, each twelve feet high and strung with razor wire overhanging both inward and outward.

Other buses were coming in at a steady pace from the north, dropping off their human cargo into the depths of a living hell. Residents from Tucson and beyond, Robin thought. Two fresh soldiers hopped into Robin's bus and the others in the fleet, then they quickly drove off to gather another group of subversive evacuees.

Robin's group was ordered to move forward. They stayed close to each other and were pushed through the wired gate into a single compound. Some were diverted to other nearby buildings. The fence was locked behind them. Buckets of water sat on the ground inside the fence line. The adults scrambled to the buckets. An inch of solid ice topped each water pail. Men kicked the ice with their fists and feet, breaking it into chunks. They stuck their bare hands into the painfully cold water, scooping up half handfuls into their parched mouths. The icy liquid hurt their chapped lips and lined their empty stomachs shocking their lukewarm bodies.

Women elbowed their way to the buckets, dragging their children for a few drops of water. Once the young ones had their fill, the mothers drank heartily from the filthy, open containers. In the front of the group one of the men walked up to the door of the dark building, dim light from the road hitting his back. He reached for and turned the makeshift doorknob. The door creaked open a bit. The man looked back at his fellow captives and nodded, as if to say it was safe to enter.

He pushed the flimsy wood door inward. The inside of the building was darker than a coal mine. No lights, no shadows, no discernible images. There was no sound as he cautiously stepped in. Without any visually distinct lines or perceptions it was impossible to tell how big or small the room was. It was impossible to see who or what was inside. The others followed like blind people, one by one, into the unknown, clinging to one another for safety.

There was a deep cough from within, and then a chorus of several more. The crowd stopped still.

"Close the damn door, my friends. It's friggin' cold out there."

Chapter 33

The President of the United States left the briefing and returned to his office. "Get the Chinese Chairman on the line," he spoke into his phone.

"Yes, Mr. President," his aid answered.

The President sat at his magnificent nineteenth-century Resolute desk made of English oak, which was an exact replica of the original one in his Oval Office. The hand-carved panel in the front displayed the same presidential seal with its eagle motif. A thick 'Top Secret' file rested before him. General Wells, the Secretary of National Defense, sat across from him. No one else was in the room. No one else needed to hear what was about to be said.

His secure satellite desk phone buzzed. In an instant the world had changed by his own hand. His name would soon be on every human being's lips as the most courageous man in history. He was the man whose vision and daring was about to alter the course of mankind and solidify world politics. He was the man who took a broken system and would turn it into a smoothly operating organization. He was the one who would fix the deliberate faults, right the intended wrongs, revise the limited, amend the oversights, modify the old, and improve what people said could never be done.

The President took a few more precious moments before picking up the phone. He would be more popular than any man who had ever lived. More esteemed than all generals who had ever ruled the battlefields, more admired than every statesman who had ever stood before great leaders. He would be more loved than Jesus Christ himself, more respected than Buddha, more revered than Mohammad. But most importantly, he would be the most feared man in all of history. The possibilities were endless once he completed the task at hand. He would show everyone who he really was. He would prove himself to the world's stage and all would bow to him.

The President realized early on that the formidable task could not be completed without the assistance of outside sources. Allies and friends would be of no use. They would never go along with such a fantastic scheme. They most assuredly would talk, leak information and deadly details about the event. Without a doubt, they would attempt to change his mind, either through diplomacy or warfare. It always came down to survival of the fittest, self-preservation. The friendlies would be hurt nearly as much as the American nation.

Exactly! He thought.

So it was his enemies, he and his followers decided to team up with. It was that old 'keep your enemies closer' sort of thing. The deals were made, the terms agreed upon, and the deed was done. The President had to keep the players in the game until it was time to dispense with them.

He picked up the phone and spoke evenly. "Mr. Chairman, it's good to speak with you again."

"And to you also, Mr. President," the Chairman responded through his English interpreter. "I've been expecting your call." Despite the language difference there was a distinct sense of irritation in the Chairman's tone.

"I wanted to make certain that all was going well before I gave you a report on the situation," the President said coolly.

"And how well is it going?" the Chinese leader wanted to know, although he had a good sense of the chaos created via his satellite communication feeds. He had a tremendous stake in the mission's success as well. If this joint undertaking succeeded as planned, he would be ruler for life. If it failed, then he and his country would be doomed.

The President eyed General Wells. Their utter and complete contempt for the Chinese was unmistakable. The President did what he did best. He put on the charm of a true statesman determined to win, and lied to the communist leader. "Your delivery and execution of the explosive device were precise. The EMP forces have spread exactly as predicted. My team and I would like to congratulate you and your unerring forces. You are indeed a great leader."

The Chairman knew when smoke was being blown up his ass, even through the accurate translation. Patronizing one's untrustworthy opponent was one of the tools of deception and trickery. The Chinese leader was as good at it, if not better, than his American adversary. "Thank you Mr. President. Much work has gone into this operation by both sides. May I ask? Is the time schedule we agreed on still feasible in order to complete our transaction?"

"I can assure you, Mr. Chairman, within the week we will both have what we want. My people are in full control of every field operation, and we can not foresee any difficulties."

"That is good news. I too would like to congratulate you on your excellent and swift measures. Although our philosophies may differ, this venture has proven that two divergent peoples can come together for the benefit of all," the Chairman expressed while grinding his teeth.

The President shook his head. He detested this arrogant, self-righteous, egotistical dictator who at the drop of a hat would take over the United States and kill every single American, despite the temporary economic loss to his empire. Instead, in return for his part in destroying the strongest nation in the world, the Chinese Chairman would have to settle for only half the country.

"I'm sure you still have much to do," the Chairman said. "I am looking forward to the time when I will have ownership over the western half of your country, particularly California. It will be an invaluable asset for the Chinese people. My forces are prepared to take possession within the week, if your schedule is correct."

"It is correct," the President answered, enraged that the Red Dragon would even insinuate the timing was off. "As agreed, Mr. Chairman, you detonated the bomb and I gain full martial law over my half of the country. Fear is always a more powerful weapon. Everything west of the Mississippi will become Chinese territory once we gather the rest of the evacuees and turn the HAARP weather control to a more moderate climate."

"Please keep me informed and let me know if there should be any difficulties," the Chairman commented.

This was the opening the President needed. "There is one thing I should mention," the President said. "We're having some trouble with the Russians. Their troops are ignorant, unprofessional barbarians. My men have taken care of many of them on the ground. But...." He was playing the dictator.

"But what?"

"I'm concerned about the Russian subs along America's coasts. They are completely unresponsive and our communication with them has been blocked. I suggest that your naval officers be made aware of the potential danger also."

There was a long pause over the phone line. "The Russians are sneaky bastards and are not to be taken lightly. We will also monitor their fleets and remain on the highest alert against our bordering enemies. Thank you Mr. President for the warning and for your diligence. I hope we will be able to work together as comrades when we are neighbors."

"Thank you, Mr. Chairman. I will call you again in the next two days." The President hung up. He smiled at the General. "Neighbors, my ass!"

General Wells grinned. "Work together? Can't trust anything that son-of-a-bitch says."

"Never have, never will," the President added. "Now let's review our plans on how we're going to get rid of him and the Russians at the same time."

Chapter 34

"There's a book that explains everything?" Cody asked, astonished at the unlikely suggestion.

"Bet ya ass there is," Raz said. "Officially, it's called the U.S. Army Field Manual 3-39-40. Printed five or six years ago by the government, but it's really based on the earlier REX 84 documents. Describes in meticulous details every aspect of internment and resettlement of the American population once the event begins and martial law is in place. I mean, this book has it down ta each light bulb and paper clip. Ya wouldn't believe what they have planned. If I had ta say so, it's a god-damn piece of art, but not the good kind. It would impress ya ta high heaven with the amount of work they put inta it, but it would scare the shit outta ya too."

"How'd you get your hands on it?" Cody asked. "Wouldn't something like that be restricted or classified?"

Raz smiled. "Supposed ta be. Only authorized for Department of Defense personnel. Or so it says. There's even a destruction notice on the first page. Says, 'Destroy by any method that will prevent disclosure of contents or reconstruction of the document.' Never seen nothin' like it before. How's that strike ya? Our fuckin' sneaky, doin' things behind our backs government tryin' ta hide it from the American people. Not bein' too transparent, huh? Ya can be damn sure the DOD didn't want this information ta hit the streets."

"But Raz, how did you get it?" Cody asked again.

"It got leaked a few years back. There's always someone willin' ta take the risk and leak or share crushin' evidence against a corrupt government. Seen it done too many times before. Whistleblowers, disgruntled workers. Someone gits pissed off, or canned, or wants ta embarrass the administration or the Army. Or maybe they just thought the whole damn thing was wrong and they wanted ta warn us citizens.

"Anyway," Raz paused, "ya can buy it on Amazon now. Believe that? A couple of clicks and a box load of military secrets gits delivered ta ya house. Don't really matter, though. Nobody wants ta believe this shit. It's too farfetched. Reads like a Hollywood sci-fi formula, 'cept it ain't fantasy."

"So, is what's happening now laid out in the book?" Cody wanted to know.

"Pretty much, but there have been changes. Ya see, this Army manual was supposed ta train our soldiers on how ta handle disasters in the country. Ya know, natural catastrophes like floods, earthquakes, hurricanes, things like that. The soldiers was supposed ta work in conjunction with other agencies includin' FEMA, the Red Cross, ICE, DHS, even the United Nations, ta offer relief and assistance ta survivors. Housin', food, medical attention, future relocation. Things on the top of the list ta help Americans in trouble.

"The book also instructs the troops how ta contain foreign combatants. Keep 'em under wraps, feed 'em, hold 'em 'til someone trades 'em off or brings 'em ta trial. Basically, how ta deal with bad guys threatenin' the United States, or spyin' on us, or tryin' ta blow us up. Anyway, that was the original plan."

"How did it change?"

"Sounds pretty good, don't it? Well, some of it might have been good initially. It's sensible ta plan for when bad things happen. Bein' prepared is bein' smart," Raz said. "But, like everythin', when the dirty no good power hungry politicians and money grubbin' contractors and commie-liberals and greedy bastards see how they can twist and spin their filthy hands inta a god-damn jackpot of shiny gold, it's all over. They git together and act like God, thinkin' it's their right ta fuck the rest of us and do whatever they damn well please. I seen it happen too many times."

Cody stepped on the brakes of the Humvee as he swerved around a clump of brush. "What the hell is that?" he asked, looking ahead. A herd of strange animals was casually crossing the path in the pitch blackness. Two black, hairy, mean-looking creatures and at least eight baby wild pigs trotting behind stopped in front of the Humvee. They stared into the headlights, their beady eyes red as devil's.

"Ain't ya never seen javelina?" Raz chuckled. "They won't hurt ya, 'less ya want ta pat 'em."

Cody laid on the horn until the wild pigs moved on.

Raz continued. "The plans ta relocate citizens in harms way turned inta an operation ta detain 'em. They was no longer refugees or evacuees. Instead, the dislocated civilians, officially known as DCs, become military prisoners. They're no longer categorized as homeless or displaced or medically needy. The entire plan was changed ta control the population instead of helpin' 'em. Detainees are identified by their known behavior. Ya have ta remember, the government, the NSA, and other agencies keep tabs on millions of Americans, monitorin' our daily communications, our Internet searches, our lifestyles. They know everythin' 'bout us."

"What sort of behavior are you talking about?" Cody asked as he continued to drive.

"The manual stipulates that all detainees be identified accordin' ta their known conduct or political tendencies toward the central government, aka the feds. They're broken down inta groups based on potential risk levels. They're labeled either cooperative, neutral, or outright combative."

Raz laughed. "Guess which group we'd be in?"

"Maybe yesterday I would have been one of those neutral guys. But now, definitely not. Not cooperative either," Cody smiled.

"Once ya know what's goin' on, ya gotta stand ya ground. Accordin' ta the book, biometric information is collected from everyone in custody. They have these internment serial numbers, ISNs, they're called, ta identify which collection points the prisoners came from, which internment facility they're in, their ethnic background, their religious affiliation, their education level, and their affinity toward any potentially subversive groups, in particular any political ties, among other things. Sorta like a UPC bar code ya see on consumer goods, 'cept for humans. They also wear ID bands on their arms. Capture tags they're called. Ya know ya history, sonny. Don't this sound a little too familiar?"

"Wait a minute," Cody said. *This couldn't be right,* he thought. People wouldn't do this to other people. Not again. Would they? Governments wouldn't roundup its citizens, ship them off to death camps, mark them like cattle, and do what it wanted with them. There was no way in hell what Raz was saying could actually happen here. People wouldn't allow it. They wouldn't tolerate this kind of tyrannical behavior. We have laws here. We have the Constitution. We have senators and representatives and civic leaders who watch out for their constituents. We have a justice system backed by the courts and rules of law. Everything Raz said was sheer craziness.

Or was it?

Raz saw the disbelief in Cody's face. It was understandable if a person hadn't kept track of the behind the scene activities of those in charge. Raz reached into his canvas bag and showed the actual book to Cody. He aimed the flashlight on the cover so Cody could read the title. "Told ya so," Raz added, a gravely serious look on his face.

"This book is real and it's bein' used against us right now," Raz said. "It's the standard operatin' procedure for trainin' soldiers how ta identify those who should be detained. It integrates evacuation and control systems and procedures. It determines each person's status based on their ratin'. It explains how captured citizens' property and money should be confiscated and handled, includin' their savin's in the banks and investments elsewhere. It teaches techniques ta exploit intelligence from the inmates. How ta git ya ta turn on ya neighbor or family member or close friend.

"The manual calls for a quick reaction force, teachin' proper take-down techniques. The door ta door roundups, the transports. It outlines civil disturbance procedures and riot control measures where deadly force is not only acceptable, but in many cases preferred. It focuses on counter insurgency, detailin' with reducin' passive resistance and armed confrontation and re-establishin' the government's legitimacy. Ya think these people know what they're doing? Damn straight they do."

Raz stopped to breathe, and then continued. "It stipulates how ta segregate people dependin' on their behavior tendencies, but it also demands the isolation of detainees based on them bein' obvious leaders, hostiles or agitators or radicals, members of the military by grade, minors, adult males and females, and nationality. It specifies daily food rations and sanitation and medical care and prisoner treatment. It outlines special uniforms and roll calls and forced labor assignments," Raz ended his list for the moment.

Cody just drove and listened.

"It even has schematics for barracks and tent layouts. It shows how buildin's should be constructed with specific designs and materials, where fences must be located, how many security lights are needed, the number of guards for every hundred detainees, and open clear zones. It advises on the proper use of restraints, contingencies for potential prisoner escapes, dealin' with hunger strikes, and handlin' suicide attempts." Raz looked out the window, still holding his copy of the Army manual with the grip of a steel worker.

Raz continued his recounting of the manual's highlights. "This one leans toward humane treatment of all prisoners. Soldiers are ordered ta not unnecessarily restrain or harm their charges. It insists on daily nutritional food sufficient enough that inmates won't lose body weight or fall ill. It demands that all guards act in a professional manner, that any deviation from the rules of engagement shall be rigidly enforced, and that recourse for both guards and prisoners shall be heard by a committee of superiors."

"That part doesn't sound so bad," Cody said.

"The problem is," Raz said, "this book and all its detailed policies and procedures ain't bein' followed by the new people in charge. Madmen have changed the rules. They've thrown out all the humanity called for in here," he lifted the book, "even in a confined environment, and enforces the severe and brutal measures of a narcissistic dictator."

"Oh."

"That's what we're up against, my friend. And we better be ready."

Cody had a twisted look on his face. "But tell me, why would our President do this? Why would he and his men betray us? We believed in him. We supported him. It's us who voted him into office."

Raz shuttered. "Just for the record, it wasn't *us*. Never trusted the guy from the git go. Let me tell ya somethin', Cody. And ya need ta remember this. People believe in the wrong people all the time. People sometimes throw their support behind leaders for the wrong reasons. People regularly vote for the wrong guy based on frivolous or false information. Most assholes in this world have a horde of backers. But, they're still assholes.

"The President is not solely in charge. Ya think a nobody from the back streets of Chicago with absolutely no leadership experience could become the President of the United States without a powerful and rich support basis? This President didn't win the presidency. It was given ta him. It was handed ta him with certain conditions attached. Shit flows down hill, sonny. We're on the bottom, but the President ain't at the top, even though that's what most people think.

"I assure ya that the President is takin' orders from someone or some people much higher up the food chain. There's too much at risk ta take a chance. The big boys runnin' the show have bought and paid for their man, and if he don't do what he's supposed ta do, then he goes away too."

"So, if that's the case, then who's the real boss?" Cody asked.

"Not exactly sure, though I have my suspicions." Raz grunted. "That's what we have ta find out. But first things first."

Cody nodded and continued driving the Humvee.

Chapter 35

Raz checked the map again. "Looks like we're ten, fifteen minutes from the camp. Think I can make out a dim haze of light up yonder."

There was a faint halo effect of reflective mist a couple miles ahead. It came from the security lights at the detention center bouncing off the low hanging sky.

"What do we do when we get there?" Cody asked.

"One step at a time, sonny," Raz grumbled. "One step at a time."

The men were tired and hungry. It was nearing midnight and they would have to rest before they took any action at the camp. They had no idea of what they were heading into and could not imagine what they were about to see.

The path wound around a clump of desert creosote brush, scrub mesquite bushes, and ocotillo cactus. Cody eased up on the gas. The Humvee suddenly slid off the dirt road and dove forward a dozen feet into the hard desert sand. Everything went black. Cody's chest struck the steering wheel with a severe brunt force. Raz's head banged into the unpadded dash and windshield, his hands blocking his body from most of the impact. Both men were dazed from the unexpected crash, but they seemed uninjured.

"What the hell?" Cody yelled. The contents from the back seat had slammed forward over the front seats, blocking his view of Raz.

Raz looked out the window straight into compacted earth. "Ya okay?"

Cody tossed some supply boxes and water bottles behind his chair. "Think so."

It took several seconds for them to shake off their dizziness. Raz caught his door handle and shoved. The headlights were still on, although they were half buried in the desert dirt. He rolled out of the vehicle and rested on the ground for a brief moment. Then he maneuvered around the Humvee toward Cody's side. He cracked Cody's door then pushed it forward.

"I'm fine," Cody said. "Took it in the chest, but I'll live."

Cody got out and stood unsteady on his feet. "Where the fuck's the road?"

There was a twenty foot gap in the dirt path, like a monsoon wash had wiped it away during a torrential thunderstorm. But it hadn't rained in months. It would be impossible to get up the bank on the other side. Cody and Raz inspected the damage and quickly assessed their situation.

Raz spoke first. "This hole in the road ain't caused by no gully washer." He could see the trail had been dug out. "There're tire tracks everywhere. The son-of-a-bitches trenched out the road with heavy equipment ta prevent access ta the camp from this direction. Dirty bastards!"

"Now what?" Cody asked in frustration.

"We could walk, but we can't carry much with us," Raz growled.

Cody climbed back into the driver's seat. "We need this vehicle," he said. The engine was still running so Cody jammed it into reverse and stepped on the gas. The rear wheels spun wildly, barely touching ground. He tried to rock it forward and drive, but at such a sharp angle resting on the edge of the road dipping into the gap, it was no use. He turned the engine off and almost threw the key away, but he didn't. "Damn thing!"

"Let's git what we can carry," Raz recommended. He didn't like the circumstances either, but they had to keep moving. "Shit happens and ya just have ta deal with it," he said in a gruff voice.

They were digging through the pile of supplies for only the absolute necessities. Rifles, pistols, ammo, flashlight, binoculars, water bottles. As if they didn't have enough to worry about, what happened next came as a huge surprise.

Two sets of headlights quickly came up from the rear and stopped a truck length from the Humvee. The first thing Raz thought was, they were sentries from the camp patrolling the nearby perimeter. But they were on the wrong side of the gutted trail. He automatically unslung his rifle and aimed it toward the trucks.

Four large figures exited the trucks, which appeared to be older Dodge pickups, and stopped. "Hold on right there boys," Raz said to them. His and Cody's rifles were aimed dead center. They had been through this routine too many times for one night.

"We ain't lookin' for no trouble," Raz informed them.

"Whoa, amigo," one of the men calmly said. He put his hands in the air as a friendly gesture.

"What ya doin' here?" Raz yelled across.

"I was going to ask you the same question," the stranger said.

Raz answered. "We're just goin' 'bout our business."

"You're on our land," the big man said. "Just wondering what you're doing here."

"Ya land? This here's government property," Raz growled.

"Afraid you're wrong, friend. Last I looked this piece of miserable desert was given to our people by your government."

"Reservation?" Raz asked, realizing his bearings may have been off kilter.

The big man moved closer to the tilted Humvee. "Yup. Every square foot paid for in blood, sweat, and misery. You're on the Pascua Yaqui Reservation."

Raz and Cody lowered their weapons. They had no beef with the Indians. "Just passin' through," Raz said.

The rest of the tribe came up behind the first man. They smiled in a non-threatening way even though it was cold as an ice storm. "Name's Pete," the man said. "These are my brothers," he pointed to the other men.

Raz introduced himself and Cody. "Ran inta a bit of a problem, as ya can see." He turned toward the disabled transport. "Damn road's gone!"

"Yeah, the Army did that awhile back," the Pascua Indian said. "Not the real Army, never saw uniforms like that before. They cut the road to stop any intruders from this direction. It's our land, but they do whatever they want."

"Tell me 'bout it," Raz said, his bearded jaw tightening up. He spit on the ground.

"Where are you headed on such an awful night?" Pete asked.

"There's a detention camp up a ways," Raz volunteered. "We have some business ta take care of."

Cody jumped in. "They kidnapped my family."

Pete nodded and looked at his brothers. "It's more like a prison, if you ask me." He pointed into the darkness. "It sets just over that ridge. We've been watching it for some time."

"So ya seen it," Raz said.

Cody perked up.

"Yup. Been real busy over there since this morning," Pete began. "The lights are on, lots of guards, Army and school buses going back and forth dropping off hundreds, maybe thousands of people into the night. The prisoners don't look too dangerous. Lots of old men, women with their children. No soldiers as far as we could see. I don't know what they're doing there, but it can't be good."

"Believe me chief, it ain't good," Raz added. "We been chasin' the buses from the fort down south. They probably beat us here."

Pete spoke up. "Some Army buses came in through the southern road. A couple of hours ago, I guess. There were four of them. The last one was shot up pretty bad. Windows blown out, bullet holes in the sides. Must have been some trouble along the way."

Cody had an alarmed look.

"But," the Indian began to explain, "people got off. Most of them were put into the last building," Pete said. "Saw a bunch of kids too."

"That could be Robin's bus," Cody said to Raz. "We found them!"

"Not so fast, sonny," Raz stopped him. "We'll have ta check it out."

"Right under our own noses," Pete said. "They started building that place years ago. It was small at first. Never had too many people, but there was always something going on. Over the past year there's been lots of new construction, crews and trucks coming and going. It was as if they were in a rush to get ready for something. Guess we know what for now. The place is huge. I'd say it could contain twenty thousand prisoners, maybe double that if they pushed."

Raz and Cody looked at each other in disbelief. That many people? Prisoners of the government? Held in the middle of nowhere? The situation was getting worse by the minute. How in the world were just the two of them going to even find Cody's family? Nevertheless get them out?

Pete motioned to one of his brothers. The men went to their trucks, turned them around, and returned with a length of hefty coiled rope. They tied it to the Humvee's rear tow rings, then went back to their pickups to secure the rope evenly between the ancient pickups.

"Good looking vehicle," Pete said to Raz. "Where'd you get it?"

Raz grinned. Pete was okay. "I consider it my tax refund."

"I figured something like that," Pete responded. "Let's yank it out of the ditch." At that point he gave his brothers the signal and they hauled the Humvee onto solid ground as easy as dragging a downed elk from the woods.

"Thanks," Raz said. " 'Preciate the help."

"No problem friend," Pete mentioned. "You still planning on going to the camp?"

"You know it," Cody answered.

"There's another way around, but we want to stay out of sight. Follow us and shut down your lights when I do," Pete advised. "Ready?"

Raz got in the Humvee's driver seat while Cody jumped in his side. They stayed close to the Indians' Dodges eating desert dust as they moved forward. They drove down a sharp sandy slope into the dry wash and maneuvered around some dead and down willow trees. Minutes later the three vehicles angled up a gentle incline back to flat earth. From there they continued up a hilly grade scattered with loose stones and boulders. The forward trucks' lights went off and Raz followed suit. Then the trucks came to an abrupt stop below the rim of a mountain ridge.

A glow of faint light hung low over the confined valley where the camp was located. The four Pascua Yaqui brothers climbed the hill up the last few rugged feet of terrain to peek into the hidden desert basin. Raz and Cody struggled to reach the Indians.

"Take a look," Pete said to Raz.

Raz peered over the rocks and couldn't believe his eyes. "Well, I'll be damned."

Cody did the same. The camp was lit up like a ballpark. Large buildings starkly stood in separately fenced compounds. Rows of structures lined narrow sentry roads throughout the camp. Armed guards walked the perimeter and stood fast at sentry points blocking the north and south entrances. Buses continued to roll in with more prisoners and shortly thereafter departed empty back into the desert.

The complex had grown tenfold since Raz had last step foot there.

"Damn huge, isn't it?" Pete said to Raz.

"Un-fuckin'-believable."

"That's the best description I've ever heard," Pete added.

"Must really piss ya off that they put this death camp right next ta your reservation," Raz mentioned.

"No," Pete said. "It pisses us off because they built this monstrosity *on* our reservation land without even asking."

"They what?"

"Yup. Like every other time. They do exactly what they want. Our people have been getting fucked by the government for generations. They take our land, our freedom, our language, our children, and our dignity. In return we get to open casinos, smoke shops, and gift centers."

"Sorry 'bout that," Raz said somberly.

"Yeah, well, we're used to it. Still doesn't make it right."

Raz bit his lip. "Let's go tear their fuckin' throats out."

Pete grinned. "Not tonight. You need to rest and we all need to come up with a plan. We'll come back at dawn. Then we'll tear their fucking throats out."

The two men laughed. Cody and the brothers did too. Apparently it wasn't going to be just Raz and Cody against the new Army.

"I'll get the tribe to help us," Pete said.

"Great," Cody said. "How many in your tribe?" He was imagining a massive army of wild redskins, hooping and hollering, circling the wagons on horseback, and attacking the evil empire.

Pete looked at the young man. "Just under four thousand."

"Really? That will work," Cody said, pleased with the numbers.

"That's a damn army," Raz interrupted.

Pete shook his head. "Not really. We only have about a hundred rifles."

Raz nodded. "So that makes it a hundred and two against the dirty bastards. Odds are gettin' better."

"Come," Pete said. "We'll go back to my house and work out the details. Tomorrow we'll take them down together."

"Show us the way," Raz said.

Chapter 36

The trucks veered southeast toward the small Pascua village. The open, desolate territory was uninviting even in the dark. In minutes the men were driving down a sandy road bordered by modest single level homes which all looked alike. There were dried up, rotting wood fences surrounding some of the houses. A few had three-sided barns in the rear housing malnourished horses corralled with hand-woven ocotillo fencing. Every residence had at least one old pickup truck parked in front or to the side. More vehicles were on blocks waiting for repairs that would never happen. The entire place was depressing, as if hope had abandoned the village long ago. There were no lights in the village either.

Pete and his brothers braked at a small dingy white house with a collapsing front porch. Raz pulled up in his Humvee. "And we think we have it rough sometimes," he said to Cody. "Makes ya sorta humble, don't it?"

Cody looked around and agreed. "Yeah. These people have been worked over."

"See what happens when ya at the mercy of the government," Raz added. "Ya live like ya in a third world country, 'cause nobody gives a damn 'bout ya."

"But why?" Cody asked.

" 'Cause no one says nothin' ta stop it. This is what ya neighborhood is gonna look like soon. 'Cept no people live in ya hood no more."

Cody shook his head in disbelief as Pete waved them into his house. "Bet ya don't read 'bout this in ya history books," Raz grumbled to Cody.

They followed the Indians into the house. It was warmer than outside because of the fire in the fireplace. Two kerosene lanterns, one in the living room, the other in the kitchen, cast off enough light. The brothers sat on worn sofas as Pete introduced his wife, Luza, to Raz and Cody. She poured hot coffee for the men, left the pot on the handmade coffee table, and went out back to the working grill.

"Lost power yesterday," Pete said. "No one has electricity except for that camp."

"They got protection for their electrical things," Raz said. He didn't think it was important to get into the workings of a Faraday cage. "Seems all government agencies have power."

Pete sat down near the fireplace. "So, tell us what happened."

Raz relayed most of the story, bringing Pete and his brothers up to snuff on the situation. At the end he added, "Had ta fight our way outta a few pinches and we ended up here."

Luza brought metal platters of hot steaming rice, pinto beans, some stringy beef, and flat bread, for the boys. She smiled at the white men.

"Thank you, Luza," Cody said politely.

"Like wise," Raz offered.

"Let's eat and talk about tomorrow," Pete suggested.

Over the next hour the men worked on their plan to get inside the detention camp and eventually agreed on the best course of action. First, they would further scout it out in the morning light. They needed to study the layout, get a count on the number of soldiers, see where the prisoners were held, and check for any heavy fire power. They knew they would be outnumbered. If there really were upwards of twenty thousand prisoners, at the rate of one guard per hundred captives that meant the camp could have at least two hundred troops.

Maybe many more.

But now Raz and Cody had the Pascuas on their side.

They also had the element of surprise. None of the guards would ever think the camp in the middle of the god-forsaken desert would come under attack. The foreign troops had never encountered a proud and resilient people who had been kicked off their lands, stripped of their possessions, denied their god-given rights, forcefully kidnapped from their homes, and falsely held as criminals of the country they so dearly loved.

Those troops would soon learn of the power of common solidarity and ingrained rugged individualism inspired by legends in history. They would see what real don't-fuck-with-us Americans were made of.

The American soldiers guarding the camp, the traitors that they really were, side by side with the Russian and Chinese mercenaries, would shortly learn a brief lesson in dogged American spirit. They were the ones who had sold their souls for fortunes of war and turned their backs on their friends, families, and earlier generations. They would soon feel the sharp edge of death and the ruthlessness of ordinary people determined to remain free and unburdened as they tried to wipe out the American character and fortitude they so clearly disdained.

Those treasonous soldiers, the ones born and raised in this great land, would be the first to bleed as they asked for mercy from their attackers and received nothing less than they deserved.

That's what Raz was thinking as he ate the welcomed food offered by the gracious Pascuas. That's what Cody was thinking too, as he sat in the warm adobe house of his new friends. That's what was passing through the minds of Pete and his brothers, as well. They were Native Americans used, ignored, and killed by the very likes of those camp soldiers, as they shared bread with the white men they were about to fight with side by side.

It was almost two in the morning. Pete stood up. His brothers had gone to their homes nearby. "You can stay here tonight. We all need to rest. At dawn we will have breakfast and fight."

Raz looked at his host and fellow warrior. "Thanks for the food and for ya help."

"You are welcome," Pete said as he left the room. "We must stick together."

"Yeah, thanks for everything," Cody said.

The fireplace was roaring and the lanterns' flames were turned down. "Good people, huh?" Raz mentioned to Cody who found a warm spot in the living room corner.

"Real good people," Cody agreed. "We're a small army now."

Raz grinned in the flickering orange light. "I think we might have more than that."

Everyone in the house slept for a few hours. By five in the morning when it was still dark, Raz smelled strong coffee brewing. Luza had once again cooked on the outdoor stove. The men downed their coffee and warmed tortillas smeared with a meat sauce.

"Time to go," Pete said.

The men gathered at their trucks. It was as cold as last night. "Check ya ammo," Raz reminded Cody. "Gonna be a busy day."

Raz walked over to Pete to discuss something.

Cody filled the Humvee gas tank from the five gallon cans packed in the back. He reloaded the rifles and pistols. He secured the supplies in the back of the Humvee, leaving the back seat open for his and Nick's families once they rescued them. When he was done he turned to Raz. "Ready."

Pete went to his Dodge. Only one of his brothers was with him.

"Where're the boys?" Raz had to ask.

"Don't worry. They'll be here soon," Pete assured him. He checked his watch. "We should go."

Pete and Raz drove toward the same ridge from where they had viewed the camp last night. Raz had his binoculars, and once settled behind the high rocks he took a good look at the detention camp as gray daylight appeared. He was more astonished at the site than before.

The camp was laid out in a long rectangle stretching at least two thousand yards. Two long rows of rough wood-sided buildings ran from end to end. Raz could see few windows on the front of each building and a single entrance in the middle. Ten buildings were on each side of a central road down the middle of the entire complex.

Each structure was individually fenced with razor wire straddling the top.

"Wow," he let slip out.

Guard shacks were stationed at the two entrance points and six sentry towers loomed over the prison. The interesting thing Raz saw was every guard tower had a stationary mounted machine gun facing inward to the camp yards. They appeared to be M2-Browning 50 caliber rapid fire weapons, as best he could tell. Bright lights from every angle blanketed the entire compound making it near impossible to slip in unnoticed.

"Damn," he said, involuntarily.

Despite the early hour and raw cold a few captives were roaming outside their units. There appeared to be outdoor toilets open to the world set near the back fencing. No vegetation grew within each fenced unit. There was no place to hide, no trees, no out buildings, just a long row of empty plank tables in the yards.

Raz refocused his binoculars to the far end of the prison. Six Army buses were entering camp. They were full of people. Other buses were leaving the area. It confirmed what Pete had told him. Thousands of citizens were being relocated here at a hasty pace. More than one could imagine.

"Jesus Christ!" he whispered.

Cody looked over his shoulder. Even from this distance without binoculars he could make out the activity. "Wow!"

"Damn big, isn't it?" Pete said.

"Ah huh."

Raz slowly scanned the grounds. Front to end, side to side, counting the visible guards bundled in their winter gear. A total of sixty, maybe seventy, guards were at their stations. But Raz knew there had to be sufficient housing units for enough guards to cover all shifts. Outside the fenced compound were more buildings. The largest one had to be the military barracks. It seemed big enough to hold a couple hundred soldiers. Adjacent to it were two smaller quarters, most likely segregated for the officers. Another building could be the admin shop, or interrogation center.

Two large army troop carrier trucks were parked near the barracks. Raz also saw three Oshkosh M-ATV vehicles near the officers' quarters. It was strange to find these armored vehicles out here in the desert, but Raz knew they were frequently used as smaller utilitarian transports, similar to the older Army jeeps.

Raz handed the binoculars to Cody. The young man took his time searching the complex. "What's that over there?" he asked and pointed to an excavation point a hundred yards beyond the guards' residence.

Pete spoke up. "We've been watching some backhoes digging that huge ditch over the past two days. Have no idea what it's for. They might be digging an underground bunker. Maybe a trash dump."

Cody gave the field glasses back to Raz who eyed the recent dig site. He studied it for half a minute, and then lowered the binoculars. "Ah…guys," Raz hesitated. "Don't think that's a bunker or landfill."

"Well, what the hell could it be?" Cody said.

"If I had ta bet," Raz stopped for a second. "I'd have ta guess it's a mass grave waitin' ta be filled."

The men looked at Raz. "Impossible," Pete wondered aloud. "Why do you think they would go through all the trouble of gathering those people, transporting them here, and stuffing them in these buildings just to kill and bury them?"

Cody turned to Raz for the answer.

Raz cleared his throat. "I don't think they intend on killin' all the captives. But protocol demands interrogation sessions with the prisoners rated as the most troublesome. Prisoners deemed as subversives—those working for the old government, military personnel, war veterans, business owners, educators, media personnel, foreign sympathizers, senior citizens, religious leaders, and conservatives—their families too, are the first ta be grilled."

Pete was stunned. "But why would your government do this to its own people?"

Raz stifled a short laugh. "Ya're askin' me after what ya've been through? First of all, it ain't my government. This here's a new breed who don't give a shit 'bout no one else. Second, the people I just mentioned are the ones most likely ta stir up the survivors. Ya know, cause an uprisin', a revolution against the new order. Hell, there's a public list of seventy-two suspicious activities the government considers potential terrorist activities. Even includes people who buy a Starbucks coffee with cash. Believe that shit? I guarantee that grave ditch is for the ones who refuse ta cooperate or ta give up any important information."

"We need to stop those bastards," Cody said. He was ready to storm down the hill like a wild man shooting anything that tried to stop him.

Raz put his arm out, holding him back. "Stand down, boy. We have ta stick ta the plan if we want ta have a chance in hell of rescuin' 'em people. Ya'll git ya opportunity ta kill some more bad guys."

Cody stayed on the cold, hard ground, simmering in the heat of anger.

Several other men from the Pascua tribe climbed the hill to the scouts. They had bandanas covering their foreheads, thick streaks of black and red war paint on their faces, and a wolf-like readiness in their black eyes. Pete spoke to them in a sing-song language indecipherable to Raz and Cody.

"Our men are ready," he said.

"How many ya got?" Raz asked.

"Couldn't get a hundred like I said," Pete remarked.

Cody immediately let out a deep breath.

"Instead, we have nearly two hundred men, young and old, prepared to fight," Pete said. "They want to stop this madness more than you do. They want to kick these evil people off our lands. They want to help you save your people."

"Thanks again," Raz mumbled.

"Today and from hereafter, we are brothers," Pete proclaimed. "We will fight together, and if the spirits decide, we will die together in our pursuit to eliminate this wickedness not of this earth."

Cody liked what he heard. He was more than ready. "Does this mean we're blood brothers?"

"If you say so," Pete said.

"Should we do that thing with a knife, cutting gashes in our hands and joining them, then swearing allegiance as blood spirits?" Cody questioned him.

Pete grinned. "No. We don't do that kind of thing anymore."

"Why not?" Cody asked.

"Because it hurts like hell."

Raz laughed along with his new friend. "Let's git this game started."

Before getting up to leave, Raz took one last look into the camp. "Holy shit!" he yelled.

"What? What is it?" Cody asked as the rest of the men nearby peeked down the hill. "People are exitin' the buildin's." He focused on the end building, the one Pete saw people entering from the bus that had arrived last night with shot out windows. "The guards are pushin' the captives toward a row of tables set up outside." Raz scanned the large group with his binoculars. He was looking for Cody's family.

"Let me see," Cody insisted, wanting the field glasses. Maybe Robin and the kids were there.

"Wait!" Raz searched the mob, examining each face as quickly as he could. No one looked familiar. Finally he stopped. "I see her, Cody! I see ya wife." From his perch hundreds of yards away he watched the woman with two children standing next to her.

Cody grabbed the glasses from Raz. "Where?" There were too many people in the ragged line facing away from them.

Raz pointed. "Halfway toward the tables. She has a scarf on her head, two kids with her."

"I don't see them," Cody said loudly. A second later he found them. His head was spinning. His eyes widened. His heart pumped wildly as he refocused and looked closer. The woman turned her body to the side as they moved. Cody's face suddenly went blank. "That's not her. That's not my wife."

He dropped back allowing Raz to pick up the binoculars. Raz kept searching. Everyone was looking down to the dirt or at the tables before them. Then, without notice a loud rattling of a machine gun filled the morning air. He saw the mass of prisoners dive to the ground. He moved the glasses back and forth in a frantic search of victims. Three men next to the fence fell limp.

"They just shot three prisoners. Don't know why," he relayed the action from the scene below to the other men near him.

Cody wiped his eyes. He had to hold it together.

"Wait a minute," Raz jerked. "I see a kid, a little boy. He's runnin' away from the tables. There're some open latrines in the back. Yeah. Cody, I think it's ya boy."

Raz handed the glasses to Cody who immediately sighted the young boy. "That's him! That's Jeffrey!" He watched his son rush back to the line of people who had apparently received their meals after the shooting. His son back with his mother, Cody could see Robin saying something to their daughter. A huge sense of relief overcame him. "We found them, Raz! We found them!" He grabbed his rifle and attempted to get up.

"Not so fast, sonny," Raz said as he held him back. "Ya runnin' down there ain't gonna do ya or 'em no good. We stick ta the plan."

"But…they're right there!" Cody persisted.

"Yup, and tagether we're gonna git 'em out. Trust me," Raz said as he patted his friend on his shoulder. He turned to Pete and his new brothers. "Okay, boys. It's time."

Chapter 37

Robin stirred from an uncomfortable sleep. She felt light-headed, her lips were chapped and bleeding, and her stomach had a hollow aching sensation. Her eyes were unfocused in the strange environment, her body was cold and numb, her back and legs hurt. She woke up uncertain of where she was.

The room she laid in was dark and had a distinct, over-powering odor of human bodies, unwashed and unsanitary. She brushed her nose, but the horrid smell remained. Shadows appeared all around her. She began to panic, as if waking from a nightmare attacking her groggy senses. Shades of movement nearby caused her to cringe as she heard hacking coughs, whining whimpers, and eerie moans fill the strange space.

Suddenly, reality hit her. She began to remember. She was in some sort of camp far from home, forced here by unsavory men in uniforms. Men with guns. Foreign soldiers. People had been shot and killed. That was real. Only hours earlier she had been shoved into this place with her children hanging onto her side. Her children! She looked to both sides and felt small shivering bodies nestled under her coat.

She tried to speak, but her dry mouth was void of saliva making it impossible for her voice to work. She licked her lips and swallowed a bit, then whispered in a raspy voice, "Jeffrey. Jennifer. Wake up." She gently rocked them from their needed slumber. "Wake up children."

Jeffrey woke first and jumped to his feet, startled by his mother tugging at him. He rubbed his weary eyes, and then held his stomach. "I'm really hungry, Mom." He looked around the large open room. The morning light seeping through the wood siding cracks was clearing out the shadows. "Where are we Mom?" he asked.

Robin pulled him down to her. "I don't know where we are, son. We should be having breakfast soon," she said, trying to assure him.

Jennifer woke too and began crying. She nestled her head deeper into Robin's warm coat.

Robin held her little girl tight. "What's wrong Jennifer?" she asked, combing her fingers through her daughter's tangled hair.

Jennifer continued crying. She sniffled and said, "I wet myself."

Her mother hugged her tighter. "That's okay honey. It was an accident. It's okay."

"Sorry Mommy. Don't get mad at me," Jennifer cried.

"I'm not mad at you sweetheart," Robin replied. "I could never be mad at either one of you. Both of you have been strong and very brave." She wrapped her arms around the two wishing this was a nightmare that would soon end.

"I feel scared," Jeffrey said looking at the other people near him.

"Me too," Jennifer whimpered. "I'm scared too."

Robin began crying herself. She felt helpless, vulnerable, lost. "I'm scared too. But we are together, and for right now that's all that matters."

Jeffrey stared into his mother's eyes and asked, "Is Daddy coming?"

"Yes, your Daddy is coming. We'll stay here and wait for him. Okay?"

"Okay," Jennifer said.

"Okay too," Jeffrey repeated. "But I hope he hurries."

"Me too," Robin said. "Me too."

People in the room began rising and walking about. A din of hushed voices spread through the cold building. Constant sneezes and thick coughs filled the air. A cloud of contagious sickness hung over the crowd. Children cried and old folks moaned their pains away.

Robin had to find food for her and the children. She also wanted to locate Lisa and her girls. She stood up and said to her kids, "You children stay right where you are. Don't go anyway."

"Where are you going Mama?" Jeffrey asked.

"Don't go Mama," Jennifer begged.

"I'm only going to talk to some people here. I'll find out when we eat. You'll see me every step. Okay?"

"Please Mama!" the little girl pleaded.

"It's okay," Jeffrey said. "I'll take care of her."

"Thank you Jeffrey. You're acting like a young man."

Jeffrey smiled and turned to his sister. "You hear Mom? I'm the boss of you."

"I'll be right back," Robin reminded them.

She moved along the lengthy wall of the structure making out hundreds of bodies lying on the floor. She tripped over outstretched legs and stumbled into groups still prone on the wood floor, apologizing each time. She found a familiar face in the massive crowd and approached a man who had been in the front of her bus. He was part of the group who attacked the soldier and was lucky enough to survive the shooting.

"Hello, do you remember me?" she asked the gentleman. "We were on the bus together."

The man nodded without saying a word. He was too tired and drained to respond.

"Do you know if there's any food?" she asked.

He simply shrugged his covered shoulders, a sense of defeat on his face.

Robin looked back at her children as she moved on. The room had to be two hundred feet long and a hundred feet wide, but nearly every square foot was occupied. She recognized several more people who appeared scared and confused. It was clear none of them knew what was happening.

Robin continued to work her way through the mass of humanity asking questions, searching for her friend, seeking answers, wondering if food or water were available, wondering what was next. She asked dozens of people the same questions, receiving the same blank stares and non-answers each time.

She noticed no one had blankets or bedding. In fact, there were no beds, no chairs, no furnishings at all in the building. There also were no bathrooms or private areas. She didn't see any kitchen section, no place to prepare food, no place to eat. Worse of all, there was no heat in the place. Basically, the structure was just a huge shell of a prison functioning strictly as a holding cell for the detainees.

The place had no real windows either. The few openings were covered with primitive shutters to keep the cold from blowing inside. Robin opened one of the shutters a bit to look out. She saw several guards walking along the dirt road between buildings. They were smoking cigarettes and laughing as they passed.

Robin moved to return to her children. "They feed us at six," a man hidden in the shadows of the crowd spoke up. "And again at six in the evening."

"Oh," Robin said, happy to have someone's help. She introduced herself. His name was Joseph. "Inside or outside?" she wanted to know.

"Only been here a day," Joseph explained. "Most of us were transported here early yesterday morning. We were the first group they caught from Tucson. Then your group came in last night. Anyway, that's when we ate yesterday. Nothing to write home about. They line us outside for the slop of the day." He held back a muffled laugh.

Robin was pleased to know they would soon eat. But she had one more urgent question. "Where are the bathrooms?"

Joseph grinned. "They're outside too, opposite the food line. Not real bathrooms, but that's what we got."

Robin shot a smile at Joseph. "Thank you for talking with me. Maybe I'll see you later."

"Same to you, ma'am," Joseph said gracefully. "Oh, one more thing Robin. Do exactly as they tell you. And don't ask them any questions."

"Why not?" she naturally asked.

"Because the guards answer all questions with their guns. I watched it happen too many times yesterday. Lost about thirty people."

Robin stopped. "Oh. Thank you." She returned to her children and thought about what Joseph had just told her. She checked her watch. It was almost six o'clock, time to eat. Five more minutes went by. People who knew, were getting restless, waiting for the word to get into the food line.

The front door suddenly slammed open causing each person inside to look. He was a huge guard wearing battle gear and a rifle held high. "Out, out, out!" he yelled in a thick Russian accent. Everyone rose, ready to shuffle outside. All except for those poor souls who didn't survive the night. Those without their medication, the sick, the aged, the hurt, were the first to succumb to the cold and brutal treatment. Dozens of limp, pale bodies lay lifeless on the floor. Some of their husbands or wives, parents or children, friends or just good Samaritans, stayed with the departed.

"Out, out, out!" the soldier shouted again. There had to be a thousand people standing in the structure, maybe double that. It was impossible to count. Ragged, cold, hungry, sick. Scared. They slowly edged their way out the door into the dreary morning light. The brittle air hit them hard. Several other guards yelled and shoved the prisoners into a sorry line.

Those who had been delivered yesterday remembered the routine. Pick up two metal cups from makeshift tables in the middle of the compound yard, stay in line, move toe to heel without saying a word. Dip one cup into a huge metal pot containing some sort of cold watery rice soup, then dip the second cup into a water bucket. Keep moving until you either find a spot outside to eat or return to the building away from the wind.

Some people couldn't wait, so they ran to the toilet holes. Several men simply leaned against the fence and defiantly pissed through the chain link onto the sentry road. A tower guard saw the men, manned his mounted machine gun and fired the six-hundred rounds per minute weapon. The men dropped immediately, slumping against the fence, their privates still exposed to the elements.

Everyone in line ducked as the shots were fired. Hearing the short screams of the dying men they stayed down until the noise dispersed.

With heads low, the hungry prisoners proceeded through the line hoping they wouldn't be shot in the back.

Robin held on to her children as they gradually made their way to the tables. They filled their cups the best they could as they were rushed forward.

"I have to go pee," Jeffrey told his mother.

"Not now," his mother whispered.

"But I have to go real bad."

Robin took the rice and water cups from her son. "Hurry up," she said to him as he dashed off toward the line of nasty holes in the ground.

When he ran back Robin asked Jennifer if she had to go too. "No Mommy," she said. She had to go, but she was too afraid to use those toilets. There was no place to sit.

Most of the captives carried their cups and moved inside to find a spot on the floor. Joseph, the man who had spoken to Robin earlier, walked by her and her children. "Told you it was nothing to write home about," he said, referring to the terrible meal.

She offered a small smile and nodded.

"Later they'll be taking people out in groups to process them," Joseph said, like he was an authority on camp procedures. "They'll get your information, give you a number, and an arm band. Don't give them any crucial information. If they think you know something or someone important, they'll interrogate you, maybe torture you until you tell them. Lot of the people didn't come back yesterday."

"What kind of information?" Robin asked. She didn't know any secrets. She didn't have anything important to hide. She was a housewife married to a college teacher. She knew nothing they needed. There was no reason to hurt her or her kids.

Joseph went to his spot and said, "I'm just telling you for your own good. Stay silent."

Robin and her children sat down and leaned against the inside wall. They ate their food, which was horrible tasting, and drank their small portions of water. Robin, like all the other prisoners sat talking quietly, wondering what would happen to them next.

Chapter 38

The President and General Wells were discussing the Chinese-Russian situation. China was promised the western half of the country for its role in activating the EMP. In return, the three trillion dollar debt owed to the Chinese would be dismissed. The Russians were promised trillions of dollars for their part in helping the new American government take over the country under martial law and further the agenda of those in charge.

Neither side could be trusted to be satisfied with their take. They both would want more. Lots more. And with the country in a weak defensive position for some time into the future, China and Russia had a distinct military advantage. The President wasn't a stupid man, however. There was no way in hell he was going to allow those commie bastards to stay on American soil. He would string them along as much as possible until the final blow was absolutely necessary. In the meantime, he and his closest advisors would make certain their plans were ready.

There was a knock on the President's door and the Deputy of the NSA entered. "Excuse me Mr. President. You wanted to review a few things with me. Is this a good time?"

"Perfect timing, Mr. Deputy," the President said. "Please come in so we can talk."

"Thank you sir."

The President spoke. "General Wells will be sitting in with us also."

The Deputy offered a polite bow to the Secretary of National Defense. He took a seat next to the General.

"You have something to tell me," the President said.

"Yes. We have several developing concerns. The least of all are the pockets of domestic insurgents in various locations throughout the nation, as General Clayton had indicated. These are small units of loyal, old regime soldiers, veterans' groups, a few rebellious mobs of older men." He hinted at a laugh. "The old guys call themselves 'DOM.' Dangerous Old Men. But I assure you that none of them are very serious threats to us or our plan."

The President and General snickered at the acronym. *Dangerous old men, my ass,* the General thought.

"A few sole renegades are out there trying to gather a force, cause trouble, slow us down. But these people have no communication network, no means of transportation, no strategic planning. They're just insignificant nobodies trying to be heroes. I've been told by the Military Operations Commander that he has these loose ends well under control, Mr. President," the Deputy reported.

"But these people, these supposed patriots and DOMs, they have weapons. Do they not?" the President asked.

"Yes sir, some."

The President looked across his desk at General Wells, then back at the Deputy. "I told everyone in the briefing I wanted these 'loose ends' dealt with immediately."

General Wells interjected. "I assure you, Mr. President, that these traitors will be dead and done with shortly."

"Thank you General. I will hold you to that. Now, Mr. Deputy, what about the foreign issues?"

"These are more pressing matters, sir. Our intelligence shows that both the Chinese and Russian military forces are preparing for a full out war on several fronts. Their air, ground, and naval forces are on full alert. Twelve Chinese infantry, tank, and armored brigades are forming along the North Korean border. We have undeniable proof through our intelligence networks that the Chinese have moved KN-08 medium-range mobile missiles near South Korea. Hundreds of Chinese warships have been ordered to the East China Sea. It appears they may attempt to control the waters around South Korea and perhaps as far as Japan.

"To the west, at least five Chinese armed divisions have been mobilized along the Indian border up to Afghanistan. Only two of their nuclear subs remain in the Gulf of Mexico while the rest of their subs are heading toward our west coast. It appears they are preparing to take on two fronts. One against the U.S. and one against the Russians." The Deputy seemed extremely nervous. These weren't trial war games.

"The Chinese long-range nuclear warheads are ready to launch once their leaders feel we are completely helpless. Although our intercontinental ballistic missiles are operational, the Chinese are waiting for an opportune time to launch. Our operatives in the Middle East have also confirmed that China is sending long-range nuclear weapons to their allies in Iran. You know what that means, sir. Israel is nervous as hell."

The President listened intently. This was nothing new to him. In fact, he had expected every Chinese move. Like a deadly chess game he was several steps ahead of his worldly opponents. He was willing to lose some of his pieces, particularly his pawns, in order to win in checkmate.

The Deputy turned to the issues with Russia. "The Russians, too, are on high alert. They already have mobilized upward to five-hundred thousand troops who are stationed along their entire western boundaries. They appear to be ready to drive into Kazakhstan down to Georgia up through Ukraine, and possibly into northern Europe. No doubt they are employing their tactical advantage due to America's problems.

"The Russian President has ordered aircraft carriers and battleships to secure ports on the Caspian and Black Seas. Eight of their advanced nuclear submarines are pushing across the Atlantic toward our east coast. They already have several subs in the Gulf and within sight of California. They apparently have decided to set forth their entire strategic nuclear arsenal. We are in one hell of a predicament, if I may say so, Mr. President."

"It appears so," the President said, seemingly not too concerned.

The Deputy had more to report. "Fortunately, China and Russia both want the entire spoils of war. Each country is waiting for the right time to make their move. The consensus is that both countries are determined to wipe out the other, along with America, in an attempt to be the sole king of the hill. So it may be possible to pit the two countries against one another.

Although they have similar political philosophies and agendas, they are still mortal enemies and will, as witnessed before, refuse to work together for the benefit of both. I believe that is our one advantage we have, sir."

"Point well taken," the President added. "But we have that covered."

General Wells gave a serious nod of agreement to the President.

"Have our troops abroad been ordered to return home?" the President asked the NSA Deputy.

"Yes sir. Our forces from Europe, the Middle East, and Asia, including our fleets in the Pacific, North Atlantic, and the Mediterranean, have been recalled. We will have a whole new military force of over 350,000 soldiers and sailors outraged at the attack on their homeland. They will follow you to their deaths sir, to further protect their families and country from the supposed communist aggressors. Within the next few days we will have one hell of an angry force ready and willing to take out the Chinese and Russians."

The President locked his fingers together and rested them on his chin as if to mull over the scenario. "Excellent work. Now we continue going forward with our plan and wait for our men to come home."

The chief executive rose from his seat. "Thank you gentlemen. We shall talk soon."

General Wells and the NSA Deputy left the room. The President sat in his comfortable chair and savored being alone with his thoughts of becoming the supreme global leader.

Chapter 39

The men crawled down from the steep hill and assembled at their trucks. They checked their watches. It was nearing seven A.M. According to Pete a new shift of guards would come on duty at seven. The team wanted to gain entrance to the camp before the new guards arrived. The night shift would be tired and inattentive, eager to get out of the cold, so now was the ideal time to hit.

"Good luck brothers," Pete said to Cody and Raz.

"Won't need no luck if we all follow the plan," Raz grunted.

Their weapons were primed, their vehicles set, their will to fight on the edge. Raz drove the Humvee with Cody riding shotgun. Pete and his brothers took their pickups and went to the far side of the concentration camp staying out of sight behind the hills. The rest of their army, the two hundred armed Pascua Indians, disappeared into the desert and hills. Everyone had a special job to do.

After getting their meager breakfast the majority of the detainees had returned to their buildings where it was a bit warmer than outside. Some stayed in the yard, smoking their last cigarettes, complaining about everything, consoling each other, pacing the length of the fenced compound like trapped animals. Dozens were waiting to use the latrine holes while others hurriedly took care of their business at the primitive facilities.

Guards were walking adjacent to the double fence with no sense of danger from the locked-up prisoners. The lack of urgency was evident in their casual manner. The complex was very quiet considering it held tens of thousands of kidnapped citizens. Raz heard heavy equipment running beyond the buildings outside the fenced perimeter. Backhoes working on those tremendous holes, he guessed.

Raz turned onto the dirt road leading straight into the camp from the south side. He drove slowly toward the sentry shack as if he belonged there. Right now he figured he did. Attacking in plain view. It was a tactic often used in such circumstances. The big green Army Humvee would throw the guards off long enough for it to get real close to them. Worked before with those cockroaches near the border, Raz recalled. He was sure it would work again.

He looked over at Cody. The young man would do anything for his family. He would give his life to save the ones he loved from those evil bastards running the camp. Raz knew that. He admired the boy. Cody reminded Raz of the soldiers he had worked and fought with. They would do anything for their families and country too.

The kid had changed over the past day. It was hard to believe that all this crap began just yesterday. Cody had learned there really are bad guys out there. There were too many of them and they were everywhere. Even in your own backyard. The kid hadn't seen enough death and dishonesty and deception in his short life to realize what lives beyond the night's door. He was an innocent school teacher who hadn't learned to hate yet.

Raz kept thinking, as he approached the guards with their hands held up signaling to stop. Cody hadn't learned to hate like the Pascuas who were helping them. They had earned that right. He had never had his possessions stolen from him. He had never been confined under the control of sick bastards. He had never been stripped of his human rights and dignity because he was different from the rest. Up until this journey, he had never been in a life or death situation.

What Cody was about to encounter would change all that. In the next few minutes he would see how the world really was, with its psychopaths and freaks and egomaniacs and paid mercenaries and greedy assholes.

These things Raz knew too well.

Raz hated the wickedness around him even more than his Indian friends, if that were possible. He hated national leaders who create false flag threats, bogus disasters, phony terrorist attacks, fake national defense breaches, all just to scare a fragile population into easy submission. He hated a government that fabricates wars to enrich close business associates, politically connected contractors, and wealthy bankers who generously contribute to the right candidates. He hated a ruling class who kills young men and women under the pretense of national security and weeps phony tears at their funerals for the cameras.

He hated everything there was to hate when his only son Jason was slaughtered on the battlefield in foreign sands, all in the name of oil contracts and big business. He despised those who were responsible for his dear wife dying from cancer at a much too early age. All under the pretense of prohibitive medical costs, while billions of dollars were given away like candy to foreign countries who loathed the United States.

Hatred drives people to correct the wrongs they have seen and endured. It grows into a fierce need for revenge and festers into a monster eating from within. It motivates a person to do crazy, sometimes stupid, illogical things. It also kills people inside. Raz felt bad that Cody would learn to hate as much as he had.

But it was his turn.

He stopped at the guard shack and watched the sentries move to each side of the vehicle. It was déjà vu all over again. Predictability and routine were deadly in the game of vengeance.

"What you want?" the small Chinese man said impatiently. He had only ten minutes left at his station. This American weather was worst than back home.

Raz didn't answer. He was waiting.

"Where you go?" the guard yelled. The Humvee proved to be an open invitation to the camp, but an old bearded guy and young man out of uniform was unusual, suspicious. Who the hell were these guys bothering him at the end of his miserable shift?

Raz turned toward Cody. They had their pistols cocked and ready to shoot, but they didn't want to create a scene and alert the rest of the guards. Not now, anyway. It was too soon. Raz simply smiled at the Chinaman, buying time. *Where the fuck are they?* He thought, wondering when Pete's men would join in. Two more seconds and he would have to shoot. He gripped his gun and began to pull it from his side.

He couldn't wait any longer. The guard was about to say something when both Raz and Cody heard a high speed sound sailing through the air.

Whoosh!

Then a second one.

Whoosh!

The guard's beady eyes went wide, as if his pupils had been transformed into orbs of hardened, shiny black glass. He stood still for a moment, not looking at the old man in the military vehicle. Instead, for an instant he looked down at his chest, a surge of blood spurting through his winter jacket. The guard fell backwards onto the road, his rifle dropped and clattered to the ground. A feathered arrow shaft was deep in his back, its razor sharp tip protruding through his chest.

Cody's guard had the same surprised reaction, except an arrow had pierced his neck, front to back, not exiting all the way through. Raz looked up at the nearest tower guard expecting movement. The guard's body slumped over the wood railings, a victim of the same silent killer.

"Guess that means it's okay to go in," Raz grinned.

Two more guards up ahead were on the ground, lifeless. The Indians were busy and accurate.

Cody said, "Must be some of Pete's people who can't handle a rifle."

"Damn good with 'em bows," Raz commented.

"Thank God," Cody added.

"Nah," Raz said. "Thank the Pascuas."

Robin's building was a hundred feet farther up the road. Raz drove slowly forward. Look normal. Cody kept an eye out for more guards. The next tower was empty. A body was sprawled out at the base of the wooden lookout. Two more contorted bodies lined the road nearby. Cody saw people mingling in the yard surrounding building number one. No one had any idea what was happening. That was good.

Everything so far was working as planned.

Except for one unexpected turn.

Hundreds of yards ahead Raz saw a bunch of uniformed soldiers exiting the guard residence and getting into two troop carriers. It was time to change shifts.

Raz hoped Pete and his warriors were ready.

Chapter 40

T he truckloads of day shift guards were about to leave for the far ends of the compound. Once they found their dead comrades an alarm would sound. There would no doubt be some confusion about the arrows in the bodies, but all hell would break loose as the battle began.

Raz stepped on the brake. It was five minutes before seven. Why weren't the troop carriers moving?

He looked through his binoculars, then stopped to think. Pete's men were supposed to shoot every guard during the transfer. During that short fleeting moment when most of the enemy in the entire camp were out in the open, vulnerable. Two hundred guards, two hundred Indians. Pretty good odds. The sides were fairly matched, but the Indians had the element of surprise.

The Pascuas would shoot, with a gun or apparently with arrows, every troop at the sentry points. Every tower sentinel would be taken down as they left the machine guns unmanned. Every soldier watching the captive compounds would be killed. Every man checking the fences would be laid out. Every guard patrolling the road would be dropped. Every enemy leaving the men's quarters would be stopped. Every specialist exiting the interrogation building would be terminated. Every officer from their separate residences would be executed.

Every single one of these son-of-a-bitches was supposed to be dead in the next ten minutes. That's what was supposed to happen if everything went as planned, which it rarely did. That's what Raz was thinking about.

Cody picked up the field glasses and watched nothing happening with the trucks. He heard a faint sound and scanned up toward the third tower. Two arrows had struck the guard, center chest, causing the man to shriek and tumble off the platform backwards onto the razor fencing below. His limp body caught on the coiled wire making it dangle like a bloody rag doll. Cody looked to the hill tops and saw no one.

"Did you see that?" Cody asked.

"Yup," Raz said. He was not too concerned with the guard. "Keep ya eyes on 'em trucks. Somethin's up."

Cody re-focused. He was worried about other soldiers seeing the dead guard hanging in mid air.

"It don't make no sense," Raz grumbled. He drove forward ever so slowly trying not to attract attention.

"A bus just turned in," Cody said. It came in from the southern route. "Here comes another one."

Raz could see the buses too, but not as clearly from this distance.

"There's three more. Wait! Four more!" Cody added. "Why would they park there, near the guards' quarters?"

Raz considered the move. It was odd to see the buses not simply roll up to the prisoner buildings to drop off their catch.

"Oh, oh!" Cody uttered.

"What?"

"I see soldiers getting off the first bus," Cody explained.

"There's always gonna be guards on 'em buses," Raz reasoned.

"Yeah, but...."

"But what?" Raz asked, getting irritated.

"There's no people on the buses. I mean no prisoners."

"What the hell ya talkin' 'bout?" Raz said. "Give me 'em glasses." He checked the out of place transports. "Ya right, sonny. Mmm. Nothin' but soldiers comin' out."

Cody ran a quick mental process. Six buses, fifty or so men per. "Holy shit! Must be close to three hundred troops there."

"Reckon ya right."

"But why?" Cody was baffled.

Raz had to contemplate the situation. He knew military tactics. He understood warfare strategies. Move troops from cleared targets to strengthen more critical positions. Mobilize forces from captured and secured regions to troubled spots. Be mobile, be fluid. Stay ahead of the enemy. Defeat and advance. Attack and destroy.

"They're throwin' duffel bags from the buses," Raz mentioned. "They're gonna settle in, is my guess."

Cody was confused. "Makes no sense to have that many soldiers to cover this place."

"They come in from the south," Raz stated. "I figure they're from our neck of the woods. Probably took care of most of the population down there. They were damn busy, weren't they? No need for that many troops ta clean up. I'll betcha they're holdin' up here for the night, then headin' north ta the big cities. Tucson. Phoenix."

Cody shook his head. "Well, hell. We have to hurry."

More prisoners began exiting their buildings wondering what the noise was coming from across the complex. Loud motor engines, a mix of voices, things being thrown around. Within the fences word was spreading about the dead guards. Some of the captives began screaming and shouting, excited about the killings. Rescuers were there to help them, to bring them home. Finally, this horrendous ordeal was about to come to an end. It was past seven o'clock. There were no day shift guards, but a shit load of them were across the road in large numbers.

In minutes the buildings emptied into the yards. Hoards of prisoners crowded the fences, yelling for help, creating a raucous uproar. They saw Raz's Humvee on the road. Two white guys, obviously not guards. They were there to release the detainees. Freedom was moments away.

The yards turned exuberant with cheerful captives.

"USA!"

"USA!"

"USA!"

The chants grew louder as more people gathered in the open spaces, rattled the fences, cheered at the sight of the guards with the arrows in their bodies. Men spit through the fences onto the nearest dead captors. One man pissed on a dead man's corpse. Women held their children's heads away from the gruesome sights. A few weaker people threw up their rice swill breakfast.

"Oh shit, Raz! The trucks are moving. One turned right to the end of the camp while the other turned left heading our way." The men had maybe a minute, two tops, to find Robin and the kids before the soldiers drew closer and discovered their dead comrades.

It was impossible for Raz to drive forward. He would run into the guard truck up ahead. The road was too narrow to turn around on. The only avenue out was to back up to the unmanned sentry shack where the road widened.

"Cody," Raz began, "we have less than a minute. Find ya family. Now!"

Cody jumped from the vehicle and ran to the first prisoner building. Almost two thousand terrified and excited detainees mobbed the fence gate. Faces of all ages looked at the lone man running toward them, hoping to be saved.

"Robin! Robin Gordon!" her husband screamed.

"Robin, Jeffrey, Jennifer!" he yelled as he grabbed the chain link and searched inside. Time was running out. The shift truck moved closer, dropping off and picking up guards along the way. In seconds the truck would reach the third tower, close enough to see the guard hanging on the fence.

No familiar faces looked back at him. The clamor was growing louder as Cody rushed past the wild horde. He kept calling his wife's name, but there was no answer.

Raz stuck his head out the window. "Cody! We need ta go. Cody, git back in here. They're comin'."

Cody barely heard Raz, but he didn't care. He was so close to his family. One more minute and he would find them. A few more seconds and his wife and children would be safe and leaving this god-forsaken place. The crowd was growing even louder, the truck inching closer.

Five seconds more, that's all he needed. Please God.

Raz sped up to Cody. "Get ya ass in here right now ya damn fool or we're all dead."

The guard on the next tower saw the agitated crowd two buildings away. An Army vehicle was chasing a man running down the road. Uniformed bodies littered the ground. He threw himself against the mounted 50 caliber Browning and turned it toward the Humvee. He ordered something in Russian and began shooting. The shots ripped holes in the road in front of the vehicle. Bullets ricocheted off the thin armor. Several rounds plugged two inch holes through the windshield. Raz ducked, unharmed.

"Git the fuck in!" he shouted an order to his friend. Cody spread-eagled against the fence trying to avoid the spraying gunshots. He couldn't find his family. He knew he had to run back.

He dashed back to the Humvee. Raz was already backing it out. The guards in the approaching truck tumbled out the back, hugged close to the vehicle and started shooting toward the invaders. The machine gunner didn't let up on his shelling. He poured all he had into the impenetrable Humvee.

Zigging back to Raz, Cody was in the open a second too long. He reluctantly glanced back at the mob of captives, still looking for his family. Bad decision. His left shoulder caught a red hot round, tearing away a chunk of flesh and shredded jacket. The impact slammed him into the ground. He fell on his back, blood gushing from his wound. All he could see was gray sky. Above the noise of the blasting gunfire, the yelling from the guards, the racket from the inmates, he heard Raz calling him. His mind went blank and his eyes closed tight, as if to stop the piercing pain.

Cody tried to shake off the dizziness, but he was disoriented. He turned and found the Humvee. It was forty feet away. Could he reach it? He pulled himself up by grabbing the fence. Holding his shoulder he crawled toward Raz. There was no protection, no place to take refuge. Another shot ripped into his side, knocking him down again in twisted agony. He felt the cold earth and tasted dirt. Bullets pelted the ground around him. He heard high pitched screaming. It sounded like his wife Robin crying to him, calling his name.

And then Cody passed out, lying motionless in the middle of the narrow road, a perfect target for the pack of angry, hostile guards quickly moving in.

Raz watched his friend go down. He saw the young man, his new son, dead in a spreading pool of blood. Bullets kept pinging off the vehicle. Raz saw Cody roll slightly to his side. The young man was still alive. He had to get to him. He had to save his dying friend.

The enemy assault was relentless. A shower of bullets kept the Humvee separated from Cody. Raz heard gun fire from the hill tops, but it failed to stop the soldiers' onslaught. *No one left behind,* Raz kept thinking, a truth all soldiers carry with them into the battleground.

No one.

Raz opened his door, using it as a shield from the assault. "Cody! Cody!" he shouted. But there was no response. A man his age should not be able to move as quickly as he did, but Raz reached his friend. He struggled to lift his buddy and carried him to the Humvee. He opened the back passenger door, shoved loose cases and duffels to the floor, then lifted Cody's body onto the seat. The side windows were blasted out from the shooting barrage.

Glass shattered around him. Bullets whizzed past him. One hit his pants without grazing his leg. A second sliced through his sleeve and drew blood, but not nearly enough to stop the man. Raz ignored the cut. He hopped into the driver's seat and kicked the gas pedal to the floor watching the speeding dirt road through the rearview mirror.

Hundreds of soldiers from the new buses ran in mixed formations toward the war zone. A hundred arrows soared silently through the air from behind the hills, at least half of them hitting their intended targets. Soldiers turned and tried to hide from the invisible wave of death. But there was no place to hide and nothing to shoot back at. Gun shots rang from the rocks above as more guards fell by the dozens. Volleys of rifle fire and streams of arrows ravaged the unprotected troops.

The prisoners scrambled back into the safety of their prisons as the battle raged on, stumbling over each other as they attempted to save themselves. The machine gunner and his fellow tower guards dropped as their hearts exploded from unending flurries of arrow shafts.

Raz raced in reverse through the checkpoint, yanked the steering wheel, and pulled forward. He had to get out of range, but most importantly he had to save Cody.

Chapter 41

From their higher vantage point the remaining tower guards could see Pete's men pop up over the ridges as they fired into the camp, picking off the uniforms one by one with their rifles or in tight clusters with their simple, but true, bows and arrows. Groups of ten or twenty Indians marked with their thick war paint briefly rose from the rocks at different spots to shoot into the valley of guards.

The enemy machine guns heartlessly tore into the hilly peaks decimating the archers and riflemen. Casualties quickly mounted on both sides, but the machine guns held the advantage and cut the Pascuas to pieces. The momentum of the battle suddenly favored the uniformed troopers.

Pete lowered his rifle. He had watched too many of his people shot dead or wounded. With the arrival of the unexpected soldiers, they were far outnumbered and out-powered. He would fight to the end just as his men would, but now, with too many killed or dying friends surrounding him, he decided to regroup. The Pascuas desperately wanted to defeat the soldiers who had blatantly taken their land, but not at the cost of wiping out every warrior in the tribe.

There had to be a better way to fight.

At his signal, Pete's men retreated from the hills. They drew back from the camp, helping or carrying their wounded and assembled on the far side of the wash where the road had been dug out. Many of the standing Pascuas were bleeding, limping from their injuries, shot or cut up from the sharp rocks blasted into them. There was still a burning fight in their eyes and a readiness to attack the camp head on. But the raw truth was in the numbers. Of the two hundred warriors, sixty had been killed, and close to that number wounded.

Pete spoke to his fearless followers. "Men, you have cut into the enemy's forces. You have fought a brave fight and have shown the evil white men your skills in battle. We have lost many brothers today, but we will avenge those who fire upon us and hold the captive families of our friends. Every one of you should be proud for your display of courage against an overwhelming army. Your ancestors are proud of you. And today I am proud to be a Pascua Yaqui by your side."

His men yelled an Indian chant and held their weapons high in defiance against their foe. They would return into the heat of battle and finish the job they had come here to do. Every warrior waited to hear more from their chief.

"We shall care for our wounded and prepare our weapons once again," Pete said. "Be ready, my brothers. We shall soon engage our enemies, and this time we shall be triumphant."

Pete walked to his pickup truck. He needed to come up with a plan, one which would not inflict such damage to his tribe. He refused to accept defeat, but for the moment he could not figure out how to engage their considerable opponent.

Raz emerged from the wash driving the Humvee up the sandy bank like a mad man. He braked short of the Indian gathering. "We need a doctor here!" he shouted to the group.

Halfway en route he had stopped to see how Cody was doing. The young man was alive, moaning from the deep pain, but he had lost much blood. From the aid kit Raz put a compress bandage on Cody's wounded side. It helped to slow the bleeding, but that would not last very long. He then dressed Cody's mangled shoulder with yards of gauze and medical tape. He gave his friend a quick shot of pain killer to lessen the throbbing. It would relax the man as well. Cody was alive, but he was in bad shape.

"My family…" Cody had muttered. "Where's…my family?"

"Ya just stay still. Hear me?" Raz told him. The old man had never been scared in his life. Today was different.

"But…."

"But hell!" Raz said. "Ya can't help no one if ya dead. I need ta git ya ta a doctor or somethin'."

Raz had given Cody a few sips of water and covered him with his jacket. From the camp it had taken over fifteen minutes to reach Pete and his men, during which time Cody had slid into a state of unconsciousness.

Several of the Pascuas jumped into action when they saw Cody. They gently moved him from the Humvee and put him into the back of one of the old king cab pickups. Three men, still in their war paint, rode with the wounded white man toward the Indian village.

"Don't worry," Pete assured Raz. "We have people who can take care of your friend."

"He needs a real doctor, not a damn witch doctor!" Raz growled. "I want that boy ta live, ya hear me?"

Pete gave Raz a stern glare. "He'll be okay. And we don't have witch doctors. We have healers."

Raz grumbled without saying a word.

Pete saw the blood on Raz's sleeve. "You okay, old man?" he asked.

Raz had forgotten about the cut. He touched it and grimaced. "Ain't nothin'."

The chief called one of his men over. "Take care of this senior citizen," he told the man with a smile. "And get him a jacket."

"I'll be back in a few minutes," Raz said to Pete as he trailed behind the young Indian. "We have lots ta figure out."

And they did have lots to figure out.

The element of surprise against the camp's security was gone. The Indian forces were halved, though surprisingly, their sense of determination seemed even stronger. Cody was out of the picture. The guards were royally pissed off and could turn their anger on the prisoners. If that happened there would be a massacre. Things were going badly. Twice as many soldiers were in the camp than before. Robin and the kids weren't found. Were they in the last building? And if so, why didn't they run to Cody? Why didn't they call back to him? And where was Nick's family?

The biggest question for Raz and Pete now was, how were they going to get back into the camp and then get out again?

"God-damn son-of-a-bitchin' bastards!" Raz shouted to no one in general as a young Indian woman in the village tended to his minor arm injury. She cleaned the laceration and applied a generous handful of some smelly natural cactus ointment directly on the cut. Using a clean piece of white cloth she gently wrapped his wounded arm, tying the ends together to secure the makeshift bandage.

"That crap smells like year old dead fish," Raz said, as the girl cared for him. He smiled at the pretty nurse.

She smiled back at the old geezer, thinking he smelled worse than the medicine. "Stop complaining. You sound like my baby brother," she sternly told him. "It's good for you."

Raz wasn't used to a female talking back to him like that, least of all a little Indian girl. "Just sayin'," he added sullenly.

"Well, you keep that on your arm. You understand me?" the girl admonished him.

Raz stared at the black haired woman. He would have laughed if the whole friggin' thing wasn't so serious. He moved his arm in a small circle. It felt better already. "Damn good job, sister."

The girl stood up, collecting her medical aids. "First, I'm not your sister. Second, you do as I say," she said like a mother hen hovering over a sick chick.

Raz decided to let it go. "Yes, ma'am," he answered. *These Pascua Indians are tough cookies,* he thought to himself. He quickly rose and headed back to Pete, ready to fight the less intimidating camp soldiers.

Pete, his brothers, and Raz sat in the running Humvee with the heat cranked up. They were pooling their brainpower to come up with a strategy to attack the concentration camp. Bottles of water were passed around.

Raz began. "So what ya boys thinkin'?"

"You ever hear the story of Yaqui Creek and the Circle of Fear?" Pete asked the white man.

"Can't say that I have," Raz grunted.

"It's about our brave ancestors hundreds of years before we were born, working together to run invaders off our lands," Pete began explaining.

"This ain't no time for ancient history lessons or fairy tales ta scare little kids," Raz insisted.

Pete paid no attention to Raz's comments.

"In the 1500s the Spanish army was moving north through Mexico into territories now known as the southwestern regions of America. It was Yaqui land, sacred and protected by our early grandfathers. The Spaniards were in search of legendary deposits of gold as never seen by mankind. The Seven Cities of Cibola. I'm sure a smart guy like you knows about that."

"Yeah, yeah. I heard that myth," Raz said, shaking his head.

"It's not a myth. It's not what you call a fairy tale either," Pete continued. "It's true. The Cities of Cibola did exist and the Spanish wanted to find them. For many years they searched and took land that wasn't theirs. They burned villages and tortured my people trying to get to the gold. They enslaved and killed the native inhabitants. They sent more soldiers, more guns, and more explorers. They only wanted the gold and nothing else mattered. Nothing or no one could stop their advance."

Raz grew quickly impatient. "Great. How the hell is that gonna help us?"

"Please listen, my friend," Pete said calmly. "My Yaqui ancestors were nearly wiped out by the swords and guns and diseases of these greedy white men. Until the battle at Yaqui Creek."

"Okay," Raz said, trying to keep peace. "Tell me."

Pete told the story. "After years of fighting, most of the Yaqui warriors had been killed or captured by the Spaniards. The soldiers kept searching for the treasures of gold, vast cities with walls made of pure gold, so they believed. One spring they made camp in a small valley fed by a mountain creek. Yaqui Creek. Eight hundred soldiers stayed there and used the camp as a jumping off point to search other nearby regions. It was surrounded by small hills to the south and taller mountains to the north. A safe place to hold up in. Or so they thought."

Pete's brothers in the back seat remained quiet, listening to the tale as if it was the first time they heard it.

"The soldiers' guns outmatched our peoples' primitive weapons and our smaller force. Not much different than what happened to us today," Pete recalled.

"So what the hell happened back then?" Raz asked. They were wasting time.

"If the Yaquis attacked head on they would be slaughtered. If they stood ground on the hills they would be picked off by the soldiers. There was no way to fight without losing, no possible way to win against such a large army. But," Pete stopped for a second, "a young warrior came up with a plan to defeat the Spaniards."

"Now ya got my attention," Raz commented.

"The handful of Yaqui men with their spears and bows 'surrounded' the camp on the hill tops. A scout had been sent back to their village with an urgent message. Every member of the tribe was to go to the hills above the camp. It took a full day for over two thousand Yaqui Indians, made up of old men, the sickly, women, and even youngsters, to travel to be with their men on the ridges of those hills and mountains," Pete said.

"How could they possibly help?" Raz wanted to know.

Pete smile. He liked this part of the story.

"The soldiers were ready to finish off the remaining warriors once they showed themselves. But, the young warrior, the one with a plan, had his people spread around the hillsides just out of sight from the camp below. When it was time, every Yaqui tribe member lifted a spear or a bow just enough so the soldiers below could see the weapons without seeing the old men, women, and children holding them. It became a huge circle of Yaqui weapons on the peaks ready to fire down upon the soldiers followed with loud chants of war. It must have been quite a sight for the Spaniards.

"Seeing so many weapons the soldiers believed they were vastly outnumbered. From around the high circle our armed warriors kept shooting and killing the frightened Spanish invaders. Large numbers of Spaniards were killed. Some Yaquis too. After a long, fearsome night of waiting, the soldiers packed up most of their gear and left the camp the next morning. Eight hundred armed troops against a few Indian fighters and a village of people. The Circle of Fear," Pete ended.

"Pretty damn impressive, if ya ask me," Raz said.

Pete nodded. "That young man who saved his people later became the chief of the Yaqui Nation. He was called Chief Running Creek. He was my ancestor."

Raz looked at Pete. These were not only strong and brave people, but they were smart too. "What ever happened ta the soldiers that got run out?"

Pete offered a grin. "They didn't get too far."

"What 'bout the gold?"

"Still where it belongs," Pete said.

Raz chuckled. "I think we have a plan, boys."

Chapter 42

During the shootout between the camp guards and the men trying to rescue the prisoners, the captives stampeded back into their buildings. They had seen the dead guards pierced with arrows. Who in the world would attempt to overrun the camp by shooting arrows? Sure, many guards were killed in the attack, and that was a good thing. But the mystery liberators had been beaten back, run off into the desert.

Some of the prisoners were afraid the remaining guards would turn ugly and pull them into the yards looking for information. Or maybe they would simply go on a killing spree, taking out their rage on the innocent and unarmed hostages. Security personnel would want to know who attempted the failed rescue. And they'd want to find out quickly. People were terrified of what might come next.

Everyone inside huddled against the walls and each other. No one spoke for fear they would be heard and singled out. Women and children were crying after watching gruesome death before their eyes. Questions ran through many of their minds. Were Indians attacking the camp? Was this a Native American reservation? Who were the men in that Army vehicle? What did they expect to accomplish? Why were there so many new guards who showed up all of a sudden?

And finally, the big one.

Would they ever get out of there alive?

The soldiers on the ground eventually completed their shift change. The tower guns were once again manned and readied should the Indians return. The rest of the guards remained alert and diligent, believing the attackers would not dare show their faces again. They stripped the gear and weapons from the dead guards and forced prisoners to load their lifeless bodies and those of the massacred inmates into the backhoe front buckets. The bodies were then transported to the large open trench. Dead mercenaries were as expendable as civilian inmates. Squads of soldiers climbed the hills to find layers of slain Indians. Some of the men laughed at the unnatural sight. It was the first time they had ever seen a real American Indian in the flesh.

The additional guards scoured the entire camp and surrounding area for any other potential attackers. They found pickup tire tracks leading away from the complex and followed them more than a half mile into the desert. They stopped where the road fell into the wash and then returned to base camp. The soldiers would next be ordered to interrogate prisoners, everyone in the camp if necessary, to determine who the attackers were and where they were hiding.

Robin was startled when the front doors to her building were kicked in. Several armed guards stormed inside. She grabbed her kids and covered them the best she could with her jacket. She was sure she had earlier heard her husband Cody calling her name, looking for his family. But the large crowd against the fence prevented her from getting closer. She wasn't able to see him, but she knew it was Cody. She screamed and screamed, answering back as Cody ran down the length of the fence, searching. But the deafening noise from the wild chanting had drowned out her cries.

Then the shooting began.

Bullets were flying everywhere. Guards went down. Machine guns were peppering the ground, battering humans, good and bad. Shots hit and ricocheted off the Army vehicle, failing to find their mark. Blasts of lead tore into the fenced area, killing dozens of inmates jammed against the chain links. People were screaming and running, looking for cover from the constant shooting. Inside their prison they waited and waited. Robin knew her husband was out there somewhere and would return for them again. She peeked through the opened shutter and realized the Humvee had gone. She had no way of knowing if Cody was safe or not.

Every detainee in the place lowered their heads to avoid eye contact with the four guards who had entered. The soldiers booted people on the floor. They jabbed the butts of their rifles into lowered heads. They moved in closer and elbowed some men standing up, knocking them to the floor. Then the guards grabbed four men by their collars and shoved them out the doors. One of them was Joseph, the man who tried to help Robin. He said nothing as he and the rest were thrust down the steps into the yard. He simply looked down with fear plastered on his face.

The forewarned inmate interrogations were about to begin. Retributions were certain to follow.

Squads of soldiers escorted collected inmates down the long center road toward the interrogation building. As prisoners were being pushed inside, the rest of the captives watched in suspense. Robin watched them from the doorway. Would they return? Joseph had mentioned that some never came back. Would the guards come back for more inmates? What if they took her? She had nothing to say. Would her children be safe without her?

She saw there were extra guards at the nearby sentry point. The troop truck was at the entrance blocking the road. More guards walked the perimeter, far more vigilant than earlier. The backhoes on the far side of the interrogation building were dumping dirt in the hole, layering the bodies with fill dirt.

Obviously there was no escape route now that the camp was on high alert.

Robin returned and sat with Jeffrey and Jennifer. She glanced around the large room. No one stopped to look at her, not like in the transport bus. There was no fight left in these people. They had already given up, dismissed any crazy thoughts of escaping. Instead, the people around her huddled close to friends and loved ones, hoping they would not be plucked from the barn to be served to the enemy.

Robin remembered hearing a term she had never liked, never agreed with. Sheeple. She had heard it on the radio, read it in some books, ignored it in conversation. Maybe they were right, she thought, gazing at the defeated mass of neighbors. These were the sheeple she had heard about.

But not her.

She refused to be one of them. She held her kids tighter and tears leaked down her cheeks. She would not give in. She was not going down so easily.

Then she heard several gun shots in the distance. The killings had begun.

Chapter 43

The President and the First Lady were enjoying a lovely dinner prepared by their private chef. General Wells and his wife had been asked to join them for the late meal as well. When they had finished their fresh Maine lobsters and perfectly grilled Kobe steaks, the men excused themselves from the ladies and retired to a small adjacent sitting room. They had business to discuss.

The President poured two glasses of scotch and handed one to the General. "To our success," the President lifted his glass in a triumphant toast, though it was probably still too soon to declare victory.

"Wow," the General said. "That's good."

"Royal Salute," the President said. "Fitting, isn't it?"

"Yes sir."

"What's going on, General?" the President asked. He had decided to get an update on the procedures above ground from the man he most trusted, rather than sit and listen to the other Deputies and Secretaries. General Wells was at the top of the chain and he knew all that was happening.

The General downed his drink. "Mr. President, you are aware of the situations with the Chinese and Russians. Until recently, there have been enormous measures taken by our adversaries to make strategic moves on America and some of our closest allies. Of course, our network of ICBMs and our nuclear armed squadrons of airborne bombers remain at peak operation and are still considered calculable deterrents by the communist and terrorist regimes."

The President nodded, quietly holding his glass. *Tell me something I don't know,* he thought.

"It appears sir, over the past few hours China has withdrawn several of its nuclear subs from our western and southern coasts. Half of their brigades along the North Korean border have been ordered to pull back and they are now being re-routed north toward Mongolia. Three of their five infantry and tank divisions near the Afghanistan border are also being diverted north to Kazakhstan, which as you know, borders Russia. It seems, according to our intelligence sources, the massive Chinese offensive movements have changed into defensive lines."

"Is it my understanding, General, that the Chinese are more concerned about our nuclear strength than was earlier expected?" the President wanted to know.

The General shook his head. "Not exactly sir. If I may, I'd first like to let you know about the Russians."

The President sat back and waved his hand, as if to say 'continue'.

"The Russians are changing their tactics as well. Troop alignment along the borders of Eastern Europe and the newer states, which were once a part of the Soviet Union, has eased up. Large portions of these Russian armies are being mobilized to southern Russia, closer to the edge of China. Four of their subs have left our shores also and are heading home. Speculation is they are on course to the Sea of Japan and the East China Sea."

"Looks as if the enemy of our enemy has become our friend, at least in this case," the President remarked. "And, only temporarily," he added.

"Yes sir. Neither side is satisfied with their deal, and they both want the whole of America for themselves. Like two dogs fighting over a bone. It's come down to one having to destroy the other in order to win the big prize. They've taken their eyes off the ball, so to speak, to clash with each other. Then, the victor can easily come back into our waters for their trophy with no resistance. Or so they think. This is a battle, sir, for singular superpower status," the General stated.

The President smiled like a master chess player facing his weakened opponent. The proper pieces were in play, just as he had predicted. Neither side, Chinese nor Russian, would be able to declare checkmate. "Excellent work General. Let the bastards annihilate each other, fucking greedy, conniving sons-of-a-bitches. This gives us time to eliminate both foreign assholes from our sights."

The General went to the wet bar and poured another drink for himself and his boss.

"This calls for a celebration," the President raised his glass, waiting for the General to do the same.

"Well, sir. Maybe not just yet," the General said in a low tone.

"What aren't you telling me, Joe?"

General Wells knew when the commander-in-chief called him by his first name he should be worried. The major problems of enemy nations attacking America was at arms length for the moment. In their place were domestic wildfires spreading out of control in many towns and cities in the country. It was an internal windstorm traveling both independently and collectively throughout the land with a force far superior than any organized army and far more determined than any hostile force with a dedicated purpose.

The Army officer was afraid to say it, but he had to explain the new insurgent developments. "We have another dilemma, sir." He hesitated, then reluctantly continued. "If you recall earlier, we had several skirmishes with outlining renegades. Small citizen groups exchanging blows with the authorities."

"I was assured those insects would be squashed," the President said angrily. "And they have guns and seasoned soldiers."

"Ah...yes sir. Veterans' service clubs like the VFW, American Legion, AMVETS, DAV, and hundreds of other affiliates are gathering their ex-military members in efforts to fight back. They're causing havoc at evacuation centers, road checkpoints, even at detention camps," the General explained. "And most of them are armed."

"A bunch of drunken old farts, all of them." The President was furious. "I told the damn Congress I wanted to confiscate every gun in the civilian population. But they backed down, fearful of the publicity, afraid of losing votes. Fucking pussies! We wouldn't have this problem if we had insisted and followed through on complete gun control."

"Yes sir, but…."

"But nothing. You know I'm right. We have the god-damn Chinese and Russians under control and you're telling me we can't stop a few splintered factions of over the hill…what'd you call them before? Dangerous old men? Come on General. What do we have to do to stop them? Take their fucking Social Security checks away?"

"Yes sir, I mean no sir," the General was all over the place. "It's not only them. There're cowboys in the west, the rednecks down south, the patriots up north, police forces from numerous cities. Rebels are coming out of the woodwork, sir. Hell, even people in California are rebelling. I'm afraid we underestimated their reaction or their ability to unite."

"Well, how in the hell did that happen?" the President wanted to know.

"Apparently they do have transportation and communications. We've received reports of motorized caravans approaching major detention camps. Some of the collection centers have been overrun. Many of the dissenters must have been preppers, you know, citizens who stock up on provisions and weapons in case of natural disasters or potential uprisings against the government."

"I know what the fuck preppers are, General Wells. They're a bunch of god-damn conspiracy theorists. Whackos. Instigators," the President shouted. "No good useless eaters who want to go back to the old way."

The President tightened his stare. "Why weren't all these troublemakers rounded up in the first place?"

The General had no answer.

The President began yelling. "They think they have sacred rights? They think they're so fucking special because they live in America? They think they can stop what we've worked so hard to create? We'll show every one of them how god-damn special they are."

The General lowered his shoulders in a show of submission. "Yes Mr. President."

Chapter 44

It was mid-morning, a few hours after the first attack. The outside temperature was actually warming up. Raz, Pete, and the entire remaining Pascua tribe were preparing once again to face the camp soldiers.

This time the outcome would be different.

"How's my boy?" Raz asked one of the men just returning from the Indian village.

"You can ask him yourself," the young man said. "There he is." He shrugged his shoulders and pointed down the trail.

A pickup pulled up to the men in a circle. From the passenger side out slid Cody. He looked like a rag tag soldier all taped and bandaged up. His wounded left shoulder and arm were held chest high with a makeshift cloth sling hung around his neck. His chest and side were tightly wrapped under his jacket making him look like a mummy. And he still had the bandage on his forehead from the glass cut.

"Ya look like hell," Raz grunted.

"Great, because that's exactly how I feel," Cody remarked.

"What the hell ya think ya doin' here?"

As he moved, Cody scowled from the pains in his body. Every part of him hurt. "I'm going back in there with you guys. Don't try to stop me old man."

Raz shook his head. "I ain't gonna try ta stop ya. A fool does foolish things."

"Ah…thanks, I think," Cody said.

"Ya ain't gonna be no help, though," Raz added.

"I can still shoot," the young man reassured him.

"Yup, from way behind me," Raz ended the conversation and turned toward the Humvee.

Pete yelled out, "Okay men, get your tired asses ready. It's time to cause some pain to the white guys. When we get to the hills have the rest of our people line up as we planned."

Raz got in his car. Cody was moving slowly. "Hey boy, ya comin' or not?"

"Hold your horses John Wayne."

The group fired up their vehicles and drove toward the camp. The other Pascuas, the old men, the women and children, followed on foot behind the caravan of trucks. Once they reached the camp, it would take them maybe fifteen minutes to set the circle on the ridges.

Looking down from the peak Raz noticed through his binoculars there was lots of activity in the detention camp. Guards were hurriedly escorting prisoners from every building. Five or six at a time. The yards were empty, but the doors were wide open. People were being pushed into the structure outside the fence. The interrogation building, the killing center. If anything, Raz knew it was more like a torture chamber. The backhoes were covering up something in the ditch with more buckets of dirt. He heard gun shots, the echoing sounds delayed a few seconds because of the distance.

People were being shot inside.

"Somethin's up," Raz said to Cody who was still struggling up the hill.

Guards were pulling out more prisoners from their safe havens. Those who refused or struggled were shot on the spot. Those who fell to the ground out of sheer panic were shot. This was no regular questioning process.

"This ain't good," Raz said with a sense of urgency in his voice.

"What is it?" Cody asked, as he reached his friend.

"The detainees goin' in that buildin' ain't comin' out standin' up. See there." He pointed at the back of the structure so Cody could see what he was talking about. It was difficult to see everything, but Cody could make out people carrying something, bodies, out the back. They were tossing the things into a pile for the backhoes to scoop up.

Raz rubbed his weary eyes to be certain what he was watching. "Yup, they're carryin' dead bodies out. The bastards must have asked them a few questions and got no satisfactory answers. Son-of-a-bitch! Those people don't know nothin'."

He yelled down the hill. "They're innocent, you fucks!" But it was good that he wasn't heard down in the compound.

Raz watched most of the guards, laughing and talking, return to the prisoner buildings, ready for another group of walking dead inmates.

"Ya people almost in place?" Raz turned to ask Pete. "We ain't got much time ta fiddle around."

"A few more minutes, my friend. If we're going to do this right, we have to be a hundred percent ready," Pete explained.

Raz looked at his watch. It had been more than twenty minutes getting all the tribe in place. "People are dyin' down there, for Christ sake!"

Members of the tribe reached their positions and settled on the ridges, staying out of view from the guards below. Each non warrior held a spear or a bow, or maybe just a long stick, prepared to join the battle without firing a shot. The armed warriors positioned themselves in intervals of twenty to twenty five Pascuas. In minutes the Circle of Fear would surround the entire camp complex. Fewer than a hundred and fifty men with their rifles and bows and arrows would create the facade of a massive force firing down on the three hundred plus soldiers.

However, in reality there would be closer to three thousand other Indians displaying their weapons and ability to wipe out the much smaller force of guards. Every one of the Pascua Yaqui tribe, except for the seriously wounded, had volunteered to enter the battlefield to help defeat the foreigners and regain their rightful lands. From the valley floor the odds would appear to be closer to ten-to-one, in favor of the Indians. Pete hoped such a false appearance would scare the hell out of the invaders, just as in the five hundred year old legend of Yaqui Creek.

Pete moved several paces from Raz's side, his rifle primed. He raised his hand ready to signal his people to fire and make a hell of a racket. He looked into the small valley. The guards were more concerned with their duties and seemed completely unaware of the Indian presence hovering above them.

Raz took one last look through his field glasses. "Oh shit!" he grumbled. He dropped the binoculars and shouted at Pete. But the Indian chief was in the zone, thinking of nothing else but battle.

"Wait!" Raz screamed. But it was too late.

All eyes were focused on Pete. People would no doubt die in the next several minutes, but death in battle was looked upon as an honorable end for the proud Pascuas as they fought to protect their home.

Cody had heard the old man scream. *Why did he want to wait?*

"They have ya wife, Cody! They're takin' her to interrogation," Raz hollered to him.

Cody squinted his eyes. Sure as hell the guards had returned to pull more prisoners and were dragging them from the buildings. Three other prisoners surrounded Robin, all going to their death sentence. But where were his kids?

He had to do something.

Now!

Pete lowered his hand, signaling his large army to fire at will. The sharpshooters and expert archers stood on the rise and picked their marks. The first to drop were the tower guards, eliminating the most dangerous firepower. Next, the guards in the road and those forcing the prisoners out of the buildings were targeted.

Soldiers looked to the hills and saw thousands of weapons thrust into the air. Arrows and lead rained upon them from every angle. They were surrounded, ambushed from above.

"Watch outside the fences," Pete yelled to his men near him. Guards near the interrogation building and the residences hid behind the structures and the parked buses, taking aim at the overwhelming forces encircling them. Shots from inside the torture chamber rang out. Each blast meant another prisoner was killed.

The uproar from the Pascuas in the hills was deafening, echoing like heavy thunder bouncing off the valley walls. Some of the soldiers steadied themselves and with quick aim shot painted warriors as they popped up to fire. But, there were too many Indians and most of the guards simply scattered for protection. Troops with their handful of prisoners hid behind their captives, using them as human shields against the blitz. Harried detainees and guards alike fell to the constant onslaught.

Cody focused on the three men using his wife and the other captives as a screen against bullets and stone tipped shafts. Steadying his rifle he took aim at the soldier and fired. With only one good hand he missed by a long shot. He tried again. He needed to save Robin. This time he rested the rifle on a large stone, bearing down on the cowardly soldier.

Lying beside him on the irregular ground, Raz reached over and pushed Cody's rifle barrel to the ground. "I'll handle this one, sonny," he said.

"No, I have to…." Cody protested.

"Hush! I don't need no distraction," Raz mumbled. He clutched his rifle firmly and sighted the guard. He took a deep breath and held it in. In his silent patience he watched the guard pulling his hostages closer to him, making a shot nearly impossible without killing one of the good guys.

"Steady. Steady ya son-of-a-bitch," he whispered, waiting for the right moment while bearing down his barrel sight. His bare finger rested on the trigger like a feather caressing a baby.

"Shoot him! Shoot him!" Cody screamed.

"Not yet. Not just yet," Raz said calmly. The noises around him had faded away as if turned off by hand. He blocked out all sounds around him. His sharp vision funneled to one spot on the guard's exposed forehead. Robin's head was two inches from her tormenter, almost touching him. There was terror in her face and tears in her eyes.

Then there was a loud blast as Raz discharged his weapon toward the panicky guard some two hundred yards away. It took less than a second before the shot exploded into the man's head, perfectly placed between his darting eyes and bushy brows.

"Bingo," Raz said smugly. "Take that, ya bastard."

Blood splattered onto Robin's face and the other prisoners. She screamed as if she too had been shot.

Both Raz and Cody heard her terror over the clamoring sounds about them.

Cody reacted without thinking. "You shot her!" he shrieked. "You shot Robin!"

"Here," Raz said, giving the binoculars to his friend. "Take a look."

Cody found his wife lying on the ground, bloodied from the close encounter. Turning to the dead man she pushed his limp body away from her. "You god-damn son-of-a-bitch!" she shouted. She looked up toward the hill, but couldn't make out her savior. Instead, she and the prisoners around her huddled together with the fear of still being killed.

"She's okay, Raz! Robin's not hit," Cody rejoiced.

Raz adjusted his rifle, taking aim at another guard not far from the first and fired again. "Yup. Now we need ta take the fight down there."

Raz motioned to Pete that it was time for them and some of the warriors to enter the camp. Pete nodded as he and half his men withdrew down the far side of the hill.

The old man looked at Cody whose face was pale white. "Can't wait for ya, kid. Some things we have ta take care of."

"I'm coming," Cody said.

"Meet ya in hell, kid," he said as he slid down the steep slope.

Chapter 45

T he Indian cries in the hills, the primitive stick weapons wildly pounding the sky, the barrage of death and destruction raining down on the camp were relentless. Guards were being slaughtered in every corner of the camp, arrows coming from nowhere, shots ringing from unseen red devils.

But the soldiers were unyielding and ruthless in their sharp response. Old men, women, and some younger members of the tribe, foolishly looking over the rocky rims of the protective hills, curious at what was happening in the valley, met their death by seasoned soldiers below.

Prisoners peeked through their doors and shutters watching the battle from a safe distance. Those in the open ran for any nearby hiding place, of which there were few. A handful of survivors from the interrogation building raced into the desert looking over their shoulders for fear of being shot in the back. Some fell into the giant death pit landing on still warm, discarded bodies. They lay there, motionless, in order to remain undetected and alive. Robin tried to get back to her children, but she was hopelessly caught in a constant pounding of crossfire gun shot.

Dead and injured soldiers littered the compound yards and roads. Lifeless uniforms lay on top of one another in their failed attempts to escape the merciless Indian attack. Squads of foreign guards threw their weapons to the ground, eventually unwilling to die for a cause they didn't believe in. Dead men could spend no money. They ran past the outer sentry points hoping to find their way through the unfamiliar Sonoran desert. The Oshkosh vehicles were racing into the desert as well, filled with runaway guards trying to save themselves.

The majority of those left alive, those whose duty was to control the camp, continued shooting wildly into the hills.

Raz and twenty Pascuas worked their way into the complex from the south end. Raz's only purpose for the moment was to grab Robin, find her children, and then get them the hell out of the camp. It was his unspoken promise to Cody.

Following their chief, another twenty or so warriors backed up Pete as they reached the northern portion of the detention camp. Their plan was to make their way toward the southern team and meet up at the interrogation center, while protecting all prisoners and eliminating every hostile in their way.

As Raz and his band entered the camp road they saw an Army truck racing toward the sentry exit. Three soldiers were in the cab, but none of them fired their weapons. A chorus of Indian rifles rang as they pelted the escaping truck. The driver slummed over the steering wheel, killed by the first bullet. Another guard grabbed the wheel, but both front tires blew out from gun shots causing the two and half ton truck to lose control. The truck rammed forward hitting the sentry shack broadside. It flipped over on its side, slid a hundred feet farther, and burst into flames. Raz's men let the guards in the cab and the dozen or so hunkered in the back burn to death. The Pascuas cleanly shot those who tried to run.

Robin saw the flames and hoped someone was coming to save her. She rose and ran toward her building, passing dead soldiers along the way. Bullets whizzed past her from every direction. One guard on the ground was wounded, his leg shot off at the knee, but he was still alert. He grabbed Robin's jacket and pulled her down. He violently stuck his pistol into her temple and yelled something in Russian. Robin didn't understand his words, though she knew the danger she had fallen into. The man was crazed with rage and pain. She knew she was going to die before seeing her children or husband again.

Pete was halfway through the camp. He had lost three warriors to hidden soldiers sniping away, desperate to survive as the camp was being overrun. A guard had climbed up one of the twenty foot tall towers and turned the machine gun on the tribe. Two Pascuas were immediately shredded to pieces by the big gun. Seconds later four arrows pierced through the guard's body, putting an end to the killings from above.

About four dozen enemy troops held strong in the interrogation building and the adjacent guards' barracks. They kept shooting through the open windows and doors into the oncoming tribal sweep. A few more of Pete's men were killed, including his youngest brother. Several others were severely wounded. The mounting bloodshed and death only pissed the Indians off even worse, making them more determined than ever to kill every trooper in sight.

Raz saw Robin a hundred feet ahead, a pistol jammed against her head. He stepped closer. When he was within earshot of the guard he went into his interrogation mode, learned and processed over so many years, an expert in calming people down on the worst day of their lives.

"Put the gun down," he yelled at the guard, getting his attention. "Listen here fella, ya put the gun down and I'll let ya go free."

The guard heard him, but didn't move. Robin froze in fear. She was surprised to see and hear Cody's old friend. She hadn't seen Raz Hunter in years. Confusion set in. How did he get here? Where was Cody? She wondered.

"Ya understand me?" Raz asked the guard. He put his hands in the air as if to show the man he was in no danger.

"Yeah," the guard responded. "My leg!" he screamed out.

"We'll git ya some help," Raz assured him. "Ya understand me?"

The guard nodded his head, but pulled Robin closer to him. "I understand."

"Good. That's good. Ya drop ya gun and ya can go."

The guard was nervous as hell. Should he trust the old man. He didn't want to, but he wanted to live. He had already lost his leg. If these men came toward him he would kill the woman. But he would be a dead man too. So he decided to do the right thing. "Okay. No shoot. I put gun down," he answered in broken English.

Raz's crew was beside him, their rifles and arrows aimed at the Russian soldier dead set on killing one of the hostages. "Easy now, pal. Put it down slowly," Raz spoke to him evenly, gently, as he moved closer. Raz motioned to his team to lower their weapons in good faith.

"We're not gonna hurt ya. My men won't shoot," Raz tried to reassure the desperate soldier.

The man removed the pistol from Robin's head and leaned over to slowly put the gun on the ground. "See," he said with a worried smile. "No problem. Okay? No shoot."

"Okay," Raz said.

Out of nowhere came a loud explosion. A rifle blast from behind Raz and his men echoed in the camp. The Russian guard slumped against the wire fence he was leaning against. Half his head had been blown off. Blood and sticky brain matter and pieces of hairy skull covered Robin. She began screaming as Raz looked around to see who had fired the shot.

Cody hobbled past the men and tossed his smoking rifle to the road. Each step hurt his side. He limped toward his wife. "Robin, Robin."

"Is that you Cody?" she asked in disbelief. "Is that really you?"

"Yup. It's me," he smiled. He staggered toward Robin and helped her get to her feet despite the pain in his shoulder.

"What happened to you?" Robin had to ask, seeing his numerous bandages.

"Been a rough day."

"Are you hurt?" he asked his wife.

"No, just shook up. I thought I was going to die," she said.

"I'm so glad to find you." He hugged his wife as best he could without twisting his rattled body. "We knew you were here someplace."

Robin looked over at her prison building. "The children, we have to get the children."

Cody and Robin quickly shuffled to the front gate. With his sidearm Cody shot off the lock and pushed it inward. The front door of the building creaked open and a few people stepped out. The good guys were here.

Raz and his men moved past Cody toward the sound of more gunfire. "Ya good?" he asked the young man.

"Great," Cody responded as he and Robin entered the yard.

"Git ya family, we got business ta finish."

Chapter 46

T he President of the New United States was fuming while eating his late breakfast. He had the situation with China and Russia under control. Once that battle was settled between the two communist aggressors his newly established nation would be strong enough to take out the winner.

His real problems were much closer to home. They were, in fact, the homegrown domestic do-gooders. The lousy constitutional backers, the pesky self-proclaimed patriots of a defunct system and outdated policies that were a major thorn in his side. These disloyal subversives were flaunting their supposedly unalienable rights and fluffing their feathers in a show of defiance, as if their puny offenses could take down a powerful new order.

The commander-in-chief took this outrageous display of insolence as a personal affront to him personally and a sign of contempt directed at the prestigious position of the most powerful man in the world. He turned to General Wells who was silently reviewing his reports, letting his coffee go cold, wishing he was any place else except with the President being berated like a teenager who had fucked up in school.

"General, you of all people should realize how much effort has been exerted for us to have arrived at this point. It's been no easy task. We've lost some battles, but what is more important is that we've won even more. I don't like to lose and I hate insubordination. Tell me, General. Am I wrong?"

"No sir. You are absolutely correct." He believed it too, but he hated being a doormat to the President. "You've done all the right moves, sir. Your building of alliances with politically opposing forces has been ingenious. The United Nations, the international bankers, the labor unions, and the old money establishments have all supported you extremely well.

"Your plans to alter the nation are nothing less than visionary. Your priorities have been straight on since the very beginning. Your calculations regarding how both our allies and enemies would react have been nothing less than prophetic. I must tell you sir, that I have never seen such a fabulously successful campaign either on the battlefield or in the political arena."

"Thank you for your vote of confidence," the President said. He truly enjoyed hearing such accolades, but now he was all business. He didn't want to hear any more excuses from his man in charge of national defense. He wanted results.

The General had some good news to break the ice. The engineers in the Weather Modification Program had, at the President's order, adjusted the HAARP effects on the weather, thereby increasing the temperature toward the freezing mark. This would make the Army's attempt to capture or run down these renegade patrols much easier. The arctic cold had done its job in frightening the public and allowing most of the citizens to be rounded up rather easily.

"Sir," the General began, terrified by what he was about to tell his boss next. "Reports have come in confirming some collection points are being attacked by groups of armed militants. Initial numbers show a hundred forty three smaller evacuation centers are on the verge of being lost to renegade dissenters."

"A hundred forty three?" the President screamed like a mad man.

"Yes sir, but that's out of over three thousand collection centers. A very small percentage."

"I don't give a shit how many we have! Those loses are totally unacceptable," the supreme executive shouted. "How many men have we lost?"

The General frowned and cleared his throat. "Nearly twenty thousand troops dead or wounded, sir. The majority of them are foreign hires."

"I still don't like it."

"Yes sir. There's more. We've just received word from Station Two in Colorado that a sizable concentration center, Camp 49, some miles south of Tucson, Arizona, has been all but wiped out by radicals."

"Tell me General. How the fuck were they able to do that?" the President wanted to know.

"Indians, sir. From a small, local reservation. And a couple white guys in an Army Humvee," the General responded. He wished he could shrink down to the size of a dust speck and disappear into the woodwork.

"Indians? Like Native Americans? How in the hell did that happen? And where'd they get their weapons?" The President's face was screaming red.

The General squirmed. "They mostly had bows and arrows, and spears, sir. It seems they were being led by two Caucasian males, heavily armed and knowledgeable in warfare tactics."

"That's just fucking great!" the President shouted. "Two guys and a band of Indians are taking over my camps."

"Only one camp, sir," the General cut in.

"I heard you the first time. Tell me. Are there any more wild bands of Indian tribes trying to destroy my control?"

"No sir. I mean, I'm not sure sir."

"You're not sure?" the President was livid. "General, let me remind you. I am in charge. This is my plan, my agenda. Once the EMP hit I was the one who declared martial law. By doing so I immediately eliminated opposition to my administration. No more legislative branch, no more senators or representatives, except for a few hand selected. No more judicial branch. I am the one who decides what is legal and what isn't. I shut the media down. No more pain in the ass FOX News, no more subversive conservative radio talk. When the country is up and running again there will only be government media allowed to broadcast what I deem is necessary for the surviving populace. No more Limbaugh, Savage, Jones, and their damn followers. Martial law also allows me to remain President indefinitely, giving me the unprecedented opportunity to guarantee our long term goals can be met. You do understand that, right?"

"Yes sir." The General remained still, taking in everything his boss was throwing at him.

"You are aware of the big picture. Plans for today's success have been established over the previous several decades. The NSA, Agenda 21, REX 84, the DHS, the NDAA, the Patriot Act, FEMA, even my own presidency. You don't think all of these just happened. Do you? Everyone of these events were meticulously set in place. And now we are experiencing the results of these historical maneuvers.

"I've authorized the NSA to collect and compile untold bits of communication throughout the world. Its sole purpose has been to capture records on all persons of interest, including American citizens. In direct response to my executive orders, the National Defense Authorization Act gives me, your President, the power to round up any American considered a potential terrorist against the government. It allows me to field occupational forces throughout the land. Without going through Congress I can now use my military forces to indefinitely detain any dissidents who are or may act in a seditious manner. They can be charged and rendered guilty as needed. There is no time to be wasted with trials. The judicial system is dead. With this law I can even conscript Americans into work brigades to later reconstruct our nation the way I see fit."

The President was on his soapbox counting off his newly acquired powers one by one for his own satisfaction and to remind his Secretary of National Defense who the boss was.

He continued.

"I now have complete control of the American economy and will run it according to our new policies. The United States Constitution has been suspended. The Bill of Rights is null and void. The rule of law is what I say it is. Both documents are useless, outdated policies, antiquated principles. Americans have been too caught up in the past. That is changing. I control all modes of transportation. Highways, air travel, railroads, inland waterways and seaports. Every form of communication is now subject to my rule, including the Internet, which should have never been made available for public use. All methods of energy production now fall under my regulations. I shall determine a prudent energy policy for the country."

The General watched his commander-in-chief, admitting to himself possible mistakes and wondering if he had made the right decision to side with the new order.

"My government controls every aspect of food in the country, from the farms to supply lines to local distribution. It is I, and I alone, who determines who gets to eat and who shall face starvation. Can you even fathom what kind of power that is? Once our nation is rebuilt and opened for business again, I shall stipulate who will receive health care and education beneficial to the state. I also shall control the flow of our new currency, the ability to benefit from commerce, and the privilege to work. There's no end as to what can be done."

The President was elated with himself. Every future decision for the nation rested solely on his shoulders.

"And finally, General. I have the Army. If a man has the guns, he has the power. That's been a standard banner throughout history. We should have been more diligent, more aggressive, in banning guns. I've said it before and I'll say it again. I don't believe people should be able to own guns and under my rule those who survive will not."

The President paused. "I have all these things at my feet, Mr. Secretary, and you tell me a few roughshod rebels are trying to take it away from me? That my plan is under siege by an Indian tribe of drunken losers with sticks and some wannabe heroes trying to save the world? Don't be so god-damn ridiculous. I am ordering you to stop these attempts to rebuff my authority."

"Yes sir," the General acquiesced. "Except, there's something else you should know."

Chapter 47

With his wife at his side Cody entered the dark building. The number of prisoners inside was unbelievable. It took a few seconds for his eyes to adjust to the weak light and the dismal rabble of citizens. A mob of detainees surrounded Cody as if he were the liberator of Europe after the fall of Germany. They were grabbing him and shaking his hand. They thanked him profusely and prayed to him for saving them.

Cody called out for his children. "Jeffrey. Jennifer."

From behind the crowd he heard a young voice. "Daddy, Daddy!"

The two kids pushed their way through the wall of people and hugged their father. They wrapped their small arms around his waist and chest, hurting him because of his injuries, but it was a good hurt.

"Oh Daddy." Six year old Jennifer squeezed her father. "I was so afraid."

"I know sweetheart," Cody said. "There's no need to be afraid now."

"Mommy said you would come and take us home. She kept saying that Daddy was coming, and I believed her," his daughter explained, excited and talkative and so innocent.

Cody's eyes welled up with tears of joy. "That's good."

Jeffrey held onto his father like he had never done before. He was trying to be brave, but he began crying too. "I wasn't afraid," he said, struggling to act like a little man. But, being older than his sister, he had been afraid, because he saw what was happening around him and understood.

"You're a very brave boy," Cody said to him.

"I'm very hungry too," Jeffrey said. His stomach was grumbling.

Jennifer added, "Daddy, the toilets here are so gross."

Cody couldn't help but laugh. Robin put her hand on Cody's good shoulder. "You're bleeding."

"I'll be okay," he told her. Carrying his daughter with his good arm Cody stepped outside with his son and wife. He promised himself he would find his family, and he did.

"I love you Cody," Robin said, finally letting her emotions run loose after the horrible ordeal they had been through.

"I love you too, Robin, more than ever before."

Together, Cody and his family walked through the enclosed prison yard followed by the rest of the incarcerated people. Gun shots were still being fired on the far side of the camp. Cody could see some of the Pascuas firing back.

He looked at his wife. "Where's Nick's family?"

Robin looked lost. "After we got off the bus, they must have moved them and some others to another building. She wasn't with us."

Cody stopped walking.

"What is it?" Robin asked, knowing something was wrong.

"It's just...I promised Nick."

"Nick?" Robin said with tears building up. "Where is he?"

Cody held back. "He's gone, Robin."

Robin hugged her husband in the road. "His family is here someplace. We'll find them."

Cody would tell Raz about Nick's family still being in the camp. They would find Lisa and her girls in the enormous crowd.

Raz had left the Humvee just outside the camp. Cody took his family to the vehicle. There they would be safe from the gun fire which was still being exchanged in the center of the complex. Hundreds of other captives ran into the desert beyond the hills waiting for the shooting to stop.

Pete's men were pinned down on the north side of the compound. Soldiers laid down a barrage of gun fire from the interrogation center and the guards' buildings. Having sufficient cover they had a distinct advantage. Several Pascuas fell mortally wounded. Pete moved his remaining men around the buildings, surrounding the hundred or so troops inside. Hostiles in the second guard truck racing toward the Pasquas were taken out with arrows. The truck swerved off the road, crashed into a guard tower, and toppled it to the ground. The disabled troops were quickly taken out by the warriors.

"We can't get to them this way," Pete said to his middle brother. It was time to go back to old school tactics. This was one circumstance where arrows were better than bullets. He yelled some orders to the band of warriors around the buildings. When they were in place, he nodded. This would flush out the camp soldiers.

"Light them up," he shouted loud enough for his men to hear. Each of the Pascua warriors lit their wrapped arrows. At will, they shot the fire sticks into the wooden buildings, pounding them with hundreds of death blazes. The tinder dry wooden interrogation and bunkhouse buildings caught like dried brush in a drought. It took less than a minute for the roofs to turn into raging flames. The exterior walls quickly became engulfed in fire as well.

Soldiers continued to shoot from the open windows, but their aim turned erratic. Acrid black smoke rapidly filled the interiors, causing the troops to gasp for air or head for the exits. Those who could find them. Pieces of the roofs began to collapse, rafters and sheathing from the structures falling within. The Pascuas heard shrieks and screams from inside. The soldiers were being burned to death in their own safe havens.

The archers ceased firing and stood still watching the blazing infernos' leap to life. The sounds of burning, crackling wood and the disintegration of the buildings were as loud as mountain thunder. The heat from the fires warmed the Indians even at a distance. It felt good to them.

Ultimately, one by one, the remaining soldiers stumbled out the doors. Some fired their rifles nowhere, attempting to escape. But there was no escape, only death. Others staggered to the ground in coughing fits, their lungs filled with deadly smoke and heated gases. Several soldiers dashed from their buildings, engulfed in flames, their odies writhing in unbelievable pain. A few lurched through the doorways, their hands up high in surrender.

But the Pascuas had no intention of capturing their foes. They would not treat their enemies as their enemies had treated their captives. No. The guards would die a quicker and less painful death. The Pascuas stretched their rigid bows and let loose their arrows into the defenseless soldiers. Each trooper reaching open ground was punched with a dozen shafts. Moans and pleas, cries and screams fell on deaf ears as the Indians finished off the invaders.

The enflamed buildings' walls caved in on themselves, feeding funeral pyres for the remaining men inside. The warriors turned to their leader. There was no time to rejoice in their victory. Shots were still being fired near Raz and his men.

"Let's end this, men," Pete said as he directed his braves toward the southern portion of the camp.

They left the crumbling blazes and shifted to the road running down the length of the camp. Raz and the men with him were fighting it out with the last few guards. Raz saw Pete's men two hundred yards away. The two groups slowly worked toward one another, picking off troops as they went. Some guards retreated into prisoner buildings to hide. They were quickly overrun by the people inside, kicked, punched, and stomped to death by common, everyday people fighting for their freedom. Within the next ten minutes most every soldier in the camp was dead.

Raz and Pete met at the middle of the compound and shook hands. Thick, sooty smoke was blowing around them. The men looked dirty and tired, but happy.

"Damn good job ya boys done over there," Raz said to Pete. "One big ass Injun barbeque. Felt the heat way over here."

"Think we got most of them, old man," Pete said with a smile. "But we also lost some good men."

"Yeah," Raz grunted. "It ain't never easy."

"You can say that again," a familiar voice said from behind.

"I thought I told ya ta git out of here," Raz said to Cody as the younger man limped toward his friend.

"My family's safe back there in the Humvee," Cody said, tilting his head beyond the camp. He was carrying a weighted rucksack with his good arm.

"What's in the bag?"

Cody smirked. "I thought this was the right time for this." He reached in the bag and pulled out the bottle of Johnny Walker.

Raz had a wide grin. "Ya a man after my own heart. Give it here."

Raz cracked open the bottle and took an extra long tug. "That's the ticket. Like mother's milk." He wiped his bearded lip with his sleeve and passed the bottle to Pete. "Can ya handle some firewater, chief?"

"Give me that damn bottle, white boy," Pete said, then laughed. He wiped the mouth of the bottle dry just to piss off Raz. "Don't want to catch anything." When he was done he handed the bottle back to Raz.

"Hey. What about me?" Cody yelled.

"Ya old enough, sonny?" Raz played with him.

Cody grabbed the whiskey from Raz and took a sip. He coughed and shook his head. "Whoa! Strong stuff."

The men laughed. It had been a tough day. Pete's men were scouring the camp, picking up rifles and sidearms from the dead soldiers. They popped open the front fences to the rest of the prisoner buildings. The people slowly emerged from their dark quarters, watching the fires burn down, seeing the dead littered everywhere. They hugged and rejoiced, dazed at what had just happened. They were free. But what was next? Where would they go?

"I have something else," Cody commented after taking another sip of whiskey. He tossed the bottle to Raz and one by one grabbed something from the sack. "These are for you and your people, Pete." He handed his new friend the two heavy woolen socks stuffed with silver coins.

"What is it?" Pete asked.

"It's not much," Cody said. He looked at the man. Pete was the only true blue Indian Cody had ever known. "I just wanted to say thanks to you and your tribe for what you've done. I would never have seen my family again if it wasn't for you."

Pete accepted the unusual gift. "Thank you Cody. We all worked well together today for many good reasons. My people can use this."

They shook hands, but then Cody hugged Pete for a long moment like a true brother.

"I have a knife," Pete said. "You want to do that blood brother thing?"

Cody backed off. "Ah, no. No thanks."

"Okay," Raz interrupted. "What are we gonna do with all these people?"

"Oh," Pete said. "In all the excitement I forgot to tell you. My guys intercepted a message on our citizens band radios from some soldiers down your ways. Apparently a large group of detained soldiers from Fort Huachuca escaped and took over the base. They're one really pissed off group of patriots. They know their families are here at this camp. They're headed this way to get them. Bringing food, water, supplies, and plenty of guns. I feel sorry for anyone who tries to stop them."

"Wait a minute here," Raz jumped. "Ya mean ta tell me ya have workin' CBs and ya never told me?"

Pete stared the old man down. "Ya never asked," he said, mocking him.

"Well, I'll be damned."

"I'm sure you will be," Pete ended.

"So now what?" Raz had to ask.

"I guess you guys can go home now," Pete said. "As for us, we're headed west. Heard there's another detention camp over in Tohono O'odham country a couple hours from here. We figure we'll go help our brothers out of a similar jam. We've learned a few things here and maybe we can make a difference. With what's been going on, somebody's got to do something about it."

Hearing Pete's comment, Raz turned to look at Cody. The old man's eyes lit up and he grinned. "Cody, ya take ya family back ta the safe place we left. Ya know what I'm talkin' 'bout."

Cody knew he meant his homestead in the woods.

Raz turned to Pete. "Mind if I tag along?"

"Can always use the extra help," Pete said.

"But Raz...." Cody said, and then he stopped. It was the right thing to do. "Thank you Raz. You're like a father to me." The men embraced each other and patted one another on the backs, like men do.

"We got a lot of work ta take care of, so I'm goin' with Pete and his men," Raz ended.

"I'll miss you," Cody said to his dear friend.

"Yeah, well. I'll be back. Someday. And if I ain't, that's okay too. It's time ta help set a few things straight." Raz reached in his pocket and tossed a ring of keys to Cody. "Now ya git."

Cody turned south and limped back to the Humvee where his family was waiting while Raz and Pete went to the north side of the camp to gather the rest of the tribe. They would help organize the crowds, find any available food and water in the camp for them, and help with the sick and injured. They would do the best they could until the cavalry arrived. Raz promised Cody he would find Nick's kin.

Chapter 48

"Something else?" The President roared. "Jesus Christ, what else do I have to worry about?"

The General hesitated and then thought, *what the hell, let the shit hit the fan.* "Reports are coming in about our base south of Tucson. Fort Huachuca. It's a huge Army facility and…we have been told that a large military fighting force which was detained there during Operations Rescue and Clean Sweep has broken out of the containment area. They've taken over the base and are preparing to reach the detention camp which was overrun by that Indian tribe, sir."

"Fucking shit! Is everyone I deal with completely incompetent? Where are my officers, my men in charge? Who the hell is running that place anyway?"

The General looked down. "I'm afraid they were all killed or captured, Mr. President."

"How many troops are we talking about here?" the President shouted. He was beyond pissed.

"Over three thousand, sir. Three thousand, four hundred and fifty five, to be exact. Mostly veteran soldiers, well trained and well educated. We run the Intelligence and Technology Centers there. And the 9th Army Signal, JITC, and the Electronic Proving Ground. These people are some of our finest leaders. A majority of them have battle experience. Gulf Wars One and Two. Iraq, Afghanistan."

"And you say they're going to that desert camp? Why would they go there?"

"We think that's where their families were taken, sir," the General supposed.

"You think? General, you're not paid to think," the President asserted. "You're paid to know. Earlier you said some of these renegade forces had weapons. What do you know about these soldiers making a move?"

The General cleared his throat and took a sip of water. "We know they have access to an arsenal of weapons, small arms and larger. They have trucks, personnel and armored carriers. They also have satellite communications capability taken from the troops running the base. Unfortunately sir, there are also tons of provisions stored on the fort for training exercises."

"So, am I correct in assuming they are a force to contend with?" the commander-in-chief asked, already anticipating the answer.

"Yes sir. They could cause trouble."

"What in the hell do you mean 'they could' cause trouble?" The President was furious at what was happening. "They already are causing trouble."

"I'm afraid they aren't the only ones, sir," the General whispered. "Communications from all sectors of the country are notifying us that other military contingents are rebelling against the new central order. Units of soldiers from Fort Benning in Georgia, Fort Bragg in North Carolina, Fort Campbell in Kentucky, Fort Hood and Fort Bliss in Texas, Fort Lewis in Washington, and others are taking up arms. They're attacking area evacuation centers and prisoner camps. Some have taken control of regional power plants, airports, and interstate highways. We may have miscalculated the strength of these pockets of American militia, sir."

"General. I want every one of these uprisings terminated at once. Use any and all lethal forms of force to eliminate these…these rebellious elements…these treasonous factions. I don't care what it takes. I don't care how much it costs. I don't care what has to be done. But, by this time tomorrow I want every member of every seditious group, including those two son-of-a-bitches, those DOMs who started it all, to disappear. End of story."

"Consider it done sir."

Chapter 49

Walking out of the camp, Cody thought about what Raz had said right before he left. "Time to help set a few things straight." His friend was right. It was time. It was time for him to stand up for what he truly believed in. It was time for him to do something, make something happen. It was time to fight for his rights, the rights and lives of his children and his future grandchildren. For the first time in his life he knew what the Founding Fathers must have felt.

It was his time to become part of the solution.

He had made a decision. He would take his family home. Well, to Raz's place. They would be safe there. Everything they needed was in the trailer or the bunker. Food, drink, heat, protection. A real bathroom. Even a CB radio. No one would find them in that off-beaten location. Once they were settled and comfortable, he would have to leave them and catch up with Raz and the Pascuas.

Nick's family would be found too. He was sure of it. They would be safe with the American soldiers liberating the kidnapped evacuees. Later they could join Robin and the kids and all would be right.

Cody would return to fight with Raz and the Indians, because ever since he, Nick, and Raz had gone after their families, things had changed. With the help of Pete and his people, his strong and brave tribe, they had saved thousands and thousands of Americans. In this little unimportant corner of the nation they had wiped out the invaders of their country, the domestic enemies and traitors of the good people who lived and grew up and died here.

It was at that very moment that Cody remembered those perceptive words spoken by Thomas Jefferson. Words which were written on that scrap of paper by his neighbor Jack. Words which he used to briefly breeze over in his history classes. Words which previously had little meaning. Back then those words sounded noble and honorable, but meant nothing to him. But now, they meant everything. They gave a true purpose to living.

"Bad things happen when good men do nothing."

Over this long and cold Thanksgiving holiday weekend, Cody had discovered what people believed was worth fighting, and perhaps even dying for. He had experienced the fear of nearly being killed and the anguish of killing. He had felt the rage of foreign shots ripping his body with intent to kill. He had watched his friends die and others being murdered. He had seen the terror and panic in his wife's eyes, and the sweet innocence robbed from his children. He had seen hatred raise its ugly head on both sides. He had watched and lived through battles of good verses evil, right against wrong.

But in the end, Cody had learned one thing that would forever change him as a man. He had learned that *that someone* who should do something was actually himself.

Cody walked slowly back to where he had parked the Humvee a quarter mile from the fighting. He had left the vehicle running to keep his family warm. He had helped his kids slip into the sleeping bags thrown in back.

"These are cool," Jeffrey had told him. "Can we keep these, Dad?"

"Of course you can," Cody had answered.

"Mine's nice and soft, Daddy," Jennifer had said.

"They'll keep you warm too," her father had smiled.

Robin had smiled back. She had wrapped herself with the last sleeping bag without getting into it.

Cody had searched through the scattered supplies in the back. He had first passed bottles of water to his family. "Don't drink too quickly," he had told the children. "There's plenty of water here." Then he had dug up a box of crackers, a jar of peanut butter, a plastic bag of jerky, and boxes of energy bars. With these, Robin had done her best to prepare finger meals for the kids and herself. Everyone had remained quiet, eating their way through the welcomed brunch.

"You guys doing okay back there?" Cody had asked his kids from the driver's seat.

"Yes Daddy. This is fun," Jennifer had responded.

"What are these, Dad?" Jeffrey had wanted to know, after finding the boxes of MREs.

"There're pre-packaged meals for soldiers," Cody had explained.

"I want one," the boy had said.

"Me too," his sister said.

Robin had looked at her son. Jeffrey was back to normal. "Not now," she had said. "Eat your crackers and drink up."

She had leaned over to her husband and had pulled back his jacket. It was sticky with fresh blood. "Let me take care of that." She had taken her time removing the old bandages from Cody's side and redressed the wound. "There," she had said. "That should hold you until we get back home."

"Feels better, honey. Thanks," Cody had said. "Before we leave, I have to go back to see Raz," he had told her.

Robin hadn't asked him why? She had sensed her husband knew what he was doing. "Will you be long?"

"I'll return shortly, hon." He had emptied a tote bag and put a few things inside. "You kids stay put." Then Cody had turned toward the camp.

He heard several gun shots echoing from the camp. Pete's men *clearing enemy stragglers*, Cody thought.

Now, returning to the spot where he had left the Humvee, Cody couldn't see the vehicle. He moved closer, picking up the pace despite his injured side. He stopped at the location where his family should have been safe inside the Army transport.

But the vehicle was gone.

"Where the hell?" he said out loud.

This was the spot. Large tire tracks covered the desert dirt. A power bar wrapper clung to a mesquite bush. Where were they? He wondered. Why would Robin move the vehicle? He looked around. Maybe this wasn't where he had left them. But he knew it was. Calling his wife, he walked in circles searching for his family. Again. He followed the Humvee's distinctive tracks. They veered off into the vast desert and disappeared beyond the hills.

Cody stopped in the middle of nowhere. He looked toward the scrub trees in the distance and saw no sign of the Humvee. He squinted his eyes and searched the far off hills. He scanned the road back toward the camp and saw nothing. Robin would never have driven off. He was sure of that. She knew he would return soon, so why did she move? Where did she go?

Unless. He suddenly thought.

Unless she had sensed danger.

Cody began to panic. He felt a large knot in his stomach. The pain in his shoulder and side increased. His eyes scoured the desolate land for a hundredth time. His family was gone. "Robin!" he yelled over and over, which came out a whisper that nobody heard.

Then he took his time to think through the situation. It was possible that some soldiers from the camp managed to escape. They may have come this way. They would be desperate to flee the bloodbath in the camp. Was it feasible that Robin and his kids had been taken by runaway troops? Yes, he reasoned. The Humvee was loaded with weapons and supplies, and was an easy getaway.

Nothing else made any sense. His family had been kidnapped again, and he was completely helpless to save them. Convinced that they were gone, Cody turned and raced back to Raz for help as quickly as possible.

Chapter 50

Cody hobbled past the demolished guard shack into the camp. He saw a group of men farther up near the center of the patrol road not too far from the still burning and smoldering buildings. The prison yards and roads were overcrowded with freed detainees roaming aimlessly. Many of the men were picking up rifles and pistols from the dead guards. He noticed some of Pete's men lowering the 50 caliber machine guns from their tower mounts. A few of the warriors were securing the heavy weapons onto the beds of several old pickup trucks. They were preparing to head west toward the other FEMA concentration camps.

"Pete!" Cody shouted, as he moved closer to the burning wreckage. "Pete!"

The chief was standing next to the troop carrier truck riddled with bullet holes. There was still too much noise from the considerable gathering of people. They were being instructed by members of the tribe to stay calm and to wait for the soldiers coming up from Fort Huachuca. Large clusters of the released detainees moved closer to the smoldering hot ruins in an attempt to warm up.

Cody pushed his way through the crowd and approached Pete. Scattered shots were heard through the camp. He was tired and hurting, but his biggest, more urgent worry showed in his expression. "Pete, Pete. I need a truck!" he gasped.

The chief had knelt to his knees. He was looking down at several people lying on the ground who had just been shot. There were tears in his rugged eyes, a sense of rage in his weakened body.

Pete saw Cody as he came to his side. "Oh, Cody," he said in a grim tone. "I'm glad you're here." He had a grave look on his craggy face.

"They took my family!" Cody yelled. Three or four bullet ridden bodies were entangled before him. The sight of death had not yet sunk in. "I need one of your trucks to catch up to them." He was wheezing hard, gasping for breath. "They can't be more than a half hour ahead of us." He stopped again to hold his aching side. "I think I know which way they went."

Pete saw the panic in the young man's presence. He heard Cody's words, but they didn't register. He was more concerned with the fallen man at his knees. "Cody," Pete spoke softly.

Cody glanced down, his eyes refusing to believe what they were seeing.

Pete struggled to help. "It's Raz, Cody. A sniper from one of the towers shot him. He got it in the head."

Cody looked at his friend. "Raz," he said. For a split second he had almost forgotten about his family. Raz was covered by the bodies of three captives shot in the back by a cowardly guard. His bloodied head rested against the cold dirt. There was no movement.

Pete gently but firmly moved the mutilated captives off his friend.

Several Pascuas stood above the old man who had inspired them to fight their enemies, allowing them to take back their land and their pride. Death was always difficult to accept, but even more so for such a worthy warrior.

Cody dropped to his friend's side. "Oh, Raz." The man's eyes were closed and dark brownish blood covered his dirty gray beard. Cody looked at Pete, his reddened eyes pleading for a miracle. This couldn't be happening. Not to Raz.

"It looks bad," Pete said. The stoic warrior chief gritted his teeth and failed to prevent tears for this brave man he had recently come to care for.

Just looking at Raz, Cody knew what was coming next. Cody had seen the face of death more than he would like. He placed his good hand on Raz's warm chest and began crying like a young boy. Why was all this happening around him? Why were so many people dying?

None of the men near him said a word. They were touched by Cody's love for his hero, and they too felt the same.

Raz opened his glassy eyes. "Stop ya cryin', son." He fought to get the words out. "I ain't gone yet," his words gurgled.

Cody and Pete couldn't help but release a short chuckle. Right to the end Raz wouldn't give up.

Raz panted to grab short gulps of air. His refusal to go quietly forced Pete and a few of his men to turn away. He blinked his eyes a few times and made one last effort. "Cody," he barely whispered.

"Yeah Raz," Cody softly answered, trying to hold back his emotions. He loved this man as much as he had loved his father.

Pete was suddenly pulled away from the circle by one of his men. Cody didn't notice him leaving and only looked at his dying friend.

"I'm real proud of ya, son. Ya did somethin' good," Raz said. The dying man slowly moved his shaky hand to Cody's. He tried to move, but he couldn't. "Now git me the hell up off this damn ground," Raz growled. He grabbed his left ear which was half torn off. Good men are hard to kill. "That was a damn close one," Raz added as Cody helped him sit upright.

Raz looked at the surrounding dead bodies that had protected him. "Friggin' animals! Damn shame they had ta die like this after all they been through." There was noise in the background. People screaming, kids crying.

Cody looked at the overturned bodies. "Oh my god!" he caught himself. He recognized one of the dead.

"What?"

"It's Lisa, Nick's wife!" Cody heard children's cries. "Mama, mama!" Nick's twin daughters were looking for their mother.

"Oh shit!" Raz said, still shaking off the daze from his close call.

Cody shifted gears. There was nothing he could do for the dead. "Pete!" he turned and called. "I have to get my family back." It was time to fight for the living.

The chief returned to the ring of men hovering over Raz. "Sorry Cody," was the best he could say.

"Can you help me?" Cody asked.

"My men just told me they found the Humvee and your family. They're okay," Pete blurted out the good news. "They were chasing the trucks that got away and ran into your Humvee. Those soldiers won't be hurting anyone else," Pete added.

Cody was stunned. "Really! Where are they? Where's my family?"

"They're coming up the road now," Pete commented.

Cody twisted and saw the green Humvee inching its way through the crowd, driven by one of Pete's men. Robin and his children were crying out and smiling. They were where they belonged.

Before the Humvee reached him Cody turned to the Pascua chief. "You've done so much. I don't know how I could ever repay you and your people. I'm sorry about you losing so many people. I'm sorry about your brother."

Pete rested his hand on Cody's good shoulder. "I've gained another brother."

Cody heard Jeffrey and Jennifer call out to him. He asked Pete, "Would it be okay if I joined you and Raz?" His voice was chocked up with feelings.

"We would be honored, Cody," Pete answered. "But first, you take care of your family. And these two little ones." He handed over Nick and Lisa's children who had worked their way through the crowd. "They'll need a family of their own."

Cody looked at the two beautiful twins. Caitlin and Tanya were both crying.

"When you're ready, you'll find us," Pete said.

Cody had a difficult time containing himself. He would take Nick's girls home with him and Robin. There was too much going on. He shook Pete's hand. All he could say was "Thank you."

"No," Pete added. "Thank you."

Cody looked over at Raz. His friend, his mentor, his hero. "I'll come back to help," he promised. Then he turned toward his family.

Chapter 51

T he word had been spreading throughout the country like wildfire. CBers and ham radio operators let Americans know what was happening in different parts of the nation. They were under attack from within. Like most government regulatory agencies, the FCC was out of action, so preppers, truckers, and a multitude of amateur radio enthusiasts relied on the low frequency airwaves.

Millions of them transmitted on a minute by minute basis the travesties and injustices imposed against the American people by the illegitimate new government. Millions still broadcasted attack strategies, tactical plans, and personal vendettas. Millions more took to arms in defense of their lives and their way of life.

The news on the streets was that the treasonous leaders of the new order were in hiding safely below the Capitol Building and they were controlling the entire operation of destroying the country from their secure bunkers. Government secured radio messages were being intercepted and deciphered from sophisticated satellite relays between Stations One and Two. Revealing pieces of top secret information were decoded, exposing the President's devious plans to the world above.

Americans were quickly learning the truth about their civic leaders and they weren't very happy about it. Death and destruction had blanketed the country. Its people, those who were still free to move about, meant to do something about the devious, traitorous bastards.

A nationwide revolution had risen from the spark of necessity and obligatory duty, manned mainly by citizen militia, much like the first rebellion for independence some hundreds of years earlier.

Everyone imaginable from all regions of the nation, from all walks of life, were joining together to stop the insanity.

Units of armed soldiers, adhering to their solemn oaths, led attacks on government secured facilities, gaining control of strategic facilities and valuable military hardware.

So called cowboys in western states rode on detention centers, freeing the captives and annihilating the hired security ranks.

Underrated rednecks from down south raided collection centers, took over hospitals, re-opened churches, and eliminated opposing forces in violent manner.

Hillbillies from the back country gathered in hundred-member clans fought viciously to open the schools to the freed prisoners, to protect the grocery and drug stores from plundering marauders, and to terminate all subversives against their fellow Americans.

Veteran's groups formed up once again, though their bodies much slower this time around, to fight the domestic enemies in their backyards.

Rambling groups of dangerous old men recaptured airports and runways, clearing them of the obstructions for incoming loyal troops.

Truckers, many with their aging rigs, flooded the nation's roads and guarded the highways against roaming intruders.

Hundreds of Indian tribes in every sector of the country, unified as one, bravely fought for their and their neighbor's lands.

Every class of the nation's population gathered in motley crews and organized factions and independent parties to defend their heritage, to reinstate their birthrights, to uphold their patriotic sense.

Soldiers and airmen and sailors and marines led their townsfolk in proud and inspired tradition.

Store clerks and doctors and carpenters found shovels and sticks and bats and arms to defeat the evil in their cities.

Fathers and mothers and grandparents gathered to stop the unholy danger imposed on their young ones.

Teachers and students, priests and believers, shop owners and cab drivers backed one another up as they stood tall and took back what was rightfully theirs.

Thousands of Americans and immigrants and visitors mobbed the streets and stormed the lit-up White House.

People of all colors, black and white, brown and red, united for one purpose. To save their America.

The poor and the rich, the homeless and the fortunate moved as one to halt the taking of their beloved country.

Christians and Jews, Muslims and Buddhists, agnostics and atheists worked together against the depriving forces.

Returning American soldiers joined forces to attack the evil that had stolen their country from them.

Unspoken words pushed each one of them forward. An inexplicable spirit from within inspired every true American to fight.

Few people could quote the exact words written by America's Founding Fathers about the greatest nation on earth.

> *"We hold these truths to be self-evident, that all men*
> *are created equal, that they are endowed by their*
> *creator with certain unalienable rights, that among*
> *these are life, liberty, and the pursuit of happiness."*

Although they may not have known the words, they knew of the driving strength, the essence of being an American, the passion for individual liberties, the privilege of living with guaranteed freedoms.

A mixed army of Americans surrounded the Capitol Building. They filled the tunnel to the underground bunker with dirt and rocks and debris and street signs and road barricades until it was impossibly shut closed, blockading the only exit. The shafts of the high speed elevators descending twenty stories beneath the surface were permanently disabled, never to run again.

The people tore down fencing from every section of town to build around and cover the ground above the safe zone, known as Section

One. They built a huge cage of chain link fencing and meshing and screening. They draped an entire acre of land directly above their notorious leaders trapped in their luxury death crypt.

In the fury of freedom a young boy attached an American flag to the fencing. He understood the significance of what was happening. Another patriot had written on a bed sheet tied to the fence, "We the people...."

The largest Faraday cage in the world prevented signals from entering the bunker, its simple principles deflecting all forms of electronic communication from the murderers within. And just like a microwave oven, the hastily tied-together shield stopped all contact to the outside world.

Everyone standing fought for what they believed in, for their loved ones, for their principles, for their God-given rights. Because many of them knew, or had recently learned, that there are always and will always be bad people doing bad things. They had learned as well, that *someone* always has to do something to preserve what is right, that certain things in life are precious and worth fighting or dying for.

That freedom isn't really free.

Epilogue

In his plush private office deep in the belly below Washington, D.C., the President was yelling into his phone. Panic set in as he failed over and over again to connect to his armies, to talk to his commanders, to confide with his sources, to secure his new world order above.

His life was caving in almost as fast as his ominous plan.

"Where the hell is everyone?" he screamed like a madman.

"What the fuck is going on out there?" He looked at the phone in his hand. He was ready to bust a blood vessel.

"I am the Commander-in Chief! I am the President of the New United States, god-damn it!" he kept shouting into the mouth piece.

"Someone talk to me!"

But no one answered.

The End--

--For Now!

Coming Next!

Treasonous Behavior
The Reckoning

by

Robert A. Johnson

About the author:

> Robert A. Johnson, businessman, entrepreneur, educator, and author, was born and raised in the Boston area, birthplace of early American patriotism. He believes in the enduring American spirits of free will, self-determination, and rugged individualism. He divides his time living in the high deserts of Arizona and the central plains of exotic Thailand with his lovely wife.

Novels by Robert A. Johnson

Looking For Eddie

Last Bus To Korat

Johnny's Fortune

Treasonous Behavior
In The Beginning

Made in the USA
Las Vegas, NV
24 December 2020